A BEASTLY KIND OF EARL

MIA VINCY

A Beastly Kind of Earl

Ebook ISBN: 978-1-925882-02-5

Paperback ISBN: 978-1-925882-03-2

CONTENT WARNING: REFERENCES TO A CHARACTER (DECEASED) WITH BIPOLAR I DISORDER AND PSYCHOSIS

Cover: Studio Bukovero

Editing, Sensitivity consultant: May Peterson

Proofreading: M.Ute Editing

A BEASTLY KIND OF EARL

*For anyone who ever believed a story about themself
that turned out to be untrue.*

CHAPTER 1

Thea Knight had never been one to follow rules unquestioningly—or at all, if she could help it—but she always adhered to three firm rules of her own.

Namely, her Rules of Mischief.

First, mischief must be conducted only for a good cause—and certainly, Thea's present mischief served no lesser cause than her younger sister's happiness. For that excellent cause, she had resigned her position as a private nurse, donned a set of men's clothing—complete with a many-caped greatcoat that weighed a stone and reeked of pigs—and journeyed halfway across England to meet Helen in this cramped room in a coaching inn in Warwickshire. Thea had even stopped laughing long enough to be laced into tight stays for the first time in three years, so she could wear Helen's stylish gown to its best advantage, while Helen took her turn to dress as a swine-scented swain. All as a prelude to the grand mischief: While Thea was at Arabella's house, claiming to be Miss Helen Knight, the real Helen would be eloping to

Scotland with her beloved Beau Russell, thus evading the long reach of Beau Russell's father, Viscount Ventnor.

Which led to Thea's second Rule of Mischief: One must trick only those who were villainous, powerful, or—as was most likely the case—both.

Her conscience rested easy on that point, for Lord Ventnor practically *leaped* into the third category. The things he had said about the Knight family! That Helen was a "sly, scheming seductress" and "too distastefully inferior" for his heir, because Pa was a "grubby merchant" and Thea a "dreadful scandal." Ventnor had then packed his son off to a shooting party, and sent men to follow Helen and stop her if she tried to sneak away to meet Beau. Even now, two ruffians sat in the tavern downstairs, waiting for Helen to emerge.

Thea had her own reasons for loathing Lord Ventnor, though she preferred not to think about that ball three years ago, when Percy Russell spewed his lies and Ventnor called her horrid names. To think that, of all the men in the world, Helen intended to marry Percy Russell's elder brother! Thea shuddered at the thought of being thus connected to her enemies, though it was probably perfectly normal for the Russell family. After all, the aristocracy had been marrying and murdering each other for centuries, sometimes on the same day.

But she bit her tongue and started no quarrels, because of her third Rule: When engaging in mischief and trickery, one must always enjoy oneself. Because enjoyment led to good memories, and Thea wanted only good memories of these precious stolen minutes with her sister.

"Heavens, Thea, where did you get this hideous greatcoat?" Helen held the offending item at arm's length, her face an exaggerated grimace of horror. "Did you buy it directly from the pigs themselves?"

"If you please!" Thea protested. "I'll have you know that greatcoat was worn by the finest pigs in all of England."

"They certainly have the finest smell!"

Laughing, Helen shoved her arms into the sleeves. Thea helped her arrange the lapels and capes, then stepped back to admire the result.

The greatcoat truly was a stroke of genius. Its bulk broadened Helen's shoulders and concealed her shape, and its fragrance would deter anyone from coming too close. Hunched into the greatcoat and with a broad-brimmed clerical hat pulled down low on her face, Helen could travel without drawing attention, just as Thea had done.

"How did you survive wearing these clothes in this heat?" Helen said, taking up the clerical hat and spinning it around one finger. "I swear, after days sweltering in stagecoaches, I shall arrive at the border as roasted as a loin of pork, and Beau will stick a fork in me to see if I am done."

"What an excellent test of true love! If Mr. Russell still wants you when you smell of stewed pig, you can be sure he will want you always."

"If his father's fury could not tear us apart, I daresay a smelly greatcoat will fare no better."

How wonderful for Helen, to be so loved and wanted. Thea could hardly argue with *that*.

So once more, she swallowed her concerns and instead made a show of inspecting her sister, circling her slowly. Helen looked as comfortable in men's clothes as Thea had felt, though it was a good ten years since the sisters had last dressed as boys. "Ted" and "Harry" they had been, hair cut short under their caps, dashing out after their lessons to run errands for Pa, gather news at coffeehouses and the docks, and earn a coin wherever they could. Because that was how the Knight family worked:

3

Everyone did their part on the long, rocky road to security and wealth.

Then the year Thea turned twelve, Pa made his fortune again, and the time came for her to stop pretending to be a boy and to pretend to be a genteel lady instead.

And look at her now, as genteel as you please in Helen's expensive moss-green carriage dress, from her manner to her accent to her walk. It still felt like pretending, though, so why not use a pretend name too? Their switch would not fool any of their acquaintances, despite their matching chestnut-colored hair and blue eyes, but they had only to fool Ventnor's men. Ma and Pa believed Helen to be Arabella's guest, Arabella's other guests knew neither of them from a jug of ale, and as for Thea... Well, no one gave a flying farthing about her whereabouts now.

No self-pity, she scolded herself. Not when she was about to put everything right, not only for Helen, but for herself too.

"We are doing very well," Thea declared. "Ventnor's men will never suspect we have swapped clothing, so they will not even notice you leave, let alone stop you from meeting and marrying Beau."

Smiling, Helen leaned toward Thea, eyes wide. "They will not stop us," she chanted.

"They cannot stop us," Thea replied automatically, and together they chorused: "For nobody stops a Knight!"

Thea clapped once and laughed. Nobody stops a Knight, indeed! How often had she muttered the family chant to herself during the years of her exile? Whenever the loneliness became too much and grim thoughts crept in, she would draw on that family spirit. On the memories of Ma hugging her, or Pa fondly pinching her chin, as they reminded her that, together, the Knight family would succeed, and never again have to worry about the roof over their head.

"Do you remember when the Little Ones learned the Knight family chant?" Thea asked Helen now. "Jemima would bang her spoon, and Andy would howl." Oh, how she missed those impish sweethearts. Her smile faltered. "I suppose they aren't so little anymore."

Helen touched her hand. "We still call them that," she said gently. "They remember you, you know. They ask after you."

"And what do Ma and Pa say to that? Good riddance to bad rubbish, I suppose."

"No! They miss you, Thea. Every night, we dine with your empty place."

And every night of Thea's exile, she had dined alone. "Nurse and companion," Mrs. Burton's advertisement had stated, but it had turned out the old woman had no interest in Thea's company. The other servants had deemed Thea too grand for them, what with her refined accent and manners, and in the three years she'd worked in that isolated house, she had made no friends. As for everyone she had known before, only Arabella and Helen ever wrote.

Thea turned away and traced the long, curved brim of Helen's poke bonnet. Thea's bonnet, now. She must not quarrel with Helen, not now, not when she had only a few minutes to enjoy her sister's company, not when she loathed arguments, and yet—

"They should have believed me," Thea said.

"But you are always making up stories, and remember you even said—"

"Exactly!" Thea whirled around. "They know I make silly jests, so they should have believed me when I said I spoke the truth. Instead, they chose to believe Percy Russell's nasty lies. Now his life goes on as merrily as it always did, while I was cast out of home."

"Pa offered you money."

"I don't want their money! I want them to believe me."

Thea hated to disappoint her parents; all her life, she had tried her best to please them and contribute to the family's success, but when Percy Russell came strutting along and sought Pa's permission to court her, the arguments had begun.

"If you marry into the upper class, Thea, the whole family will be secure," Ma had said. "Not just you, but Helen and the Little Ones too. Your Pa has made his fortune again, but he's lost it before, and in this world, only those in the upper class can be sure of their position."

But when Thea protested that she did not like Percy Russell, Ma only said, "Give him time. With time, he'll grow on you."

"Like fungus?" Thea had retorted.

Indeed. A toxic fungus that poisoned her whole life.

"Never mind," Thea said now. "Soon, everyone will know the truth. I am going to put the world right," she announced, with more confidence than she felt. After all, to put the world right, she must first convince the world that it was wrong. And if there was one thing the world hated, it was being told that it was wrong.

Helen narrowed her eyes. "Thea, what mischief are you up to now?"

Before Thea could reply, someone rapped at the door. Helen yanked the clerical hat down over her braided hair, and Thea hastily pulled on the poke bonnet. Its long, curved brim was designed to completely shield the wearer's face from the sun—and, conveniently for their purposes, from any prying eyes. The effect was like blinders on a horse, and she had to rotate her entire body to see who entered.

But it was only Arabella, sliding through the door and shutting it silently behind her, before turning to assess them with cool, critical blue eyes. Arabella had traveled only a few miles from her family estate to collect Thea, but her royal-blue pelisse, adorned with little white tassels down the front, was elegant enough for a promenade with the queen. Atop her dark hair, and a perfect foil for her pale, angular features, was a matching cap, from which sprouted a single, superb ostrich feather. Arabella was unfashionably tall, but she wore her outfits to such perfection that Thea was sure the fashions must be wrong. Even in Helen's stylish new outfit, with its smart rows of frogging, Thea felt shabby by comparison.

"You'll do," Arabella drawled in her imperious manner. "I can hardly see your faces. We are all satisfied that neither of you has met anyone on my parents' guest list?"

"Agreed," Thea and Helen chorused.

"Then all that remains is for Mister Helen to travel north, and Thea to come home with me where Ventnor's men cannot follow."

Helen peered out the window at the yard, where the next stagecoach north waited. "First, Thea," she said, turning back and pulling on her gloves. "I have just enough time for you to tell me about your other mischief."

Thea couldn't help chuckling. "I have penned a pamphlet telling the true story of what Percy Russell and Francis Upton did to me," she said. "Arabella has a publishing connection in London who has agreed to print it and deliver a copy to every aristocratic and genteel household in Town. I'll place copies in every coffeehouse, and advertisements in every newspaper, and prints in every bookseller's window. I'll pay hostesses to discuss it in every salon, and debt-ridden gentlemen to whisper of it over every game of cards. Enough of the *ton* will be in London for the Little Season in September that word will spread to everyone in society. And oh, if only I could ruin them," she spat. "Ruin Percy Russell and Francis Upton like they ruined me."

Only a few hundred people had been in Lord Ventnor's ballroom that night to witness her downfall, but they had spread the false story like a disease. Everyone else had believed the rumors without question, of course, never caring that a life was destroyed. Well, time for Thea to turn the rumor mill to her advantage instead.

Excellent mischief, indeed! And it complied with her three Rules: It served the admirable causes of justice and restoring her reputation, it would expose Percy Russell's vileness, and she would enjoy every last minute.

"It will be chaos," Helen said.

Thea sighed happily. "I know."

"It will be expensive," Arabella said.

Thea sighed ruefully. "I know."

"It will enrage Lord Ventnor," Helen said.

Thea grinned. "I know."

Arabella shook her head just enough to make her ostrich feather quiver. "We must plan it very carefully. Lord Ventnor will not appreciate you saying such things about his son."

"By 'such things,' you mean 'the truth.'"

"Another truth is that Ventnor is a powerful man. He may be only a viscount, but he boasts the ear of several dukes and the Prince Regent."

Thea waved away her doubts. "The pamphlet uses false names, with only a note in the foreword inviting the reader to guess whose story it tells. Ventnor cannot accuse me without admitting the story is about Percy. Helen will be married to Mr. Russell by then, and he'll protect you from Ventnor's ire... Won't he?"

"Of course he will," Helen said, without a moment's hesitation. "I promise you, Thea, Beau is a good man."

"You say that, but..." She would not say it. She would not quarrel. She would not— "Oh, Helen, are you sure about this?" she blurted out. "I know you are in love, but when you marry Mr.

Russell, you get his whole family."

"They are not so bad," Helen said. "Lord Ventnor terrifies me, of course, and Beau says Percy was always vile, even as a boy. But his mother, Lady Ventnor, is lovely, and his younger sister is too. He says he still misses his elder sister, Katharine, although 'tis nine years since she died." Helen glanced out the window again, and when she turned back to Thea, a wicked gleam lit her eyes. "They say her husband murdered her."

"No!"

"Yes! Some say it was poison. Others say he is a witch and killed her with sorcery. They say he bears the Devil's mark upon his face, and it was the Devil himself who killed his father and brothers that he might become the earl."

"The earl?" Thea repeated, looking from Helen to Arabella.

"She speaks of the Earl of Luxborough," Arabella said. "Although when he eloped with Katharine Russell, he was only the earl's penniless third son."

Helen's eyes were comically wide under her clerical hat. "And since he became the earl, they say he keeps to his estate in Somersetshire, where he practices his sorcery, making potions and poisons, keeping company only with foreigners and heathens and witches."

"What utter nonsense," Thea declared. "You cannot believe such rumors are true."

"Rumors about other people are always true," Arabella said. "It's the rumors about oneself that are false. But some of that story is fact: About thirteen years ago, he ran away to America with Ventnor's daughter. After a few years, they returned to England, she died in mysterious circumstances, and he left again. Now he is back, he never goes into society."

"But the claptrap about witchcraft and the Devil?"

Arabella pursed her lips thoughtfully. "I have not seen him in

9

person, but they say his face is indeed scarred, not by the Devil, mind you, but by..."

Thea leaned in. "By?"

"By...a cat."

"A cat?" Thea glanced at the fine white lines running up the back of her hand, a souvenir from her childhood attempt to befriend a stray cat that did not wish to be befriended. "Then I have the Devil's mark too," she scoffed. "To think him a witch for a mere cat's scratch."

"Good grief, Thea, he is an English aristocrat, and would never suffer the scratches of an ordinary cat," Arabella scolded lightly. "He was attacked by nothing less than a jaguar, while in the forests of New Spain."

"Ja-gu-ar," Thea repeated, trying out the strange word in her mouth. How unfortunate that her limited education had taught her only how to be a lady, and omitted any mention of strange cats and foreign forests. "What is a jaguar?"

Helen drew on her slightly more extensive education to explain, "A jaguar is a very big cat. With very big claws, and very big teeth, and very little sense of humor."

"Impossible," Thea said. "If it is a cat, then it doubtless believes it has an excellent sense of humor and it's the humans that cannot take a joke."

Arabella almost smiled. "I daresay you can ask the earl all about jaguars and their jokes when you meet him."

"I am happy to say that I have no desire whatsoever to meet the Earl of Luxborough."

"Unfortunate for you, then, that he is arriving at my parents' house this evening too."

Before Thea or Helen could respond to Arabella's astonishing announcement, a call from the yard warned that the stagecoach north was about to depart. Helen grabbed the small bag Thea had brought, gave her a one-armed hug, said, "Wish me luck!" and dashed out the door on a waft of happiness and swine.

Thea darted to the window, Arabella by her side. It felt like an eternity until Helen emerged. With her clerical hat pulled down low and her greatcoat flapping about her breeches and boots, Helen jogged across the yard and jumped into the coach. Thea hardly dared breathe, praying Ventnor's men had not noticed that the fellow in the greatcoat was Helen. Other passengers boarded. The carriage door slammed shut. The coachman hollered at the team of six horses, and the huge stagecoach rumbled off. Still Thea and Arabella waited, until the stagecoach was well out of sight. No one followed.

Another coachman maneuvered a stylish barouche into the yard. A liveried footman and an inn employee carried out a traveling trunk and lifted it into the barouche. Thea recognized the trunk as Helen's. Well, her trunk, now that she was Helen.

Arabella tapped the glass. "No one is chasing Helen, and my barouche is ready. Assuming Ventnor's men did not notice her leave, we need only smuggle you past them without them seeing your face."

"IF THIS EARL OF LUXBOROUGH never leaves his estate, how is it that he is visiting your house?" Thea asked Arabella's back, as they filed down the narrow, stuffy stairs toward the tavern and its din of chatter and calls.

"I hesitated to mention this before, but Lord Ventnor is giving the earl some rare plant specimens," Arabella replied, her ostrich feather sweeping the air as she half turned her head. "As Warwickshire falls about halfway between their estates, Ventnor has sent them to our house for the earl to collect. Apparently, Lord

Luxborough is a keen botanist when he is not wandering through the Americas being attacked by giant cats."

As they reached the bottom of the stairs, Thea pulled Arabella to a stop. "Lord Ventnor sent these plants to your house, at the same time that he believes Helen to be your guest," she said in a low voice. "Does that strike you as more than coincidence?"

"It does, rather. On the other hand, Lord Ventnor has a finger in hundreds of pies. There is no reason he should not make such an arrangement with Lord Luxborough, given he is his father-in-law, or with Papa, given their acquaintance. Either way, the Earl of Luxborough cannot possibly know who you are, and it is too late to stop your scheme now." Arabella shot a glance at the door leading into the noisy tavern and extended her left elbow. "Ready?"

"Ready."

Thea slipped her fingers around Arabella's elbow and looked down, the tunnel formed by the bonnet's brim revealing little more than the toes of her half boots and a circle of uneven flagstones. She swung her head but all she could see of Arabella was the blue skirt of her pelisse, the little white tassels down the front perfectly aligned.

"When I came in, Ventnor's men were seated at a table that will be on our right as we leave," Arabella said softly. "Remember, chances are they will identify you only by your dress and not bother checking your face, but no need to give them the opportunity to prove they are not complete muttonheads. Whatever happens, keep your head down and do not look at anyone."

Thea was already fighting the urge to look up. "I shall try, but it will tax my resources immensely, and I'll likely faint with exhaustion at the end."

"Duly noted. If you manage to cross this room without looking up, I shall commend you to the Crown for a medal of valor."

Arabella set off, and Thea let herself be guided into the tavern like a horse in blinders, eyes on the floor, which did not bear such scrutiny well; it could use a good scrubbing. The thick air dried her throat; a man ranted about a missing box; the smell of burned toast filled her nostrils. Through it all, Thea did not look up.

"Ventnor's men have seen you," Arabella drawled in a low, bored tone. Thea did not look up. "Keep walking. They are watching you, but they do not seem suspicious. We are almost— Oh dear."

Arabella stopped abruptly. Thea stopped too and zealously studied the floor.

"What?" she hissed. "What is it?"

"Nothing. Don't look up."

Thea looked up.

First, she saw boots. Men's boots, dusty and scuffed. Their toes were pointed toward her and Arabella, from which Thea deduced the rest of the man must be facing them too. Even with her limited education, Thea could discern a finely crafted boot of expensive leather: Whoever this man was, he was not one of Ventnor's rough hires.

And as though someone had attached a string to her bonnet and was pulling on it relentlessly, Thea's gaze traveled up, up that expensive, dusty leather to the top of those boots, up the man's long, powerful, buckskin-clad legs, to an exquisitely tailored dark-blue coat—he was definitely facing them, and definitely not moving, and he was not only sufficiently big to block their path, but also sufficiently rude. This man was an aristocrat, Thea decided, for only an aristocrat would stand so nonchalantly in their way.

Up, up her gaze traveled, racing against the brim of her

bonnet, up past the rows of buttons spanning a broad chest, to the white neckcloth and collar, to the darker hue of his long, angular jaw.

To his scars.

Ah. Now she understood. This man must be the Earl of Luxborough.

The thick lines, too jagged to be truly parallel, began on the high crest of his left cheekbone and continued relentlessly down, over the hollow of his cheek, narrowly missing his ear to disappear under his neckcloth. Another two thick marks scored his temple.

These scars had long since settled into his skin, but Thea could not help but imagine how they might have looked once. What a horrifying experience it must have been! And what a monstrous great cat, to have paws the size of a man's face!

A sharp point in her side made her jerk: Arabella's elbow. Ashamed for gawking, Thea dragged her gaze off the earl's scarred cheek and gathered an impression of tangled dark hair tumbling haphazardly over a high forehead, before she found herself looking into his eyes. He was staring right at her, his gaze intent, his eyes golden-brown against his thick lashes and straight, lowered brows. He could not have been much older than thirty, but those eyes—those eyes were ancient, as though they had seen a million things and wearied of them all.

Those tired eyes pinned her to the spot, as he took one deceptively lazy step toward her, and another, until he filled her narrow vision, both fascinating and terrible. His haunted eyes, his careless hair, his coiled energy, his storied cheek. His air of utter indifference to anything but her. Thea felt uncomfortably aware of the tightness of her stays, her scalp itching under the bonnet, the warmth of her cheeks.

Then a smile tugged at one corner of his mouth, a secret half smile, for himself and not for her. Before she could find words, or breath with which to speak them, his gaze slid to Arabella.

He inclined his head in greeting. "Miss Arabella Larke, I presume," he said, his voice low and rough like smoke.

Thea could not see whether Arabella nodded in return, but certainly she did not curtsy. Arabella was famously difficult to impress; even an earl would not induce her to bend a knee, or to rouse herself to more than a drawl to say: "And you must be Lord Luxborough."

"However did you guess?" he said wryly.

Belatedly, Thea remembered their mission, and in the absence of Arabella's commentary, she had to fight the urge to look for Ventnor's men. Not that they would accost her now, in the company of an earl. A man like Lord Luxborough would easily keep such men at bay, and ensure quick service and polite treatment, and make the whole world fall into line. Indeed, an earl would make quite a useful pet, but all things considered, she'd rather have a cat.

Then his eyes slid back to Thea, a knowing, triumphant gleam in their depths that set her heart pounding anew.

Beside her, Arabella shifted slightly. "Allow me to present my good friend, Miss Helen Knight."

Thea hastily lowered her head and bobbed a curtsy. If his lordship deigned to favor her with a nod, she didn't see, but she doubted he would. An earl was one of the highest-ranking men in the land, and earls did not bow to merchants' daughters, however hard their parents tried to turn them into gentry.

"The infamous Miss Helen Knight," he murmured, and she did look up then, meeting that knowing gleam. She opened her mouth to demand his meaning but Arabella, ever prescient, smoothly spoke first.

"My father informs me you have come to collect the plants

sent here by Lord Ventnor," Arabella said. "They have arrived safely and await you in the conservatory."

Lord Luxborough looked irritated by Arabella's interruption. "And your father informs *me* that you will guide me to them, Miss Larke. Indeed, he informed me that you will show me his entire estate, which you will inherit, although I cannot fathom why he might have mentioned *that*."

His dry tone indicated that he knew very well why Mr. Larke had mentioned Arabella's inheritance. Poor Arabella, to be married off to a rude, unpleasant man like this! Arabella could handle him, of course—Arabella could handle anything—but Thea had to speak nonetheless.

"But you have not traveled here to meet Miss Larke, have you, my lord?" Thea said.

Arabella elbowed her again, but she ignored it, unable to look away as those tired eyes flicked back to meet hers.

"Hmm?" he said.

"You are not here for Arabella," Thea persisted. "You are here for your plants."

He half groaned, half sighed. "Actually, Miss Knight, I am here for you."

CHAPTER 2

Rafe watched the expressions flit over Miss Knight's face, or rather, what little of her face he could see down the shadowy tunnel of her bonnet. He could just make out dark brows over blue eyes, a narrow nose, wide mouth, and pointed chin, all of which were looking divertingly outraged.

He ought not have said that, of course, but then, he ought not be here at all, given that his purpose was to engage in a little fraud and mischief. But when he had discovered what trick the Knight sisters were planning, Rafe could not resist seizing the opportunity to play a trick of his own. Now that he was here, looking into Thea Knight's big blue eyes, while Helen Knight headed to the border disguised as a man—well, there was no rule saying one could not entertain oneself when engaging in a little fraud and mischief.

"How can you be here for me?" Thea Knight asked. "You cannot even know who I am."

"You are Miss Helen Knight, are you not?"

"You heard Miss Larke say that to be so."

Well played, Thea, he might have said—a clever way to avoid telling an outright lie. But then he'd already known she was clever. According to the content of letters provided by an enterprising servant in the Knight household, Thea Knight was the architect of this entire scheme to fool Ventnor by taking her sister's place. A risky scheme, to be sure, but so far successful, given that Helen Knight was already on her way north while Ventnor's men sat like hairy potatoes, one eye on the ladies, the other on their tankards of ale.

The bonnet was clever too, irritating though it was; he wanted to see her properly, this woman who would unwittingly help him. But never mind: He would have plenty of time to study her in the coming week, and she would have plenty of time to stare at his scars.

Although she was not looking at his scars now; rather, her eyes were roaming over his entire face. As she studied him, she caught her lower lip between her teeth, then let it slip away.

It occurred to him that Miss Larke had spoken. He looked back at her. "Hmm?"

Miss Larke sniffed. "Perhaps you would be so kind as to explain your meaning, my lord."

"Perhaps I would be so kind," Rafe said. "But it's unlikely."

Enjoying their matching expressions of indignation, Rafe excused himself with a nod, and headed toward Ventnor's men, a space mercifully opening up around him as he crossed the sticky tavern floor.

Of all the places to end up—a blasted coaching inn in blasted Warwickshire. Definitely not what he had expected when he traveled to London in search of a lump sum of capital. There, he was surrounded by would-be geniuses, who all offered the same genius solution to his money problem. "Get married," they all said, one after the other, the bishop grinning, his solicitor shrugging, his man of affairs scratching his chin. Get married, and he would meet the conditions of the trust set up by his mother with the express purpose of encouraging her sons to wed.

Or, as the bishop had put it: "Why not, my boy? You need only say 'I do,' and you will have ten thousand pounds."

"I will also have a wife," Rafe had pointed out. "And what the hell would I do with one of those?"

A mistake to ask, because the bishop was full of bright ideas for what, exactly, Rafe might do with a wife.

"You could contract a marriage of convenience," his solicitor had suggested, ever looking for loopholes in the law. "Simply marry some lady who wants to be a countess and forget about her."

A nice theory, but in reality, something was sure to go wrong, and Rafe would end up having to take care of his wife anyway. If life had taught him anything, it was that he did not need to look for trouble, because trouble would find him. Maybe if Rafe were a different man, he would take that risk, but he was not a different man.

He was still surprised that the solution had come from Lord Ventnor, of all people. Rafe preferred to ignore the viscount's existence, but when he had heard of Ventnor's rare orchids, and how Ventnor's ignorant gardeners were murdering said orchids, Rafe had felt compelled to offer his advice for keeping the plants alive. At which point, Ventnor promised to give Rafe the orchids in exchange for helping to keep that social-climbing seductress Helen Knight away from Ventnor's precious heir until he could find the boy a more suitable bride. It had been a small matter, in the circumstances, to send a man to learn more about Helen Knight, only to discover the scheme she was plotting with her sister. How nicely it all came together: Helen Knight would elope with Beau Russell, and Thea Knight would adopt a false name, thus giving Rafe a way to get married and get the money, but not end up with a wife.

Oh, and Ventnor would be apoplectic with rage. Excellent.

First, though, Rafe must get rid of Ventnor's men.

They were big, uncouth-looking fellows, the sort Rafe would expect Ventnor to use; former soldiers, probably, who lacked property, a trade, and a conscience. Thanks to ruffians like these, Ventnor could conduct his dirty deeds, while keeping his soft white hands spotless. The pair had been watching the two ladies, but as Rafe bore down on them, they turned to stare at him, eyes wide, spines straight.

"It's Luxborough," he heard the bearded one hiss, as they exchanged panicked looks. "They say he..."

The words trailed off before Rafe had the pleasure of hearing which of the delightful rumors the man had chosen to share.

A glance over his shoulder revealed that Miss Knight and Miss Larke had made it out the door and were climbing into the waiting barouche. Ventnor's men dropped their tankards and began to rise. Rafe pressed his hands to their shoulders, and they sank back down in their seats.

Rafe would have preferred not to have been cursed with title, scars, and outlandish rumors, but he had to admit, they had their benefits. People tended to become conveniently docile in his presence. When they weren't trying to run away, that is.

"Lord...Lord Luxborough," the bearded one said with a gulp.

"In the flesh," Rafe agreed. "Or what's left of it."

He hauled a chair from a neighboring table and dropped into it. With a jerk of his chin toward the bar, he had the barkeeper pouring a round of drinks.

"'Scuse us, m'lord," the other one said, "but we hafta— You see, that lady..."

"Miss Helen Knight, you mean?"

"Thass the one. Lord Ventnor told us to keep an eye on her."

"And what an excellent job you have done. But I'll take it from here. As per my own arrangements with Lord Ventnor."

When the server set down the fresh drinks, the men eyed the tankards as if they were poisoned, and then, once more, the bearded one spoke.

"I don't want to argue, my lord."

"But you will anyway."

"Just that Lord Ventnor didn't tell us you was coming."

Rafe nudged a tankard toward the man. "I was not aware that Lord Ventnor or I were required to apprise you of our movements."

"But Miss Knight—"

"Is on her way to Vindale Court, residence of Mr. Larke and his family. Did you intend to follow her there? Have you obtained an invitation? Hmm? Lady Belinda Larke, earl's daughter and famed society hostess, just happened to add you to her guest list, did she?"

"I s'pose you have an invitation," the man grumbled.

"I don't need one. I am welcome everywhere."

"Because you're an earl, I s'pose."

"No. Because of my good looks, charm, and cheerful disposition."

The two men exchanged another look. Rafe didn't want to be here, not in this blasted coaching inn, nor staying at Mr. Larke's house, nor anywhere else that involved spending time with all these people and their incessant talking. He didn't want to commit fraud, or play tricks on Miss Thea Knight, or jump through hoops to get the money from his mother's trust. But he did want to do something useful with his plants—and the devil knew he was good for little else—and if this was the price he had to pay, he might as well take his entertainment where he could.

Miss Larke's barouche was long gone by now, and habit had Ventnor's men curling their hands around their tankards. Rafe reached into his pocket and pulled out the two papers there: One was the marriage license prepared by the bishop, allowing Rafe to marry Helen Knight, and the other was Rafe's note telling Ventnor he had done just that. A trifle premature, as the marriage had yet to take place—or even the proposal—but that was a small matter. Sometime tomorrow, he would invite Thea Knight for a walk in the rose garden or some such thing, call her "Helen," and invite her to be his wife. If she married him using a false name, the marriage would not be valid, but she—the scheming, social-climbing outcast, whose attempt to trap Percy Russell into marriage had failed so spectacularly three years earlier—would see another opportunity to catch herself a nobleman and rush to agree. And once the trustees had released the ten thousand pounds, Rafe would "discover" his wife was not who she said she was, feign shock, and send her on her way.

Rafe returned the license to his pocket and dropped the letter onto the table, along with several coins. "Return to London immediately, and deliver that note to Lord Ventnor."

They exchanged another look. "But Lord Ventnor told us to wait and watch if Miss Knight left."

"And I am telling you there is no need." Rafe patted the note and stood. "Miss Knight does not know it yet, but when she leaves Vindale Court, she will leave with me."

THE SUN WAS HOVERING over the pink horizon when Arabella's barouche turned between the towering hedges marking the entrance to Vindale Court. At Thea's request, they had made the trip with the hood down. The brim of her bonnet prevented her from properly admiring the scenery or feeling the breeze on her face, but she enjoyed the fresh summer evening nonetheless. They would not be expected at dinner tonight, Arabella had said, and Thea, tired from her journey and all the excitement, was relieved she would spend the evening alone in her room with a hot bath and a supper tray. She had no interest in talking to anyone other than Arabella tonight.

Well, she did have questions for one other person, perhaps.

"But what on earth could the earl have meant, saying he is here for me?" Thea wondered out loud, for approximately the twenty-seventh time.

And for approximately the twenty-seventh time, Arabella replied, "I daresay he will tell us when it suits him."

"I deeply resent that we must follow his schedule."

"As do I. But it would not do to let him know that you care."

That was Arabella's pride speaking, of course. She was one of those aristocrats who nurtured indifference as if it were a pet. Which reminded Thea of another question.

"The note that Luxborough mentioned," Thea said. "It sounded as if your father wants you to marry the earl."

"Oh, Papa always wants me to marry someone."

Arabella kept her eyes straight ahead. Her profile revealed nothing.

"Arabella, is your father—"

"But recall, Lord Luxborough seemed much more interested in you."

"Yes, but what—" Thea stopped. Clearly, Arabella did not wish to discuss her father, and there was little point in wondering, yet again, what the earl might have meant.

Yet even without his unsettling words and the inexplicable promise gleaming in those eyes, there had been something about Lord Luxborough that made her feel... Oh, she didn't know what it was. Something about the way he was so large yet so at ease with himself; the way he had crossed the tavern floor with such strong, sure-footed grace; the way he seemed not to give a flying farthing what anyone else thought.

Were it not for those scars, one would never imagine he had ever been weak. Yet for all that he was an earl—and therefore, by definition, a villain—he was also a man who had suffered. Somehow, he had recovered from that weakness; if only she could ask him how to do that, how to regain one's faith when the world had been whipped out from under one's feet.

Thea tried to shake off the discomfiting feelings his memory aroused, but the towering hedges lining the driveway offered no distraction, and her thoughts strayed back to him again.

"When a man is attacked by a giant cat," she said, "do you think he becomes infected with the nature of the beast?"

Arabella turned her head slowly and raised one eyebrow. Cheered by this response, Thea continued.

"Consider it to be like the legend of the werewolf. Most of the time, he appears to be a perfectly normal gentleman." She gripped Arabella's forearm and lowered her voice for dramatic effect. "But at nightfall, he turns into a giant cat. He prowls through the shadows and pounces on humans like mice."

Arabella gently reclaimed her arm. "If Lord Luxborough is a were-jaguar, then I do hope he is house-trained. I should not like him scratching the furniture and making a mess in corners."

"If you please!" Thea protested. "A jaguar is far too noble a beast to do anything so vulgar as that."

"You speak with great authority, considering you do not even know what a jaguar is."

Thea sniffed haughtily. "I do not need to be an expert to share my expertise."

"Fair point. Ignorance has never stopped anyone from talking knowledgeably about a subject."

Any response Thea might have made died on her lips, as the barouche swung around a corner and the house came into view. House? Such a paltry word did not serve. The sprawling white pile boasted such an array of ornate wings and spires, Thea would sooner call it a palace. Arabella said nothing—it was her childhood home, after all—so Thea willed herself to stop fidgeting and feign nonchalance. She would not think about the daunting grandeur of this house, or about the lies she would tell the people inside it. She would think about something else instead.

"If I could turn into any animal at all, I would be a cat," she announced.

"An ordinary house cat?" Arabella sounded appalled by the idea.

"There is nothing ordinary about a house cat. A cat is playful but fierce and doesn't care what anyone thinks. Why, what would you be?"

"I would be a hawk." Arabella tilted back her head and studied the twilight sky. "I would soar up high, where I could see and know everything. I would find my enemies and watch what they did."

"And then?"

"I would swoop down and tear out their eyes."

"Um."

Arabella looked back at Thea with a faint, self-mocking smile, and that was their last quiet moment, for they had reached the house and the barouche came to a stop. Servants streamed out to assist them, and together they climbed the steps and entered a marble cavern that passed as a foyer, where a maid relieved Thea of her horrid bonnet and handed Arabella a letter. Arabella read the letter as she led Thea through a maze of stairs and corridors to a large, handsomely appointed chamber.

"You will have everything you require, as my guest," Arabella said. "There is no need to be nervous: If I say you are Helen, no one will doubt it."

"Thank you," Thea said softly. "I realize that if this goes wrong, you will be disgraced."

"Nothing will go wrong. Nevertheless, do not draw attention to yourself."

"I never—" Thea caught Arabella's sharp look and sighed. "I shall try."

"And don't get into trouble."

"I shall try."

"And don't go near Lord Luxborough. He might think you are a mouse and pounce."

"He might rub up against me and purr."

Arabella's eyebrows shot up and Thea considered her statement.

"That didn't come out quite as I intended," she said.

"I am serious, Thea. I shall not repeat those absurd rumors about sorcery, but something happened to his wife, and who knows what stories he has heard about you. Whatever he wants with you—or with Helen, rather—do not let him find you alone."

Arabella was right, of course. It was just that Thea had so many questions.

Which she would not ask. She would not.

"Then I shall stay out of trouble by finalizing the plans for my pamphlet and deciding how I shall live when the truth is out and my reputation has been restored."

Arabella waved the letter. "My publisher in London advises they have had to alter their schedules. They have an opening to print your pamphlets and whatnot this week. Otherwise, you may have to wait several weeks or even months. They recommend a Mr. Witherspoon to manage your publicity campaign. You must send your manuscript and instructions to London tomorrow, with a guarantee to cover the full costs."

Thea's heart sank. "So soon. I thought it would be after Helen returned from Scotland, so she could help me gather the money."

Arabella considered. "I can speak to Mama, on the remote chance she will advance me a sum without asking questions, but otherwise, I am afraid money is one area where I cannot help. It is a source of considerable embarrassment to me that I shall inherit one of the finest estates in the middle of England but I cannot lay my hands on five pounds."

"You have helped so much already. I'll figure something out. I have to," Thea added, almost to herself. "I have no family, no money, and only one friend. I might win, I might lose, but first I have to try."

When Arabella had left, Thea explored her room, concluding her tour at one of the large windows, studying the expansive view in the lingering summer twilight. On a hill in the distance, past a million acres of garden, parkland, and forests, the famous ruins of Longhope Abbey were silhouetted against the pink sky. Below her, her window looked out onto one of the other wings, a length of stone arches that ended in an expanse of glass walls: the conservatory. The Earl of Luxborough's rare plants waited for him behind those glass walls.

As Thea watched, a male figure crossed the lawn below her, heading toward the conservatory with the long, graceful strides of a man who could move quickly while seeming to make no effort at all. He wore no hat, revealing untamed dark hair.

Lord Luxborough had also arrived.

The nerve of the man! That the first thing he did was check his plants! Who did he think he was, to smile that gleeful smile, and speak those mysterious, menacing words, and then waltz off to *check his plants*?

Well, most likely, he thought he was an earl, and could say whatever he wanted, and waltz off to do whatever he pleased.

Arabella was right: The sensible thing would be for Thea to wait for Luxborough to make his next move in whatever rum game he was playing. Because those were the rules: He was the earl, and she was the merchant's outcast daughter, so he was the one who chose the time and place, and all Thea could do was wait. Oh, how she tired of waiting. For three long, lonely years, she had waited, waited for someone to come for her, waited for her life to fix itself. No one ever came for her. Her life never fixed itself. She had had to brew plans to fix everything herself. And now this— this *earl* had come prancing along and started some game that threatened to ruin everything, and she was expected to—what? Sit quietly until he was ready to explain himself? Until he fetched her? Until he crooked his little finger to command her to come running?

Below her, he disappeared into the conservatory.

Thea was not going to be at his beck and call. Without another thought, she threw a shawl around her shoulders and made for the door.

IN THE CONSERVATORY, heavy air settled over Thea's skin, and she breathed in soil and leaves. The plants were packed densely, and she could see little through the rows of thick, lush greenery. She wandered through the aisles, trailing her fingers over the leaves as she passed.

As Thea's sum knowledge of plants was that they were mostly green, mostly pretty, and somehow produced fruit and flowers, she could not begin to guess which of these might belong to the earl. Certainly, nothing here seemed interesting enough for that big, sure-footed man with the tired, gleeful eyes. When Luxborough did not appear, Thea concluded that she had missed him and may as well head back to her room.

Then she entered an alcove whose single bench bore a dozen plants, including a flower unlike anything she had ever seen.

Closer inspection revealed it was not a single flower, but half a dozen yellow blooms clinging wearily to a single stem. The stem emerged from thick flat leaves that drooped around their pot like yesterday's stockings. Each flower was no wider across than her little finger, and each had petals in three different shapes and colors: round, yellow petals at the front; long, purple petals behind; and a central dappled point that looked hairy like an animal's snout.

How splendid they were! Dropping her shawl on the table, Thea bent to examine the flowers more closely. She reached out, eager to know the texture of those unusual yellow—

"Hands off!"

With a yelp and a jolt, Thea snatched her hands back close to her throat and spun around, heart pounding.

It was Lord Luxborough, of course, a large looming silhouette of tousled hair and broad shoulders and impatient legs. As he advanced, his face came into view. He looked tired and annoyed.

Annoyed with her, she supposed.

Well, she was annoyed with him, lurking in shadows and scaring her like that.

With an effort, Thea lowered her hands, straightened, and tried to behave as if this was perfectly normal. But nothing about this man was normal, not given his inexplicable words back at the inn and the haunting questions of what he knew and what damage he might wreak.

"You startled me. My lord. Um."

"Do not touch that flower," he said, in his low, rough voice, its smoky edges sliding down her spine.

He prowled closer and she managed to stand still, but such was the intensity in his eyes that she had to look away, back to the flowers, whose delightfully odd faces surprised her all over again.

"Is it a flower, then?" A silly sentence, but a coherent one at least, and her voice was not quite a squeak.

"No, it's a monkey. Of course it's a blasted flower."

"I've never seen a flower like it in all the world."

"And you've seen all the world, have you? You just happened to be passing through Bahia?"

"Bahia? Yes, I see, Bahia, yes," said Thea, nodding and ignoring his horrid sarcasm.

"Have you ever even heard of Bahia, Miss Knight?"

"Of course I have."

"When?"

"You mentioned it just now."

He leaned a hip against the table, arms folded like a sentry, and examined her as if she, too, were a specimen he had never before seen.

Defiantly, Thea examined him back. Despite everything, she liked looking at him. Something about his surly roughness appealed, the way he was battered and worn, yet strong nonetheless. Like a castle that had endured storms and sieges and battles, yet remained impervious and indifferent, a place one could seek shelter, if one but dared to draw near.

She would not draw near. They should not be alone together, here in the fading light, but she could not leave, not until she discovered what he knew. As she sought the words to ask, her eyes strayed back to the flowers. The purplish petals at the back were ruffled, puckered like sewing when one pulled the thread too tight. She reached out and—

"I said, don't touch!"

She snatched back her hand. "Sorry. I forgot."

"Forgot? I told you barely a minute ago."

"It was a very crowded minute."

Despite his scowl, he seemed perplexed, as though he did not know what to do with her.

He might think you are a mouse and pounce.

He might rub up against me and purr.

Thea whirled about and put a few steps between them before facing him again. She was growing used to him, and that made it easier to speak.

"I wouldn't hurt it," she said.

"Orchids are delicate. It does not need you poking at it."

"What did you call it? An awkward...what?"

"An orchid."

"Orchid." She tried out the word, savoring its shape in her mouth. "What an odd name. Orchid."

"It's from an ancient Greek word," he said irritably. "*Orkhis.*"

"Oh. You're going to educate me. Very well."

She folded her hands and waited politely.

"You don't sound thrilled," he remarked.

"On the contrary, my lord. I'm always thrilled when a man wants to tell me all the important things he knows." His brows hitched a fraction. "I suppose now you will tell me what the word means and where the plant comes from, and if I'm very lucky, you'll explain at length how you know more about it than anyone else."

That little half smile curled his lips. The scars on his cheek twisted slightly to accommodate it.

"No, I wasn't going to tell you what the word means, actually."

He shoved off from the table and strolled around her, coming to a stop by a pillar. He fell back against it, arms folded again, and regarded her as patiently as if he had all night.

Thea waited. He added nothing. She looked about, looked back at him, studied her hands, glanced up to meet his eyes. Still he said nothing.

She would not speak first. She would not speak first. She would not speak—

"You have to tell me now," she said.

"Hmm?"

"One cannot throw a foreign word into the conversation and not explain it. That's bad manners."

"Hmm."

"*Orkhis*," Thea repeated, since apparently this was going to be a one-sided conversation. "It sounds like a hideous spider, with hairy black legs and gleaming red eyes. Or—or some slimy sea creature that rides up on the waves and makes glub-glub sounds. Or—or—or—"

"Testicles."

"I...beg your pardon?"

"*Orkhis* is the Greek word for testicles," he said. "The species of plant was so named because the roots of an orchid look like a man's testicles."

"Um."

"Shall I stop educating you now, Miss Knight? Or would you like me to explain testicles too?"

Thea knew she should be scandalized—Arabella would give him a glare so withering his hair would fall out—but her mind was already occupied with assessing her relevant knowledge.

There were animals, of course, which were not known for their modesty, and the secret etchings she found in Mrs. Burton's library had filled in a *lot* of gaps in her education, and Billy Nash, the butcher's son, had shown her his testicles when they were both ten, because he had them, and he was proud of them, and Billy really, really liked to share.

So while Thea was certainly no expert, her education in testicles was sufficient for her to conclude that, whatever else might be said of them, they were not, well, *pretty*.

"Allow me to confirm that I have understood correctly," she said, her puzzlement overriding her nerves. "Here is this gorgeous, magnificent flower, and some man—who for unknown reasons is put in charge of naming it—he looks at this gorgeous, magnificent flower and he says, 'By George, that looks like my bollocks.' And then he says, 'You know what the world needs now? The world needs more things named after my bollocks.' So he names this gorgeous, magnificent flower after his bollocks, and all the other men look at it and say, 'How excellent, it is named after our bollocks.'"

His expression was unreadable as he studied her. She would not be surprised if he stalked off in disgust at her unladylike speech.

"I must admit," he finally said, "that us men are immensely fond of our bollocks."

Something like amusement crept into those tired eyes, perhaps a hint of playfulness. Thea did not know what to make of his look, so she wandered away, ending up in front of the orchid again. It really was gorgeous and magnificent, although not at all soothing like an English wildflower. She reached out and—

"Don't touch it! How many times must I tell you?"

Once again, she snatched back her hand. "Sorry. I forgot."

"Again."

"What happens if I touch it?" she asked, winding her fingers together. "Will I get poison all over my hand? Will monsters come and take my soul? Will anyone die?"

He pushed off the wall and came back to the flowers, stopping by her side, stirring the air around her. With one broad, strong hand, he caressed the space around the delicate blooms.

For once, the flower could not hold Thea's attention. Her eyes trailed up his arm to his face, his profile suddenly as touchable as the flower: the individual curls of his dark hair, the contrasting textures of his skin and scars, the defined shape of his firm lips, the angle of his jaw. She should not stand so near to this surly, disagreeable man. She did not move away.

His eyes remained on the flower. "I told you, orchids are delicate. This one is not as well as it looks. It has been carted across the world, and then nearly murdered by an arrogant, ignorant Englishman, arrogant and ignorant being the worst possible combination in a human. It needs special care and attention, not the poking fingers of a lady with the curiosity of a cat and the concentration span of a puppy dog."

"Oh."

His words were grumpy, but his tone was gentle. As though he cared. How intriguing that he cared about a flower, this big, gruff man, who must have gone to wild places and seen wondrous things and done terrible deeds, because one did not get mauled by giant jungle cats by sitting nicely in one's club in St. James.

His unexpected tenderness toward the flower made the last of her nervousness disappear.

"You have not said why you sought me here," Thea said. "Or how you know anything of me."

"Lord Ventnor told me you would be here."

"The plants..."

"A mere excuse."

He straightened, but did not explain. He simply studied her thoughtfully, intently, tapping his mouth with his fist.

"For what?" she prompted, her nervousness blooming anew.

"One cannot say something like that and not explain it. It's insufferable."

Then he shrugged and let his fist fall. "Might as well do it now, I suppose," he muttered.

"Do what?"

"Apparently, your Beau agreed with his father not to marry you, and obediently went north to a shooting party to recover from his heartbreak. Yet Ventnor fears that his son will need only one look at you to lose all reason and elope anyway. I am here to make sure you don't go anywhere and give him that one look."

Wonderful, Thea thought. Their plan was proceeding superbly. In truth, Beau Russell had only pretended to do his father's bidding, as the shooting party had placed him conveniently close to the Scottish border, making it easier for him to steal away to marry Helen. And along came this earl, believing Thea to be Helen and himself to be so clever.

"And what does Lord Ventnor bid you do in this matter?" Thea asked pertly. "No doubt he had excellent suggestions."

"Not at all. One of his suggestions was that I kidnap you."

"Gosh! I've never been kidnapped. That sounds terribly exciting."

"It sounds terribly tedious, not to mention troublesome. Another suggestion was that I seduce you."

"Also terribly tedious," she said hastily. "And very, very troublesome."

His eyes flicked over her. "I'm inclined to agree. Fortunately, I have my own plan for ensuring you do not marry Beau Russell."

"Do tell."

"Why, I shall simply marry you myself."

CHAPTER 3

S he might have looked pleased, or calculating, or any number of things. But not Thea Knight. Of course not. No.

Thea Knight laughed.

Peals of bright laughter bounced off the glass walls before she covered her mouth, while her shoulders shook and her bosom quivered, and a glossy lock of chestnut hair swayed against her neck. Even in the fading light, Rafe could see her eyes sparkle. Throughout their ridiculous conversation, he had been unwilling to tear his eyes from her face; he found himself surprisingly captivated by the way her entire countenance conveyed her thoughts, from the active dark brows and lively blue eyes, to the mobile mouth and the teeth that occasionally nibbled at her full bottom lip.

And now she laughed, freely, generously, holding nothing back. Rafe would not call Thea Knight a beauty, necessarily, but she had a beguiling freshness about her, like the plant that was best placed, that received a little more sunlight or a little more water, and was just that little more lush and alive.

Yes, that was it: The *vitality* about her, the way her whole face and body welcomed the world's delights.

Suddenly, he sympathized with her urge to touch the orchid, to confirm that something so marvelous was real. His fingers twitched, his arms became restless, as if he could reach out and capture her laughter. Hold it, taste it, share it.

A surge of irritation had him balling his hands into fists instead.

Blast it. This was not how she was meant to react to his proposal. This was not how he was meant to react to her.

If a woman earned a reputation as a wily, ambitious seductress, then she should bloody well have the decency to act the part. She should flatter and flirt and... Oh hell, he didn't know. Cast coy looks under her lashes, perhaps; present her figure to its best advantage, and declare him clever and handsome in a manner so sincere that he even began to believe it himself.

She was not meant to make fun of him, or appear scatterbrained and silly one moment and biting and crass the next. Why had no one thought to mention that she had mischievous eyes and a playful smile and a tendency to break out in satire?

He scowled at her. "A marriage proposal from an earl amuses you, Miss Knight?"

She shook off the last of her laughter. "It is such a male way of solving your problem: 'Should I kidnap this woman or seduce her? By George,' he says, 'I'll do both at once and just marry the girl.'"

"How gratifying that you find my proposal diverting. But I assure you, I am quite serious."

"Yes, you look quite serious." Another light laugh escaped her lips, and she tapped them with two fingers to make them behave. "You're not very good at proposing, are you?"

"You're not very good at accepting."

"If you were better at proposing, I might be better at accepting."

"If you were better at accepting, I wouldn't need to be good at proposing. Why do you not leap at this opportunity? If you married me, you'd be a countess."

Ideally, she would not realize that if she married him under a false name, she would not legally be his wife. But even if she did know the marriage wouldn't be valid, surely she could see how to turn this to her advantage? Surely, her past scandal had ruined her so thoroughly she would be desperate enough to try to make this marriage real. Get close to him, charm him, play on his lust or honor or gullibility so that he married her anyway. None of which she would ever manage to do, of course, but surely she would take the chance to *try*.

"Precisely," she said. "You would prevent me from becoming a future viscountess by raising me to the higher position of countess instead."

Rafe shrugged. "Men like Ventnor get all excited about lineage and breeding and whatnot. I don't much care whom I marry, so long as she's female and she... No, that's it. Just so long as she's female."

And Thea Knight certainly qualified on that count.

"Besides, you'd have to haul me off to Scotland to marry me quickly," she added. "And I don't want to go to Scotland."

"Neither do I. Scotland is very far and I want to go home. And since, as you point out, English laws preclude us from marrying quickly in the normal way, I came prepared: I have obtained a common license."

"A common license. I see. Yes. Right."

"Do you know what a common license is, Miss Knight? I could

tell you," he added, "but then I'd be educating you, and we both know how little you enjoy that."

Ignoring her glare, he slid the license out of his pocket and offered it for her inspection. She caught one edge of the paper between two ink-stained fingers and stretched to peer at it. A hint of her strawberry-sweet fragrance tantalized his nose; he kept his eyes resolutely on the page.

"This license authorizes us to marry immediately. The details are all there." He pointed to each item as he spoke. "Rafe Alexander Landcross. That's me. And Helen Elizabeth Knight. That's you. There's the name of the parish where this permits us to marry. And the name of the bishop who issued the license: the Bishop of Dartford. He's my father's cousin. When I told him I was journeying to Warwickshire to meet and marry Miss Helen Knight, he was more than happy to prepare this for me."

"Yes. Right. I see." She nodded knowledgeably and released the page. "That seems to be in order. Well done."

As he returned the license to his pocket, she paced away from him, glanced at him over her shoulder, then turned back, frowning and drumming her fingers against her chin.

"This is absurd," she finally said. "Is this a prank?"

"Do you think I have nothing better to do than travel for days to play some prank?"

"We've barely met and you're not very nice."

"True, but I am an earl."

"And?"

"Are you saying you do not find me interesting?"

"Not nearly as interesting as you find yourself."

"You followed me in here for this encounter." He waved an arm at the plants and glass walls. "An intimate *tête-à-tête* in the twilight. What did you seek, if not a marriage proposal?"

"I sought an explanation for the words you spoke in the inn."

"Hmm?"

"One cannot make cryptic comments without explaining them. It's exasperating."

"Are you saying you don't want to be a countess?"

Something flickered in her eyes, a hint of confusion, indecision.

Rafe waited. What the hell did she want, then? Unless the rumors were wrong and she was not the scheming social climber that her reputation suggested? But she must be. Look at her current efforts to help her sister catch a viscount's heir. And her own scandal was more than rumor. Scores of people had witnessed her disgrace. It was all perfectly clear to Rafe. If only she would do what he expected her to do, so he could get this blasted matter over with and go home.

"You must be very eager to please Lord Ventnor, to go to such lengths," was all she said. "I had no idea earls were so biddable."

"When the reward is sufficient, we are positively servile." Her contempt should not bother him, but still he found himself adding, "If I marry, I get access to a large trust fund."

"You were already married."

"My mother established the trust to encourage her younger sons to provide legitimate grandchildren. Unfortunately, I was a widower by then and did not qualify, as dead wives are not known for producing live children."

But she did not seem to be listening, as a calculating gleam lit her eye. "That must be quite a sum."

"It's big."

"How big?"

"Very big."

"I see."

Rafe did not bother asking what she thought she saw, for one thing she would not see was a penny of that money.

"There you have it, Miss Knight. Early tomorrow, we rouse the vicar, marry, and then leave for my estate."

"Your estate?"

"Brinkley End, in Somersetshire."

"But I'd need to live with you."

With that, she was backing away.

"And heirs," he lied desperately. "Earls have to make heirs. Surely you can see the opportunity this presents."

"By George," she might say to herself, in that way she had. "If I seduce him and he gets a child on me, he'll have to marry me for real."

Perhaps he had found the answer, for her face softened. Yes! She was going to accept! But she shook her head and turned away.

"What is the trouble?" he demanded.

For an agonizingly long minute, she stood silently, facing away from him. Several tendrils of hair had escaped their pins to caress the bare skin of her neck, brushing the edge of her gown and the buttons that kept it fastened.

"The trouble, my lord, is that was a terrible proposal." Levity had entered her tone, and when she twirled back around, mischief once more danced in her eyes. "Do they not teach you how to propose at earl school?"

"'Earl school'?"

"Yes. Lessons in proposals, after your lessons in posturing, prejudice, and pomposity."

"No need," Rafe said. "No matter how an earl proposes, there are only three possible answers: 'Yes, my lord,' 'Of course, my lord,' or 'I'd be honored, my lord.'"

"And yet again the nobleman gets what he wants without having to work for it."

"I have no interest in courting you, Miss Knight. If you yearn for pretty words and nice sentiments, you can provide them yourself."

"Very well, I shall. 'My dearest Miss Knight—'"

She paused and looked at him expectantly. Rafe met her gaze and said nothing.

She broke the impasse with an overwrought sigh. "A pretty state of affairs, indeed, when a lady must dictate her own marriage proposal. Once upon a time, it was chivalry and gallantry and poetry, but oh no, not with these modern earls."

Damn her. Why could she not simply behave like a caricature of a social climber? Why did she insist on having a personality? But what else could he do? He was an earl, yet she could make him dance like a carnival bear.

"Fine, I'll play your blasted game," he muttered. "My dearest Miss Knight."

"'The mere thought of your ankles makes me swoon.'"

"You want *that* in your marriage proposal?"

She eyed him defiantly. "I rather like the idea of a man swooning over my ankles."

"If he swoons over your ankles, he won't be good for much else. I assure you, they are not your most interesting feature."

"Whatever can you mean? My ankles are *fascinating*."

Rafe glanced down, but her ankles were hidden by the shadows under her hem. He was suddenly and irrationally curious about them, how they would look, how they would feel in his hand. Bloody hell. They were ankles, for crying out loud.

Maybe she was better at this than he thought.

He dragged his eyes back to her face. "Your fascinating ankles make me swoon."

"'The sight of you makes my heart go pitter-patter like raindrops on a—'"

"No. Enough. Let me emerge with some dignity."

"Your aim is to emerge with an engagement; your dignity is of no consequence."

"Anything to end this agony. Pitter-patter heart raindrops. What else do you want?"

Her expression changed again. The mischief faded, replaced by something like sorrow. Rafe's arms tensed with the improbable urge to offer comfort. She stared at the orchids, and then brushed her thumb over one petal. He bit back his scold. Her fingers were so gentle and reverent, her touch alone might help the orchid recover.

"I want..." She trailed off, and he caught himself leaning forward. "Say: 'I promise you a lifetime of laughter and kittens and syllabub, and a warm, safe, loving home.'"

Kittens? Syllabub? What?

"Enough!" he snapped. "You have had your entertainment, making me say ridiculous things, but that is too much. You can use this opportunity, so stop playing games and just bloody well agree to marry me."

A sad smile curved her lips as she nodded. Already she had stopped playing, and he didn't understand what had changed. How he had lost her, when he had never had her. How he had missed something, something important. Misunderstood, miscalculated, got something horribly wrong.

"No, my lord," she said softly. "I won't."

She snatched up her shawl, backed away, and then turned and ran. A moment later, the door opened and closed, and her figure hurried up the path, a blurred ghost disappearing into the last of the light.

Damn it. Why didn't she just agree? What kind of inept social climber was she, if she didn't seize a chance like that?

A wave of fatigue washed over him, as if only her presence had kept him from wilting like the orchids' leaves.

Maybe she needed a night to think it over. And tomorrow he'd invite her for that walk among the roses and she'd beg his forgiveness and say she was overcome and something something blah blah blah. She was right about one thing at least: He was not very good at this.

And he would not get better overnight.

Blast it, no. No more games. No more pretty smiles and pretty proposals and pretty ankles.

Rafe had another option. Thea Knight was not the only one who knew how to play tricks.

THE EARL OF LUXBOROUGH was likely mad, Thea decided, as she darted off in search of Arabella to tell her about the encounter.

That whole encounter had been, well, rather thrilling, if she was honest. How demanding he was, never imagining that she tricked him. And how marvelous for him, to be so sure of his place that he could issue a marriage proposal as carelessly as a dinner order. Perhaps he saw a wife as being of as little consequence as a meal.

Really, he had nothing to recommend him.

Except the money.

Oh, the money.

If somehow she could turn his proposal to her advantage and wangle some money from that trust, then she could go ahead with her publishing scheme immediately.

No. No regrets. Refusing was sensible. Her fascination with him was silly. The fact was, he had been awful to her, and she was rather tired of noblemen being awful to her.

Thea got lost several times in her attempt to locate Arabella's room, and might have spent the rest of her life wandering through the enormous house had a servant not rescued her. Arabella had not returned, so Thea left for her own chambers. She ate the supper left for her, bathed, and prepared for bed. But as her mind continued to torment her with "what-ifs" and "yes-buts" and memories of intense eyes and an amused half smile, Thea pulled on a wrap and went back to Arabella's room.

Which was still empty.

She sat and stood and sat and stood, and was about to leave when Arabella drifted in, looking even paler than usual.

"Where have you been?" Thea asked. "What's wrong?"

"Why on earth would anything be wrong?" Arabella said, only to stop short and stare at nothing.

"Arabella? Are you ill?"

"Worse."

"Are you dying?"

"Worse."

"Are you already dead and I'm conversing with a ghost?"

"Worse." Arabella inhaled with a hiss and blew the air back out. "I am engaged."

"What?"

"To be married."

"What?"

"To the Earl of Luxborough."

"That lying, cheating, hypocritical cad!"

That shook Arabella out of her daze. "Not quite the response I had anticipated," she said dryly, sounding more like herself.

"The earl already proposed to me," Thea told her.

"He did? Does he know you are not Helen?"

"On the contrary: He is sure that I am. He had even prepared a marriage license with Helen's name."

"How did he— Oh, his father's cousin, the Bishop of Dartford, I suppose."

Thea almost asked how Arabella knew the earl's cousin was a bishop, but of course, the aristocracy held everyone's family trees in their heads the way Pa held the last decade's price of gold.

"If you'll forgive my perplexity, Thea, why on earth would Lord Luxborough want to marry Helen?"

"So she can't marry Mr. Russell. He's here at Lord Ventnor's bidding. And if he marries again, he gets money from some trust set up by his mother."

"Clearly you didn't accept him."

"Of course not. But..." She felt unjustifiably betrayed. His proposal had been insulting and preposterous and yet... "What kind of beastly cad proposes to one woman and, as soon as she refuses him, proposes to another? If you had refused him, would he have worked his way through every unmarried woman in the house? And why didn't you refuse him? Wasn't his proposal dreadful?"

"He never issued one. He simply told my father he would marry me, and Papa agreed. I have just now had an interview with him and— Why, Thea, he is utterly detestable."

"What did he say?"

"That he wants my enormous dowry and..." Arabella burst into activity, straightening everything in sight. "I must remain on his estate, with no allowance, pastimes, or guests, until I have produced four sons. And how his eyes gleamed, as though it thrilled him to upset me."

"But your father won't make you marry such a man."

"Papa doesn't care. All he wants is a grandson."

Hands in fists, Arabella glared at her perfectly neat room. Thea helpfully pushed over a stack of books.

"What about the Marquess of Hardbury?" she asked, as Arabella tidied the books with zeal. "You've been promised to him since you were a child."

"No one has seen him in so long they say he might be dead, and Papa grows tired of waiting."

"You can refuse."

"Yes, and be disinherited and cast out. And then what? I shall make a formidable peeress, but I am of little use for anything else."

Her tidying frenzy passed, Arabella crossed to the window and touched a hand to her reflection. She was too restrained to shatter the glass with her fist, but her glare could well do the trick.

Thea wanted to weep for her friend, who would twist herself into knots to help others and never seek help for herself. Who hid her kindness under a proud facade and a sharp tongue. And these men—they reduced her to nothing more than a means of making more men.

Even Thea's parents had dismissed her, when Thea had come back from her year at the Winchester Ladies' Academy and announced she had a true friend in Miss Arabella Larke. "She is excessively proud and aloof and so elegant she makes my eyeballs ache," Thea had gushed. "But she is uncompromising and principled and good."

Ma and Pa had shaken their heads in despair. "Miss Larke has excellent connections but no brothers," they had said. "What use is a friendship if it does not grant you access to a circle of young noblemen?"

Thea had hated to disappoint her parents—she understood their ambitions were for the good of the whole Knight family—but never would she regret her friendship with Arabella. If only Arabella had not been in Italy the year of Thea's scandal. Arabella always knew what to say; she would never freeze in fear. She would have looked down her nose at everyone in that ballroom and dealt Percy and Francis such a scathing set-down they would have fallen right through the floor.

"You were always very efficient," Thea said brightly. "Perhaps you could arrange to have two sets of twins in two years." She sought a positive note. "And he didn't threaten to slit your throat and throw your body down a well."

Arabella was not cheered by this perspective. "No wonder it is the fashion to marry for love. When a man may exercise such control over his wife, it would be nice if one's husband felt a modicum of affection."

"Then I shall marry him after all," Thea announced and ignored the protestations of her suddenly pounding heart.

Arabella swung around. "No, you will not. Besides, his license bears Helen's name. If you use a false name, the marriage won't be valid."

Thea waited.

"Oh." Arabella drew the sound out. "The marriage...will not... be valid."

Her face almost betrayed a smile, and Thea grinned in response. A terrible trick, indeed, to marry a man while using a false name, but it did comply with her Rules of Mischief. First, it served several good causes: saving Arabella from a horrid marriage, deflecting attention from Helen, and hopefully providing funds to pay for her pamphlet. Second, she had no qualms about tricking an earl, when he was powerful and had proven himself villainous. And third, well, why not enjoy life as a counterfeit countess for a week or two?

"He would have no legal rights or control over me at all," she said excitedly. "I need only pretend until Helen's return."

"And Papa can hold a grudge for a century, so Luxborough could never propose to me again."

Thea danced across the room. "And if I could channel some of his money toward myself..." An idea struck her. "Perhaps I shall uncover his dreadful secrets and he'll pay thousands for my silence."

"Yet to deceive an earl. Possibly even steal from or blackmail an *earl*."

"Oh, who cares? He is only a man, and not a very agreeable one at that. *I* shall not bother my conscience over him. And neither should you. After all, he is planning to slit your throat and throw your body down a well."

"No, he isn't," Arabella said patiently. "You made that part up."

Thea sniffed. "Just because I made it up doesn't mean it's not true."

"It is too dangerous, Thea."

"Not at all." She thought of the way Lord Luxborough's features had softened when he spoke of the orchids. Of his warm solidity at her side. "I am sure his lordship is as sweet as syllabub under all that growling."

"And I am sure he is not. If he believes you are legally his wife, he may—" Arabella cleared her throat. "Claim his conjugal rights."

"Um. Yes. He did mention heirs."

His large body, covering hers, like in the etchings in Mrs. Burton's library. She remembered his big hand, cupping the flower; would he be so gentle with her? Would she touch him too? That dark, curling hair, that scarred face, those broad shoulders... And his firm-looking mouth, with the little half smile on his defined lips...

Thea had been kissed before, but only by Percy Russell, whose chaste kisses had been tolerable at best. She had tried hard to like him, for the sake of her whole family, yet with Percy, she always felt awkward, as if she had too many arms. With the earl, even when he had stood so close that she caught his scent, she had felt not awkward but...right.

"The invalid marriage will last only until Helen returns safely married, a week or two at the most," Thea said. "If he comes near, I shall scream and faint. Or I shall tell him I have my monthly courses and send *him* running in fear."

"But he is odd and reclusive. The things they say about him."

"No. I refuse to listen to more rumors."

Arabella raised her brows. "Not to mention the fresh rumors this will start about you, if word gets out."

"But word needn't get out, given Luxborough avoids society," Thea argued. "Besides, Ventnor and Luxborough are sure to hush it up. They will never admit to being outwitted by the daughters of a mere merchant. True, our behavior as a pretend married couple will break all the rules, but one cannot be concerned with propriety in such a situation."

Arabella considered. Thea could almost see her spinning out the implications and ramifications, dozens of moves in advance.

"This plan is flawed," she concluded.

"We must treat it as a game," Thea said.

Finally. Today, everything changed. After three lonely years of waiting, aimless and scared, Thea had purpose and a plan. She would have this adventure, she would finagle some money, she would publish her pamphlet and tell her story, and in a few short weeks, she would find her way home.

Arabella gave a single sharp nod: decision made. "I shall send a manservant to accompany you for safety, and you will write to me every day. Do you need money?"

"I have a few pounds from my wages."

"Carry it always. Sew money into your stays so you can run at any time."

"I am out of the habit of wearing stays."

"Your hems, then. I still don't like this."

"You cannot stop me," Thea said quietly. It was risky, but better her than Arabella. "And he's not entirely unappealing. What's the worst that can happen?"

"He could slit your throat and throw your body down a well."

"That doesn't sound so bad, then, does it?" Thea patted Arabella's hand. "In one single, bold move, I shall save you, Helen, and myself. I truly am a Knight in shining ribbons."

"Oh, good grief."

Thea grinned. "Now, help me pen a note to Lord Luxborough, in which I inform him that I shall marry him in the morning."

CHAPTER 4

T he vicar protested that it was highly irregular when he opened his door early the next morning, unshaven, bleary-eyed, and smelling of sherry, to find a wedding party on his doorstep. At first, he quibbled over the license and bleated about irritating, inconsequential things like rules, but Rafe quieted him with a mention of the Bishop of Dartford, and Miss Larke's imperious impatience did the rest. Throughout the argument, Rafe's fake-bride-to-be, wrapped in a blue cloak and carriage dress, yawned and rubbed her eyes.

No one giggled during the meaningless vows or the paperwork, and soon Rafe was in possession of an invalid marriage certificate. Business concluded, the vicar marched into his house and slammed the door. Miss Larke headed after him, and Rafe strode toward the road to await the loaded carriage.

"Must you walk so fast?" Thea called from behind him.

He glanced at her over his shoulder. The hood of her cloak was pushed back and the morning mist gathered in droplets in her chestnut hair.

"This is how I walk," he said, and kept going.

"It makes it difficult for me to walk beside you," she complained.

"So don't."

"But that's what people do."

"I'm not people."

A few more steps brought him to the ivy-wreathed gate, and he paced by the roadside. Thea joined him and brushed her damp hair off her face. Now that she was fully awake, her eyes were bright, and as blue as the cornflowers blooming in his garden.

Blast it. He had miscalculated. With his attention on the practical details of his scheme, Rafe had failed to consider Thea Knight as a real woman. A woman whose skin promised to be soft, and whose smile promised mischief, and whose curves promised that her ankles were definitely not her most interesting feature. He had not even thought how to address her now she was his counterfeit countess. Neither "Thea" nor "Helen" was acceptable, and he would not call her "my lady" when she was no such thing.

Whatever he called her, he suspected she would not be easy to control. How inept to assume otherwise. She would not placidly obey, but neither would she argue or cajole. She would tease and trick and torment, and Rafe would somehow have to survive.

"The fact is, we did just get married," she said, as though continuing a discussion that, as far as Rafe could recall, had not started. "So it would be as well for us to—"

"Not necessary."

"But I'm your wife."

"Which does not require further discussion."

"And a countess too." With an impish smile, she executed a neat pirouette, her skirts swishing around her. Brown half boots covered the famously fascinating ankles, but he caught a glimpse of shapely, stockinged calves. "Isn't that exciting?"

Rafe looked away from her legs. "No."

"Is it exciting to be an earl?"

"No."

"But being a countess will be exciting."

"Unlikely."

"I shall have lots of new gowns."

"Not a one."

"But I must." She gave him a haughty look. "The best countesses are very elegant."

"The best countesses are very quiet."

"But—"

"They never talk."

"Oh."

A shape appeared in the mist at the end of the road. That had better be his blasted carriage. He would put Thea in it and ride alongside and never speak to her again.

Back at the vicarage, he saw, Miss Larke was in conversation with the vicar's wife. Even Rafe had heard of Miss Arabella Larke, the notoriously proud heiress. How had Thea secured such a lady's friendship? Miss Larke hardly seemed the sort to suffer sycophants or be easily duped, and Thea's scandal should have kept every respectable lady away.

"Now, I have my doubts," Thea said, "but Ma and Pa always said that a title is the best thing in the world."

"Congratulations, Countess. You passed one whole minute without talking."

She frowned. "I don't think that's the correct way to address me."

"I shall address you however I please."

"Of course, because you're an *earl*. So you must be happy to have a title."

"No."

"But—"

"I am the third of five sons. I neither expected nor wanted to be earl. My eldest brother John was an excellent man and an excellent earl and if there were any justice he would never have died."

"Then your next brother—"

"Philip was an awful man, and if there were any justice he would never have been born. But if there were any justice, the title would have skipped me and gone to my next brother, Christopher, who is a Member of Parliament and would make an excellent earl. It's an absurd system."

"But you benefit from it."

"Which proves my point," he muttered.

Besides, he could hardly consider the title a benefit when worthier men like his father and brother John had to die for him to have it.

She lapsed into silence, and Rafe watched the torturously slow approach of the carriage. How long until she started talking again? Ten, nine, eight—

"Are you a good earl?" she asked.

"'Good' as in competent, moral, or well-behaved?"

"Any of those."

"No."

Not that Rafe could bring himself to care. A peer's purpose was to govern in the House of Lords, but politics was beyond him. All those *people*. All that *talking*. Schemes and ambitions, policies and demands. Read this. Listen to that. Sign here. Vote there. For his part, Christopher insisted he was happy as an MP in the House of Commons, where he could get more done.

And Rafe was about to become an even worse earl. As soon as he had the money from this invalid marriage, he would do what aristocrats never did: start a business. The idea alone could trigger an earthquake of genteel shudders.

"They don't teach charm at earl school either, do they?" Thea said with some asperity.

"Charm is about making oneself liked by making people like themselves, and I don't care if anyone likes me or themselves."

"But how can you not want people to like you?"

"If people don't like me, they don't talk to me."

"And you don't like anyone, I suppose."

"On the contrary. I like everyone who doesn't talk to me."

She cocked her head, considering. "But what about society?"

"Society? You mean people chittering and twittering like so many blasted birds? A whole world of wonders out there, and they chatter on about their petty concerns, the weather, their shoes, their horse, though there's no point to any of it."

No point at all, Rafe thought, eyes on the approaching carriage. One's wife would still lose her reason and ride to her death. One would still get attacked by a wild animal hunting its prey. One's brothers would still die in accidents and wars, thus transforming an itinerant botanist into an earl. He could long to hear Katharine's laugh one more time, or wish for his brother's calm wisdom, or smile at the memory of his father's bad jokes, but whining about it to the world would not help. One could cheer or complain, care or not, and it did not change a single blasted thing.

And not to forget that society repeated those rumors about him, shuddered at his face, ignored the truth about Katharine, and then had the gall to criticize him for preferring the peace and quiet of his estate.

"Discussing such small things is a way of understanding the world and oneself," Thea said, with irritating gentleness. "Of forging connections with others. It's what people do."

Rafe glared at her. "I'm not people."

FINALLY, mercifully, the carriage arrived, accompanied by Rafe's manservant and horse. Also riding on the carriage was a swarthy, broad-shouldered stranger who nimbly leaped down before the coachman had brought the horses to a stop.

"You." Rafe accosted the stranger. "Who are you and why are you riding on my carriage?"

"That is Gilbert," Miss Larke said, appearing at Rafe's side.

The man Gilbert bowed and turned to check on the luggage. Thea drifted off to chat with him.

"He is Lady Luxborough's manservant," Miss Larke added. "Formerly a champion pugilist."

"She doesn't need a manservant, pugilistic or otherwise."

"He will stay by her side. To ensure no harm befalls her."

"What harm could possibly befall her?"

"None. Because Gilbert will make sure it doesn't."

Miss Larke met his gaze steadily. Not once did her eyes flicker to his scars. Impressive, really: At first, it was a natural human instinct to look. Yet even during their excruciating interview the night before, when Rafe was painting a future so awful Thea would have to rescue her, Miss Larke's exquisite manners had never faltered. Her face was a mask; he found it unbearable.

Also unbearable was the knowledge that they feared him. Not that he could complain, given his threats against Miss Larke. It was frightening enough for young women as it was, to be packed off to remote estates where they knew no one but the near stranger they had married. Even bold, reckless Katharine had feared her father's plans to marry her off, so that crossing the Atlantic with Rafe had seemed preferable.

Worst decision she ever made.

"She will come to no harm," he snapped.

"It would be remiss of me not to be concerned," Miss Larke said calmly. "Given the stories about your first wife."

Rafe turned his worst glare on her. She did not flinch.

"Stories, Miss Larke?"

"You are being willfully obtuse, my lord."

"Am I."

"Some say you poisoned her. Others say you killed her through sorcery."

He had to unclench his jaw to respond. "You disappoint me, Miss Larke. You strike me as too intelligent to listen to other people's stories."

"An intelligent person always listens. People tend to betray themselves through the stories they tell."

Bloody hell, she was exhausting. He was not going to waste his day trying to match wits or stares with his fake bride's demanding friend.

"She will come to no harm," he repeated.

Miss Larke glanced at Thea, and her expression softened ever so slightly. "She can be impulsive. She has a tendency to try to save people, a blatant disrespect for rules, and a gift for seeing through others' claptrap. If she were shipwrecked alone on a rock, she would find something to entertain her. Do not mistake her playfulness for foolishness."

"Your recommendation is unnecessary."

"You will not interfere with her manservant. She will write to me daily and you will allow it. And for the first month, you will not—" She stopped short, then nodded meaningfully and made a rolling gesture with her hand.

"I'll not what, Miss Larke?"

Miss Larke did not sigh, but she gave the impression of having sighed. "Again, my lord, willfully obtuse."

Past her, Thea was peering through the carriage window,

cheerfully remarking to Gilbert on the presence of the plants inside as her traveling companions. Rafe felt strangely glad that Thea had such a fierce and loyal friend.

Yet he could hardly reveal that he had no intention of even talking to Thea, let alone bedding her. It was a fine line he trod: to maintain the pretense he believed she was Helen and hence truly his wife, while giving Thea no cause to demand a real marriage.

"I will not touch her for one month," he said.

Miss Larke nodded regally. Without another word, Rafe covered the few steps to the carriage and yanked open its door. Thea said her final farewells and joined him.

"How do you know Miss Larke?" he asked abruptly.

"We met at the Winchester Ladies' Academy." Thea bit her lip. He suspected she had answered as Thea, not Helen. "Mr. Larke sent Arabella there in the vain hope of making her more demure. My parents sent me to gain some extra polish."

"And to meet high-born ladies, I suspect. A time-honored tactic for social climbers."

She narrowed her eyes. "I suppose you begrudge my family their ambition, though it is only what our society demands."

Rafe shrugged. "If people are foolish enough to believe that joining the upper class is worth that much trouble, that's their problem."

"I suppose people always want what they cannot have," she said. "Not you, of course, because you're not people."

"No." He held out a hand to help her into the carriage. "Your carriage awaits, Lady Luxborough."

"Lady Luxborough," she repeated with great amusement, and placed her gloved hand on his, warm and alive. It occurred to him with some surprise that this was the first time they had touched. She laughed lightly, and her laughter shot into his hand and up his arm like an electric charge. "Lord and Lady Lucks-bor-ough. Oh—Do they call you 'Lucky'?"

"Astonishingly enough, they do not."

Again, she laughed, as she stepped up into the carriage. He let her go, still feeling her warmth and weight, and watched as she arranged her cloak and skirt and sat back, looking about her with delight. She had blankets, as well as a basket of food and drink, and the company of the orchids.

She smiled back at him. "Gilbert says you will travel by horseback, and not in the carriage with me."

"I daresay you will find the plants' conversation more stimulating than my own."

"Oh, you're not that bad," she said cheerfully. "I could almost enjoy talking to you."

He could travel with her, he supposed. It would be more comfortable riding in the carriage than on horseback. They could chat, or not. She could come up with nonsense, and he could pretend not to be amused. He could simply look at her.

Rafe stepped back, slammed the carriage door shut, and made for his horse with such briskness that the startled creature shied away.

A DAY RIDING DID little to improve Lord Luxborough's disposition, Thea observed, when they stopped at an inn for the night. Without giving Thea so much as a nod, he left the men to deal with the carriage and strode inside.

The innkeeper took one look at the earl and greeted him as "my lord." Scowling, Luxborough insisted that he was Mr. Cross, traveling with Mrs. Cross, and demanded separate rooms. The innkeeper began to protest, but a quelling look persuaded him that he could find some rooms, if his lordship, that is, Mr. Cross, didn't mind waiting.

"We'll wait in the private parlor," Luxborough said, and marched straight for it.

The innkeeper scuttled after him. "I'm afraid it's occupied, m'lord, I mean, Mr. Cross. You see, a small party—"

"Tell them to get out."

Luxborough threw open the door and froze, aghast. Thea hurried to his side to see what horror lay within. A horror indeed: four women and two children, nearly all of who were weeping.

"What the hell is this?"

The earl shot a furious look at the innkeeper, as though the man had pinched the women to make them cry, purely for his inconvenience. Then one of the children, eyes on Luxborough, cried, "Auntie, it's the Devil come for us!" and emitted an ear-piercing scream.

Luxborough slammed the door shut.

"Some kind of tragedy, m'lord, I mean, Mr. Cross," the innkeeper whispered. "They can't afford the parlor, but I put them there so as not to upset everyone. Weeping women puts people right off their food, it does. It's the economics of it, m'lord, I mean, Mr. Cross. A man's got to think of his economics. But if your lordship insists. I mean, Mr. Cross. Sir."

The innkeeper flashed a worried smile at Thea, who tried to return it. Luxborough made a growling sound and dug out some coins.

"How's this for your blasted economics? This'll cover the cost of the parlor for them," he said irritably. "And send them in food and drink too."

The innkeeper eagerly took the coins. "Too kind, m'lord, I mean, Mr. Cross. Now, wait one shake of my tail and I'll have a table cleared in the main tavern."

"In a corner," Luxborough called as the man bustled away. "I don't want any attention on us."

He drew a deep breath and rubbed one shoulder.

"That was very kind of you," Thea said tentatively.

"Least I could do after terrifying the children." For the first time since they stopped, he looked at her, a surprising glint of humor in his expression. "But let the record show that the women were already crying *before* they saw me."

"Actually, they stopped crying when they saw you."

"That's me," he agreed glumly. "Bringer of good cheer."

But his unexpected good humor faded in the doorway to the tavern. It was full of rowdy ale-cheered travelers. The air was smoky from pipes and thick with the smells of stew and, well, travelers.

"This is hell." Luxborough massaged the back of his neck. "These *people*. This *talking*."

"It's a normal tavern," Thea pointed out. "And you don't seem shy."

"I'm not. People exhaust me." He shook his head at the room. "Forget fire and brimstone. Hell is eternity stuck in a stuffy, smoky tavern full of loud Englishmen determined to enjoy themselves, despite having nothing but bland stew, warm ale, and each other." He slid her a sideways glance. "But you cannot go in alone, can you?"

"No."

"Right. Hell."

Shaking his head, he shoved through the crowd to where the innkeeper had cleared them a table by one wall.

No sooner had they sat than a serving woman brought them food and drink. Thea, hungry and happy not to dine alone, showed her gratitude by not talking, despite Luxborough's new provoking manner of casting her thoughtful glances.

As soon as their plates were empty, the server—perhaps paying them special attention because of the economics—quickly cleared their table and refilled their drinks, after which Luxborough abruptly said, "Your sister."

Thea's hand jerked and wine sloshed onto the table.

"My sister?" she squeaked, busily wiping up the spill.

"Dorothea, I believe, is her name."

"Ah. Yes. Thea. Right."

"Rumor has it she developed a scheme of seducing noblemen in an effort to trap one into marriage," he said. "But she tried it with more than one at a time and they found out."

How very succinct he was, Thea thought, and poked at a remaining droplet of wine.

"So what is the full story?" he asked.

She looked up, startled. "You want to hear the story?"

"That's what I said."

Oh. Only Arabella had ever asked her for the story. Warm pleasure spread through her like wine, and she sat back to consider her approach. How odd to narrate her own story as if it had happened to someone else. Unless—yes! She would be like the narrator in her pamphlet, telling the tale not of Thea Knight but of the heroine, Rosamund.

"Very well," she said. "I shall tell you the tale of...a winsome lass."

"Winsome?" He regarded her skeptically. "Do you even know what that means?"

"Of course I do."

She'd never given it much thought. Winsome was just one of those things that lasses were.

"How is, ah, Thea winsome?"

"Um. Because she win some, lose some."

"I'm sorry I asked." He briefly closed his eyes. "Very, very sorry."

Drunk on his interest, Thea laughed. "Anyway," she continued, using her hands for dramatic emphasis. "This winsome lass is attending a picnic, and—"

And she waved her arms, slamming her knuckles into the wall. Ouch. She could not tell her story like this, hemmed in as she was. She pushed back her chair and stood.

"What are you doing?" Luxborough snapped. "Sit down."

"I need space to tell the story."

"No, you don't. You sit in your chair and talk. It's really quite simple."

"But I can't..." The chair dug into the back of her knees and she pushed it back further. "I need—"

"'Ere you," came a male voice from behind her. "Wotcha think yer doin' then, eh?"

Thea spun around, mortified to realize she had jostled the man at the next table.

"I do beg your pardon, sir," she said. "But I am telling a story and I need space."

"Oh, I like a good story," said the man. "What's this story about then?"

"No story," Luxborough called sternly. "You, man, turn around. You, wife, sit down."

Thea and the man ignored him. "It's about a winsome lass," Thea said.

"Oh, I like a winsome lass. And the theatre. I saw Miss Sarah Holloway perform in London once, years ago. Splendid actress. Shame she disappeared. But I do like a nice spot of theatre after a day on the road."

"This isn't theatre," Thea hastened to correct him. "I'm just telling a story to my, um, to him."

But the man was already shuffling back his chair so he could hear her story too. In doing so, he upset his whole table.

"Oi, Joe," cried the people at the table. "Watch what you're doing."

"Make some space," said the man named Joe. "This lady here is telling us a story. There'll be some theatre tonight."

The people at the table welcomed this news loudly, for they, too, liked a spot of theatre after a day on the road.

"What's this story about, then?" one of them asked.

"It's about a winsome lass," said the man named Joe. "Who —" He turned back to Thea. "What happens to this winsome lass?"

A dozen keen faces turned to her. People stuck in a coaching inn, after a long day of tiresome travel, desperate to be entertained. Thea risked a glance at the earl, who was looking murderous. Everything was fine there, then.

"She is cruelly wronged by a pair of dastardly knaves," she told her new audience.

"Boo, poor thing," said the people. "Let's hear this story, then."

They shoved back their table, its feet scraping on the floor, to rearrange their chairs. This upset other patrons, but they were soon mollified by the news that they were about to get a story, and everyone liked a spot of theatre after a day on the road.

"What are you all doing?" asked the innkeeper, bustling in. "Messing up my room. It's not good for my economics."

Several patrons informed him that this fine lady was going to tell them a story.

"This is the taproom, not a theatre." The innkeeper jerked his chin at Luxborough. "If people are watching theatre, they're not talking. And if they're not talking, they're not drinking. It's the economics of it, m'lord, I mean, Mr. Cross. A man's got to think of his economics."

With more dark muttering about hell, Luxborough offered another handful of coins. "Get them all drinks."

It didn't take long to refresh everyone's drinks and clear a space for Thea. Luxborough lounged against the wall, apparently resigned to this hellish development, and Thea considered how to proceed. Her family, like many households, enjoyed performing plays at home to while away the evenings, but it was another matter to perform alone.

She was still considering how to begin when the man named Joe, who had started all of this, bounded onto a chair and hushed the crowd.

"Friends and fellow travelers, listen well," he said in a rich voice, waving his arms with pleasing dramatic effect. "For tonight's theatre performance, this fine young lady will tell us the story of a winsome lass—"

"Ooooh," everyone said.

"Who is cruelly wronged—"

"Awwwwww," everyone said.

"By a pair of dastardly knaves."

"Booooooo," everyone said.

"I present to you 'The Tale Of—'" He paused, arms in the air, and frowned at Thea. "What's her name, then, this winsome lass?"

"Rosamund," said Thea.

"Can I be Rosamund?" called out a serving woman, a plump fair-haired woman in her thirties. "I've always wanted to be an actress. And you can't do it all on your own, miss."

Before Thea could agree, the woman was at the front of the room, curtsying to the crowd.

"I am Rosamund," she called out. "I'm a winsome lass"—she pressed one hand to her forehead—"who was cruelly wronged"—she clasped both hands over her heart—"by two dastardly knaves."

66

Again, the crowd cheered. Thea's confidence grew. They were apparently very easy to entertain.

"I want to be a dastardly knave!" called a young man, leaping to his feet, followed by another man saying, "Me too!"

"Of course," Thea said, because what else could she do? "You are Percy," she told the thin, sandy-haired one, who did bear a passing resemblance to Percy Russell. "And you are Francis," she told the stout, balding one. "And remember, you are arrogant, dastardly, and very, very knavish."

While the two men got into character, which meant puffing up their chests and strutting around to the cheers of the crowd, Thea darted back to Lord Luxborough and his baleful glare.

"The knaves in question are Percy Russell—that's Lord Ventnor's youngest son; I suppose you know him as you married his sister—and Francis Upton, heir to the Baron Bairstow."

"Those are the two whom, ah, Thea reportedly tried to trap into marriage," he said.

She waved an admonishing finger at him. "Just listen."

The man named Joe put his chair to one side and then helped Thea climb onto it. She looked out over the faces turned to her in eager anticipation.

Waiting to hear her story.

The last time a roomful of people had stared at Thea, it was in Lord Ventnor's ballroom. Now, after three years of her being silenced, spoken over, sent away, people wanted to hear her story.

She cleared her throat and smiled. "Now listen, all, to the tale of Rosamund, a winsome lass—"

"What's that mean, anyway?" interrupted the woman playing Rosamund. "Winsome."

"Why," Thea said, "it means you win some, lose some."

The eager, tipsy crowd cheered again. Thea flashed a smile at Luxborough and began her tale.

CHAPTER 5

R afe let his head fall back against the wall with a thump. This was meant to be a quiet evening.

But not with Thea Knight, who couldn't sit in a simple blasted chair and tell a simple blasted story without involving every blasted person in the entire blasted room.

And were they involved! Awaiting their entertainment as eagerly as in a real theatre.

He used to enjoy the theatre, Rafe remembered suddenly. How had he forgotten that? Even as a boy and a youth, he loved watching the frequent amateur performances by his parents and their friends. The magic of it thrilled him, the way his imagination would take over, making it real, so when it ended, he would blink with surprise to find himself seated in the middle of a crowd.

And then—what happened? In America, even when he and Katharine had no money, he had stopped for performances in markets and fairs by traveling theatre troupes. But since Katharine's death, he had not watched a single play. It was a simple pleasure, yet he had let it be taken from him.

"Rosamund," Thea explained to her tipsy audience, "is the brave, honorable daughter of a rich merchant. One day, at a picnic, she overhears the two knaves making secret plans. She hides in the shrubbery to listen."

"Rosamund" curled her hand around her ear in a dramatic portrayal of eavesdropping.

The audience was enthralled.

"These two knaves are noblemen," Thea said, as the knaves strutted about. "They are scoundrels, utter villainous blackguards who deserve to have their—"

The crowd cheered and booed, drowning out Thea's words. Rafe didn't need to hear the words to understand the rage simmering under her good cheer. He found himself sitting forward on his seat.

She calmed the crowd and continued.

"Rosamund overheard these knaves placing bets on who could first ruin fair Lady Letitia, by seducing her and telling the world."

Bored gentlemen were known to make dubious bets, although this sounded worse than most. He remembered little of Percy Russell—Percy had still been a schoolboy when Rafe eloped with Katharine—but he recalled her saying that her brother had been almost sent down from Eton over a betting scandal.

"One hundred pounds says I can ruin the lady first," said "Percy."

"One hundred pounds says *I* can ruin the lady first," said "Francis."

Boos from the crowd egged them on into a torrent of coarse euphemisms.

"I'll feed her pussycat!" one yelled.

"I'll visit her at Bushy Park!" cried the other.

"We'll honeyfugle!"

"We'll fuddle!"

69

"We'll splice!"

Thea banged a knife against a metal tankard to bring them to order. They muttered apologies, the crowd quietened, and Thea continued. "Brave Rosamund knew she must warn Lady Letitia."

"What dastardly knaves they are!" cried "Rosamund". "I must warn Lady Letitia!"

"Oh!" cried the other serving woman, running onto the makeshift stage. "I'll be Lady Letitia!"

"Then who's going to fetch our ale?" someone yelled.

"Fetch your own bleeding ale," she yelled back. "I'm an actress and a lady now."

To demonstrate this, she stuck her nose in the air and pointed one boot-clad toe in a dainty manner.

"I must talk to you, Lady Letitia," said the woman playing Rosamund.

"Do not talk to me, merchant's daughter. I'm too good for you."

The crowd booed and hissed. Thea, looking worried, waved her hands and said, "No, no."

Too much, Rafe thought, and surrendered to his imagination, letting the taproom melt away and the play unfold.

NARRATOR: No, no. That isn't what happened.
ROSAMUND: Fine, I'll let them ruin you, then.
CROWD: *[Cheers.]*
NARRATOR: No. Rosamund does not say that. She's our noble heroine and she must warn Letitia.
ROSAMUND: Very well. I must warn you: Those knaves have a plot to ruin you.
NARRATOR: The two knaves approached Lady Letitia and sought to woo her.
[The knaves go to Lady Letitia and take her hands.]
PERCY: Fair lady, let us play the game of see-saw.

FRANCIS: Beautiful lady, let us dance the goat's jig.

NARRATOR: Gentlemen. Please.

LETITIA: You have made a bet to ruin me. I shall not be seduced.

NARRATOR: The scoundrels' game was ruined! They were furious and demanded to know who told.

PERCY: I am furious!

FRANCIS: I demand to know who told!

LETITIA: *[points at Rosamund]* It was Rosamund, the merchant's daughter.

NARRATOR: The dastardly knaves vowed to get revenge.

PERCY: We must get revenge!

FRANCIS: Revenge on the merchant's daughter! Bwah-hah-hah. *[Pause]* How do we get our revenge then?

Thea looked around at the crowd. "We need someone to be the rich merchant, Rosamund's father."

A graying man jumped up and strutted across the stage. "I am very rich. I feast on roast beef every day."

Unfortunately, this boast set the crowd to booing.

"No, stop," Thea said. "He is not a bad man, but he is very ambitious, and he desperately wants his daughter Rosamund to marry a nobleman, for the good of his whole family. May we continue?"

NARRATOR: Percy, to get his revenge, asks the merchant for permission to court his daughter, which pleases the merchant.

PERCY: I am a nobleman. I want to marry your daughter.

MERCHANT: Right you are. Ahoy! Rosamund! Shake your tail with this nobleman then.

NARRATOR: Rosamund doesn't like Percy the Dastardly Knave, but she does want to please her father.

ROSAMUND: Very well. You may seduce me.

PERCY: Let's have a nice game of bob-in-joe.

NARRATOR: No! That's not what happened. He doesn't seduce her.

PERCY: What? Why don't I get to seduce her?

ROSAMUND: And why don't I get to be seduced?

NARRATOR: Wait and you'll see. Settle down.

PERCY AND ROSAMUND: Oh, very well, then.

NARRATOR: So Percy took Rosamund and her father to a fine ball, where Rosamund and Percy danced.

There followed an interlude where the crowd sang and clapped a rhythm, and "Percy" and "Rosamund" danced. Rafe fell back against the wall, his unease growing. Thea caught Rafe's eye and shrugged, apparently cheerful, as she continued her narration.

"But Percy's father—a great lord, mind you—was very angry!" She stopped. "We need a great lord to be very angry."

Two men bounded forward, both loudly insisting they had the necessary anger to be the great lord. While they argued, Thea dashed over to Rafe.

"That's Lord Ventnor," she whispered. "But it didn't happen quite like this."

"Did it not? You astonish me."

"I mean, I—" She stopped short and bit her lip. "*Thea* only knew about Francis Upton and another man, so she had no idea Percy Russell was involved. I simplified it so as not to confuse anyone."

Rafe looked past her, to where the two men were rolling around on the floor.

"No," he agreed dryly. "We wouldn't want to confuse anyone."

"This is going very well, I think," she said.

Before Rafe could respond, she dashed away, sorted out the

two men fighting, leaped back onto her chair, and the play resumed.

NARRATOR: The lord was very angry and stopped his son from dancing with Rosamund.

LORD: *[separates Percy and Rosamund]* Son! How dare you dance with a merchant's daughter!

NARRATOR: At which point, with every eye on the ballroom upon them, Percy loudly announced that he would marry her, for he had seduced her.

PERCY: What? But I didn't seduce her.

ROSAMUND: You said he wasn't allowed to seduce me.

NARRATOR: Precisely. He told everyone he seduced her when he didn't.

PERCY: You mean, he *lied*?

NARRATOR: Dastardly knave, remember?

PERCY: Very well. I had a brush with her and now I shall make her my bride.

LORD: Oh no you won't.

PERCY: Oh yes I will.

NARRATOR: Then the other knave, Francis, runs on and— Where is the other knave?

FRANCIS: *[puts down drink]* Sorry. What?

NARRATOR: Francis tells everyone that he also seduced Rosamund and intended to marry her.

PERCY: What? How come he got to seduce her and I didn't?

FRANCIS: Because I'm better at it than you are.

NARRATOR: He didn't seduce her! No one seduced her! It was a plot. Their revenge.

Thea's words were greeted with uncomprehending silence.

Everyone stared at her blankly, actors and spectators alike. Her exasperation palpable, she tried again.

"The two of them *told* all of society that she lay with them both, separately, to trap one of them into marriage," she said. "But she didn't, you see. It was all a lie."

More blank faces.

Thea looked around desperately. "If she lay with only one of them, he would be honor-bound to marry her," she explained, almost frantic. "But if she lay with *both* of them, then neither would have to marry her, and she would be ruined and called names besides. Don't you understand?"

Finally, they understood. Jaws dropped and spines straightened, and the audience members launched into a round of enthusiastic booing.

CROWD: Those dastardly knaves! Cads! Villains! Boooo!
FRANCIS: We played a game of pully-hawly. She might be carrying my baby.
PERCY: We played a game of rankum-spankum. She might be carrying *my* baby.
FRANCIS: I'll knock your teeth from your skull.
PERCY: I'll tear your guts from your body.

The two knaves hurled themselves at each other in an exuberant mock fight. The spectators cheered, the other actors laughed, and Thea...

Thea watched, one hand over her mouth, looking lost. She made no move to intervene.

"So does either of us marry her?" asked the man playing Percy.

Thea said nothing.

"Miss?" prompted the other knave. "Who does she marry?

Again, Thea said nothing.

Faced with Thea's silence, the actors continued alone, the script an old one, already well known. Thea watched the scene unfold, her light gone, as if her life was yet again falling apart before her eyes.

It was the man playing Lord Ventnor who spoke first.

LORD: She will not marry either of you, since she lay with you both. And who knows how many others there were? Once these women start, they never stop.

ROSAMUND: But I didn't!

LORD: Women like you always say that.

ROSAMUND: They're lying!

LORD: My son and his friend would never lie. You tried to trap them. Everyone knows your father wants you to marry a nobleman. You harlot!

PERCY: Ha ha! She is ruined!

FRANCIS: We have had our revenge! Ha ha!

CROWD: Booooo. Hissssss.

MERCHANT: But what about me? She's my daughter.

NARRATOR: *[says nothing]*

MERCHANT: Oi! Miss! My daughter. Don't I say something to help her?

NARRATOR: No. You don't say anything. You hide in the crowd.

CROWD: What?

ACTORS: What?

MERCHANT: *[looking around, bewildered]* But she's just standing there, with these toffs telling filthy lies. Where's her family? These people are saying shameful things, and she's all alone.

NARRATOR: Yes, she is, isn't she?

The spectators muttered, confusion on their faces, and the actors exchanged looks, full of questions. The whole room waited for Thea to elaborate. She said nothing.

The man playing the merchant scratched his head, face screwed up. "But I'm meant to be her father. I should stand at her side. I should knock their teeth out. I should... I should..."

"But you don't," Thea said softly. "You hide in the crowd and pretend you don't know her. You just leave her there, standing alone."

The crowd fell silent as understanding crept through the room like an icy November mist.

Rafe realized he was leaning forward, tense from his jaw to his shoulders to his thighs. He wanted to smash heads against the wall, starting with her father, because Thea's *joie de vivre* was a gift that she gave to the world, and they had robbed her of it.

Something inside him ached, something he could only call his heart. Ached for that bright young woman, whose life had been ruined in such a malicious, meaningless way. Who continued to bear the burden, because of people like him, who nodded and asked no questions because they thought they already knew. That was the genius of the plot against her: People would believe that a scheming woman had used wiles to trick a man, because that was one of the stories people always believed.

And Rafe, damn his own eyes, had chosen to believe that too. Hell, he had believed it so deeply he had based his entire scheme upon it. But watching her now, he could not doubt she told the truth.

Yet still she teased and laughed and played, even with this scar upon her heart.

She was a survivor. When people talked of survivors, they meant battle-scarred soldiers and shipwrecked sailors, people like Rafe, who wore his trauma on his face. But how many other survivors walked through the crowd? Unmarked, unnoticed, keeping their scars hidden as they went about their daily lives.

Pasting on a brave face, putting others at their ease, hiding their pain beneath a smile. Of course: Life treated most people roughly, once in a while. Who didn't, at some point, feel like they had been mauled by an indifferent beast?

The crowd grew restless, murmurs swelling, and the serving woman playing Rosamund waved at Thea.

"Miss?" she called. "What happens to me, then?"

"Your parents cast you out," Thea replied dully. "Your presence in their home jeopardizes your younger siblings' futures."

"But when I tell them."

"They do not believe you. They demand that you leave. You find a position in an isolated country house. You make no friends there, and you never quite belong."

"What about us?" demanded one of the knaves. "How do we get our comeuppance?"

Thea said nothing. The crowd muttered and shifted angrily.

"Miss?" the other knave persisted. "We do get our comeuppance, don't we?"

Thea shrugged. "No. Why should you? You are the sons of wealthy noblemen. There is a small scandal, but it soon blows over. Your life continues the same."

Then the man playing the merchant said, "What about me?"

"You have another daughter. Perhaps she will fare better in helping the family."

"That's a rotten story," said the first man, the man named Joe. He leaped to his feet and paced about. "It was a good story and then it turned rotten. Whoever heard of the heroine not triumphing? Whoever heard of the villains not getting their comeuppance?"

Thea said nothing.

The grumbling grew. The crowd stirred angrily. Some stood. Others banged the tables. A riot was brewing.

Rafe lurched to his feet. The angry faces swiveled toward him and quieted at his glare.

"She jests," he said. "Of course that's not how the story ends."

"So how does the story end?" demanded the man named Joe. "What does she do next?"

"Next she...she..." Bloody hell. How did he end this story? "She gives them both a kick in the bollocks."

The crowd erupted into cheers and applause. Shrieking with delight, Rosamund threw herself into her task with glee, while the knaves sought to evade her. Some audience members decided to take part, and then the innkeeper was in the fray, yelling at them to stop, because broken furniture wasn't good for his economics, so Rafe paid for more drinks, and helped settle everyone down, and when he looked up, Thea was gone.

THEA BREATHED in the cool night air. The beech trees beside the inn were silhouettes against the sky, lit by a valiant half moon. She wandered onto the road, and when she looked back at the inn, with its noise and yellow pools of light, it seemed eerily removed, as if she viewed it through a glass. Lord Luxborough would like this; he would have preferred to stand out here, yet he had entered the crowded tavern for her sake. A small sacrifice on his part. Another unexpected kindness.

Wandering on, she sucked in more country air, filling her lungs but not the hollow in her stomach. What on earth was wrong with her? Finally, she had told her story. Strangers agreed she had been wronged. Surely she should feel some satisfaction or vindication? Yet all she felt was an aching sorrow for some other girl.

Around her, the fields were silent and still, the darkness thick and endless. An owl hooted. A gust of wind tugged at her skirts. She turned and, for a panicky, disoriented moment, feared she had lost sight of the inn. But there it was, a distant glow. Thea headed back, her regrets dancing at her side.

If only she had trusted herself. A little voice inside her had whispered that Percy Russell was rotten, but she had allowed her parents to tell her she was wrong. Thea had never been averse to the idea of marrying into the upper class, for the sake of her whole family, but until Percy Russell it had only been an idea, and then she faced the reality of marrying a man she disliked. Everything had changed with Percy, especially Ma and Pa; the thought of Thea marrying a viscount's son had gripped them like a fever and they'd stopped listening to reason. And Thea, hating to disappoint them, hating to let down the whole family, had tried to suppress her dislike and accepted his attentions, but not without arguing first.

Would that crowd still have cheered if she had confessed to the next part—the part where she began saying foolish things? "Why should I stop with charming Mr. Percy Russell to induce him to marry me?" she had snapped, as Ma, seeking to "improve Thea's charms," pinched color into her cheeks. "Maybe I'll expedite matters and simply seduce him instead. Maybe I'll seduce the whole jolly lot of them." But she never dreamed Percy and his friends would hit on a similar idea, as punishment for her good deed. Never dreamed her bitter jokes would come back to haunt her, and prevent Ma and Pa from believing a word she said.

Reaching the yard to the inn, Thea paused and breathed deeply, shoving away the grim thoughts before she once more faced the world.

Then a shadowy figure caught her eye, slinking between the carriages. Pausing at the Earl of Luxborough's carriage. Easing the door open, disappearing inside.

"Hey you!" she called out. "Stop! Thief!"

She ran in search of help, one eye on the carriage, one on the figure emerging with a box of plants. Again she called out, as the thief ran. And ran.

And stopped.

For his way was blocked by a tall, broad man with tousled hair.

"Put down that box," the earl said calmly.

The thief nimbly darted to the side. Luxborough was there before him. The thief darted back the other way; his path was once more blocked.

"I do not much care for dancing," Luxborough said. "So put down that box and if you run very fast, perhaps you'll escape with your life."

He loomed, head raised, the moonlight hitting his scarred cheek. Thea heard a whimper and the sound of the box hitting the ground and then footsteps as the thief fled. Luxborough immediately dropped into a crouch by the plants and began inspecting them. He did not look up as Thea approached.

"Are they unharmed?" she asked.

"Hmm."

"Would you really have killed him?"

"Hmm?"

"You threatened to kill a man over some plants."

"The plants are irreplaceable," Luxborough said. "Yet that ignorant thief would probably just feed them to the pigs."

"And then what?" she demanded. "The pigs would poop diamonds?"

He shot her one of his looks, and went back to tenderly inspecting each plant, each clay pot. Hands that a moment ago had been ready to take a man's life now cupped a yellow flower as tenderly as if it were a newborn kitten.

"Those plants are so fortunate," Thea heard herself say softly. "To have you to protect them and look after them."

In a swift, fluid movement, he stood, and she realized again how big he was. His chest and shoulders were vast and his arms looked strong. Perfect for hugging, really. How selfish of him not to invite closeness. Surely it was his civic duty as an earl to offer a hug to any citizen who required one.

Starting with her.

"That story you told in there," he started.

"It was the truth, you know." Belligerence made her voice too loud. "I suppose you think it's silly, for m—my sister to cry over a ruined reputation."

"Hmm?"

"'By George, you think someone laughing at you is bad. You should try being attacked by a wild animal.'"

"Hmm."

"Forgive me." She glanced down at the flowers and back up. "It is impolite to mention it."

"I imagine scars this pronounced are difficult to ignore."

Behind them, the inn door opened, releasing the noise inside, which became muted again as the door slammed shut. The inn was settling for the night, and the yard was quiet but for them and the owl.

"Yet why should we ignore them?" she asked. "I do not wish to pretend your scars are not there. Our scars are our stories, and stories should be told."

"Then my story must be a frightening one, to match my face."

"But that's it." She stepped closer to him. "The attack must have been horrific, but now you seem so strong and fearless, and I wish I knew how to... You wear those scars like a challenge. As if to say, 'Yes, I tussled with a wild animal with paws as big as my head. What did *you* do this morning before breakfast?'"

He did not seem to mind her words, for that half smile curled his lips, and the corners of her own mouth tugged upward in response. The streaks of his scars looked almost shiny in the moonlight. She was already used to them, she realized, yet she longed to touch them, to pretend she could ease his past pain, to pretend he gave a flying farthing for hers.

She tangled her fingers together at her waist.

"Actually, I find it a benefit, that my face makes children run away," he said. "Although their screaming gives me a headache."

Encouraged by his self-deprecating joke, Thea ventured a reply. "And if ladies swoon at the sight of you, you are spared from having to talk to them."

"Precisely. Although that raises the question of the etiquette of stepping over their prone bodies."

"And the men?"

"Ah, the men." He scratched his chin. "They say something jovial, like, 'Spot of bad luck there, what?' as if my cricket match was rained out."

Thea laughed, the sound a lonely one in the deserted yard, but he was smiling, just a little, and she liked having someone to smile with again. Then his smile faded, for he was searching her face with questions in his eyes, and the silence grew as heavy as the dark. She should go in, but she was not ready to leave him, not while there was the smallest chance they might smile together again.

"The selva is intense," he said abruptly.

"The... I beg your pardon? What is the 'selva'?"

"The tropical forest. It teems with life. Everything is bigger, brighter, bolder. One can encounter snakes longer than a warship, butterflies as big as a man's palm. One can almost see the plants growing. With so much life, death is closer too. There is no past,

82

no future, only the present, as one avoids the myriad of ways to die."

She tried to understand what he was saying. "So one knows, when one goes into the selva, that one might not make it out alive." Laughter bubbled up in her throat. "It is rather like a ball, then."

He made a small sound that might have been a chuckle. "All those poisonous flowers. Vines that will choke you."

"Man-eating animals."

"Precisely. I'd risk the selva over Almack's any day." He paused. "The point is, I knew the dangers beforehand. No one betrayed me, unlike y–your sister. That makes my loss easier to bear."

His words stole her breath and a pang shot through her heart. He didn't understand. Ma and Pa thought *she* had betrayed *them*.

Yet he was being kind. Again.

Before she knew what she was doing, Thea's fingers were untangled and she was moving forward. She placed one palm on his scarred cheek. He did not flinch or object, so she let it rest there. His skin was like her skin, warm and alive and soft, but for stubble of his beard. These scars were not ugly; they were simply part of him. She placed her other palm on his other cheek, and she cradled that bold face in her hands.

"You're just a man," she whispered.

He studied her with a faintly troubled expression, as though she was a puzzle he had already solved a dozen times, yet still did not understand. She wished she had the right to ask what thoughts were forming behind those eyes of his.

Then he covered her hands and gently lowered them away from his face, his fingers big and warm as they curled around hers. He was so close, all delicious solidity. If he could wrap his arms around her, pull her against his chest... Oh, how she yearned to be held. It had been so long since anyone had held her.

Too long, clearly, if she looked to him for comfort! She must not forget she was nothing but the means to an end for him, as he was for her. He would never be her friend.

She tugged her fingers free and edged away.

"You need not fear me," he said, clasping his hands behind his back.

"You threatened my friend."

"I never intended any harm. That was merely a maneuver to force your hand."

"It was badly done of you."

"I daresay it was."

"You don't seem sorry."

He shrugged. "I wanted something. I went after it. I got it. In this case, what I wanted was you."

A thrill coursed through her and she fought to quell it. How the moonlight made her silly!

"You mean, you wanted me to agree to marry you, so I could not marry Beau Russell and you could get some money."

"Exactly." He wiped a hand over his eyes. "I promise, you will be safe."

How marvelous, to feel safe again. She had always believed herself safe, until those minutes in that ballroom, when her world was whipped out from under her and she learned that everything she believed in could disappear in the blink of an eye.

"Sometimes I wonder if someone like me can ever be safe," she said. He frowned and she did not want to talk to him anymore. "I'm tired, my lord. I trust you and your plants will sleep well tonight."

Thea turned away to go inside, and had taken barely three steps when—

"Countess!"

She turned back.

"Those people in there were right," he said. "Percy and Francis should get their comeuppance."

She must be more tired than she realized, because all she could think was that the world didn't work like that. Her scheme seemed silly, so puny and hopeless.

But in the morning, she would feel brave again. So she pretended it was already morning and she was already feeling brave.

"They will," she said.

Then, before she could do something foolish—something like throwing herself into his arms and pressing her face to his broad chest—she turned and ran inside.

CHAPTER 6

Ah, London. Rafe muttered curses as he cut through the commerce-fueled hubbub of the City two days later. Grime, stench, noise, *people*. As usual, London put Rafe in a foul temper, which had the effect of arranging his face into an expression that made people scurry to obey.

So it was with pleasing speed that he and his solicitor—a co-conspirator in Rafe's fraudulent marriage scheme—convinced the trustees that he truly was married and secured their agreement to release the funds. But such things took time, the solicitor advised: Rafe should keep Thea close to allay any suspicions before the money was definitely his.

"Easily done," he snapped, ignoring the memory of her hands in his, her palm on his cheek. He would put her on the other side of his house at Brinkley End, where he would never see her or talk to her, or be tempted to touch her again. His plans had no place for Thea and her infectious smiles.

Nevertheless, since they were near the Exchange anyway, an impulse inspired Rafe to call on Thea's father at the man's office. It went against all his plans, not to mention common sense, but Thea's story had roused his curiosity about the kind of man who abandoned a daughter for his own ambitions.

Mr. Knight turned out to be stout and brightly dressed, with a skip in his step and an appealing shrewdness in his eyes. When Rafe informed Mr. Knight that he had married Helen—"met her in Warwickshire...very taken with her...couldn't wait"—the man seemed to become younger by ten years.

"By my buttons! Our Helen, a countess!" the man repeated, then clapped and laughed and clapped again. He pressed his hands to his chest and murmured, as if to himself, "The girl has done it. We may all rest secure."

"You have another daughter," Rafe interrupted. "Thea, I believe is her name?"

Mr. Knight shook his head. "I do not know where we went wrong with Thea."

"Did it never occur to you, Mr. Knight, that those men in her scandal might have lied?"

"The trouble with Thea, my lord, well, she was always up to some mischief or other, and that time she went too far. We never could make a rule but that she would find a reason to break it. But don't concern yourself, my lord—our Helen is quite different, and she will be a credit to you. Why, when Miss Larke invited Helen to her house, we never imagined she would end up married to an earl." His eyes brightened. "But you must dine with my wife and me tonight!"

Even if that were possible, Rafe would rather dive headfirst into a piranha-infested pond. His face must have helpfully indicated as much, for Mr. Knight actively recoiled.

"Forgive my impertinence, my lord," he hastened to add. "I would never dream of imposing."

"My bride and I return to my estate in Somersetshire

tomorrow. We wish for complete privacy while our marriage is new." Rafe lowered his voice to a conspiratorial tone. "For the first month, the marriage will be *our secret*, Mr. Knight."

"By my buttons! A secret with my son-in-law, the *earl*."

At which point, Rafe should have left, but instead said, "My solicitor desires to discuss the settlement."

His solicitor, having not been aware of this desire, looked surprised, but Mr. Knight didn't notice. He launched into a story of how he had set aside a portion of fifteen thousand pounds for each of his elder daughters, to be protected even if he lost his fortune again, but considering he now had only one daughter of marriageable age—and why, she had married an earl!—his lordship could have the full thirty thousand.

"Fifteen thousand will suffice," Rafe said.

From there it was a matter of tedious paperwork, but fortunately Rafe's solicitor took a perverse pleasure in paperwork and briskly made arrangements for receiving the funds. Back on the street, the solicitor agreed to open an account in Thea's name, in which to deposit her dowry. Secret, Rafe insisted: The lady must not be informed of her new fortune until Rafe was ready to tell her. If she knew, she would leave, and he had to keep her close.

Close. He shook off the memory of her cradling his face. Not that close, he scolded himself, a scold he had to repeat, several times, all the way home.

Where he discovered that London had not finished torturing him yet.

William Dudley was back on the street outside Rafe's townhouse. As he had previously, the actor wore tattered black robes and his hair was in disarray. He curled his fingers into claws as he screeched about sorcery and poisons and how the Earl of Luxborough was a demon made flesh.

A very convincing performance, Rafe had to concede. One

could almost believe Dudley to be a genuine zealot, like the many other men and women who shouted their messages in market squares around the land. It was all very well for the upper classes to pride themselves on their rationality, in these oh-so-enlightened times, but in the absence of widespread education, superstitions ran deep. No wonder tales of a devil-scarred witch in the aristocracy spread faster than typhoid.

Rafe stopped right in front of him. Dudley gave him an apologetic nod, before continuing.

"Behold the evil sorcerer," he screeched, clawing at the air. "He who rains demons down upon the innocent!"

"Heard that one before, Dudley," Rafe said. "Haven't you a new script?"

With a nervous glance down the empty street, Dudley dropped his voice to a normal tone. "Sorry, my lord. No time to prepare one. Lord Ventnor didn't know you would be back in town and he sent for me in a hurry."

"He pays you well, I hope?"

"Beware the witch! Bears he the mark of the Devil!" Dudley screamed, then, after another furtive glance, whispered, "'Tis good work, my lord. 'Tis hard for an actor these days. Especially in summer, when everyone's out of town."

"Everyone" being the upper classes, who escaped the city's heat and stench for the seaside, a fashionable spa, or their country estates. Unfortunate, then, that Ventnor still skulked about town.

"If the neighbors were here, they would have tossed you in jail," Rafe said. "Quiet it down, would you? Ventnor won't know."

The actor scanned the pristine street, as though the viscount lurked in a drainpipe. "Lord Ventnor knows everything. What he'd do to me if..."

"Yes, I know," Rafe sighed, and went inside to wash off the London grime.

RAFE EMERGED from his bath to learn that the Bishop of Dartford was taking tea in the front parlor.

Furthermore, the butler informed him nervously, a pile of bills was growing on his lordship's desk, which matched the pile of parcels growing in the countess's sitting room. In the time it took the butler to explain what the countess had got up to that day, three more deliveries arrived from smart Bond Street shops: parcels for the countess, bills for him.

Clutching the bills, Rafe wandered into the front parlor, where Nicholas was seated before a plate of cakes, pouring himself tea from a floral-painted teapot, the voluminous sleeves of his bishop's shirt billowing at his sides. He looked up, eyes twinkling over the fragrant steam, thinning gray hair a mess.

"Rafe, my boy, lovely to see you," Nicholas said.

"You too," Rafe replied, full of fondness for the old rascal. "What mischief are you up to now?"

The bishop beamed, the picture of pink-cheeked innocence— if innocence was a ten-year-old boy who had just put a frog in his governess's bed.

"I don't know why you put up with that." Nicholas gestured with his teacup at the window, through which came the faint strains of Dudley doing his job. "Accusing people of witchcraft is against the law."

"It's Ventnor's doing. If I had Dudley put in jail, Ventnor would simply replace him with someone else."

"Dudley? Oh, that's William Dudley, of course." He put down his cup and crossed to peer out the window. "That's where I recognize him from. The theatre. I saw him playing opposite Sarah Holloway. Marvelous actress. Shame she disappeared. Such splendid red hair and a wonderful pair of—"

"Nicholas."

"—lungs." Nicholas grinned. "You used to enjoy the theatre. Come sometime with Judith and me."

"Maybe I will."

"A miracle! Rafe Landcross has agreed to be sociable!"

"I agreed to go to the theatre," Rafe corrected irritably. "Where I shall be exceedingly unsociable. I'll not talk to a single person, and I'll scowl so hard the actors fall off the stage."

Chuckling, the bishop returned to his tea. Rafe lounged against the window and perused the bills, to see what Thea had bought on his account. Silver buttons. Lace handkerchiefs. Snuff boxes. All small items, very easy to resell. No, indeed, he would never make the mistake of thinking Thea Knight a fool. She would have a tidy sum when she resold this lot.

She must really need money, though, to have jeopardized her scheme like this, with the risk of anyone discovering she was not Helen. If only he could tell her that she would receive her own dowry.

"The smoky flavor of this tea is heavenly," Nicholas said. "Judith would adore this."

"You can have it. It was a gift from my new father-in-law, Mr. Knight."

Nicholas lowered his cup with a clatter. "You talked to him? I thought you intended to keep your mischievous scheme quiet. Or does he know the truth?"

"No. He believes I married his perfect Helen. I got Thea her dowry. They just cast her out, and did not believe her side of the story. She deserves better, for all that she is a royal pain in the neck."

"Is she, Rafe? Is she a pain in the neck? Because that look on your face when you say her name..."

Rafe waved the bundle of bills in his hand. "She took the

Luxborough carriage and a servant in Luxborough livery, told everyone she is the Countess of Luxborough, and has bought up half of Bond Street."

"I like her already." The bishop smiled like the angel he wasn't. "What about you? Do you like her, Rafe? Do you?"

"Oh no, you don't."

"Don't what?"

"Don't you put on that innocent face for me, old man. If you're hoping to meet her, forget it."

Nicholas pouted over his teacup. "Only to check she's good enough. I should meet the girl you've married."

"I haven't married her! You knew I had no intention of marrying her when you issued the license. So stop it. This is not a real marriage."

"Not yet it isn't," he replied, singsong.

"That's it. Out now. Out."

"But I haven't finished my tea."

Rafe grabbed the teacup and emptied it into a potted palm. "Yes, you have. Look. All gone. Now—out."

"You can't talk to me like that," the bishop protested through his laughter. "I'm a holy man."

"You're a holy pain in the neck. And when you start nagging me to marry, it's time for you to go."

Nicholas merely poured himself more tea. "So you don't find her appealing, then."

"Of course she's appealing. She's... She's..."

Thea in the moonlight, bright and brave and all alone in the world. Her palms cupping his cheeks, standing so close he could have slid an arm around her waist and pulled her into his embrace.

He caught himself pressing his knuckles to his cheek and lowered his hand.

"She's perfectly nice-looking," he finished.

"Does your face frighten her?"

Rafe snorted. "She jokes about it."

"And would she hate to be married to you?"

"Don't even think it," Rafe said. "I've told you a thousand times, I'm not getting married again. I'm not good at it."

"It's marriage, my boy. No one's good at it. That's what makes it so much fun." Nicholas sipped his tea, his bright eyes fixed on Rafe. "This girl sounds perfect for you."

"We are lying to each other."

"So perfect."

"Besides, she likes people."

"Oh, heaven forbid. Not *people*!"

"One week at Brinkley End and she'd be moping about, desperate to get back to London."

That was all there was to it: Rafe did not have it in him to make someone happy. He had one wife buried on his estate. He did not need a second one there too.

"You don't know that," Nicholas persisted. "Let me ask her."

"No! You're each as mischievous as the other, and who knows what you would cook up together." He shuddered. "You should go before she gets back."

"I'd behave myself."

"You have never behaved yourself."

Nicholas drained his cup and stretched his arms with a loud yawn. "Very well, I'll be off. I wish you wouldn't run back to Somersetshire so soon. Judith complains she never sees you."

"Tell her I look the same as I did last time she saw me, but older and more miserable."

"You should have gone to the seaside with Christopher and his family. Christopher's boys have been asking about you. They want to learn how to hunt a jaguar."

Christopher was one of the few people Rafe felt truly comfortable with, but the thought of his younger brother's family —Christopher's beloved Mary and their gaggle of children, three or four or twenty or however many they had now—unsettled him.

"I don't know how to hunt a jaguar," Rafe said. "In case you hadn't noticed, the jaguar won."

"If the jaguar had won, you'd be dead."

"Right. And Christopher would be earl, and there'd be a proper family in Brinkley End again, and all would be—"

"Don't say it!" Nicholas slapped his hands down on the table and the tea things rattled. He launched to his feet, suddenly serious, fury flashing in his eyes. "Don't you dare say it, Rafe."

From outside came screeching about witches; from inside the banging of a door. Rafe's jaw ached with the effort of locking down his throat.

He unclenched his jaw. "And all would be right in the world," he finished defiantly.

"Brinkley End—"

"Is not my home," Rafe said. "It never was. It never will be."

"Not if you think like that it won't."

That sounded like something Thea would say. What a pair they were, Thea and Nicholas, chatty and sunny and knowing nothing at all. Rafe wheeled away and paced across the room.

"You did all you could for Katharine," Nicholas said.

"This has nothing to do with Katharine."

"Her death was not your fault."

Rafe stopped short. "She rode recklessly through a storm to escape from me. I promised to look after her and I failed."

"You keep telling yourself this story, but what if it isn't true?"

"I was there, Nicholas. I know what is true."

"You allow your guilt—"

"Guilt has nothing to do with it. I'm simply not made for...for marriage."

"Katharine's situation was unusual. There is nothing more you could have done."

Rafe shook his head, tired of this argument. It suited the bishop to absolve him, but Rafe would never escape his failure to look after his wife. He would never escape the truth that he could look after nothing more complicated than a plant.

Their thick silence was broken by the sound of a carriage pulling up outside.

"Is it her?" Nicholas dashed to the window, eager as a boy at Christmas. "Oh, it's her!"

Rafe found himself at the window too, watching as Thea's manservant Gilbert helped her down from the carriage. She certainly appeared the part of a countess, in a sleek blue-striped pelisse and large, elaborate bonnet. The wide-brimmed bonnet did a fair job of hiding her face, until she paused and looked up to admire the house. The light caressed the angle of her jaw and slid down the smooth column of her throat.

"She looks delightful," Nicholas said. "Please, may I talk to her? Please, please, please?"

"No!"

With both hands on the laughing bishop's back, Rafe marched him into the hall and ordered him to leave through the kitchen. A moment later, the butler had opened the door and Rafe was in the doorway, looking at Thea.

"Begone, fair lady!" Dudley screeched at her, bouncing on his feet. "We be in the Devil's lair!"

Thea paused mid-step. "Oh, is that what they call Mayfair these days?"

"Here lives a wild man! He consorts with demons!"

"Don't be silly. He doesn't consort with anyone. All that *talking*."

Behind Rafe, Nicholas chuckled. "This one's going to liven you right up."

Rafe twisted around. "I told you to go."

"Not a chance, my boy. I wouldn't miss this for the world."

CHAPTER 7

Thea had intended to walk straight past the man in black. As a Londoner, she was familiar with such men. Every market square in the city had people like this, yelling warnings at the world, while the world either ignored them or threw slops at their head.

Besides, her day in London had left her weary. First, she had gone with Gilbert to deliver her manuscript to Arabella's publisher and to meet Mr. Witherspoon, the man who would oversee her advertising campaign. He was as excellent as Arabella promised: He listened to her wishes and suggested improvements, before briskly stating how he would achieve each item, how many delivery boys he would hire, which artists he would commission, and, of course, how much it would all cost. The amount made her heart sink, but she confidently assured him the money would be forthcoming, and dashed off on her risky shopping expedition, praying no one would recognize her.

She had hoped to get home before Luxborough did, so she

could plead a headache, lock her door, and avoid awkward questions about her shopping.

And perhaps she would have succeeded, if not for her rash decision to have the carriage stop in Warren Street, a little down from the blue door with the brass mermaid knocker. Ma had planted pink flowers in the window boxes and changed the curtains upstairs.

As Thea sat watching, that blue door had swung open to reveal Ma, as if she sensed in her heart that her eldest daughter had come home. But then Pa had dashed up the stairs with his usual vigor and they were both laughing as he whirled Ma about, and they laughed harder when Pa clutched at his lower back.

Thea had blinked away tears, though she smiled for them too. It was too soon to hear from Helen, so the Knight family must have scored some other victory. If only Thea could share in their celebration! If only she could skip through that blue door, wink at the brass mermaid, and know that she was home.

But then another carriage had rumbled past, blocking her view, and when it had passed, her parents were gone and the blue door was shut.

Nothing to do but wait until her pamphlets were ready, and never forget that the Earl of Luxborough was her enemy, and it signified not at all that he was kind to weeping women and plants.

Neither did it signify, she reminded herself sternly, as Lord Luxborough stepped through his front door, his dark hair curling damply over his forehead and collar, that his lordship looked deliciously fresh after a bath.

Dismay shot through her. At least, she thought it was dismay, though it felt like a mix of excitement and pleasure. Their eyes met, and she was reminded of their very first encounter, for that same glee lit his brown eyes as he slowly descended three steps.

Suddenly, Thea didn't feel so tired after all.

She was preparing to greet Lord Luxborough, when she was distracted first by the appearance in the doorway of a grinning, gray-haired man, whose sleeves marked him as a bishop, and then by the zealot, who addressed her again.

"Yet you visit his devil's lair, my lady," the zealot said, continuing their peculiar conversation. "Be you a witch?"

She bestowed upon him the imperious look she had been practicing all day. "If you please! I am the countess."

After a quick glance at Luxborough, the man recoiled in horror. "You came back from the dead!"

"I did what?"

"First did he kill you with his sorcery!"

"He did what?"

"Then did he raise you from the grave!"

Thea hesitated. As ludicrous as the rumors about Luxborough's first wife were, she could not quell her curiosity about the kind of woman he had married.

"I am his second wife," she said quietly, so Luxborough could not hear. "What can you tell me of the first one?"

"He poisoned her, ensorcelled her, enslaved her to his devilry."

"That sounds like a lot of work. Why would he do all that?"

"Because he is a demon! A witch! A sorcerer! A—"

"Yes, yes, I comprehend that part," she interrupted impatiently. "But if he has all this power, why use it to harm his wife? This has always puzzled me. Consider, if you will, the plight of a woman accused of witchcraft because two days after she argues with her neighbor, the man gets a pox on his tickle-tail. And this man, he says, 'By George, that woman must have caused this pox through the power of the Devil. If she can do magic, she won't use her magic to get a decent house or some gold, by George no, her only use for magical powers is to put a pox on my tickle-tail.'"

The zealot blinked at her, then tugged at his hair. "Have you a demon inside you, my lady?"

"I am rather hungry. Does that count?"

"Beware the beast! Kill you, he will!"

Oh, for pity's sake. Thea was hungry and her feet hurt, and the best way to stop nonsense was with more nonsense.

"But after he kills me, he will raise me from the dead," she proclaimed loudly. "Like he did his first wife. Like he did a thousand women."

"He... What?"

"Oh yes!" she cried. "A thousand women, killed and raised to make an army of the dead! Beware the day when an army of dead wives marches on London. Beware, little man, beware."

The zealot stared at her, wide eyed, and when he spoke, his tone was perfectly rational. "You're mad." He looked past her to the earl. "She's mad."

Thea turned. Up on the steps, the bishop was laughing, holding his belly as his shoulders shook. Luxborough elbowed him in the ribs, which only made the older man laugh harder.

Yet a smile played around Luxborough's lips too, as he came down the last steps toward her. He was in his shirtsleeves, which might be why his shoulders looked so broad, and his wine-red waistcoat hugged a narrow waist and hips. How fascinating it was, that a man could have such broad shoulders and powerful thighs and yet such narrow hips.

Until Luxborough, Thea had never noticed how fascinating men could be.

"You continue to astonish me, Countess," Luxborough said. "That you make such a response."

She dragged her gaze off his torso and looked up to meet his eyes, humor glinting in their brandy-colored depths. Again, she felt that little skip of dismay-masquerading-as-excitement. "Response to what?"

"You were screaming at Dudley about an army of dead wives."

"Oh. Yes. Right. I forgot." Then his words sank in. "Dudley? You know him?"

"His name is William Dudley and he— Oh hell." Luxborough's curse startled her. He gripped her forearm, and she was so surprised by the firmness of his fingers that she did not seek the cause of his alarm, until he said, "It's Ventnor. Go inside now."

Needing no encouragement, her knees so weak she feared they might fail her, Thea picked up her skirts and ran inside. She raced straight past the bishop and into the front parlor, where she stood behind the curtain to watch, heart racing, nausea building, as Lord Ventnor's carriage arrived.

IT WAS A GRAND COACH-AND-FOUR: a shiny black carriage pulled by four perfectly matched gray horses. The viscount's coat of arms was emblazoned on the side, and on the back rode three footmen, also perfectly matched: all the same height and build, dressed in the same royal-purple livery, with the same white wigs on their heads. They leaped down the moment the carriage stopped. One pulled open the door, one folded down the steps, the third unrolled a royal-purple carpet on the street.

Then they lined up along the carpet, as if for the Prince Regent himself.

From the depths of the cavernous carriage emerged a long, thin, silver-tipped ebony stick.

Then one long, thin, black-clad leg.

Then all of Lord Ventnor, long, thin, and impeccable in a

silver-and-gray striped waistcoat and black coat, with a tall black hat on his long white hair.

He stepped down onto the carpet. Planted the silver tip of his cane and rested both gloved hands on the silver knob. Raised his chin and tapped one foot. In perfect unison, the three footmen bent at the waist in identical deep bows. Only when they had straightened did Lord Ventnor step forward to greet the earl.

He looked exactly as he did in Thea's memory of those nightmarish minutes in the ballroom, which played over and over in her mind like a never-ending cotillion. That night, Ventnor had seemed to stretch to ten feet tall and everything became too close and yet so far away. Her confused mind had struggled to understand, to argue, to find just one word—No! Liars! False!—but shock had stolen her voice, and so she'd simply stood, like a hunted rabbit, until Lady Ventnor gently guided her out of the ballroom, and Percy Russell gloated.

And he was there too: Percy Russell himself. Stepping down onto the carpet, smirking at the footmen as they bowed for him too. His clothes were the height of fashion: a bottle-green coat over a mint-green waistcoat, with the high, starched points of his collar scraping his pink jaw. The years had been good to him, but then cads like him always prospered, for it was not only coats and boots that were tailor-made for them; it was the whole world.

"I hate him. The *Honorable* Mr. Percival Russell." She slid a sideways glance at the bishop. "I know it's wrong to hate someone."

"Eh," he said, in a tone that suggested otherwise.

"Aren't we supposed to love everyone?"

"We're supposed to, but..." He shrugged. "Some people are such vile snots."

A surprised laugh burst out of her mouth and she hastily stifled it. He met her gaze serenely.

"I'm sorry," she said. "I thought you were a bishop."

He grinned. "It surprises me sometimes too. What *were* they thinking?" He stepped back and bowed with a flourish of his sleeves. "Nicholas Landcross, Bishop of Dartford, at your service. Rafe's father was my cousin. Which means you and I are family now."

"Um."

"Don't worry. I'm not as terrible as they say."

"I mean…"

A glance around the curtain showed Percy lounging against the carriage, while Luxborough and Ventnor faced each other on the street. Luxborough looked completely at ease, while Ventnor brandished his walking stick. She had never seen him use the stick to walk; as far as she could tell, he used it only to menace other people.

It occurred to Thea that Luxborough had no reason to hide her from Ventnor, unless he knew the viscount would be unkind and he meant to protect her from any unpleasantness.

If only she had had the courage to stand up to them all that night, when Ventnor called her names and his elegant guests stared at her as if she were horse dung on their shoes. She hated her own weakness as much as she hated them. Her life had never been in danger, but her body reacted as though to a real threat. But if someone had stood by her side—as her parents would have done, of course, if they'd known the truth—then she might have found her courage.

How lovely it would be, to have someone always at her side, who thought her worth fighting for. Someone big and strong and powerful, who could fight off savage beasts and civilized lords. Not Lord Luxborough, of course. But someone.

"I have something to confess," she said to the bishop.

"No, no. Please don't."

"I'm doing bad things. I'm lying and stealing and...bad things."

He sighed. "A physician friend of mine cannot pass an hour with the newspapers in his favorite coffeehouse without someone telling him about their ailments. I suffer a similar problem: Everywhere I go, someone wants to confess their sins."

"Oh, I do beg your pardon." Thea considered this. "Actually, that sounds rather delicious."

"It would be, but most people's sins are terribly dull. So, my dear, I understand your conscience is bothering you, but you need not let it bother me too."

"It only bothers me sometimes, when I fear I'm tricking someone who is good, for I have vowed to trick only the villainous and powerful. Should I feel bad?"

The bishop shrugged. "Eh. Why bother? It's probably good for them. Yes," he added, his expression growing thoughtful. "I think it is probably very good for them indeed."

His look unnerved her, so she peeked around the curtain. As she watched, Ventnor spoke to the zealot, who turned and ran, and Ventnor and Percy laughed.

How farcical, that the zealot had called Lord Luxborough a demon, when true demons like Ventnor and Percy stood right there.

"Some people have done truly hurtful things, yet no one wants to hear about that," she said. "Why do some people get to tell their stories and others don't? Why do some people get to say what is truth? And why doesn't *he* stop it?" She jabbed a finger at Luxborough. He and Ventnor appeared to be arguing. "It's one thing for people like me to put up with rumors, but why him?"

"Because Rafe believes it too," the bishop said.

Her head whipped around. "He believes he's a witch?"

"He believes he has done something wrong, so he does not argue when people say that he did. In truth, his only sin is to be as flawed and human as the rest of us. But he tells himself he has failed and is not enough."

"Failed how?"

He didn't answer.

"You care about him," Thea said.

"He's like a son to me. You'll look after him for me, won't you?"

"Look after him?"

The bishop's eyes flickered to the window. Ventnor was stalking back to his carriage.

"I must go." The bishop slapped on his hat and hooked his coat on one finger. "He's a good boy. But he's caught up in false beliefs. It would be lovely if someone would set him free." He half turned and hesitated. "That jaguar saved his life, you know."

"How?"

"Ask him about it sometime."

And with those cryptic words, the Bishop of Dartford swung his coat over his shoulder and sauntered out the door, whistling an unfamiliar tune.

LORD VENTNOR WAS SO ENTRANCED by his own countenance that he did not so much as glance at the two faces at the window, their features indistinct through the glass.

"I say, Luxborough, congratulations on your marriage," Ventnor said, hooking his cane between two fingers so he could offer a few sarcastic slaps of applause. "To a shop girl! I did try to warn you about these women, with their coy looks and flattery. But then I daresay a man such as you—" His gaze lingered pointedly on Rafe's ruined cheek. "—would be more susceptible to flattery than most. And so—dare I say it?—Helen Knight sank her claws into you."

If only Rafe could see Ventnor's face when he learned whom Helen Knight had really snared.

"I thought you'd be more grateful," Rafe said guilelessly. "I sacrificed myself to save your little boy Beau."

Past the viscount, a smirking dandy with hair the same sandy color as Katharine's lounged against the carriage, looking pleased with himself. The dastardly knave Percy Russell, no doubt.

"That selfish boy! Fancies himself in love, and cares nothing for the harm such an inappropriate match would do to our entire family." Ventnor looked Rafe up and down. "I suppose it hardly matters to you, though, considering how you blithely sully your own once-noble title."

Rafe glanced at Dudley, who looked like he was praying for the earth to swallow him up. "You certainly assist me on that point, Ventnor, with these tales you spread about me."

"Did you like the little gift I sent you? Useful creature, isn't he?" Ventnor pointed his cane at Dudley. "You have served your purpose. Go."

Dudley shot an apologetic look at Rafe and fled, his black robes flapping about his heavy boots.

"Look at him run." Ventnor turned to Percy, and father and son shared a laugh. "I say a word and like little rabbits they run." He looked back at Rafe. "You are not amused, Luxborough? My abilities do not impress you?"

"Anyone can start a false rumor. If you wish to impress me, make the falsehoods stop."

"If you want me to try, you already know what to do: Retract those heinous lies you published about my daughter."

"That pamphlet contained only the truth about Katharine, and you know it. Katharine was tormented, and no one should suffer that alone."

Bold claim, but in truth, Katharine always had to suffer them alone, those private horrors inflicted by her mind. Even when she was well, she lived in fear of her mind betraying her again. To this day, Rafe could feel her hands clutching him, hear her terrified whisper, "What is happening to me, Rafe? I no longer even know who I am." All he could do was hold her, and try to soothe her, and hide his own fear. And when he published a pamphlet about Katharine and the need for better treatments for all those similarly afflicted, Ventnor had swiftly countered by spreading the message that nothing natural ailed his daughter: He claimed Rafe had turned Katharine's mind through cruelty or poison, and published those lies to cover his villainy. All credit to the viscount. He was dedicated and deployed a creative array of methods, from actors planted around the country to sly anonymous letters to editors and the occasional satirical cartoon. And all those blasted people, so busy gobbling up outrageous rumors that they had no appetite left for the truth.

"I shall retract nothing," Rafe added. "Never will I deny Katharine's truth, or pretend she never happened because that makes you feel more comfortable."

"You selfish boor!" Ventnor hissed. "What about my younger daughter? Daphne is satisfactorily married now, but no man would have chosen her had I allowed your stories about Katharine to stand unchallenged. And I daresay you never spared a thought for my future grandchildren. Can you imagine what cruel treatment they might endure if people knew?"

"Then use your influence to change people's views. Then we can treat those afflicted as Katharine was with compassion, rather than locking them away in horrendous conditions in shame."

"Naive fool!" Ventnor spat. "It is easier to convince the world that you are a witch than that madness is not to be feared. So what if it is nonsense? Most people could not get out of bed if they did not have some nonsense to sustain them. I will do what I must for my family."

Rafe looked at him steadily. "How afraid you are, Ventnor."

"How dare you!" His whole head quivered. "Those rumors might die away on their own if you behaved like a normal human being, but instead you fuel them, by hiding away on your estate, brewing strange concoctions with heathens and foreigners. But then you always were odd. How your father puzzled over you, the dark, silent boy who preferred to run through the woods like a commoner than behave like the son of an earl." He sighed. "Shame."

Ventnor stalked back to his carriage, where the trio of matching footmen still stood to attention. He paused as he stepped onto his little carpet.

"Oh, and you have not yet thanked me," he added to Rafe, in the affable tone of a man doing another a favor.

"Hmm?"

"For the orchids. If not for me, you would never have come by such fine and rare specimens. So thank me."

"Hmm."

Looking uncertain, Ventnor emitted one shaky "ha." He glanced up at the window, at the indistinct faces of Thea and the bishop. "And for your merchant bride, of course. How desperate you must be for a body in your bed."

As the viscount climbed back into his carriage, Rafe sauntered over to Percy Russell. Shamelessly, Rafe used his greater size to loom over the younger man, who stretched up like a weasel, leading with his chin.

"I don't like you, you miserable, sniveling—"

"You cannot harm me," Russell whimpered. "My father won't allow it."

"Hmm."

Rafe didn't move. The youth sidled away crabwise, then leaped into the carriage. The footmen performed their ritual in reverse, and the coach trundled off.

On his way to the door, Rafe realized he still held the bills from Thea's shopping expedition. Her purpose was plain enough, and he secretly applauded her ingenuity. And yet... It would be highly diverting to see what excuses she offered. Just a little teasing would do no harm, and it would take his mind off Ventnor and Katharine and the blasted hopelessness of the lot.

Feeling suddenly and uncommonly light-hearted, Rafe headed back into his house.

CHAPTER 8

Rafe found Thea in the hallway, tugging at the bow of her bonnet, letting the ribbons flutter against her throat. As she lifted the bonnet from her head, her bosom rose and fell. A hairpin clattered onto the floor and a thick lock of chestnut hair tumbled down her neck.

Rafe twisted the bills in both hands. "Has the bishop gone?"

"Yes. He's unusual, isn't he? For a bishop."

"What did you talk about?"

"I don't recall."

She put down the bonnet. One by one, she released the five buttons of her pelisse, the fabric parting to reveal the summer gown below, pale blue with a shiny royal-blue ribbon under her bust. Perhaps he should help her, slide the pelisse off her shoulders and down those smooth, bare arms.

He did not move, except to concentrate on untwisting the bills. He ran his eyes over the words and numbers so he would not think about shiny ribbons and satiny skin.

"I shall retire, my lord," she said. "I am terribly tired."

"Too tired to tell me how much of my money you spent today?"

She tossed her head. "I'm sure I have no idea. The best countesses never count money."

"But the best earls always do."

He waved the sheaf of bills meaningfully, earning a thrilling glare.

"How utterly detestable to ask a question to which one already knows the answer." Her chin came up. "I shan't stand for it. Because you did that, I refuse to reply. No, do not argue. You have brought this upon yourself."

She whirled about and marched for the stairs. Her exaggerated hauteur magnified the sway in her hips. Rafe sauntered after her, watching the fine cotton of her gown swirl around her legs and ankles. Her fabulously, famously fascinating ankles.

"Five dozen silver buttons," Rafe said to her back, as she started up the stairs, the movement of her gown around her rear even more fascinating than those ankles. "Why would you need sixty buttons?"

"It is cheaper to buy them in bulk, as any good merchant's daughter knows," she retorted. "One would think he would be grateful, but no, I get nothing but complaints."

Rafe fought a smile as he climbed the stairs after her. "One jeweled music box," he read.

"All the best countesses have jeweled music boxes."

"And do all the best countesses take snuff? You bought a hand-painted enamel snuffbox inlaid with pearls."

She sniffed. "That was a gift for you, but you've upset me so thoroughly, I shan't give it to you now."

Maintaining her haughty air, she started up the next flight of stairs to the bedrooms. Rafe followed, enjoying himself far too much to stop.

"One pair of mother-of-pearl opera glasses," Rafe read out.

"What else would a countess take to the theatre? Oh!" She whirled about so abruptly that Rafe stopped only a few steps down, looking up into her bright blue eyes. "Let's go to the theatre!"

She looked so earnest and excited that Rafe almost agreed. But of course they couldn't go to the theatre. They'd both taken enough risks today. Had she forgotten? He could not tell if she genuinely forgot things, or if it was a ploy to distract him.

"No," he said.

With a sigh, she resumed walking. "I suppose you don't like the theatre."

"Yes, I do," he said, vexingly stung at her disappointment and annoyed that he cared enough to defend himself. "But being around you is theatre enough."

In the doorway to her dressing room, she turned back. "You like the theatre?"

"A dozen lace handkerchiefs."

"You cannot announce something astounding like that and not elaborate. It's insufferable. Do you really like the theatre?"

"Why is that so hard to believe?"

"Theatre is so frivolous and you..." She frowned, studying his face. "You never really smile."

"I smile." He realized his brows were drawn together so deeply he could see them. He smoothed them out. "Very well," he said, resuming the game. "Let's go to the theatre. Tonight."

Her eyes widened in alarm. "Well, we can't go *tonight*." She spun and traipsed into her sitting room, with its small heap of parcels by one wall. Rafe followed her. Not quite proper, given they weren't actually married, but to hell with it. No one would know. For now, they were sheltered by the fiction of their marriage.

"Why not go to the theatre?" he asked.

"Because I don't have any jewels. London would be horrified to see a countess with no jewels. 'By George,' they would say, 'it must be true he's a devil, because only a devil would not buy his wife jewels.' No," she added firmly, shaking her head. "I simply cannot have them speaking of you like that."

"How thoughtful of you."

"I am an excellent wife."

"You are not. You're not even a good wife. As a wife, you are of little use to me at all."

Thea's eyes flickered down to his chest and a faint blush colored her cheeks. He guessed she had understood his meaning. It was wrong to tease her in this way, but he could not bring himself to stop. Not yet. In a moment, he would stop.

She looked back up, nibbling at her lip. She took a step backward. Rafe took a step forward. She brushed her knuckles over her jaw, glanced down at his chest, and away.

Again he stepped forward. Again she stepped back.

"Do you know why men marry women?" he asked.

"Because they're not allowed to marry their horses?"

Her gaze flickered to his lips, and he realized he was half smiling. "Because among women's many delightful attributes, they have—"

"The ability to embroider buttons," she finished, too loudly.

"That too," he agreed.

Another step forward, another step back, and her shoulders were against the wall. Her gaze roamed over his face, then dropped to his mouth, then lower to his chest. Her skirts brushed against his legs: She was twisting her fingers in them. Her cheeks were a little pink.

"Am I frightening you, Countess?"

"No," she squeaked. "Though you act like you are hunting me."

"Ah, but man is a hunter."

She snorted derisively. "If man is a hunter, why does he sit around expecting other people to serve him? 'By George,' he says, 'I could hunt the cow myself, but instead I'll send the wife for roast beef.'"

Rafe leaned one forearm on the wall by her head, catching her sweet strawberry scent. He kept his other hand, with its clutch of bills, behind his back, so he would not test the softness of her skin, or catch a curl of her hair. She tilted back her head and made no attempt to flee.

"I promise never to send you for roast beef. But surely I can expect a kiss. What use is a wife whom I don't take to bed?"

"It might be nice to wait until we know each other better."

"I don't need to know you better to locate your pertinent parts."

Ah, poorly done, Rafe. Now he was imagining her pertinent parts. Imagining all of her. How animated she would be, how curious, enthusiastic, fun. Her expressive face... So help him but he would love to pleasure her just to watch her face.

But he must not. He had promised she would be safe, and she would be. This was a whole new game, and one not even he was ready to play.

So he closed his eyes and contented himself with breathing her in, her scent summoning images of long, lazy summer afternoons. He was aware of every inch of her: her breasts above the ribbon, the curve of her waist below. Aware of her hips, her thighs, her feet.

Aware of her breathing. Her breath hitching. Her skirts rustling.

She was escaping. He kept his eyes closed. He must let her go.

Then soft, warm lips pressed against his.

Just pressed. Unmoving, but unmistakable. A light promise of a kiss.

Every part of Rafe was as still as stone, but for his suddenly pounding heart and the hunger stirring in his loins and the sweet sensations dancing through his gut. He dared not move, for fear of frightening her away, and he needed time, a millennium, to savor the sensation of her lips on his. Time stretched and Rafe became as big as the selva, yet as tiny as this moment: this tiny, sacred moment of two pairs of lips pressed together.

He dared to move his mouth against hers, a gentle search for more, an offering, a vow. Hunger coursed through him. He stopped. Waited. Eyes still closed.

She responded in kind, the enchanting caress of her lips as slight and self-conscious as his own. Once more, he moved his lips, perhaps this time less a kiss than a prayer, a prayer that was answered, as for another tiny, sacred moment, they kissed as lovers would.

Then the pressure was gone. She ended the kiss. His lips were cold from her absence and warm from the memory, and new and familiar and alive. He could breathe again, and he sucked in that breath, his body desperate for air, and for, oh, so many things. He kept his eyes closed, because to open them was to lose that precious, tiny moment, but he knew from the murmur of muslin and the whisper of his shirt sleeve over his skin, that she had ducked under his arm and escaped, and was lost somewhere in the room.

He opened his eyes and faced the wall. It was papered with a riot of leaves and flowers and berries.

"What was that?" he asked the ugly wallpaper.

"A kiss," Thea said from behind him. Her voice was too high and too bright, and he felt a rush of unmerited pride.

She cleared her throat and added, in her usual tone, "That should keep you satisfied for...a week."

He turned and lounged back against the wall to show he didn't care. She stood by the writing desk, fingers of one hand curled around its edge, the others fiddling with the ribbon below her breasts.

"What happens in a week?" he asked.

"Um. Two kisses?"

"And in two weeks?"

"In two weeks, we shall renegotiate."

In two weeks, this farce would be over.

But what if things were different? What if he were a different man? A man who could take a lively bride home and make her happy?

Thea at Brinkley End, lighting up the house, turning it upside down, making it a place that he longed to enter.

Thea at Brinkley End, lonely and bored, sick of him, fading away, her light dimming, her laughter gone, and him, helpless to save her.

She had lived in an isolated country house, she had said, where she had no friends and never quite belonged. Whereas he rarely left his estate these days and spent every evening alone.

Blast it. No. Desire was turning him foolish, the bishop's words confusing his thoughts.

Her face was half turned away from him as she stared down at the desk, giving him the angle of her jaw, the lock of wayward hair. He searched for words, annoyed both that he could not find them and that he cared enough to try.

But then her manner turned sharp and bright, and the last lingering echoes of that tiny moment and its elusive promise faded away.

"Look! A letter for the Countess of Luxborough," she said, lifting the paper sitting by her hand.

Rafe suspected that if he mentioned the kiss she would look at him blankly and say, "Kiss? Oh, yes, I forgot."

Fair enough. It was barely a kiss. He would forget it too, if he could not still feel her lips on his, her caress soaking into his skin like dye.

"But this isn't Arabella's hand."

Her smile dimmed. Oh, blast. It could only be Mr. Knight. A mistake to have called on the man. If he told Thea about the money, she would take it and run, and this would end too soon.

"This is my father's hand," she whispered. "How could he possibly know?"

THEA PRESSED one corner of the letter into the pad of her thumb so hard it left an indent. As she watched, the indent disappeared. Like that kiss: a fleeting feeling, soon gone, easily forgotten.

And yet, not.

Luxborough was watching her intently and more than a little warily, as if he feared she would do something terrible like kiss him again. If she had surprised him, she had surprised herself more. But when he teased her, a kiss had seemed a marvelous idea. When he advanced, seeing nothing but her, thrills had spiraled down her middle. When he stood close, her body warmed to his, even though they did not touch.

Thea was not accomplished at kissing—besides, he was tall and she had not been steady—but perhaps she had not done too badly, because the kiss still bounced around inside her, like a living thing that had become trapped in her body, bumping against various parts of her, creating...sensations.

Oh dear. That was not part of the plan. She was meant to keep him at a distance. He believed they were married, which meant he believed he had a legal right to her body. She had to put things back to how they were, when she annoyed him with her nonsense and he growled at her.

He was rather adorable when he growled.

"You called on Pa?" she asked.

"I married his daughter. Seemed right." His eyes flicked down to the letter and back again. "Give me the letter. I'll read it."

"It's my letter."

He lunged for it. She leaped away. Those same thrills spiraled through her, right down between her thighs. She did not know what to make of this, and when their eyes met, he seemed equally confused.

Then he lounged back against the wall, and she scrabbled at the letter so clumsily she tore the page.

"'*My darling Helen,*'" she read out loud.

Oh, thank heavens. Her parents didn't know what she was up to. Helen and Thea had agreed not to tell them, because they were incapable of keeping a secret. And this—this must have been the cause of the joy she had witnessed that day.

Luxborough was eyeing the letter as if it planned an attack.

"What did you say to him?" she asked.

"Hmm?"

"My father. What did you say?"

"Hmm."

Thea gave up and read silently:

How proud we are of you, to have married an Earl. Just yesterday we learned the new Marquess of Hardbury has returned to England a Bachelor, and we entertained Dreams you might become his Marchioness. But better an Earl in the Hand than a Marquess in the Bush! Thank you, our dearest—We can forget the Troubles your Sister caused, and know that even if I lose everything again, the Little Ones' future is secure. Nobody stops a Knight!

The paper was suddenly too heavy; Thea lowered it and let it dangle. The too-familiar feeling of having disappointed them lodged in her throat, as sour as old cream. She supposed if she had truly married an earl, they would welcome her home and forget what "troubles" she had caused. Perhaps, if she were a countess, they would discover they did believe her, after all. Well, she wasn't a countess, and she never would be, but soon Helen would be safely married, and Thea's pamphlet would be published, and everyone would know the truth. Nobody would stop *this* Knight.

"What did he say?" Luxborough asked.

"I didn't read it all."

This time, when he reached for the letter, she let him take it. The letter did not seem to betray her ruse. Her mind swam with the image of her parents that day, hugging and laughing. The closed blue door.

She didn't want to think about that. She would think about something else.

"The Marquess of Hardbury!" she cried.

Luxborough did not look up from the letter. "What about him?"

"He's alive and back in England."

"And?"

"You already knew?"

"Someone mentioned it today. Everyone assumes that as a peer I am interested in other peers."

"Arabella!"

He did look up then. "Are you just yelling out names like in a game of charades?"

"I must tell Arabella about Lord Hardbury's return."

"Because?"

"Because they were promised to each other as children, but

they hated each other. Then he went away and everyone thought—"

"Stop. Enough. I'm sorry I asked."

She would write to Arabella and then she would not think about her parents. Yet no sooner had Thea sat at the desk than he said, "Your parents mean to call on you tomorrow," and she bounced back up with a high-pitched "What?"

No, they must not see her.

She snatched back the letter and scanned it, saying as she did, "The Prince Regent will host a grand party in London to celebrate the marquess's return and they want me to procure them invitations. '*This year, September's Little Season will be a Grand Season, and we will be part of it.*' And he will call tomorrow."

"Not possible," Luxborough said. "We leave for Somersetshire first thing tomorrow."

"Yes, yes, of course," she said absently, her mind still on this news.

A grand party, hosted by the Prince Regent. In late August, every lord, lady, and gentleman in Britain would travel to London for that party; Town would be as busy as during the main Season in spring. Pa would not be wrong; he would know because he supplied the contractors who supplied the Crown.

Oh, but this was a marvelous opportunity! If Thea's pamphlet was distributed to every genteel house in London, then by the time of the Regent's ball, her story could be the talk of society.

Yet her charade with Luxborough would be finished. She would have no entry to the ball, unless Arabella could smuggle her in, for surely Arabella would attend. As would everyone else. Ventnor and Percy and Helen and Beau and—

"What are you up to?" Luxborough said.

She blinked, startled. "Pardon?"

"You are scheming something. You have a frighteningly expressive face."

"You must acquire invitations for Ma and Pa." Hastily, she began to prepare pen, ink, and paper. "And write to Pa. Tell him— Why aren't you writing?"

"I am an earl."

"And?"

"You cannot order me to write a letter like I'm your secretary."

"Don't they teach you to write at earl school? Classes in penmanship, alongside classes in preposterousness, peremptoriness, and parsimoniousness."

"You do realize there is no earl school."

"Then how do you know how to earl? You are in charge of running the country and they don't train you for it?"

"Precisely."

"Without even teaching you to read and write?'

"Of course I can read and write."

"Then why are you not writing?" She patted the chair. "Sit. Write. Tell Pa that if he keeps your marriage secret, you will announce it at the ball, and present them to the Prince Regent as your parents-in-law. They'll like that."

He looked disgusted by the idea. "I shall not attend any blasted ball, or beg for invitations, or present your parents to anyone."

"Do you want them showing up on your doorstep in Somersetshire? My parents, who are incapable of keeping a secret? Poking in their noses right where you are raising an army of dead wives?"

He threw up his hands. "I am not raising an army of dead wives."

"I have it on good authority that you are."

"That was your fabrication."

"Well, if I made it up, it must be true."

His eyes looked wild and she managed not to laugh. Or to catch his face in her hands again, just to feel his warmth and strength. Or to kiss him again. Her lips tingled at the thought.

"At least if I write this blasted letter, you might shut up," he muttered.

Bending over the desk, he dashed off a quick note to her father and addressed it. Then he scrawled out a separate note, tossed down the pen and wad of bills, and straightened. His eyes skated over the pile of parcels but all he said was, "We leave for Brinkley End early. Be ready."

He took two steps toward the door, then turned back. "Countess, I should advise you, some of the workers in my house and on my estate are...unusual."

"Unusual how?"

"My land steward and housekeeper have trouble finding employees because of the rumors about me. Astonishingly enough, many people prefer not to work for a man reputed to be a murdering sorcerer. But we are not far from Bristol, where people from around the world wash up, many of who are desperate or homeless or have come from situations that make a murdering sorcerer sound pleasant by comparison. We don't care where people come from or what they look like, so long as they are willing to do an honest day's work."

"You forget that I grew up in a part of London full of people from around the world."

"And the housekeeper, Sally Holt. She is...eccentric."

"Eccentric? How?"

"I assure you she is quite harmless."

"Um. That's comforting."

He paused, looked at her lips, and the kiss bounced around inside her again, as if eager for a friend, but then he wheeled about and headed for the door. In the doorway, he again turned back.

"And I apologize for my earlier behavior. You are exceedingly desirable but I promised not to importune you for a month. I assure you, you are safe."

Then he was gone.

You are exceedingly desirable.

Well.

Just as well he was honorable enough to follow his own rule, because Thea was still thinking about how delicious it felt to be near him, the way his radiating heat embraced her. At no point had she felt truly frightened when he pursued her. Indeed, she rather liked the idea that he wanted her.

Silly. She knew enough of men to understand that a man could want to kiss a woman yet not really want *her*.

Determined to forget about the kiss, Thea sat and read his letter to her father, tersely worded and penned in a precise, bold hand. The other note was for Luxborough's man of affairs in London, whom he instructed to obtain invitations for Mr. and Mrs. Knight and to pay all of Lady Luxborough's bills.

Thea sealed the letter to her father, and placed it and the note on a salver. Then she wrote first to Arabella—judiciously omitting mention of the kiss—and to Mr. Witherspoon, regarding the possibilities the Prince Regent's party presented for their campaign.

And several times she caught herself brushing a finger over her mouth, reliving the unexpected softness of his lips.

He had not pressed her over his conjugal rights. He had protected her from Ventnor's unkindness, and written to her father, and not scolded her for the shopping.

You will be safe, Luxborough had promised her, and she could almost believe it was true.

What if it could be true? What if everything could be different? If Thea could have someone who truly wanted her. Who would keep her safe, and give her a home, and hold her close, and kiss her in thrilling ways.

But no: He would detest her when he learned about her lies, and even if he didn't, he would not want a woman like her. Anyway, she didn't want him. He had married a stranger for money, and he had conspired with horrid Lord Ventnor. Thea shoved away the notion. She had enough impossible wishes, without wishing for that too.

CHAPTER 9

It took nearly two days to reach Brinkley End, though Lord Luxborough grumbled that they would arrive more quickly if Thea didn't insist on making frequent stops. Such breaks were essential, she argued, for what was the point of travel if one didn't stop to gush over the scenery, eat snacks, and torment the locals? Happily, the earl shared meals with her, and she used these interludes to pepper him with questions about his travels; he had wisely realized it was easiest simply to answer, and he enthralled her with descriptions of what he had seen.

Neither of them mentioned that small kiss; it might have never happened, except that when he was near, Thea could feel that kiss bouncing around inside her, and her fingers itched to touch him again. For all that he had called her desirable, he betrayed no evidence of desire now. Sometimes she thought he was looking at her, but then his eyes were elsewhere and she scolded herself for imagining things.

Alone in the carriage, her thoughts kept wandering back to Luxborough, but she could not enjoy such thoughts for long before recalling that he was a villain and she was a trickster, so each time, she ruthlessly turned her mind to imagining his house at Brinkley End. This task was hampered by her limited experience of aristocratic country estates, but, fortuitously, she boasted extensive knowledge of Gothic novels on which to draw.

The house would, naturally, be grim and dark, with secret passageways, haunted dungeons, and a locked tower. The butler, whose name would be Carrion or Skull or something similarly promising, would have skin and eyes as cold and white as a dead fish, and the housekeeper, Sally Holt, would compensate for her vexingly ordinary name by being black-clad and skeletal, with a cruel smile and the intently sinister gaze of a crow.

Thea so excelled at this game that she felt genuine disappointment that the sun broke through the rain clouds as they turned into the drive; she had hoped to arrive during a thunderstorm. Furthermore, the driveway did not look at all encouraging, for the road was well maintained and lined with stately, handsome trees, their leaves glossy from the recent rain. And when the house came into view, Thea huffed with dismay, for it was so unsporting as to appear not only perfectly normal, but perfectly lovely to boot.

The moment the carriage came to a stop, Thea tumbled out onto the gravel. As always, her eyes went straight to Lord Luxborough, but he was handing his horse off to a groom, so she resolutely turned and scowled at the manse. Its smooth walls, which rose some four stories, were charmingly dotted with ornamental windows and topped by picturesque Italianate balustrades. It was not huge—not nearly on the scale of Arabella's family pile—but it was grand enough to put on an impressive show, as the late-afternoon sun bathed the elegant gray stone in a golden glow. Jolly green vines clambered up the side walls, and bay windows on the ground floor glinted welcomingly.

"That's a fierce frown, Countess," Luxborough remarked as he came to stand at her side. She had not been aware of the cool breeze until his large body blocked it. "Is the house not to your liking?"

"It's not even old," she complained.

"I never said it was."

"It should be old and crumbling and gloomy, with mad monks and bats and ghosts." She shook her head. "Honestly, Luxborough. How do you manage to stay so grumpy when you live in such a beautiful place?"

"An overabundance of natural talent, I suppose."

He slid her a sideways look, laughter gleaming in his tired, brandy-colored eyes, and Thea fought hard not to smile and hug his arm. The wind was teasing his curls under his hat, and his closeness stirred more of those delicious sensations under her skin.

"It has quite spoiled my fun," she said. "I was determined to have a perfectly horrid time here, but it is not nearly terrifying enough."

"I apologize for failing to provide more miserable accommodations. If it would please you, I could hire someone to wander the corridors at night, moaning and rattling chains."

She sighed. "It is kind of you to offer, but I should not like to put anyone to trouble. I suppose I shall simply have to enjoy myself instead."

"And you certainly have a talent for that."

His tone was dry, but his look was warm, and that combination so confused her that she forgot to breathe. Then he was busying himself with removing his hat and freeing his hair, and she found enough air to say, "It's easy enough. When it is so very lovely here."

"I suppose it is."

"You *suppose*? Had you not noticed?"

"It's been here all my life," he said carelessly. "And I passed my youth wanting to escape."

Oh, but he was impossible, not to realize what he had! Suddenly irritated with him, Thea skipped away to the edge of the lawn, which sloped down to an enormous ornamental lake. Waterbirds drifted over its surface, and a Roman-style folly beckoned from a small island in the middle.

"Can one bathe in the lake?" she called.

"Of course. I swim most days when the weather permits. Down the end is a secluded area for women, sheltered by the willows."

"What is in that folly on the island?"

"Take a boat out and see."

"Oh, will you row me out there?"

"Row yourself. Plenty of rowboats in the boathouse."

"Very well, I shall."

A plague on him. She did *not* need his company, and neither did she need a Gothic atmosphere. The Rules of Mischief demanded that she enjoy herself, so she would think of Brinkley End as a pleasure garden, created for her entertainment; she would pass a merry old time these few days, and leave without a backward glance.

"I shall swim and learn to row and..."

Looking about, her gaze snagged on an empty wagon on the other side of the driveway. A large piebald horse stood between the shafts, snorting and stamping its feet.

"And I shall learn to drive, too," Thea announced, and dashed toward the horse and cart.

But the horse did not like this idea; it threw up its head and bared its huge yellow teeth. Then Luxborough was there, catching her around the waist and gently pulling her away. She was so surprised she could not resist, what with the firm heat of his hands, and his bulk at her back, and his woodsy scent that made her think of cozy nights by the fire.

"Careful," he said, his breath tickling her ear. "Tatworth's horse is a mean old brute."

"It won't be mean to me," she protested, but she stayed nestled against him anyway.

"I fear the horse will be immune to your charms, even if the rest of us are not."

Before she could pursue the fascinating topic of her charms and his susceptibility to them, he released her and moved away, a chill shivering over her back from his absence. Another thing not to think about; she was developing such a colossal list that it would require all her faculties merely to remember what she must forget.

"At any rate," he went on, more brusquely, "the cart belongs to Dick Tatworth, a deliveryman from Bristol. Ask one of the grooms to take you out in the pony gig. Ah, there's Tatworth now."

He was looking toward the nearby woods, which were separated from the garden by a stream. A stone footbridge spanned the stream; beyond it, a path disappeared between the trees. Crossing the footbridge were two people: a small, ruddy-cheeked man in a tattered greatcoat, and a taller woman with dark skin, wearing a pink dress, with a matching pink bandeau wound around her short black hair.

Excellent. Another distraction.

"Is that the housekeeper Sally Holt?"

"No. That's Martha Flores. She works here too."

"What does she do?"

"You ask more questions than a child."

"If you offered information, I wouldn't need to ask. What's in the woods?"

"Nothing."

Thea set off toward the woods, but Luxborough barreled around in front of her, blocking her view with his body made for hugging and sheltering.

"You had better not go into those woods," he said.

"The woods are forbidden?" she asked eagerly.

"Very forbidden."

"Are they dark and dangerous and full of monsters?"

"No, they are just forbidden." His expression was severe, and he stood as unmoving and unmovable as a watchtower. "This is my one rule: Do not cross that footbridge or go into those woods. There are a hundred acres of woodland on the other side of the lake, as well as fifty acres of gardens and two thousand acres of farmland and orchards. Go anywhere you please, but not through there."

"So *that* is where you bury the bodies of your victims," she said lightly.

Though she spoke in jest, a darkly bleak expression crossed his face. He pivoted away from her, and when she saw his face again, the look was gone.

Thea was fumbling for words when someone yelled, "Dick Tatworth!"

She turned to see a newcomer striding around from the rear of the house. At first glance, Thea assumed the newcomer was a man, given the outfit of breeches and boots, with a black waistcoat over a white shirt, but at second glance—

"That's a woman!" she said.

Sun glinted off the woman's red hair, which was gathered in a fat coil at the back of her head. Her clothing must have been tailored to her measurements, for Thea couldn't imagine a man having such a curvy shape.

"So it is."

Thea clutched Luxborough's arm. "And she's holding a gun!"

"So she is."

What's more, the woman was pointing the gun at the deliveryman, her arm straight and steady as she marched at him, scolding him in a strong, rich voice.

"Dick Tatworth, you rotten cad, I'll skin you alive and feed your meat to the dogs."

"Calm down, missus," that man stuttered, hands raised as he stumbled toward his wagon. "We can talk about this all sensible like."

Lord Luxborough did not seem even mildly perturbed by the unfolding drama, and Martha Flores only ducked behind the gun-toting woman to watch the spectacle with interest.

"What's going on?" Thea realized she was squeezing his arm and released him. "Do you mean to intervene?"

"She seems to have this in hand."

The red-haired woman continued her advance. "You think you can dally with one of my maids? You think her lack of family means she's not protected? I protect my own."

"She's lying!" the man shrieked, his ruddy cheeks turning ruddier. "I never."

"You never what?"

"Whatever she said I did, I didn't."

"You think I don't know you have one wife in Bristol and another in Bath? Be gone, Dick Tatworth, before I shoot you in the bollocks and let you explain that to all your wives."

Luxborough and Thea jumped aside, as Dick Tatworth leaped into his wagon and spurred his horse to a swift escape. The woman lowered the pistol and handed it to Martha.

Thea could hardly drag her eyes off her. If only she could do that! She could see herself now, pointing a gun at Percy Russell in that cool, confident way, while Percy spluttered and ran. She must learn to shoot while she was here, too.

"She is splendid," Thea breathed. "Who is that?"

"Sally Holt," Luxborough said.

"*That's* your housekeeper?"

He shrugged. "I did warn you she is eccentric."

WITH A CALL to Sally over his shoulder, Rafe took Thea's elbow and tried to usher her toward the house. This was made difficult because she kept twisting to look back at Sally, as if she couldn't get enough of her.

"Show's over," he snapped, irritated both by Thea's blatant admiration and by his new tendency to find excuses to touch her. "You'll find walking easier if you face forward."

Thea looked up at him, her face bright with excitement. Blast her and her talent for delight. It was not only infectious, but addictive. For all Rafe's grumbling during their trip, he kept looking out for sights she might enjoy. Even now he was tempted to be the one to show Thea the house and estate, if only to watch her face light up at each discovery. And after each new delight, she would seek another, and another, always seeking something new. He would do well to remember that. A man could run himself ragged offering novelties in an effort to keep her happy, and never succeeding for more than a day.

The sooner he handed Thea over to Sally and forgot about her existence, the better.

"Why does Sally Holt wear men's clothing?" Thea asked in a low voice.

"Because she wants to, I suppose."

"And you don't mind? Arabella's mother would have a fit."

"If you had met some of the people I've met in the world, you'd understand why I do not care a penny what my housekeeper wears."

"I cannot wait to see the butler." She turned her eager gaze toward the front door. "What does he wear?"

"No butler."

"Why not?"

"He objected to Sally and said either he went or she went, and I said fine. She manages without one."

"Why did you choose her over him?"

Rafe hesitated, not sure how to explain Sally. He released Thea's elbow and settled on saying, "Her father was the local schoolteacher, and she has lived here most of her life."

It was simpler not to say the rest: that as a girl, Sally Holt had been unexceptional, except for her beauty, which she attempted to conceal under plain gowns, unflattering caps, and a deferential manner. But in the six years between Katharine's death and Rafe's return—that period when Rafe went into the selva to hunt orchids and avoid the world—polite Miss Holt had transformed into a woman who said what she pleased, dressed as she pleased, and eyed the world as if she wished to deal it a good hard slap.

Rafe had never asked Sally what happened in those years that made her change so, and she never volunteered the information. By tacit agreement, they never mentioned Katharine at all.

Thea threw another glance over her shoulder, and said, "Oh, she's coming," and stopped short. Rafe had to stop too.

"My apologies for losing you a deliveryman, my lord, but I will protect the girls at any cost," Sally said, as she approached. Her words were for Rafe, but her eyes did not leave Thea. "I trust I did not frighten you, my lady."

"Not at all."

"That was not how I intended your first impression of Brinkley End. The staff were to be lined up outside to greet you. But then the maidservant was weeping and... I shall call the staff now, if you wish, my lady."

Rafe frowned at this unexpected version of Sally. She seemed almost anxious to please. Surely not.

"Do not trouble yourself, Mrs. Holt," Thea said graciously. "I was very impressed. It is much more important to protect the maid."

"Thank you, my lady. And I prefer just 'Sally,' if you do not object to the informality."

How unusual. Sally never sought *his* opinion on such matters. Rafe tried to catch Sally's eye but to no avail, for she was still talking to Thea, saying, "We are delighted to welcome you to Brinkley End. Lord Luxborough said he would never marry again, but I have long hoped he would."

"You have?" Rafe asked.

The two women ignored him. "I trust you find everything to your liking, my lady," Sally went on. "I will happily make any changes you require."

"No need," Rafe interrupted. "She will not interfere."

"Of course not," Thea agreed cheerfully. "Interfering would be work, and the best countesses never work." She turned her bright smile on Sally. "Feed me at regular intervals and I shall be no trouble at all."

No trouble? Thea? Ha! She created trouble simply by standing in one place, her hair troubling him to run his fingers through it, the fastening of her cloak troubling him to release it.

Such trouble made Rafe's arms restless, so he waved at the far side of the house. "Sally has prepared an apartment for you in the west wing. You have ample space in your rooms for your meals and everything else you need."

"My meals?" she said sharply.

"Feeding at regular intervals."

"But what about you?"

"I also feed at regular intervals."

"You expect me to take my meals alone in my room?"

Wounded bewilderment haunted her tone and eyes. No, he would not feel guilty or offer her comfort. He was not here for her passing entertainment.

"That's what I do," he said.

"I don't like dining alone. People dine together."

"I'm not people."

She glared at him, but her imperious countess look did not mask her lingering hurt.

"Get used to it," he snapped.

He wheeled about and crunched across the gravel to the carriage, where a groom was lifting a box of orchids. Rafe yanked the box into his arms and strode away, down the path and toward the woods, not looking back.

Aware of Sally's watchful gaze, Thea lifted her chin and pretended nothing was amiss. Neither should it be. Lord Luxborough was her adversary—not her friend and certainly not her husband—and she could rely on him for nothing, not even dinner. It was better that he did not behave like an interested husband, because the more questions he asked, the more lies she would have to tell.

It was just that she had never expected him to dump her like a carriage with a broken wheel.

Holding onto her pride, Thea sailed past Sally through the front door and tossed aside her cloak and gloves, looking for something to divert her. Easily done: The foyer was pleasingly spacious and symmetrical, with a staircase running up each painting-covered wall. Under the split staircase, a large double door opened onto a courtyard garden. On a pedestal sat a welcoming arrangement of fresh flowers.

Turning, she spied a trio of maids goggling at her. They giggled, bobbed curtsies, and darted away.

"Forgive their excitement, my lady," Sally said, joining her. "Everyone was so happy to hear his lordship was married."

"Um." Thea tried to swallow away her guilt. "That's very kind."

"He has lived alone for a long time. If we served dinner in the dining room, he would have little choice but to dine there with you or starve."

Thea had to smile at the housekeeper's insubordination. How diverting it would be, to conspire with Sally against Luxborough! But Sally was matchmaking and Thea was being silly.

"You are very kind, but I'm sure he and I will reach an agreement."

Avoiding the questions in Sally's eyes, Thea wandered to the open doors under the staircase. From here, she could see that the house was shaped like a horseshoe around this courtyard garden, all manicured lawns, sculpted shrubs, and colorful flowerbeds.

She turned back to Sally. "There is no need to go to any trouble. I am easy to please, and it is such a lovely house."

"Everything is in excellent condition, and the rooms are ready for your use. Guest rooms, nursery, and schoolrooms above and... Although Master Rafe—I mean, his lordship—only uses his study and occasionally the library. Shall I show you to your apartment first?"

Without waiting for a reply, Sally started up the stairs and Thea followed her. The staircase emerged into a long portrait gallery. The housekeeper turned left and continued without pausing, but Thea lingered to scan the paintings.

"Where is Lord Luxborough's portrait?" she called.

"He never sat for one. Your rooms are this way," Sally prompted her from one end of the gallery.

Thea looked toward the dark doorway at the other end. "What's through there?"

"That leads to the other wing of the house, and his lordship's rooms."

"I see."

Thea followed Sally out of the portrait gallery and around a corner to a long corridor lined with doors on one side and windows on the other. She stopped to push open a window and looked out onto the courtyard garden and the opposite wing. So, her fake husband's bedroom lay over there. How odd aristocrats were. They made such a fuss about who married whom, but once they were married, they slept so far apart, they might as well be in different villages.

Turning back, she saw Sally disappear through a doorway, so she slammed the window shut and dashed after her. But once inside the door, she skidded to a halt and laughed, despite everything. These rooms were quite the loveliest she had ever been in. They were decorated in peach and yellow, with thick carpets, elegantly carved furniture, fresh flowers, and whimsical paintings. She wandered through the apartment, amazed it was all for her: a dressing room and bathing area; a bedroom dominated by a canopied bed so enormous it had its own staircase; an even larger sitting room, which was fitted out with a daybed under the window, settees by the fireplace, and a dining table.

For her meals. Alone.

She would not be silly about this. For three years she had dined alone; another few days hardly signified. Being a fake countess would provide her with plenty of pleasure, and she would not complain.

Resolutely, Thea crossed to the window to take in its

spectacular view over the gardens, and the woodlands and fields beyond.

"None of this is as I expected," she said.

"What did Luxborough tell you to expect?"

"He didn't tell me much at all."

"He never was one for talking."

Thea whirled about. "Ooh, what was he like as a boy?"

"Quiet, solitary, thoughtful." Sally's face softened with a fond half smile. "Always going off on his own. He preferred to roam the woods than be in anyone's company. By contrast, the rest of his family were gregarious and loud and could not bear to be alone for an afternoon. Eldritch, some called him. Said there was something wrong with him."

"But there isn't!" Thea protested. "That's simply how he is. Although I cannot imagine him giving a flying farthing for anyone's opinion. And I suppose..." She trailed a finger over the window frame. "In turn, he does not label people or judge them, but rather accepts people as they are. It's one of the things I most like about him."

"He always was impervious like that," Sally said. "He let people talk, and then did as he pleased. No one was surprised when he ran away to America to avoid joining the army. Although it was a surprise he took Katharine." She stopped short and added quietly, "I ought not have mentioned her," her tone not apologetic so much as regretful.

"You must have known Katharine," Thea said.

Sally's eyelids flickered and she turned away. "You'll want to see the drawing room and library, first?"

Without waiting for an answer, she left the room.

CHAPTER 10

B y the time Thea caught up with Sally downstairs, she was already throwing open one of the doors leading off the foyer. Thea peered past her at a drawing room as lovely as the rest of the house. The bright, airy room was decorated in cream and gold, with blue carpets and upholstery. A glossy pianoforte beckoned from one corner, an ornamental fire screen covered the empty grate, and the furniture was arranged to make the most of the light and view.

Despite the room's air of expensive elegance, it felt welcoming and lived in, as though all it needed to be complete was for Thea to come in and sit down.

"Is it to your liking, my lady? We'll start lighting fires again soon, and will arrange the furniture accordingly, but we can easily make changes now."

How peculiar that they rearranged the furniture for best use in a room that was never used. The previous earl—Luxborough's elder brother—never married, so this house had had no mistress in the years since Luxborough's father died and his mother moved away. Yet looking at this room, one would think its mistress had just now stepped outside.

"This room is perfect," Thea said. "All I shall ever require is to take afternoon tea here."

"Of course. Bread and cakes are baked fresh every day, and the farms provide fresh butter, cream, jam, and honey. It will be a pleasure to see the countess taking afternoon tea. And if you have guests... The house is always ready."

Thea could almost see it, this room full of friends and family, chattering, singing, competing to entertain each other. She blinked away the alluring image and faced Sally with a bright "Where to next?"

Next was the door on the opposite side of the foyer, behind which lay the library. Thea needed only one look to fall in love.

Rich red carpets and curtains created a warm atmosphere, and the oak shelves lining the walls were stuffed with books. Two large bay windows overlooked the lawn and the lake. In one window was a cushioned seat, perfect for reading. In the other was a massive desk, with a large chair covered in supple green leather.

Thea was drawn to the desk helplessly. She smoothed her hand over its surface, thinking almost fondly of the little desk in her bare room in Mrs. Burton's house, where she had passed her spare hours, writing until her bum grew numb from the hard seat and her fingers stiffened with the cold. Only during those hours had she felt anchored to her real life; the rest of the time she felt horribly adrift. *Soon*, she promised herself. *Soon I will get home and no longer be exiled to strangers' houses.*

"And you say Luxborough does not use this desk?" she asked.

"He prefers his study."

"Ooh, I want to see his study. Is it through that connecting door?"

Before Sally could answer, Thea yanked open the door and

tumbled into a large room holding a billiard table a good twelve feet long, with a dozen or so ivory balls scattered over the green baize. Through the next door she spied a small parlor. It looked to be very much in use, and not by the earl, judging by the workbasket of sewing and the neat stack of books.

Back in the billiard room, the housekeeper stood by the table, absently spinning a ball in one hand, her expression guarded.

"Let us continue the tour," Sally said. "We have become accustomed to using that parlor in the evening, but we shall stop if your ladyship desires."

"We?"

"Martha and I."

Two friends who passed the evenings together in a parlor. Thea would not be welcome to join them. They were employees and she was the countess, so they could be friends and she could not. How silly it was, that such rules prevented even a countess from doing as she pleased.

Well, a plague on all the rules. Thea knew better than to form attachments anyway. Her family had moved so often, as her father's fortunes rose and fell, that Thea learned early that nothing lasted. Even her faith in her family, the one thing she had been sure of, had been wrenched away from her. Soon she would set the world right and start her life anew, and then she could find more friends. For now, the only rules that mattered were her Rules of Mischief, and they demanded that she enjoy herself. So enjoy herself she would.

With that, Thea pulled the door to the friends' parlor shut.

"What her ladyship desires," she announced, "is to learn to play billiards. I am sure I shall excel at the game."

Ignoring Sally's bemusement, Thea lifted a stick from the rack and approached the table, but there her pride failed her, for she hadn't the slightest idea what to do next. She poked at a ball with the unwieldy stick.

Across the table, Sally winced. "You'll tear the baize if you're not careful. Use your other hand to steady the cue while you line up your shot."

"What do you mean?"

Grabbing another cue, Sally demonstrated, making a bridge with one hand and sliding the cue into the furrow between her thumb and forefinger. She deftly struck a ball with the tip of the cue, sending the ball slamming into a second ball, which spun across the table and into a pocket. Without pause, she did it again and again, before standing back, holding her cue upright like a soldier resting his musket.

Yet again, Thea found herself envying the other woman's confidence and competence. Her dress and behavior were scandalously improper, of course, but who cared, when one was as assured as that? If Thea could learn *that* during her sojourn here, it would have been time well spent.

"And the aim is to hit the balls into the pockets?" she asked.

"Yes." Sally tapped a book on the corner table. "*A Practical Treatise on the Game of Billiards.* You can read more here."

It took Thea a few attempts to gain sufficient control over the cue, but when she finally struck a ball cleanly, it was so satisfying that she immediately did it again.

"Luxborough said you've been attached to the estate for years," Thea said, as Sally gathered up all the balls and used a wooden frame to form them into a triangle. The housekeeper had dropped her deferential manner, and Thea was glad of it.

"The previous countess—Luxborough's mother—hired me to teach letters and numbers to the younger servants and tenants' children, so I came to live in the house."

"And did you live here at the same time as Katharine?"

"Katharine never lived in this house."

Sally bent over the table and slammed her cue into the triangle of balls, scattering them over the baize.

"A zealot in London made the strangest claims." Thea affected a breezy tone to cover her curiosity. "That Luxborough killed her with sorcery."

"She died in a riding accident. He told you that, didn't he?"

"Of course," Thea lied, her mind racing as she lined up her cue. "I thought aristocratic ladies rode so well they always held their seat."

"Anyone would have trouble keeping their seat if they're riding away recklessly in the middle of a storm."

Thea's arm jerked and the cue missed the ball completely.

"Too many Gothic novels and too much imagination," she said, repeating one of Ma's recurring scolds. Her cheerful tone sounded false to her own ears. "When you say it like that, I picture some Gothic heroine wildly frightened and fleeing for her life."

But Sally did not laugh. Instead, she went still. Too still. Her knuckles where she gripped the cue were white, and her sudden tension sent a shiver up Thea's spine.

"That...that isn't what happened, is it?" Thea asked. "She wasn't...fleeing?"

Silence blanketed the room, broken by the ominous ticking of a clock. When Sally finally spoke, it was only to say, "Katharine liked Gothic novels, too." She met Thea's eyes for one tick of that clock before looking away again. "You had best address such questions to your husband."

"To my...? Oh, yes. Right. I forgot. My apologies. I ought not put you in a difficult position."

Sally gave a derisive snort. "Why not?" she muttered. "It's the position with which I'm most familiar."

They played on in silence, and soon Thea was so engrossed,

she forgot about Luxborough and his late wife. Each time she sank a ball in a pocket, a heady confidence spread through her limbs, and she danced with the cue in celebration.

"You really are not what I expected," Sally said, laughing.

"What did you expect?"

"Honestly, I could not imagine what kind of woman Luxborough would marry. But you're not…"

"I am not an aristocrat, if that is your meaning. I grew up poor. And I'm not accomplished like real ladies are. When my father became rich enough to afford tutors, my entire education consisted of learning how to pass as genteel. Pretending to be something one is not takes up an inordinate amount of time and energy."

Sally's expression grew thoughtful. "Indeed it does." She opened her mouth, closed it, and then said, all in a rush, "Master Rafe—I mean, Lord Luxborough. He is a good man. He…" She stopped. "But of course you know that. How did you two come to be married? The truth now."

The truth was Luxborough had married her for money and to please Lord Ventnor, and the other truth was, they were not married at all. With so many secrets, Thea could not tell the truth.

"Let's talk about you," Thea said.

Sally lined up her cue again. "No, let's talk about you."

"No, really, we should talk about you. You are so unconventional and you must tell me everything."

Sally struck the ball so hard it jumped off the table and landed on the carpet with a thud. When she straightened, her expression was hard, and her tone when she was spoke was hostile.

"You cannot dismiss me, my lady, whatever you think of me, or learn of me."

Thea stepped back. "I have no intention of dismissing you. I thought we could be friends."

"Indeed. Until I say or do something you don't like and then we won't be friends, will we? Then you'll be the countess and I'll be out on my ear. I wish for his lordship to be happy, but this is my home, and I'll not be made to leave again." Sally tossed the cue onto the table, where it bounced and clattered against the balls. "I'm sure you can find your own way back to your rooms, my lady."

With that, she strode out.

Thea unwrapped her fingers from the cue and swallowed away the sour taste in her mouth. Yet again, she had got it wrong. Sally was right: They could never be friends. How careless she was, to keep forgetting. As appealing as she found Brinkley End and its inhabitants, this was yet another place where she did not belong.

She did not care, she decided, as she launched her cue at the balls once more. A plague on them all. And if she must dine alone, then she would jolly well eat her dessert first!

RAFE MADE it to the footbridge before he surrendered to his urge to glance back, only to see that Thea and Sally had gone inside.

Everything was going according to plan, he reminded himself as he faced forward and strode along the dirt path through the woods. His plan had always been to ignore Thea until this fictional marriage was over. Because that was all it was or would ever be: fictional. The minute news came that the trustees had released the funds, he'd toss Thea into his carriage and send her away.

This silent lecture brought him to the clearing, as big as a cricket field. As always, his tension ebbed at the sight of his greenhouse, rising up before him like a church, and, behind it, the stone cottage that served as Martha's laboratory. This—*this*—was why he was here; he must not let himself be distracted by expressive blue eyes, or by enticing chestnut hair tumbling around a lively face, or by... No. Enough. She was the means to an end and nothing more.

In the greenhouse, the warm, fragrant air settled over him, dense and familiar, and the rows of lush plants greeted him with blessed, calming silence. He took a moment to breathe, letting the plants work their magic, then he carried the orchids to the work area, stripped down to his shirtsleeves, and pulled out his notes. Ventnor's eagerness to impress meant he had retained details of the orchids' origins, all to serve his boasting: "*This* flower comes from a secret gully so deep in the jungle that two men died blah blah blah." Self-important braggart. But at least the detail enabled Rafe to make an educated guess as to each plant's preferred conditions, and hope it would be enough to save those that had survived this long. Rafe could do little for other people, but at least he had a talent for caring for plants.

A glance at the sky through the glass-and-iron roof told him he had enough light to finish today. No one would be inconvenienced. The staff would know not to bother with a hot meal; they'd leave a cold plate in his sitting room for him to dine later.

Dine alone.

I don't like to dine alone.

The flash of hurt in those blue eyes.

Surely it would do no harm if they dined together? Either way, she—

No.

He would not change his plans.

Rafe grabbed the first orchid his hand landed on and slammed it onto the table so hard its pot cracked. It was, naturally, the drooping yellow flower that Thea had wanted to touch that first evening. The little face-like blooms eyed him reproachfully.

"Don't look at me like that," he snapped at them. "It won't

change my mind." The flowers said nothing and the space filled with the embarrassing echo of his own voice. "But at least you didn't talk back, so she hasn't driven me completely—"

A sound came from behind him. Rafe froze. Listened. A sound like...a foot shuffling. Skirts rustling. Then silence. The kind of silence that came from someone standing behind him, trying not to laugh.

Blast it.

Adopting a fierce, silencing glare, Rafe turned around.

Martha stood with her lips pressed together, the lines around her dark eyes crinkling suspiciously.

"We talk to plants now?" Martha asked in her Spanish-accented English.

"No."

"It sounded like you were talking to them."

"I wasn't."

"No problem if you were."

"But I wasn't."

He resolutely ignored her and focused on the orchids. She didn't go away.

"Congratulations on your marriage," Martha finally said. "Very unexpected."

"Any news?" Rafe countered.

He glanced up to see Martha's face break into a grin

"Great news," she said. "The blacksmith's mother-in-law came to live with him and she suffers terribly from rheumatism. Isn't that wonderful?"

"Forgive me if I do not share your enthusiasm over others' suffering."

"I mean, it's wonderful that she agreed to try my new ganja medicine, and it eases her pain and stiffness considerably.

Unfortunately, it also makes her sing, which sets the dogs howling."

"Eh. Every medicine has a side effect."

"And the blacksmith said the new Malay liniment relieves the tightness in his scars, so you must try it on yours too." Martha pinched off the tip of an orchid leaf, crushed it between her fingers, sniffed it, and tentatively tasted it. "How fortuitous that I have two of you to experiment on."

"And how fortuitous we both suffered for your convenience."

She flicked the crushed leaf into the nearest pot and sampled another one. "What are your new wife's medical ailments? It would be marvelous if she suffers great pain during menses!"

"Would it."

"Not marvelous for her, but marvelous for me. No matter. She can test the bhang anyway."

"No."

"I've changed the recipe. It's still mostly ganja, with a bit of opium, but I added—"

"Not for the countess."

"It's perfectly safe, although I cannot remove the intoxicating effects. Sally and I tried it. I need more people for testing."

"I'd rather she didn't know what we do."

The last thing Rafe needed was Thea spreading more muddled stories about his and Martha's medicine-making activities, which would only exacerbate the outlandish rumors. When it came time to sell the medicines, they would use only Martha's name; it would be better to hide Rafe's involvement—a difficult ask, given people's insufferable interest in an earl's affairs.

"I'll test it again," he said.

"Not you." Martha sampled another leaf. "It is not good for your little problem."

"What little problem?"

"I can suggest an herb for that problem."

"What blasted problem?"

"The problem that makes you put your bride's bedroom far from your own."

Rafe shot Martha a quelling look. "That is not a medical problem."

"If you're having trouble."

"No trouble."

"Most men at some stage—"

"Not me."

Trouble? Him? With Thea? The only trouble he had was remembering that he couldn't touch her because she was not his wife and never would be.

"*Bueno*." Martha reached for another leaf. "But you should be happy with your pretty bride."

"And will you stop eating my orchids?" Rafe swooped the pot away from her. "They aren't for you to make medicine from."

"Ah, that's what they are. Orchids. Pretty but useless." She followed Rafe as he positioned the transplanted orchids in those parts of the greenhouse where they were most likely to survive. "They say orchids get good prices in America," Martha continued. "Sell them, get money so we can finally start our business."

"I'm not selling them to yet another bumblehead who'll kill them with ignorance."

Rafe turned to head back to the work area, but Martha blocked the way, hands on hips.

"I came with you from Peru to this cold, damp country for a new life and to make new medicines, but you keep saying we don't have enough capital to make my laboratory bigger and start a business, and every day I get nothing but more gray hairs. You go away with promises, and return with only pretty but useless plants and a pretty but useless wife."

"She's not useless."

"I cannot use her for my experiments. Therefore, she is useless."

"That marriage got me ten thousand pounds."

Martha cocked her head. "That's a lot of money."

"It is." This time, she let him past, and he returned to the work area to wash. "Plan your new laboratory, Martha. As big as you want, with several assistants and whatever equipment you need. Those plants you wanted will arrive in Bristol soon, and more are on the way, and before long, your medicines will follow."

He dried his hands and studied the rows of plants, most chosen for their medicinal properties, their value derived from Martha's willingness to provide her knowledge. To think: All those years Rafe had passed in foreign lands, studying plants most Englishmen would never see and facing dangers most could never imagine, and he had ended up right where he began, the place that had never felt like home. He breathed through the familiar medley of guilt and grief. What a jumbled, muddled world it was, that he was the one still alive and here. Even though Rafe's father had never understood him, he had indulged him by hiring tutors in botany and horticulture; if only Father were here, to see what he had achieved.

"Maybe I can make some good from it," he muttered, as he thrust his arms into his coat sleeves.

"Not if she dismisses Sally," Martha said.

"Hmm?"

"We will get no good if your marriage brings you money, but then your wife sends Sally away."

Rafe stared at Martha, baffled. "Why the hell would she dismiss Sally?"

"Because..." Martha hesitated and frowned. "Sally says your countess will change things."

"She won't change anything or dismiss anyone. She isn't even..." She wasn't even truly married to him and would soon leave, he could say, but it was safer for Martha and Sally to remain ignorant of his fraud. "Look, the countess is friendly and full of life, and she's remarkably resilient and..."

"And what?"

"And...I don't know."

Confusing, that was what she was.

"So you *do* like her," Martha said.

"Bloody hell." Rafe strode back through the rows of plants toward the door. "I am going for a swim and then I shall eat dinner and I swear, if one person says one more word to me today, I'm going to kick the whole blasted lot of you out."

CHAPTER 11

When Thea awoke on her first morning at Brinkley End, her mood was quite restored. After dressing and breaking her fast, she headed out into the sunshine to explore the estate.

"*Brinkley End is a terrible disappointment,*" she wrote to Arabella later that afternoon.

No matter how I look at it, it refuses to be sinister. But the earl was kind enough to forbid me from entering the woods under pain of death, and that cheered me up immensely.

In the garden, she glimpsed Lord Luxborough crossing the footbridge into the Forbidden Woods, accompanied by Martha, whose position remained unexplained. Resolutely, Thea went the other way. Her enjoyable walk took her through the flower-filled pleasure gardens and back to the lake, where she found the secluded area Luxborough had mentioned, with quiet waters and lush grass hidden behind weeping willows.

For the sake of your delicate sensibilities, Arabella, I shall never reveal that I stripped to my shift and swam in the lake, so you will never know how delicious that cool water felt on a warm summer's day.

Next, Thea commandeered a pony gig, instructed by her borrowed manservant Gilbert and a helpful groom. It turned out to be terrific fun, driving around the estate. They passed fields of golden wheat and acres of apple orchards, and workers everywhere, waving and tipping their hats. Following the river, they came to the cider mill, with its great wheel slapping the water, and its foreman eager to teach the new countess how apple cider was made.

"*He gave me a taste of their finest cider,*" she wrote. "*And then another, and then another, and then I had to lie down.*"

Back at the house, Thea washed and changed, deciding that Helen's pale-green gown with the gold embroidery would go nicely with the drawing room's decor while she played at being a countess. To think that people actually lived like this! Although of course a real countess would have serious duties too.

Over hot tea and fresh cakes, she read a letter from Arabella that had arrived with the morning post, and that contained some dismaying news concerning the Marquess of Hardbury's return:

Papa wasted no time in reminding the prodigal marquess of our supposed life-long engagement, to which Hardbury replied, and I quote, 'Nothing on this Earth would induce me to marry Arabella Larke.' Alas, thus end these halcyon days of using Hardbury's absence as an excuse not to marry. Papa insists I marry before the year is out and draws up a list of names. I am as excited as a child on Saint Nicholas' Day, wondering what bridegroom I shall find stuffed in my stocking.

Thea was not fooled by her friend's flippant tone, but as Arabella would detest the merest hint of sympathy or fuss, she settled on a cheerful:

Allow me to offer my excellent services as matchmaker, based on my extensive experience of being 'married' for nearly a whole week. Luxborough is not too awful; if you like, I could send him back your way when I am finished with him.

No sooner had she written the words than she felt a pang of something like guilt mixed with jealousy. *Don't be silly*, she berated herself, and folded and sealed the letter.

Her correspondence finished, and her solitary evening drawing near, Thea perused the library shelves for books to read. She trailed her fingers over tomes on agriculture, botany, and philosophy, until she reached a shelf of plays.

A play could serve, she decided, and half pulled out the volumes, one by one, to read their titles. This sent a sheaf of loose papers fluttering to the floor. When she kneeled to gather them, she saw they were playbills for performances at a London theatre. A performance of *Macbeth*, with special billing for Miss Sarah Holloway in the role of Lady Macbeth. A performance of *School for Scandal*, featuring Miss Sarah Holloway as Lady Teazle. Indeed, Miss Sarah Holloway appeared on all of them. Clearly, someone in the Landcross family was enamored of the actress!

The name was familiar, Thea mused, as she tidied the pages. Oh yes, that night in the inn when she told her story, the man named Joe had mentioned an actress called Sarah Holloway, who disappeared. Thea glanced back down at the top playbill, and a second name leaped out at her: William Dudley. But surely that was the name of the zealot outside Lord Luxborough's house?

What an odd coincidence.

And yet, not really. If this Sarah Holloway had been so popular, it was only to be expected that several people might mention her. And London was big enough to hold two men with such a common name.

Thea replaced the playbills and moved on. She had picked out the first readable books she saw, when she came across the heavy family Bible. Eagerly, she turned to the pages listing names with their births, deaths, and marriages. There were the five sons: John, Philip, Rafe, Christopher, and Edmund. John and Philip each had a "d." and the year they'd died. Rafe and Christopher each had an "m." and the year they'd married. Christopher and his wife Mary had several children, but Thea hardly noticed them, as her eye was drawn to the name of Rafe's wife: Katharine Jane Russell, which bore not only a "d." and a year, but also a strange marking. A box had been drawn around "Katharine Jane" with vertical lines scored through it, chillingly like the bars on a jail cell. How terrible, that someone had thus defaced the family Bible!

Thea slammed the book shut and shoved it back onto the shelf as though it might bite her, grabbed the books she had chosen, and dashed back to her room.

Where she was perfectly content, she decided, to stare out the window and daydream about finding her new home, and even more content, when dinner was served, to dine alone, for there was no one to object when she ate her syllabub first.

RAFE WAS DULY INFORMED that Lady Luxborough was out exploring the estate, and, lecturing himself that she did not require his company, he and Martha began making plans in earnest. Rafe sketched out a second greenhouse, Martha listed extensions to her laboratory, and both agreed to hire a man of business as soon as possible, as neither wished to deal with paperwork or the outside world.

Satisfied with the day's work, Rafe plunged into the lake for a long, vigorous swim. On the way back to his rooms, he passed Sally and Martha, talking quietly in a hallway.

"How is the countess?" he asked Sally.

"I believe she is in her rooms."

"I asked how she is. Not where she is."

"A peculiar thing about being married," Martha mused. "A man is allowed to talk to his own wife."

A teasing expression stole over Sally's face. "He is also allowed to sleep with her."

Rafe shook his head at their infuriating grins. How the hell had he managed to form a household with two women who nagged him more than his own nursemaid ever had?

"The countess is nervous," he explained. "I am waiting until we know each other better."

"Never talking to her will help with that," Sally said dryly, and Rafe muttered dark curses all the way back to his rooms.

No sooner had he dressed and dismissed his valet than the footmen brought his dinner. Rafe drummed his fingers on the mantelpiece as they laid out his meal, following the same routine they had for years.

One bowl of vegetable soup. One dinner plate. One glass of syllabub and raspberries. One set of silverware. One goblet. One serviette.

Two chairs.

"Must you do that with quite so much sarcasm?" Rafe said.

"My lord?"

"If you've something to say, spit it out."

The two servants exchanged nervous looks.

"Ah. Dinner is served?" one of them hazarded, and removed

the last cover from the dinner plate, to reveal potatoes, French beans, and half a small roast duck.

Half. It was a blasted conspiracy.

Waving the servants away, Rafe pulled out his chair. The empty chair opposite smirked. The half fowl said nothing. The image of Thea's bright blue eyes filled his mind.

"All be damned," Rafe muttered, and replaced everything onto the tray and hefted it into his arms.

THE DOOR to Thea's parlor was ajar, so Rafe kicked it open and barged in, to see Thea alone at her dining table. She leaped to her feet, dropping her soup spoon with a clatter, and fidgeted with her dress. It was an elegant gown in pale green; it had long sleeves and a modest bodice and still managed to reveal acres of creamy, touchable skin. Matching green ribbons were woven through her hair, and her complexion flaunted a new glow from her outdoor adventures that day, as if she had brought home the sunshine.

"No talking." Rafe dumped his tray and offloaded his plates onto the table. "We will dine together, because you don't like to dine alone. But I don't like talking. So no talking. Understood?"

She nodded rapidly, her lips pressed together in an exaggerated manner. Once she had resumed her seat, he poured wine and sat too. In silence, they dipped their spoons into their soup and ate.

The vegetable soup was tasty, and Rafe tried hard to ignore Thea, but it was difficult when she sat across from him, and might or might not have an alluring dusting of pale freckles on the skin above her bodice, and so his eyes kept drifting back to her.

Which was why he saw her fierce frown as she pushed away her empty soup bowl. He followed her gaze: She was glaring at his glass of syllabub as though it had accused her of cheating at cards. Then she gave her head a little shake as if to clear it, half smiled into the air, and turned her attention to her roast duck and beans. Yet as she ate, her gaze wandered back to his syllabub. Again she frowned; again she shook it off.

This ferocious internal argument continued throughout their meal, until Rafe could bear it no more.

"What?" he demanded. "What is it?"

Her eyes opened wide. "I never said a word. You don't like talking and I'm not talking."

"You are thinking. I can hear you thinking."

"Then I shall think more quietly."

"You seem upset."

Again, she frowned, first at his side of the table, and then at her own, and sighed. "I'm not upset. I am merely...confused."

"About what?"

"I cannot help but observe that your meal includes syllabub and raspberries."

"So it does."

"But mine does not. That is all."

She carved the last of the meat from her half of the bird, shoved it into her mouth, and chewed with dignified fury.

Rafe examined the table. "True. Your meal is entirely devoid of syllabub and raspberries, or indeed, syllabub and fruit of any kind."

"No doubt there is an excellent reason why the earl has syllabub but the countess does not."

"You want dessert, call a servant for it."

"No!" Her knife and fork clattered to the plate and she tidied them. "I do not wish to antagonize them. I can live without syllabub." She heaved a sigh that would put the most tragic of martyrs to shame. "I suppose all the best countesses must suffer deprivation."

"Oh, for crying out loud." He shoved the glass across the table. "Have mine."

"I can't take yours!"

"Take it!"

"How noble and self-sacrificing of you, my lord! To go without dessert! So stoic. So honorable. So—"

"Shut up and eat your blasted syllabub."

With an impish smile, she did just that, with such blatant pleasure it was sheer torment to watch. Rafe gulped at his wine, but it failed to dull his desire. She seemed unaware of him, all of her senses engrossed in her sweet solitary pleasures. And he... Damn it, he was jealous! Of a blasted spoonful of blasted whipped cream!

The glass scraped empty, she dabbed at her lips with her serviette and smiled at him.

No, she didn't simply smile. She cast her smile over him like a fisherman cast a net. It wrapped around him and made him long to draw near.

He stood so abruptly the table rocked. "I bid you good night."

She leaped to her feet too. "Must you go so soon? We could..."

"What?"

"Um. Play billiards?"

"You don't know how to play billiards."

"If you please! I excel at the game," she protested. "That is, I shall excel, once I learn how to play. I can teach myself, from a book, but it would be much more diverting to play with someone else."

Rafe wavered. It would indeed be a pleasant way to pass the evening. He would enjoy teaching her, watching her frown of concentration, her triumphant joy when she sank a ball. Perhaps she would need guidance positioning her cue, and he would stand behind her, wrap his arms around her as he showed her how to find the angle. He would press his lips to the fragrant skin at her neck, perhaps nip at her ear so she would leap backward in surprise, and then run his hands up—

"Play with Sally and Martha," he said.

"They're staff."

"I shouldn't think you'd care about that."

"I don't. But those are the rules." She nudged the empty plate in front of her. "Rules are so unspeakably silly, don't you think? You know, when Pa made his first fortune, we moved to a nicer part of town, and I wasn't allowed to see my old friends anymore. So I made new friends. Then Pa lost his fortune, and we moved again, and my new friends weren't allowed to see me. I started again. Made new friends. And again Pa got rich, and again we moved, and so on. All these rules about who can be friends with whom and who can marry whom, when we're all just people, aren't we? But not you," she added with a wan smile. "You're not people."

"Right."

Rafe spoke automatically, seeing only her faltering smile, the way she straightened her shoulders as if bracing for more disappointment. He dragged his eyes off her, onto the empty plates between them, the debris of their fleeting domesticity. He didn't want to be yet another person shutting a door in her face. True, his original plan was to ignore her, but that was an eon ago, back when she was nothing but a name.

"Never mind," she said brightly. "I shall be quite content to read. How do you usually pass the time after dinner?"

"I read."

"Then perhaps you might enjoy one of the books I collected today." She gestured at a trio of books on the small table by the settees. "It makes no sense for you to sit over there reading, and for me to sit here reading. It's a waste of..." She trailed off as she glanced at the empty fireplace.

In cooler weather, it would indeed be wasteful to sit in separate rooms with separate fires. In winter, if they sat together reading by the fire, would the light of the flames pick up the mix of colors in her hair? Would her ears and nose turn pink when she ran in the snow? She would throw snowballs at him, of course, and he would not hesitate to retaliate; he'd aim to hit her, to make her squeal and laugh and jump back up to throw snowballs at him again. Eventually he would run at her, tackle her, and they'd fall into the snow together...

"Have I said something amusing?" she said.

"Hmm?"

"You looked amused."

"Hmm," Rafe said, and fell into the empty settee.

Thea flew into a flurry of activity, carrying over their wine goblets, then dropping into the other settee and gathering the books.

"What would you like? First up, *Leonora* by Miss Edgeworth." She flipped it open. "Oh. Some sentences are underlined."

Rafe tensed and his heart skipped a beat. Blast. He should have foreseen this. Thea appeared not to notice, as she frowned at the page.

"That reminds me. Today I saw a strange marking in the..." She flicked a glance at him, then returned to the book. "Never mind. Let's see what the previous reader underlined. '*What a misfortune it is to be born a woman!*' Well, that's cheerful. And maybe not for you."

She tossed it aside and grabbed the next book.

Rafe realized he was jiggling his leg and pushed his hand onto his knee to make himself stop. Stop. He had to stop this. Across from him, Thea chattered on, oblivious.

"Here is poetry, much more manly: *Marmion: A Tale of Flodden Field*. Flodden? What kind of word is that? Really, Walter Scott. Our intrepid reader has been here too, and has underlined... '*O, what a tangled web we weave, When first we practise to deceive.*' Um. Ha ha. Well."

Cheeks pink, eyes averted, Thea tossed the book at him. Rafe caught it in one hand and pressed a sharp corner into his palm.

Thea picked up the third book and considered its plain cover. "I begin to get a sense of our unknown friend's character. First, I deduce it was a woman."

"It was Katharine," Rafe said abruptly. "The underlining," he added, at her questioning look. "It was a habit Katharine had, underlining sentences that she said..." He hesitated. How to explain that Katharine believed the books were sending her messages? "Had particular meaning to her."

It was only to be expected that the subject of Katharine would arise, sooner or later, given Thea's curiosity. Rafe watched her turning the book over in her hands, and he was still trying to decide whether to leave or stay, when she looked up.

"She was your wife," she remarked.

"Hmm."

"Were you in love with her?"

"We agreed no talking."

She opened and closed the book a few times before saying, "You ran away to America to avoid the army, and you took Katharine with you."

"Sounds like you already know everything."

"I don't know whether you were in love with her."

"We were so young and..." No. Katharine deserved better than that. "Yes," he amended softly, and let himself remember, the

162

naive, adventurous eighteen-year-old he had been, and Katharine, a few years older and bolder. Yes, he had been young. Since then, he had aged a thousand years.

Thea's expression was soft now, and somehow that softness made it easier to speak.

"Have you ever seen a wild horse?" Rafe said. "Katharine was like that. Reckless, untamable. She refused to marry any of the men Ventnor chose for her. Her family was staying here, and she overheard me arguing with my father about joining the army, and it seemed we had much in common. When I told her I was thinking of sailing for America, she wanted to come. We sat up one night talking, spinning out tales of the adventures we would have, and by the time the sun rose, we had decided to run away together. We sailed from Bristol two days later."

How full of hope they had been, he and Katharine, standing on the ship's deck and yelling their joyful farewells to England, while the briny wind whipped at their clothes. A far cry from Katharine's final days, when she cursed him and fled. When the ship's captain married them, they had promised to look after each other always. A promise Rafe had failed to keep.

"And then?" Thea prompted.

"And then..."

The conversation unfurled in his mind, the questions Thea would ask, the answers he would have to give, hauling up the unchangeable past like some slimy, crumbling remnant of a shipwreck, turning Katharine's story into her post-dinner entertainment. Soon, Thea and her curiosity would depart for her next escapade, but those resurrected memories would remain; better they lay buried, where they were easier to manage.

"She became unwell," he finished brusquely. "It was better for her to return to England. She wrote to her parents. Ventnor came to take her home. The end."

"But you came back too, didn't you?"

Rafe stood and bowed, painfully aware of his comically stiff politeness. "I bid you good night. Thank you for your company. Now I shall retire."

He headed for the door, but with a swish of skirts, Thea skipped ahead of him.

"Please forgive my impertinent questions," she said. "It was thoughtless of me. My curiosity gets the better of me. I did not mean to upset you."

"I'm not upset."

"It's just that it was all so long ago, and you need not be lonely."

"I'm not lonely."

"Very well."

Those cornflower-blue eyes called him a liar, but her expression was caring and earnest, her lips slightly parted. His cheeks warmed with the memory of her palms, and his fingers craved to caress her sun-kissed face in turn. The edge of her pale-green gown drew his eye to the swell of her breasts, to the fine muslin cascading over the promise of a waist and hips and thighs. Rafe wasn't upset and he wasn't lonely, he wasn't, but he was a hot-blooded man and Thea was a captivating woman who made his blood run hotter; he had vowed not to touch her, but neither could he summon the will to return to his empty room.

A knock at the door had them leaping apart. They loitered awkwardly while the servants cleared away their dinner plates. No one batted an eyelash at them; all were caught up in the fiction of their marriage.

"Why was the countess not served syllabub?" Rafe asked the last footman before he left.

"No!" Thea cried. "Please don't mention it."

The man was frowning. "I don't understand, my lord."

"The countess had no syllabub on her tray."

"Her ladyship eats her dessert first, my lord. The empty glass was on the sideboard."

Where Rafe had not noticed it. *Well played, Thea.* He pivoted to face her. She stood against the wall, eyes wide in feigned innocence. The footman hurried to escape, and once more Rafe was alone with Thea.

Alone with her playfulness and mischief and delight.

A giddy recklessness washed over him, and he was advancing on her before he even knew what he was doing.

"You eat your dessert first?" he said slowly.

She pressed back against the peach-colored wall. "The best countesses always eat their dessert first."

He used his arms to cage her in, which had the added benefit of keeping himself steady, for her hands were on his chest and his legs were ready to collapse, that he might fall to his knees and slide up her skirts.

"And do the best countesses always eat the earl's dessert too?"

"The best earls always give the countesses their dessert. You, my lord, are an excellent earl."

"And you, my lady, are not an excellent wife."

Her eyes were so bright, her spirit so lively. It would be a small matter to take one more step, to brush her hair away from her face and slide his lips over hers. If he were a different man, he would.

If he were a different man, he would tease and play with his bright, lively bride; he would revel in these prizes of pleasure and delight and joy.

But he was not a different man.

How did this keep happening? He kept forgetting. One moment he was heading for the door, the next he was thinking of taking her to bed. It was as though Thea's presence transformed him somehow, but like all magic, it could never be real.

That realization hit him like cold water and gave him the strength to wheel about and march out the door.

But his own rooms had become echoing and dull, where nothing held his interest, so he sought out Martha in the parlor downstairs. She pointedly remarked on the countess playing billiards alone in the next room, but he pointedly ignored her, and demanded that she give him some bhang to test tonight. The way he was feeling now, a little pain-relieving intoxicant would go a long way.

"THERE, THAT GOT RID OF HIM," Thea boasted to the empty settees, but the furniture was not fooled; it knew as well as she did that she had wanted him to stay.

More than that. When she had stood so near to him, enclosed in his heat with her palms touching his chest, so near that his woodsy scent intoxicated her and his eyes saw inside her, she had longed to trace the contours of his body. The mysterious folds of his neckcloth had tempted her to strip it away and bare his throat, and his wicked coat taunted her with notions of sliding it aside. And the lingering sensations under her skin, where their single kiss bounced around excitedly, warned that she wanted him to do similar things to her.

So. This was the sinful desire ladies were warned about. How right they were, to call passion dangerous, for it perilously banished rational thought. But after some coaxing, rational thought returned to remind her that Luxborough believed them married, and would be furious when he learned the truth. If she succumbed, she would ruin herself, and ruining herself would ruin her plan of restarting her life as if there had been no scandal.

She calculated the days. Surely she would hear from Helen tomorrow? Surely. And tomorrow she would leave.

Resolutely, Thea laid out the three books on the table, but they only made her think of Rafe and the story he refused to tell, so she decided to practice billiards instead.

In the billiard room, she heard muffled female voices. Thea opened the door to see Sally and Martha sitting together in the neighboring parlor, one with sewing, the other with a book, and both with guilty expressions. Thea did not cast them out, and they did not invite her in, so she closed the door and played billiards alone.

At one point, she heard Lord Luxborough arrive and exchange inaudible words with Sally and Martha. She froze, straining to hear, wondering if he would play billiards with her after all, but then he left and she heard nothing more.

Finally, long after the other women had retired, Thea blew out the candles and headed back to her rooms. As she walked along the corridor, a movement in the courtyard garden caught her eye and she opened a window to look out.

In the garden stood Luxborough, half dressed, his white shirt bright in the moonlight. Thea tried to puzzle out what he was doing, but he seemed only to be staring at a pink flower. He poked the flower like a perplexed cat, and then picked it. Moving as though his arms were unnaturally heavy, he plucked a single petal, which he studied from various angles. Then he threw it into the air and watched it drift away, before repeating the process with the next petal.

With a shiver, Thea closed the window and kept walking, chilled by the baffling scene and the realization that the earl remained a mystery to her still.

CHAPTER 12

The next morning, Thea coaxed Gilbert into taking a rowboat with her on the lake, where her first efforts at rowing had them turning in circles.

"Are they treating you well, Gilbert?" she asked, once she had figured out how to make the boat go straight.

"Aye, this household's as jolly as bonfire night. Mind the reeds there, my lady," he said, his cheerful tone at odds with his nervous grip on the boat. "That Mrs. Sally, she knows how to run a house and keep the staff happy."

"She's been doing it a while, I suppose."

"Not so long. It's only a few years since his lordship gave her the position. Maybe he knew what she was capable of, from when she was his first wife's companion."

One oar snagged in the water and the little boat lurched. "But Sally said Katharine never lived in this house."

Although no one had explained how Katharine's books came to be in the library. Thea had not thought to ask.

"Maybe not," Gilbert said. "But when his brother was the earl, his lordship and his wife and Mrs. Sally lived in the Dower House here on the estate. All three of them together, cozy as puppies in a pile of hay. Until his wife fell off her horse. They say she wasn't right."

"What do you mean?"

"That's all they say, that his lordship's wife wasn't right. Then their mouths shut tighter than a poacher's snare. Ah, maybe I should take the oars now, my lady?"

Thea surrendered the oars and Gilbert rowed them back to shore. She was no longer enjoying herself anyway, and besides, rain clouds were gathering. And how could she think about rowing with this discovery that Luxborough and Katharine had lived in the Dower House, with Sally as Katharine's companion, and the vexing puzzle of why neither Luxborough nor Sally had mentioned it?

Sternly reminding herself that it was not her concern, Thea marched up the lawn toward the house. At first, when a horseman came cantering up the driveway, she paid him no mind. But then she realized from his saddlebags that he must be a fancy express messenger, and a peculiar jolt made her knees and elbows giddy. News from Helen! Then it was over. Already. Today. Of course, she had to leave, before she entangled herself further, but... Not yet. She wasn't ready for it to be over yet.

That thought was enough to spur her foolishly weak knees into a run.

RAFE SAW the messenger through a window, and he had barely thought, *Thank God, it's over,* and *Not yet, please,* before he was tearing down the stairs, skidding on the floors in his haste.

It must be news from Ventnor. Only Ventnor thought his

communications so important he would bother with an express. Ventnor's letter would inform him that the woman Rafe had married was not Helen, and Rafe must feign shock and send her away.

But not yet.

Besides, he'd not received confirmation that the trustees had released his funds. Or that Thea had her dowry. And where would she go without money?

So no, not yet. He wasn't ready yet.

He charged out of the house as if he could somehow stop the messenger from delivering the news, just as Thea came running up the lawn, pink-cheeked and panting.

"Give it to me!" she cried breathlessly, as the messenger reached into his leather saddlebag.

"No, give it to me!" Rafe countered.

What with them both yelling and running, even the messenger's well-trained horse became skittish, and in calming it, the messenger dropped two letters on the gravel at Rafe's feet. Thea launched herself at them, in a dive that would earn cheers in a cricket match, and Rafe was so caught up trying to grab the letters with one hand and stop Thea from falling with the other that they both tumbled to the ground, still scrambling for the letters, and ended up sitting side by side, with their rumps on the cold, sharp gravel, their legs tangled, and each with one letter in hand.

At which point Rafe noticed the seal on his letter. He freed his legs from Thea's skirts, trying to ignore all the places he bumped against her warm softness, and looked up at the messenger, who had his horse under control and a bemused expression on his face.

"This is from the Royal Household," Rafe said.

"Yes, my lord." The messenger was edging his horse away. "They've sent scores of messengers out across Britain."

"This one is addressed to the Countess of Luxborough." Thea sounded as dazed as Rafe felt. "Why would the Royal Household write to me?"

But the messenger's job was to deliver news, not explain it, and he looked relieved when a servant dashed out to guide him around the back for refreshments and his tip.

Rafe studied the letter in his hand. Letters sent across the country? Maybe the king had died or something. Nothing important, anyway. This wasn't over yet.

Beside him, Thea's elbow bumped against his arm as she yanked off one glove and slid a finger under the wax. The gravel was cold and sharp under his buttocks, and getting colder and sharper, but Rafe stayed seated, as he tore open his letter and scanned it. Definitely nothing important—merely a stern reminder that a peer was expected to present his new bride at Court and something something blah blah blah. Rafe scrunched the page into a ball, bounded to his feet, and dusted himself off. He extended a hand to Thea, who was staring at a thick, cream-colored card.

"Countess?"

She looked up, her expression aglow with excitement or delight, some feeling that had nothing to do with sitting beside him on cold, sharp gravel.

"'Tis our invitation," she said. "To the party."

"What party?"

"You remember. The Prince Regent is hosting a party to celebrate the return of the Marquess of Hardbury."

"He is?"

"We discussed it in London."

"We did?"

"You obtained invitations for my parents. How can you not recall?"

Finally, she noticed his outstretched hand and took it. Her fingers were chilled; he wrapped his hand further around them.

"A party with the Prince Regent and your parents?" he said, as he pulled her upright. "That sounds like exactly the sort of thing I would be at pains to forget."

"It was right after we..." She bit her lip and glanced down at their joined hands. He released her and they both stepped back. "In London. You remember?"

"No."

"After we...kissed."

"Ah. Yes. We kissed. I do remember that."

Slowly, the rest of that evening came back to him. The kiss was worth remembering; the party was not, given that neither of them would attend. Thea would not be allowed through the gates, and Rafe would prefer to be wrapped in chains and thrown into the lake in winter.

"Someone decided it should be a costume party," she raced on, her voice too high, as she shook out her skirts. "That sounds diverting, doesn't it?"

"No."

"You don't want to go?"

"No. Do you?"

"Indeed I do." A faraway look entered her eyes, though her jaw had a fiercely determined set. "Everyone will be there, all of society. All those people..."

There it was. Thea longed to be in society, surrounded by people. Rafe could count on his fingers the number of people whose company he truly enjoyed, and still have his thumbs free to twiddle.

He pivoted and strode into the house, tossing the screwed-up letter from one hand to the other. He could end this now. No need to wait for confirmation of the money or the marriage; news would arrive soon. Send Thea away to... Well, it was hardly his concern where she ended up, was it?

He swung around. She was trailing behind him, drumming her fingers on the invitation, her expression thoughtful.

She really wanted to attend that party.

But a ruined, friendless, scandal-ridden, middle-class outcast could not attend the Prince Regent's costume party. Not without help from someone who was very well connected. Or from someone who was an earl.

It didn't matter to Rafe one way or another if she went to that ball. But it mattered to her.

And suddenly, that was enough.

"There are two rooms of costumes upstairs," he said. "Take what you want."

"Costumes?"

"My parents loved amateur theatrics. Every year, they hosted huge house parties, during which the guests rehearsed and performed in plays, with elaborate costumes made specially. The village women did very well out of it."

"And you too? You will attend?"

"I'm not going to any blasted costume party," he said, and wheeled about and started down the hall.

Lord Luxborough bellowed for Sally to fetch the keys, and the three of them trooped up to the third floor. Thea watched the other two carefully, but nothing in their manner toward each other aroused any suspicions; although Sally did not pay the earl due deference, Thea detected no hint of intimacy or shared secrets. Still, she could not fathom why neither had mentioned their shared past, living together in the Dower House with

Luxborough's wife, but neither could she think of a reason to ask.

Indeed, she could hardly think at all when she entered the room, so amazed was she by the sheer volume of clothes presses and trunks crammed into the space. With her usual brisk vigor, Sally threw open doors and lids, revealing enough costumes to transform one into anything: a Roman emperor or French queen, a fairy or an animal, a criminal or a saint.

"I never imagined there would be so many." Thea eased open the heavy lid of a giant trunk to discover a treasure trove of masks within. A Janus mask, a jester's hat, a gorgeous bird's head with iridescent green and blue feathers. She looked up at Luxborough, who was peering at a toga. "You spoke of amateur theatre productions but this is astonishing."

He tossed aside the toga. "This house overflowed with guests when my parents lived here, and theatrics were *de rigueur*. My family was never happy unless making a show of themselves."

"Professional actors and actresses were invited too, to provide instruction," Sally chimed in. "And, shall we say, to liven up the evenings."

"Did you perform as a boy?" Thea asked Luxborough.

He groaned and Sally laughed. "Not he! Master Rafe would be out of the house and hidden in the woods at the first whisper of a play."

"But Sally performed, and she was as good as any of the professionals."

"How marvelous!" Thea looked to Sally to learn more, but Sally was busy rummaging through a trunk.

"She displayed a rare talent for acting," Luxborough went on. "Everyone said so, and I believe more than once she was asked to go to London."

"Were you not tempted?" Thea asked eagerly. "How exciting!"

Finally, Sally straightened. "Exciting, yes. Respectable, no. My father was very strict and disliked me even joining the productions here, though such amateur domestic entertainments are common and perfectly acceptable. And Lord and Lady Luxborough—Master Rafe's parents—always encouraged me."

Absently, Thea opened a red wooden box, and gasped at the beautiful cat's mask that lay within. It was large enough to cover her face, leaving only her mouth and chin exposed. A large black diamond shape surrounded one eye slit and a red diamond surrounded the other, with red and black diamonds on opposite ears. The remainder was white and covered in intricate swirls in gold. Reverently, Thea lifted it out.

"One of the Venetian masks," she heard Sally say. "Beautiful, isn't it?"

"Yes," Thea breathed.

This, she decided. She would love to be a cat, she had told Arabella that first evening: playful yet fierce, not caring what anyone thought. A mask would be easier to carry than a full costume, and she could wear it with a regular evening gown. Although the party was not a masquerade, she would have to cover her face, assuming Arabella managed to smuggle her in. She could drift through the crowd, eavesdropping on conversations. If all went to plan, other guests would have read her pamphlet; perhaps some would be discussing her and how Percy had done her wrong.

And perhaps there would be a gentleman, lounging against a wall, watching her. When their eyes met, his mouth would curl into an intriguing half smile. Naturally, she would favor him with a haughty look and turn her back, but a moment later, he would be in front of her, holding out his hand, inviting her to dance. His golden-brown eyes would seem ancient and weary, but for their glint of humor, their flare of heat, and—

Thea snapped the lid shut. Foolish dreams. Luxborough would never even attend such a party, let alone invite Thea to dance.

She glanced up and caught him studying her, his expression unreadable, and something in his gaze made her look away. Her eye fell on a magnificent lion's head, designed to sit atop a man's head.

Without thinking, she held it up. "And you should wear this! You could..." She trailed off at his thunderous expression. "I beg your pardon. I thought it would be amusing, but it's not."

He hardly spared a glance for the lion's head. "I told you, I'm not going to any blasted costume party. You must understand, I am not made for society."

"I do understand," she said. "It doesn't matter."

But all he did was shake his head and leave the room, his boots echoing on the wooden hallway until they faded into nothing.

Once more, Sally was witness to a husband's peculiar treatment. Thea's cheeks heated, but the housekeeper's smile was kind.

"Was there anything in particular you were looking for, my lady?"

"This cat mask will serve. Please don't trouble yourself for anything else. Although I suppose..." Thea looked wistfully at the lavish costumes. "It would be liberating to don a full costume and become somebody else entirely."

"Such is the magic of theatre," Sally agreed, tidying away the costumes. "To experience all the other people we could be."

"But lonely too. To wear a disguise."

"True." Sally paused, her hands molding some ornate fabric. Her features softened into a dreamy look. "It's a sublime miracle to go without a mask, and to be loved anyway. To have someone with whom one can be utterly oneself and accepted unconditionally."

Something tugged at Thea's heart. "Are you in love, then? Who is he?"

But somehow, she had once more chosen the wrong words. Sally's face hardened and she shoved the costume into a clothes press, slammed it shut, and spun to face Thea.

"Do you mean to stop me or send me away?" Sally demanded.

"If you're in love, that's a happy occasion, not a crime."

"I have committed no crimes."

Thea bit back her questions. It didn't matter to her. Sally was not her friend. Luxborough was not her husband. Thea did not belong here. She would leave soon and they would all hate her anyway.

"Forgive me, my lady. I shall leave you to your choice," Sally said with stiff politeness and then she marched off too. Yet again, Thea was alone.

THAT AFTERNOON, the rain poured down and Thea returned to the library shelves to seek another book to occupy her mind. None of the books in her room could hold her interest for a page, and while she suspected the problem lay with her, it was much more agreeable to blame the books.

But she hardly even saw the books at her fingertips, as her mind skipped from one question to the next like an overexcited dancer at a ball. There was so much about Lord Luxborough and Brinkley End that she did not understand. About what really happened to Katharine, and why no one would speak of it, and what lay in the Forbidden Woods, and how Martha fit in, and what secrets Sally hid, and what Luxborough had been doing in the garden the night before, and why he blew so hot and cold.

While trying to subdue these futile thoughts, she came across a collection of familiar Gothic novels. Nostalgia had her opening *The Mysteries of Udolpho*, thinking fondly of when she and Helen had read the adventures of Emily St. Aubert.

But Katharine had read this too, Thea saw, as she flipped through the pages: Scores of sentences and fragments were underlined. Opening a page at random, she read an underlined sentence: *"It was impossible for her to leave."*

What particular meaning could *that* have?

Turning to another random page, she read another underlined fragment: *"I shall be murdered!"*

And then another—*"gloomy prison"*—and another—*"horrors of a prison"*—and another—*"remained a prisoner."*

Thea thought again of the awful defacement of the family Bible, of Katharine's name behind bars, and how it reflected these terrifying fragments that Katharine had underlined.

Flipping faster and faster, Thea scanned the pages, finding dozens of such fragments, underscored with ragged black lines: *"menaces of her husband... terror had disordered her thoughts... he had a heart too void of feeling... Fly, then, fly from this!"*

"Countess."

Thea yelped and her hands jerked so hard the book flew up into the air. It landed on the red carpet, open to a page marred by accusing lines. Lord Luxborough stood motionless inside the library door. His gaze was fixed on the book on the floor, his expression as bleak as old stone. Thea gripped her skirts and held her breath, as he raised those weary, shadowed eyes to meet hers. Her heart pounded so hard, she was sure he could hear it, the thumps competing with the ticking of the clock.

He knew. He knew what lines Katharine had highlighted, and the messages that lay within.

But all he said was, "Pray, excuse me."

Then he bowed and left, closing the door behind him.

Thea did not move, her eyes on the ticking clock. When five minutes had passed, she scooped up the book and ran back to her room. Barely stopping to catch her breath, she threw herself onto a settee to study the underlined phrases.

Unsurprisingly, Luxborough did not join her for dinner, and Thea ate hurriedly and returned to the book. The fragments Katharine had chosen in this particular novel clustered around a single theme: terrors and prisons, locked doors and a cruel husband.

And if Katharine did mean something by this, then the vengeful, menacing husband, who had "a heart too void of feeling," was the earl.

Even later, as Thea lay in bed, the rain drumming against the windows, the phrases played over in her mind like a sonata. Perhaps something sinister was afoot at Brinkley End after all. The house and estate were lovely, but a lovely facade could hide horrors, just as an ugly facade could hide kindness.

Thea stared into the darkness and huddled deeper under the covers.

No. He would not harm her, or anyone. Lord Luxborough was big and surly, but he had been so gentle with his plants, so gentle with her. He had promised she'd be safe and given her no reason to fear he lied.

The fragments underlined in Katharine's books were not messages about Luxborough, she told herself. She closed her eyes and turned over, determined to sleep.

But what if they were? What if more of them would tell a full story?

There would be no more messages in Katharine's books, she told herself.

But what if there were?

Then she would look tomorrow.

But what if Luxborough removed the books tonight?

He would not.

But what if he did?

Oh, a plague on it. Thea knew herself too well. She would not get a wink of sleep if she did not check those books now. She climbed back out of bed, found a wrap and slippers, and lit a candle. Then, feeling as silly as a heroine in a Gothic novel, she slipped out into the hall.

CHAPTER 13

The silent hallway felt eerie in the aftermath of the rain, and Thea jumped at a distant rumble of thunder and her own flickering shadow cast by the candle. She scolded herself for being fanciful, but when she crept through the portrait gallery toward the staircase, her feet slowed and stilled on the cold wooden floor, and she could not help a prickle of fear.

All around her were white faces, many in white wigs, floating in the darkness like so many ghosts.

And then—a sound.

She froze, breath held, candle raised, ears pricked. Nothing emerged from the darkness, but she swore something moved. She whirled around, and again. Nothing. No sounds but the thumping of her heart. No movement but the shaking of her hand.

For the first time, Brinkley End assumed a sinister air, with these ghostly faces and the darkly gaping doorways. The books could wait, she decided. It was a far-fetched notion, that Luxborough might remove them, and if he did remove them, that was proof he was dangerous. She should definitely return to her room.

Another sound.

It was only the house. That was all. Houses made noises, and she gained nothing by agitating her already fevered imagination. Being silly was fun sometimes, but not, perhaps, when one stood alone in the dark in a room lined with portraits of dead people.

"There are no ghosts here," she said out loud. "No ghosts."

Her words sank into the darkness, into a silence that seemed to breathe. Oh, how horrid.

Until that silence was broken.

Even more horrid.

For what broke the silence was a hoarse hiss behind her that sounded like: "Ghostsssssss."

Thea froze, not daring to turn, wondering if she had imagined that sound. Nothing followed, nothing but dark, brooding silence. Fixing her eyes on the quivering flame of her candle, Thea concentrated on taking a calming breath and swallowed away the dryness in her mouth.

"No," she told the darkness. "There are no ghosts here."

"There are ghosts everywhere."

No mistaking it this time. She had not imagined that whisper, hoarse and masculine. She willed herself to turn, but her legs would not move.

"Do you see them?" the whisper added.

"My lord?" Her voice was quavering, high and hopeful.

Silence. No: not silence. Breathing. Ghosts did not breathe. If they had to exist—and she would really rather they didn't—they most certainly were not allowed to breathe.

"Luxborough?"

"So many ghosts."

Forcing her frozen legs into action, Thea turned. And there

was Lord Luxborough, barefoot, half dressed, his shirt and breeches white, his hair tousled, his face shadowed. He carried no light, and swayed like a young tree in the wind. She inched closer, holding up the candle to examine his features. His expression was distant, as if he were in a trance.

"My lord?"

He did not respond, his eyes fixed on some distant point in the darkness.

"Lord Luxborough?"

Still nothing.

"Rafe?" she ventured.

Slowly, his eyes tracked to meet hers. He blinked at her, with long, slow blinks.

"Countess," he said.

"Are you...unwell?"

"You are not a ghost."

"No."

"Not yet, anyway."

"Um."

Perhaps he was drunk. She drew closer to surreptitiously smell his breath, but the unfamiliar spicy-sweet tang about him was unlike any liquor in her limited experience. She recalled his curious behavior in the garden the night before; perhaps he had been drunk then too.

"Katharine is a ghost," he said dreamily. "And John is a ghost. And Philip is a ghost. And Father is a ghost. And Katharine is a ghost."

If not drunk, then definitely some kind of intoxicated. But his manner was so dreamy, and his presence so solid, that Thea's anxiety faded, and the notion of terrified messages in books seemed ludicrous.

"Katharine," she repeated. "Can you see her?"

"She's not here." He gestured at the portraits with a clumsy wave unlike his usual assured grace. "All of the ghosts."

So that's what he was talking about: the portraits. Which did not include portraits of either him or his late wife.

"You're not here either," she pointed out.

"Then where am I?" A tremor of fear entered his voice, and he turned in a circle, as slowly as if he were moving through honey. "Where am I? Where am I?"

"You're here." Thea caught his hand to stop him from turning. She wondered if she ought to run for help. "I'm here and you're here."

"I'm here." He sighed, calmed, and studied her. "And you're here."

Flipping his hand, he tangled his warm fingers with hers. Then he smiled, and even in the dim light it was an unexpectedly sweet smile for that scarred, surly face.

"You wanted to touch the flower," he reminisced, his fingers playing over hers. "Then I frightened you."

"Yes. You were rather beastly."

His brows drew together. His eyes narrowed. Thea tugged at her hand, but he held it fast.

Then he bared his teeth and made a sound. Like...a squeak. Another squeak, and another. It became a series of squeaks, also known as...a giggle.

The Earl of Luxborough was giggling.

"Beastly," he repeated, still giggling, his face scrunched up and his big shoulders shaking. "I was beastly."

Thea found herself laughing too, more from relief than amusement, until his giggles subsided with a deep sigh.

"Come along, Countess." His voice sounded normal now, if a little lethargic. "Come and meet the family."

He led her to a portrait and she held up the candle to see a man in a big white wig and ornate clothes.

"This was my father." He led her to another, similar portrait. "And here is my brother John. He didn't like her, but he gave us a home anyway."

"Her? Do you mean Katharine? My lord?"

He didn't answer, his eyes fixed on his brother's portrait.

"Luxborough?"

Nothing.

"Rafe?"

Sluggishly, he turned his head. The distant dreaminess had returned. "I turned her into a ghost. She was dead when she was alive."

"What happened to Katharine?"

"I couldn't help her. You saw her books," he added in a near whisper. "Her secret messages. She was scared. So very, very scared."

"What was she scared of?"

"Me."

Abruptly, he released her hand and wandered away. The cool air collided with the warmth he had left behind. Nothing made sense. Of course, he was intoxicated. Then she remembered the bishop, who clearly cared about him, who had said Luxborough had done nothing wrong, but blamed himself anyway.

Somehow, Thea could not be frightened.

"Lord Luxborough? Rafe?" She darted around in front of him. "Where is your portrait? You are the earl now. Your face should be here."

"No one wants to see my face."

"I like your face. It tells your story. How impressed your children and grandchildren and great-grandchildren will be, telling tales about old Rafe, who survived an attack by a giant cat."

"Not going to have children, so no grandchildren. No great-grandchildren. *Et cetera*."

"But you said you needed to marry to get heirs."

"I have heirs. I have Christopher. He's my other brother. I have another other brother too. Half my brothers are dead. Half my brothers are alive. I'm half dead and half alive. Where was I?"

"Christopher. Heirs."

"Christopher has lots of heirs. His wife produces them in litters, like a rabbit."

He resumed his walk, toward the gloomy passage leading to his rooms. But his gait was unsteady and he bumped into the doorjamb. He stopped short and frowned at it.

"My lord?"

He poked the doorjamb.

"Luxborough?"

No response.

"Rafe?"

Slowly, he turned his head.

"Do you need help?" she said. "Shall I take you to your room?"

"Countess. It's you."

"That's right."

"I like you, Countess. You talk too much but I like you anyway."

"Oh. Good. Are you drunk?"

"Bhang," he said.

"Bang?" she repeated.

"Bhang," he agreed.

"Like a gun? Bang?"

"Like a gun." He giggled. "Bang bang."

"You're giggling."

"I am not."

"I'll help you back to your rooms."

Again, she took his big hand in hers. He lifted her hand and placed a light kiss on her knuckles.

"Bang," he whispered.

Then, still holding her hand, he led the way through the darkness to his well-lit rooms.

In his rooms, Luxborough released her and made for a jug of water. He poured himself a glass and drank.

Thea put down her candle and waited, looking about with interest and worrying if she had made a mistake in coming here.

"Luxborough?"

He didn't answer.

"Rafe?"

"Hmm?"

"I'll go now. If you're all right. Should I fetch someone?"

He held up a hand, indicating she should wait. He squeezed his eyes tight shut and when he opened them again, his gaze seemed clearer.

"Don't fear me. I'm not mad. I'll not hurt you. I just want to know how to make it better." His voice began to drift again as he wandered back to her. "Perhaps I cannot save any lives, perhaps everything I try is useless, but maybe it's enough to take the pain away, if only for a while."

He paused to study her, and then he lifted his arms and cradled her face, those big hands warming her cheeks and jaw. She wondered if she should be frightened, but instead a sense of comfort unfurled over her like a blanket. Those hands were tender, as were his eyes as they searched hers, tired and gentle and dazed. She felt dazed too, by his touch, by his closeness. By the strange, sweet intimacy of this strange midnight moment. She felt herself sway toward him.

"Because it hurts, sometimes, and it's nice to take away the pain," he murmured. "Do you ever hurt, Countess?"

"Sometimes," she whispered, mesmerized.

"Poor Countess."

He released her face and she missed his touch immediately, but before she could react, he slid his arms around her and enfolded her against him, exactly as she had longed for him to do. He might be mad or dangerous or drunk or anything, but she didn't care. He was holding her, and she wanted nothing else.

And though Thea knew she should not, she circled her arms around his waist and relaxed into him, her eyes closed, her cheek pressed to his warm, solid chest. There was his heart, beating in slow, steady thuds.

Suddenly, she wanted to weep. Three lonely years' worth of tears, three exhausting years of putting on a brave face, of not letting herself cry because that would be giving in and letting them win, those tears welled up inside her. How pathetic she was, to take comfort from a man like this, when he was intoxicated and she was lying about her very name.

But she did not pull away. Instead, she spread her hands over his back, feeling the firm muscles through the linen of his shirt. He rested his cheek on her hair, and his arms engulfed her, strong and sure. Soon, her urge to weep melted, and peacefulness spread through her, like he was warming her from the inside. Perhaps she was intoxicated too.

His body became heavier: He was falling asleep. Reluctantly, Thea dropped her arms and pulled away. He released her and stumbled backward. When he ran his hands through his hair, she regretted not doing that herself. Her sole opportunity to experience the feel of those tousled curls and she had missed it.

"Time for bed," she said softly.

"Bed." He wandered to the connecting door. "Join me. Poor Countess. So lively and lovely. Doesn't like to dine alone. Doesn't like to sleep alone."

Chuckling, he disappeared into the darkness of his bedroom.

Thea took her candle to the doorway. In the dim light, she watched as he climbed into his bed and under the covers, and apparently fell asleep.

Already she was forgotten, but he was not. She felt him still, his arms encircling her body, that peacefulness in her heart.

She would not believe him to have done ill. But her curiosity burned brighter than ever. She would have to leave soon, tomorrow or the next day, and if she didn't learn his secrets now, she would never know.

CHAPTER 14

T he next afternoon, Thea wrapped a dark-green cloak over her gown and announced to no one in particular that she was taking a walk. Her walk took her along the stream and, when she was sure no one was looking, she raised the cloak's hood over her head and darted across the footbridge into the Forbidden Woods.

On the peaceful, sun-dappled path, she kept to the tree line, ready to hide if anyone came. By "anyone," she meant Luxborough. Or Rafe, as she thought of him now, as that was the only name he had answered in the night.

But she encountered no one on the path, which ended abruptly, spilling her into a huge, grassy clearing. There, resplendent in the sunshine, stood a church-like edifice of white iron and glass, behind which lay the green silhouettes of plants. A stone cottage sat deeper into the clearing, and several more paths led into the surrounding trees.

A greenhouse. Well. Nothing surprising or sinister about that.

Fortuitously, the place was deserted. No workers, no earl. With another furtive glance, Thea ran across the clearing to the greenhouse and edged along the glass walls until she came to a door. As she was about to ease it open, a movement made her freeze. The silhouette of a large man. Luxborough! Heart pounding, Thea ducked and, still hunched over, raced away from the greenhouse to the stone cottage, where she flattened herself against the wall. When no angry earl appeared to scold her, she assessed her options. There was nothing interesting here, so she needed to return to the house without him seeing her. Nearby was the entrance to another narrow path leading into the trees, and she dashed toward it, hoping it led back, sooner or later, to the house.

Where it led, however, was to another clearing, no bigger than a parlor, with two more paths leading away. It took Thea several ragged, relieved breaths until she was calm enough to notice what lay at the center of the clearing.

A grave.

The grass around the gray stone was carefully tended. A morning glory vine clambered exuberantly over the tomb and headstone, pink blooms winking among its glossy green leaves. A pair of little blue birds perched on the headstone, chattering at each other, before flying off to their next appointment.

Thea crouched beside the grave and she knew, even before she tenderly parted the vines covering the headstone, whose name she would see.

Katharine Jane Landcross.

She traced the engraved letters and then the dates: Katharine had been twenty-five years old when she died, nine years earlier. The only other words were from the Bible: *Come unto Me and I will give you rest.*

"What is your story?" she whispered. "What happened, Katharine?"

A sound: She spun and stood, shrinking into her cloak. Luxborough, coatless and hatless, was heading right for her, striding along one of the other paths so fast his hair bounced and his shirtsleeves billowed. His face... Oh, how awful and evident was the displeasure on his face.

"I'm so sorry," she whispered, though she knew he could not hear.

He had given her one rule—not to come into the woods—and she had broken it. The story of his late wife still haunted him, and she had barged right in. He was clearly upset and he had every right to be, and oh, she could not bear it! Before she even knew what she was doing, Thea had whirled about and was running back down the path she had come.

What a coward she was, to run like this! The right thing would be to face his anger and disappointment, but those two things had always made her weak, and now she was embarrassed and guilty too, and oh, she could not face him. So run she would, and keep on running. Run back to the house, where she would run to Gilbert and run away. Helen would surely be married, and Luxborough would not be sorry to see her go.

But back in the clearing, a glimpse of what she thought was another person had her shoving open the door to the stone cottage and dashing inside to hide. She shut the door and waited, struggling to listen over the rushing of her blood: nothing. Once her eyes had adjusted to the gloom and her lungs had recovered from her exertion, she turned.

And found herself nose to grin with a human skeleton.

With a cry, Thea leaped backward, slamming into the wooden door. A heartbeat later, she laughed at her own fright.

The skeleton hung from a hook and made no attempt to attack her, even as she sidled near. She poked one bony shoulder. It swayed and grinned. Well, it couldn't help that, poor thing.

Fascinated, Thea looked around. The skeleton's domain proved to be a single room, with a stove in one corner and dried herbs on the walls. Dominating the space was a huge battered table covered with glass receptacles and various items whose names Thea could not guess, let alone their purpose. Also on the table was a row of large jars in which floated strange shapes. She drew closer. Was that...? A snake with two heads! And a strange creature like a misshapen, half-formed baby, with thumbs on its feet and a long curling tail. And there— She lifted her eyes to a shelf holding a collection of invitingly fat books, whose spines bore the words "*Materia Medica.*"

Then the door slammed open. Rafe filled the doorway, a looming silhouette against the light.

Thea could not see his face, and she supposed he could not see hers in the gloom. Her fingers gripped the wooden edge of the table, and when he turned his head, the angle showed his clenched jaw, his tense shoulders. Sourness flooded her throat, the familiar taste of having been a disappointment.

Hands aching, she released the table, wiped her palms over her skirt, and straightened her spine. No more cowardice. That was not who she wanted to be.

"Have you found what you were looking for, then? Proof that what they say of me is true?" His voice was harsh, unlike the confused, gentle man whose embrace had calmed her the night before. "My evil sorcery? My poisons? My cruelty? How you must fear me now."

~

SHE FEARED HIM.

Rafe wanted to throw back his head and howl. Tear the door

193

off its hinges and smash every glass vessel in the room. Then she'd have a reason to fear him!

His own fault. Threatening her friend. Teasing her for a kiss. Being surly and silent and solitary. Wandering about while intoxicated on bhang. No wonder Thea feared him. Just as Katharine had feared him, at the end.

Blast it! Thea had not feared him last night.

Not when she had taken his hand, or softened her body against his. In his drug-addled memory, the feel of her danced over his skin like quicksilver. Last night she had looked after him, and trusted him. And just now, when he saw her darting through the clearing like an inept spy, he had laughed and set out to talk and tease.

Until he saw her face, with its patent apprehension.

"You found my dead wife's grave," he snarled.

"I'm so sorry." Her voice was anxious, her face pale.

Damn her, she knew he wouldn't hurt her. Damn them both, he should bundle her into a carriage and send her away forever. He should take her in his arms and kiss her senseless. But neither was possible, so he thumped the table and the glass vessels rattled.

"Do you want to know how she died, you with your endless questions? Did I poison her? Ensorcell her? Or was it commonplace cruelty that made her flee? Do you ask yourself what kind of monster I must be?" Fury stole his reason, taking charge of his tongue and turning him irrational. He waved an arm at Martha's curiosities and the instruments of her science. "You must be pleased to have found such excellent answers—Demons. Poisons. Sorcery."

"Rafe. I mean, my lord. Please."

Worried. She sounded worried. Fearful.

Rafe grabbed the skeleton's bony hand in a grotesque wave.

"Do you imagine I killed this one too? Or that these are instruments of my evil?"

He bounded across to Martha's collection of curiosities, flicked the glass jar holding the two-headed viper.

Thea edged closer, her head tilted.

"Yes, indeed, I practice witchcraft and this snake is my familiar," he snarled. The monkey fetus: "This baby is the Devil's spawn. And behold—the remains of a human sacrifice." He slammed his hand down on the jar holding a horse's heart bigger than a cabbage. "This is the heart of a virgin."

"That heart is giant," she said, eyeing it dubiously.

He glared at her. "The virgin was a giant."

She studied the heart, clearly not squeamish, and when she looked up at him, her eyes were big and round. Her lips were pressed together. Her shoulders slightly shook.

She was trying not to laugh.

Rafe's irrational rage evaporated as quickly as it had come. Bloody hell. If only he could go back, start this conversation differently. Because if it started differently, it might end differently. It might end with them laughing together. With him pulling her into his arms and kissing her as he had dreamed of kissing her last night.

Instead he... Oh, the devil take him. What a fool he was!

Hot embarrassment slithered over his skin. In a few strides, Rafe reached the door and yanked it open.

"My lord?"

He ignored her and escaped into the sunlight, blinking against its brightness.

"Luxborough?"

He kept walking through the grass, he knew not where. From behind came the sound of the door closing, the light tread of her feet.

"Rafe?"

He stopped. A note of hurt threaded through her voice and he hated that. He hated himself for hating that, when she was playing her game and he was playing his, and soon—perhaps tonight—she would be gone.

But he didn't move, except to turn toward her as she reached his side.

Her only head covering was a dark bandeau, and the sunlight brought out the red in her chestnut hair. He knew, now, how that hair felt against his cheek, how her face felt under his palms, how her body felt pressed against his.

"I don't believe you harmed your wife," she said gently.

"You fear me."

"No."

"Your face hides nothing."

"You gave me one rule and I broke it. And I...I cannot bear it when people are angry and disappointed. I'm such a coward and I'm so sorry."

Her expression was earnest. The breeze played with her hair and the hem of her cloak brushed his leg. He clasped his hands behind his back and said nothing, hot with lingering embarrassment.

"I certainly don't believe in witchcraft," she added. Her fingers were dancing again, winding around each other as she talked. "Many people still do, I know, but not me. And I saw the books: *Materia Medica*. I don't need a fancy education to figure out the meaning. Besides, I've visited apothecaries in London, and a cunning woman. Last night you said something about easing pain. You make medicines, don't you?"

"Hmm."

"I used to enjoy looking at medicine labels in shops. *Dr James's Fever Powder. Tincture of Peruvian Bark. Radcliffe's Purging Elixir.*"

She flashed him a smile. "That last one always sounded promising for an entertaining evening at home."

Doubly foolish of him to have doubted her. For all her playfulness, Thea had a practical streak. Rafe cleared his throat. "I...might have...reacted in a manner that was...unnecessary. Sometimes I lose my temper but I...I do no harm."

She barely noted his awkward apology. "Do you make your medicines alone?"

"I merely grow the plants. Martha has expertise in their medical properties. It is her family's specialty. They built their knowledge over generations living alongside indigenous people in the Spanish colonies, combined with knowledge handed down since her ancestors were first enslaved in western Africa and taken to Peru."

"So that's where she fits in. Why did she come to England?"

Rafe shrugged. "Ask her. All she said was she wanted to make a new life and she refused to say more."

"What do you do with your medicines?"

"We plan to start a business selling them. That's what the money is for. From the marriage."

"You'll go into trade?" Her eyes opened wide. "That's even worse than witchcraft. 'By George,' everyone will say, 'man's an earl, better he consort with demons than lower himself to behaving like a merchant.'"

Her charming humor loosened his tongue. "I have to do it. It's the one thing that gives me..."

The words eluded him, though the devil knew where it came from, this need to make her understand his purpose. Never before had he even tried to explain, though Christopher, Martha, and Nicholas likely knew him well enough to guess.

He gestured at his scars. "After the attack, I recovered in a village, where the people had a medicine for calming the mind, using a plant they knew. It seemed like something I could do. So I went looking for more information, and in Peru I met Martha's brother, and then Martha, and here we are."

Thea's eyes were kind as she studied him. "So if the jaguar had not attacked you, none of this would be here. Where would you be?"

"Still traveling, perhaps."

"That would be sad, never to come home."

Her thoughtful scrutiny discomfited him and he pivoted away. A stone caught under his boot; he picked it up and threw it into the trees. He had revealed too much. But her mere presence seemed to turn his own body into a stranger, as if it belonged to a different man, one who chatted and laughed and touched and played.

"Were you taking a medicine last night?" she asked.

"I was testing one for Martha, her latest variation on a concoction called bhang. The original is based on a plant that the people of Hindustan call ganja; they have extensive medical knowledge, and have long known this plant can ease pain and increase appetite, in addition to its intoxicating effect. Which you witnessed. I apologize. I fear my behavior was offensive and frightening."

"Not at all. It was—"

She stopped short and her gaze veered away. He waited. She rolled her shoulders and he indulged the fancy that she was reliving his embrace. His memories of the night before were unreliable, but he did not doubt the memory of holding her in his arms. The shared memory of that hug enveloped them, as real as the birds singing in the woods. Neither mentioned it. Neither ever would.

"The grave... It's in a pretty spot," she ventured. "In the woods, with the morning glory."

Despite her claims of being a coward, she was braver than he, but the air around them was mellow, not tense, and he found it unusually easy to reply.

"The morning glory was Katharine's favorite flower," he said. "She liked it because it grew as it pleased and could never be forced into a vase. Katharine hated being confined to small spaces, so I had her buried there rather than in the family mausoleum. Sheer folly, of course, for there is no smaller space than a coffin."

"I'm so sorry," Thea blurted out. "In London, I made those stupid jests about dead wives and your victims and the whole time she was buried here. I didn't even think—"

"It doesn't matter."

"—And I'm always bungling things and disappointing people, I know, but I never meant to hurt you."

"Hush. You have never disappointed me."

"I haven't?"

Her expression lightened. He'd done that! He'd told her a simple truth and made her world a better place.

"You impressed me," he added. "You lasted nearly three days before succumbing to your curiosity."

"Last night, you called her a ghost. Why does she haunt you?"

No. No more talk of Katharine. Whatever nonsense he had spouted, whatever his past failings, none of it belonged here in the sunlight, with this woman who was so vibrantly alive.

"So you don't believe in witchcraft but you do believe in ghosts?" he parried lightly.

"The past can haunt any of us." She lifted a hand as though to touch him. He swayed toward her but she dropped her arm. "Your eyes are tired. I thought it was because you had seen everything, but maybe it's because they're haunted."

"Maybe it's from the effort of trying to follow your thoughts."

"But they're the color of brandy in the sunlight."

"Hmm?"

"Your eyes." She smiled, playful and warm. "Has no one ever told you? That in the sunlight, your eyes are the color of brandy."

He was as silly as a girl at her first ball, to let such flattery affect him. Yet his chest swelled with undeserved pride, as though the color of his eyes was the greatest achievement of his life.

"It is a source of continual amazement that not once has anyone told me that my eyes look like brandy in the sunlight."

She laughed, and oh, how Rafe wanted to capture that laughter with his mouth, taste her joy upon his tongue. Now he should say something about her eyes. Tell her they were as blue as the sky, like the wings of tropical butterflies.

But he felt enough of a fool as it was.

"You're smiling," she said accusingly.

"I am not."

"Ha ha! Now I know the true reason why you rarely smile. You have a dimple."

"I do not."

"Yes, you do. Right there. When you smile. Smile and then—"

She poked at his cheek. He caught her hand and held onto it.

"You are determined to rob me of my dignity, aren't you?" he said.

Her attempt to appear innocent meant fighting her smile, but that only made her look more mischievous, as she dipped her head to peer at him from under her lashes, and there, beside her mouth—

"*You* have dimples," he said.

"No, *you* do."

"No, *you* do. Right here and here."

His thumb brushed the little indents. How delightful they were, these dimples that appeared only when she sought to hide her smile.

It would be a small matter, in the circumstances, to cradle her face as he had done the night before, but this time press his lips to hers, caress her mouth and coax it open, that he might taste her fully, kiss her hungrily, experience the miracle of having her kiss him. He had dreamed of such kisses last night, dreams so vivid they were almost real, but he was glad they were not real, for they had passed too quickly. It would be something to savor and anticipate, the first time Rafe kissed Thea properly.

He dropped her hand and stepped back. The devil take him, one might think a kiss was inevitable, but if he kissed Thea's mouth, it would seem a small matter to kiss her everywhere, and if he took such liberties, honor would demand he marry her, and what would someone as lively and sociable as Thea do then, living in an isolated country house with a surly, solitary husband who cared only for his plants?

The glasshouse, the laboratory: These were his purpose. He was not a family man. That was Christopher, with his beloved wife Mary and their seventy-six children. Rafe was not made for keeping a wife happy. He was made for this.

And he did mean to tell her to return to the house, but her inquisitive expression melted the words on his lips.

He had been upset, yet she had changed his mood, with her simple, undemanding friendliness. Like a ray of sunlight breaking through the clouds, lifting one's spirit. What about her spirit? Did it become tiring for her, being cheerful all the time, finding the will to play when she had lost so much? This lively woman who hated to disappoint others, even though the world continually disappointed her?

He called himself weak, but surely it was not a weakness to want to make another person happy.

So instead of sending her away, he said, "Would you like me to show you around? The glasshouse, I mean."

Her expression brightened, and he thought, *It is wrong for anyone to take that from her.* Then she schooled her face: She tried to hide her delight and failed utterly. Rafe had never been so glad to see anyone fail.

"I should like that very much," she said.

CHAPTER 15

Inside the greenhouse, Thea looked at the plants, and Rafe looked at Thea.

"Yes, yes." She nodded knowledgeably, in that way she had when she didn't know a thing. "Yes, I see."

"What do you see, precisely?" he asked.

She frowned, as though he had posed a complex and important scientific problem. "I see...plants. Definitely plants. And if I might offer my expert opinion?"

"Please do."

"They are...green."

"They are very green," he agreed solemnly. "It seems I have nothing left to teach you."

She traced the leaves of a nearby palm, ran those irrepressible fingers down its stems.

"My ignorance should thrill you, for it grants you considerable opportunities to educate me," she said. "When I was a child, the only green patch around was the scum on the horses' watering trough outside the Red Lion Inn."

"Your family never went to the countryside?"

"I remember going to a park to see a hot air balloon. I had never seen so many trees. I imagined them full of fairies."

"Did you enjoy the balloon?"

"It terrified me. When they released the ropes and the basket was no longer anchored to the earth, I cried." A troubled look crossed her face, chased away by a smile. "Ma and Pa considered buying a country estate, but they find the countryside unnaturally quiet and they prefer London."

"And you?"

"Of course," she said absently. "London is my home."

Precisely. London was her home. He must not forget that.

"Where are the orchids?" she said.

"They have their own room." Rafe headed for it, listening to her footsteps behind him. "They are notoriously difficult to grow, but English gardeners fail to respect the complexities of their origins. They think only that their countries of origin are hot and wet, so they create conditions that are hot and wet, and the poor plants are essentially stewed. I shan't save all of these, but perhaps a few will survive."

In the small alcove, he stood back to let Thea pass. Her eyes were immediately drawn to the same flowering plant that had caught her attention the night they met.

She caressed the air around the yellow and purple petals.

"It still blooms," she whispered.

"They only bloom about once a year, but the flower lasts a month."

Shaking her head, she stepped back. "I had forgotten how astonishing these flowers are. No wonder people want them."

"Some say orchids will become as valuable as tulips were a couple of centuries ago, if we can grow them reliably."

"Hence Lord Ventnor's interest, I suppose. 'By George,' he says, 'here's something rare and beautiful. Better put a price on that.' Is that why you wanted them? Or do orchids have medical properties?"

"Not that we know of. They're just beautiful."

"Beauty is healing too."

Her dark lashes were lowered as she studied the plants, and locks of hair curled around her ear. Rafe studied the line of her jaw, the shape of her lips. Healing. He didn't need healing. But nevertheless he said, "Yes."

She glanced up, caught him studying her. Something flashed across her face, but her eyes did not leave his. Her openness to the world made him ache and yearn. That openness was the source of her miracle, the source of her pain. He wanted to capture that life, that verve, keep it close, shield it from hurt.

Something stirred in him, like a long-buried bulb that sensed the warmth of spring and turned itself upright, to punch through the earth to the air. Something fierce and potent and wondrous that threatened to engulf him.

He pivoted away and pushed back into the main room, where he narrowly avoided colliding with a bench.

"What do you want to know?" he said brusquely. "Their names? Temperature? Humidity? Acidity?"

"You. I want to understand you."

His heart thumped harder. "Hmm?"

"You're an earl. You can do whatever you please. Yet you spend your time growing beautiful plants, to make medicines to ease people's pain. And you don't even like people."

"I like them well enough. In theory."

Her lips parted as if to protest, but she said nothing. She merely breathed out, audibly, like an echo of a fledgling laugh. Her eyes roamed over his hair and forehead, and down over his cheeks, which burned with the imprint of her palms. Then down his throat, down, down, and he felt her anew, still, again, forever, her face pressed to his chest, her breasts soft against his front, her hands spread over his back. Her gaze flicked up, veered away. She wrapped one hand around her throat and absently shifted her fingers into a row, as if measuring her own pulse.

"Well. I'm sure I can find something interesting here," she said.

Her voice was too bright and breathy. The short sleeves of her summer dress made him think it would be no task at all to slide them down her arms.

"Rafe?"

"Hmm?"

She was caressing a reddish-green, three-lobed leaf. "I asked, what is this one?"

"It's..." He dragged his eyes off her fingers and onto the leaf. "A plant."

"Gosh."

"It does have a name," he assured her.

"That is brilliant."

"Bellyache bush. For dysentery," he blurted out as it came to him.

When he stepped forward, she didn't move back. Her smile broadened. And suddenly, Rafe relaxed. He was not in this alone. Whatever this was, she felt it too.

"This is *Arum ovatum*," he said, indicating another plant, his voice lower. "Used for treating burns."

She reached for one of the large, flat leaves, then pulled her hand back and feigned innocence.

"Sorry," she said. "I know I shouldn't touch."

"You can touch. You can definitely touch."

Her eyes flicked up to his hair, down to his chest, and his skin tingled as if it already felt her fingers. Oh, what he'd give for her touch, for her kiss, for the right to strip off her dress and taste every last inch of her soft, fragrant skin.

She whirled away and darted up the row away from him. Then she pivoted and lowered a large, palm-like leaf in front of her face, her smiling eyes peering through the fronds.

"Melegueta pepper." He prowled closer, slowly enough for her to get away. "For colds, coughs, and stomach problems."

As he neared, she released the leaf and danced on. She grabbed a potted plant and held it between them like a shield.

"A cannabis plant," he said. "For relief of pain, rheumatism, and convulsions. Also a powerful intoxicant, unlike the related plant that grows in England. That was one of the ingredients in my medicine last night."

She regarded the spiky bright-green leaves with interest. "May I try some?"

"No. You appear intoxicated even when sober."

Tossing the pot at him, she made her escape. Rafe took his time shelving the plant; he was happy to let her escape, because he enjoyed chasing her. That was the game, and he must not catch her, however much they both wanted him to.

She skipped away to the potting area down the end.

"Oh, I know this one," she said of the small fruit trees on the table. "Tangerines."

"They prevent scurvy."

She poked at a tangerine tree, making the little fruit wobble. One fruit fell into the pot. "Oops," she said and turned away, pretending it had never happened.

There were no more plants, but before her sat a tray of rich, dark soil.

"And dirt," she said.

"Food for plants."

Laughing, she plunged her hand deep into the soil and jerked it back out, sending soil spraying.

"You'll get dirt all over you," he warned, drawing closer.

"Like you do."

"Like I do what?"

"Have dirt all over you."

Rafe checked his shirt, his hands. "I do not."

"Right here."

He was too slow. Maybe he was distracted by her radiant cheeks and impish smile. Or maybe the medicine was still in his blood. Or maybe he wanted to be slow, because he knew her intention and let it happen.

Either way, he did not even try to escape as she pressed her soil-covered hand to his cheek and smeared that gritty mud over his skin and into his hair.

That giddiness washed over him again, the recklessness of a young man who cared nothing for consequences, seeking only the joy of the moment. Thea arched back, poised to run. Slowly, deliberately, Rafe extended one arm and rubbed his hand in the dirt. She followed his movements with her eyes, as he lifted his hand, thick with dark, redolent soil.

Squealing, she danced backward. Her bottom collided with the table behind her. The leaves of the tangerine trees quivered, and the small fruits bobbed enthusiastically.

"Your hair, I think," he murmured, inching toward her. "It's much too shiny and clean."

With another squeal, Thea covered her head with her arms.

The pose was very effective for protecting her hair.

It left her front completely exposed.

So Rafe pressed his soil-covered hand firmly over her chest. Right at the spot where her breasts met. She gasped, a sound as warm and soft as her bosom against his palm. Sensations coiled up his arm and charged into his groin as a savage, clawing desire. Her heart beat madly under his palm—or perhaps that was his own pulse—and her chest rose and fell with her ragged breaths.

For half a dozen blissful beats of their racing hearts, Rafe let his hand linger before dragging it away. Her breathing fast and shallow, Thea slowly lowered her eyes, and together they admired his handiwork: a perfect handprint right over her bosom.

Rafe rubbed his fingers against his palm. The dirt clung to his skin, while the feeling of her softness slid under it, into his flesh and blood, right down to his bones.

They both looked up at the same moment. Thea narrowed her eyes, her mouth tightening.

He schooled his face into innocence.

"Oops," he said.

THEA TRIED TO BREATHE, but breathing proved difficult when laughter and the lingering heat of Rafe's impudent touch had robbed her of air. Yet air seemed inconsequential when Rafe was looking at her like that. With mischief and desire, and something else, something that made her feel special and interesting. As if whatever she did next would be the right thing to do, simply because she was the one doing it. It was a wondrous feeling, which mingled with the delicious sensations bouncing under her skin to make her reckless. More reckless, even, than when she had smeared dirt on him, merely as an excuse to touch his hair.

Not taking her eyes off his wicked face, stifling her laughter, Thea fumbled behind her. Her hands landed in the pot of a tangerine tree, with its treasure trove of soil and fallen fruit.

Rafe prowled closer. Closer. She pressed her bottom back against the table. His gaze flicked to the handprint over her breasts, and her skin burned yearningly at the memory of his touch.

Behind her, she rubbed both hands in the soil.

He drew nearer. His eyes intent. Seeing nothing but her.

She clutched a tangerine in each palm.

He stopped. The toe of his boot nudged her foot. That vast chest loomed barely a foot from her eyes. A crumb of soil tumbled down his cheek and he swiped at the dirt on his face.

A distraction. Ha! Using all her strength and weight, Thea pressed her tangerine-laden palms against his chest. Solid as a castle wall, he did not budge an inch.

Perfect!

The tangerines exploded under her palms, against his chest, and the tart scent of citrus filled the air. He yelled his protest as his arms flew up like wings on a startled bird, and his ribcage shifted beneath her hands. Relentless, she smeared the crushed fruit down the front of his waistcoat, leaving a triumphant trail of pulp and juice and dirt.

Then the giddy recklessness made her giggle, made her linger, made her hook a finger inside the waistband of his breeches. She tugged it an inch from his body, and—

"Oh no you don't!" he cried.

—dropped the crushed tangerines inside.

Her feet were light as air and she danced away before he could react, darting around to put the solid width of the table between them, from where she could gloat in safety.

When he looked up at her, his body was as still as a cat on the hunt, and his eyes gleamed with predatory intent. Thea's breathy laugh did nothing to distract him, and her body thrilled in anticipation of his revenge.

He slid a few steps to his left. She danced the opposite way, keeping the table between them. He slid back; so did she. He feinted one way, and then the other, and each time she kept her distance.

No catching her! Perhaps they would pass days this way, dancing around the table, until he—

He leaped onto the table.

A single bound of virile athleticism and he was back in control. Whichever way she ran, he had only to pounce and he'd be there first. Catching her. And then?

Thea backed away, her bottom meeting another bench, and drank in his magnificence as he stood on the table, like a sculpture displayed for her pleasure. With a wince, he tugged at his waistband, then ignored any discomfort and nimbly picked his way between the pots.

At the near edge of the table, he paused. Their gazes tangled. His eyes dared her to move. He twitched. She sidestepped. He pounced.

The second he landed, his hands slammed down on the bench on either side of her. Thea arched backward, and he leaned over her. His toes nudged hers, and his legs pressed against her skirts. He did not touch her but she felt him everywhere.

"Got you," he whispered.

One hand shifted firmly onto her waist. She responded by pressing a palm to his bicep, the firm muscle hot through the linen of his shirt.

Then his other hand slid over her cheek and jaw, the fingers sliding into her hair, caressing her ear, and gliding back down, until his thumb touched her lips. She could not look away from the compelling heat in his eyes, as he traced the outline of her mouth. A warning, perhaps, or an invitation.

She let her lips part. Her own invitation.

Again he spoke, the delicious promise in his near-whisper curling over her skin like smoke.

"Now I have caught you, what shall I do with you?"

His head lowered, unstoppable as the tide. Thea let her eyelids flutter closed as his lips settled on hers, warm and sure and open. His kiss was full of purpose and triumph, as though kissing her was a long-sought prize and the one thing he absolutely had to do that day, and he was doing it with every ounce of focus he had.

It made kissing him the most important thing in her world too.

Pushing into him, Thea fumbled for his hair, his shirt, needing to hold him tight, tug him closer. His tongue touched hers, sending new and exciting sensations swirling through her. Again she had that odd fancy—that his kisses entered her body like living things and gathered between her thighs, where they bounced around eagerly, making her tingle and hum as she yearned both to let them out and hold them in.

With a groan, he slipped his arm around her waist, pulling her against him as he kissed her deep and hard. He was everywhere, engulfing her, stoking her senses until they clamored with craving. He made another growl-like sound, deep in his throat, and she pressed harder into him, wanting more of that sound. More of him. The taste and feel of him were new, unimagined, splendid, and she needed more, more, always more.

Her hand slid inside his shirt. That was new and exciting too, and demanded exploration: the satiny skin, the firm muscles, the heat that was so like and so unlike her own. One of his thighs pressed against her, and she pushed into him, craving more of that hardness.

Then abruptly, he released her and stumbled away, robbing her of his heat, leaving her clutching at air.

Thea tried to breathe. She did not want to breathe. She wanted him.

But he was backing away, all the while hissing between clenched teeth.

"Rafe? What's wrong? What did I do?"

He shook his head, holding up one hand in a gesture of "wait." His mouth worked, and when he spoke again, it was in the hoarse, airless whisper of a man holding his breath.

"Tangerines."

Giggles bubbled up inside her and she struggled to smother them, as Rafe stumbled away. He turned his back to her, rested his forehead on a pillar, and slipped his fingers into his breeches. Thea craned her neck to look, then remembered herself and sat back on the bench.

"Um." The sound came out breathy and unsteady, matching the rest of her. "I hope the tangerines did no damage."

"Simply...a little crowded in there."

He tossed the offending fruit to the side, and Thea hastily averted her eyes. She smoothed down her skirts, as if that might soothe her unruly body, while he stood motionless, his forehead still resting on the pillar.

Then he thumped the pillar with one fist. He muttered something that sounded like, "I keep forgetting. One look and I forget," and once more he thumped the pillar, the muscles in his back shifting under his shirt.

This was not about the tangerines anymore.

Thea waited. No words came to mind, and she occupied her restless hands by rearranging her clothing. She tugged up her bodice, brushed off the dirt, and shook out her skirts. Straightened and breathed and squeezed her tormented thighs.

All the while, Rafe faced away. His broad back rose and fell with his deep breaths, and by the time he finally turned around, Thea was settled enough to perch on the bench, gripping its edges.

His expression was pained. Too late, she remembered he believed they were married, and she'd have a hard time putting him off because clearly she did not want to put him off. But she had to put him off, because...because...oh yes, because he thought she was Helen, and they weren't truly married, and soon she would leave, and while she was eager for adventures, she had not anticipated an adventure like this. As she fumbled for words to delicately imply it was that time of the month, he spoke in a harsh rasp.

"I can't. I *can't.*"

"Oh. *Oh.*"

Oh no. How naive of her, not to read the clues. Never having children, he said. Ignoring his bride. Never demanding his conjugal rights. Needing medicine to ease his pain. Indifferent to his wife's lineage.

When he said "I can't," it must be because he *couldn't.*

The poor man. No wonder he was grumpy.

"Was it the jaguar?" she asked softly.

"Hmm?"

"Did the giant cat maul your orchids?"

His chin jerked up, his eyes widened. She might have turned into a giant cat herself, he looked so taken aback.

Then he blinked, rapidly, before his face settled into a fierce glower.

"I assure you, my orchids are fine."

"Oh. Good. Um."

"I mean, we..." He half laughed and ran a hand through his hair. It came away dirty and he blinked at the soil with surprise. "I promised to wait. So. My apologies."

Without another word, he strode out of the greenhouse, leaving Thea alone with the plants and their knowing looks.

BY THE TIME Thea arrived back at the house, cloak wrapped tight around her dirt-smeared dress, she was thinking more rationally again. And rational thought informed her that she had to leave.

Now. Today. Tonight.

Rafe—Lord Luxborough, his lordship, whatever she should call him—had tried to avoid such pleasures, and now she understood why. Because once those delicious sensations slid under one's skin and into one's blood, they became all consuming. Even now, Thea did not want to be rid of them. She wanted more.

Which would lead to nothing but her ruin—when her ruin was precisely what she sought to undo. Besides, Rafe didn't want *her* or care about *her*. He didn't even know her real name. Likely, when he learned she was not truly his wife, he would merely shrug, grumble about the inconvenience, and replace her with someone else.

She would not tell herself stories that had no foundation in truth. The truth was, this was not her home and Rafe was not her husband. The truth was, Thea must leave for London tonight, but she could not travel alone, so required Gilbert's help.

An inquiry of a passing servant revealed that Mr. Gilbert was in the ballroom with Mrs. Flores. Unable to fathom what possible business Gilbert and Martha could have together, Thea headed for the ballroom.

Where she still could not determine what business they had together.

The cavernous room was cool, despite the sunlight that poured through the open curtains and sparkled in the crystals of the chandeliers and sconces. By one window sat Martha, a notebook in her lap, pencil in hand. She was periodically frowning out the window and then looking back at Gilbert, who was...waltzing?

Gilbert was a broad man, whose battered face told the story of his past as a champion prizefighter, which made the gracefulness of his dance all the more surprising.

Or perhaps not, Thea mused. After all, a boxer did have to be light on his feet. The only real surprises were that he even knew how to waltz, and that he was dancing at all, given it was afternoon and he was alone. His arms were positioned as if they held an imaginary partner, his eyes were closed, and his face wore an expression of dreamy bliss. As he circled nearer, she heard him humming a slow waltz in a pitch-perfect baritone.

Thea slipped across the room and crouched beside Martha. Martha's dark eyes narrowed as they roamed over her face, and Thea feared that the effects of the kiss were evident. Cheeks heating, she clutched her cloak more tightly and reminded herself that everyone believed she was married.

"What is Mr. Gilbert doing?" Thea whispered.

"Mr. Gilbert is dancing."

"Of course. Um. Why is Mr. Gilbert dancing?"

Martha tapped her pencil on her notebook and shook her head. "It's astonishing, isn't it? It takes everyone differently."

"It?"

"I do not have a good name for it. It's based on bhang, but such modifications I have made, it has become something else."

Thea's heart sank. "He is intoxicated?"

"Mr. Gilbert volunteered to help test my medicines. The purpose is to ease pain, and I am trying to remove the intoxicating effects, but without success. It seems to make people behave more like themselves. When Sally tested it, she laughed and laughed. I rambled for hours about natural philosophy."

And Rafe, Thea recalled, had been sweet and funny and affectionate.

"Of course, that is what intoxicants do," Martha added. "We

wear masks to survive in society, and intoxicants allow us to remove those masks again."

Thea looked back at Gilbert. With his grace and bliss, he made a lovely sight.

"He is in quite a state," she said. "When will he recover?"

"By tomorrow morning, he'll be himself again."

"I see."

If Gilbert was intoxicated, he could not accompany her to London, and Thea could not go alone. Thea wasn't leaving Brinkley End today, then. So she took a seat and watched Gilbert dance, feeling her body tingle with the memory of Rafe's touch, and her heart relax, as if she'd had a reprieve.

CHAPTER 16

The next day, Rafe crawled out of bed after a night that involved rather less sleep than he would have liked, and rather more thinking of Thea, of reliving the feel of her in his arms and dreaming of making love with her, as he could never do. He intended to go straight to the glasshouse, but stopped to terrorize a passing footman with a barked demand: Had someone gone for the post? The footman stammered that yes, someone had gone, someone always went, but he could check again if his lordship desired. His lordship, who knew he was being a pain in the neck, said only that he wished to be informed the minute the post arrived.

"The very minute, you hear?" he snarled. The footman agreed, and Rafe stayed in his study and wore out the carpet.

The very minute Rafe got his bundle of letters, he tore them open. A letter from his solicitor confirmed the trustees had released the funds and Rafe could safely end his farcical marriage; a postscript noted that Mr. Knight had not yet handed over Miss Knight's dowry. Yet another letter from the Royal Household demanding that Rafe—oh, who cared what the Crown wanted now. He tossed it aside and ripped open others.

Nothing from Ventnor. Nothing about Thea.

He calculated and recalculated the days. Surely Helen and Beau Russell were married by now. Surely word had reached London. Surely a scathing letter from Ventnor should have arrived.

But nothing.

He felt light-headed with relief. It wasn't over yet. They had at least one more day. He should not waste it.

Unless—

"What about the countess?" he demanded.

"She received a letter too."

"And?"

The footman searched the room for the right answer. "And… her ladyship has not yet read it as she has not returned from her walk."

Rafe stopped tormenting the man and went outside. He strode down the lawn, seeking Thea and not seeing her, and what would he do if he did? Take up sorcery after all so he could put a spell on his estate to freeze time? They said desire made men into fools and he was living proof. If news from the outside world never came, and she never confessed, and he never confessed, and she never left, and he never had to decide—

Decide what, exactly?

He stood by the lake and let the water lap at the toes of his boots. A dragonfly skipped over the surface; a gentle breeze gathered the water into ripples that glinted in the sunlight; a bird issued a lazy call. An idyllic summer's day. Rafe stood in this idyll and ached. Ached with indecision and desire and despair. Well, a vigorous swim in cold water could fix one of those, at least. He stripped down to his drawers, plunged into the cool water, and swam.

He swam and swam, as he did every day, his legs kicking behind him, his arms cycling over his head. Yet every gulp of air and kick of his legs, every slap of his hands slicing the water, brought a thought of Thea. Memories, questions, images of Thea in a future that could not be. Thea, who was lying to him. Thea, who longed for balls and society and London. Thea, whose vitality made him yearn to be a different man.

He swam, harder, faster, further, flipping around and doing it again and again. Every muscle in his body worked to keep him moving, until it became difficult to catch his breath. Drowning seemed excessive, so when he neared the bank once more, he stopped and sucked in air.

He dug his toes into the mud, the water lapping at his chest, his drawers clinging uncomfortably to his thighs. Gripping his wet hair, Rafe let out a bellow of frustration and turned.

There she was.

Thea sat on a flat rock hanging over the water's edge. The skirts of her blue walking dress were bunched around her knees, displaying a hint of white undergarments, and her bare calves and feet dangled in the water, intriguing pale shapes under the surface.

Her ankles. Those famously, fabulously fascinating ankles.

The swim had stolen all his thoughts, but Rafe did not need to think. Of its own will, his body turned, and he pushed through the water toward her.

IN HER OWN DEFENSE, Thea had removed her shoes and stockings and sat on the rock *before* she'd noticed Rafe swimming.

She had intended to pack first thing, but no sooner had she opened her empty trunk than she developed the notion of saying her farewells to Brinkley End. After all, she reasoned, a delay of a couple of hours would not matter, in the grand scheme of things. She was in no rush to get to London, given that her pamphlets would not be ready for days.

And it was such a warm day, and her feet were hot and tired, and it wouldn't matter if she sat for a while with her bare feet in the water.

But when she'd seen him swimming back and forth in that absurdly vigorous manner, she found she could not move.

Neither could she move when he came to a stop. The water lapped at his skin, halfway up his naked, heaving chest. She barely had time to marvel at the breadth of his shoulders, when he lifted his arms to wipe his face, revealing the shape of his ribcage, and the muscles shifting under his skin, and the jagged scars marking his shoulders and ribs. Then he gripped his hair and roared at the sky like a beast, and she wondered fancifully if he was indeed some magical, mythical beast. Until he turned and looked right in her eyes, and she knew, without a doubt, that he was all man.

A man with the intent gaze of a hunter.

Slowly, he lowered his arms and rested them on the surface of the lake, the muscles in his chest again shifting in interesting ways. He advanced. His feet, always so sure of themselves, did not miss a step. The water grew shallower as he came closer, revealing more of his naked torso as he approached. Thea's hungry eyes tried to devour all of him at once: the broad shoulders, the muscular arms, water sliding over the hairs on his chest. More ridges of muscle, like weathered bricks in a timeless castle wall. His navel. Was that more hair? And then—

He stopped. Right in front of her. The water lapped at his lean waist, vexingly hiding what lay beneath. On his arms, dark hairs gathered in wet spikes, the sun catching in the drops of water.

Thea tracked back up his body to meet his eyes, still the color of brandy, but hot brandy that stirred her own rising heat. His gaze was so intense she had to look away, to his dark hair, the curls not so wild when wet. A droplet of water trickled over his cheek and jaw, down his throat, gathering other droplets as it went. She followed its progress all the way down his body, gripping the rock so she would not catch that droplet on her finger and touch it to her tongue.

A strange longing hit her so forcefully she forgot to breathe.

A fierce, hungry longing to dive down inside him, like he himself was a lake and she could travel deep under his surface and discover what marvels lay beneath. Surely, she'd find some magical kingdom, within his depths, where she could begin to understand the workings of his mind, his heart, his body, his soul.

It started with his eyes, she knew. So she gathered her courage and looked back at his face.

"You were swimming," she said, her voice too high.

"Hmm."

"I never saw anyone swim like that before. All that splashing."

"I learned that method from watching members of a Native tribe in America." His voice sounded rougher, smokier than usual. A little breathless; from his exertions, no doubt. "It enables one to swim with more power and speed."

"What is chasing you?"

"Hmm?"

"You do not swim to a destination, so surely you require speed only if something is chasing you?"

Thea thought she made an excellent point, but Rafe had that look again, as if he didn't know what to make of her, yet enjoyed her anyway.

He sidled another few inches toward her. Perhaps if she straightened her legs, she could wrap them around his waist.

"It's the crocodiles," he said solemnly.

"You have crocodiles in your lake in Somersetshire?"

He edged closer. "Don't worry. They're mostly friendly."

"Friendly crocodiles?"

"Mostly friendly."

Under the water, he grabbed her ankle. She yelped then slammed her mouth shut. His hand was firm and sure and oddly warm, and as he traced her bones with his thumb, sensations sizzled up her legs.

"So..." His eyes dropped to her ankle in his hand, still under the water. "The famously, fabulously fascinating ankles."

When he released her foot, it came to a natural rest against his hip, where his skin burned her and the waistband of his drawers tickled her. He ran his fingers up her calf to the back of her knee, then down again. Up and down.

And perhaps it was those sizzling sensations, or the defiant thought that she had as much right to touch him as he did her, or the desperate knowledge that soon she must leave, she must confess, and never again would he spout nonsense about crocodiles or argue about dessert or hold her ankle in his hand— whatever compelled her, Thea touched him too.

She poked at a sunlit droplet of water on his shoulder and smeared it over his skin. Her fingers brushed the edge of a ragged scar.

"The jaguar got you here, too," she murmured.

"Hmm."

Spreading her fingers wide, she pressed her whole palm over as much of his shoulder as she could.

"It was in a tree and pounced on me from behind," he said. "I heard it and spun, and it caught my face."

"And then?"

She trailed her fingers along his collarbone. He didn't seem to mind. He was still running his hand up and down the back of her calf. And even when his touch slid down, the sensations kept going up and up and up.

"The other men were there with the dogs and guns. The jaguar decided I wasn't worth the trouble and leaped up into the trees. It was over before I understood it had begun."

"They didn't shoot the jaguar, did they?"

"It was too fast. Besides, I cannot blame it; I was in its forest, stealing its flowers."

Gently, he lifted her ankle, straightening her knee. Her leg looked small in his big hand, his weathered skin darker than her own. Though he touched her only in the one place, she felt his touch everywhere, from her throat to her breasts to her quim.

"You look a little flushed," he murmured, his eyes knowing and intent.

"It's warm today, don't you think?"

"Swim with me. Right now."

"My gown..."

"Leave it on. Take it off. I don't care."

She caught a droplet hanging from his hair. "Swimming fully clothed... That seems rather impulsive."

"It won't be impulsive if you keep bloody talking about it."

"You are so grumpy."

"I am not."

But he was smiling. Properly smiling, dimple and all. Thea slid an arm around his neck and gave him her weight. He lifted her down into the water, blessedly cool against her hot, tormented skin. Her skirts bunched around her; laughing, she pushed the air out of them and they grudgingly sank below the surface to swirl heavily. Her foot bumped him, and she slid it up his leg, over the roughness of his hairs. Those assured legs did not falter as he pushed back through the water, sweeping her away with him. Her feet did not touch the bottom, but she did not need firm ground to stand, not when he held her in his sure, strong arms.

His forehead pressed against hers, and he freed one hand to tug pins from her hair and run his fingers through the strands.

Next, he would kiss her again. Kiss her, and he did not even know her name.

She couldn't do this.

She was deceiving him, and oh, how she wished it could last forever, this magical day, the sunlight, the water, the sheer folly of swimming in her clothes, his arms, his caress, this unexpected moment of bliss.

She wished it could last forever, but nothing in her life ever did.

"Rafe," she whispered.

"Hmm."

He trailed his lips down the side of her face and nuzzled her neck. Thea tangled her fingers in his wet hair and tugged.

"I have to tell you something. About...me."

"Tell me tomorrow."

"I have to tell you now."

"No," he murmured against her throat. "Tomorrow. It can wait until tomorrow."

The water swirled and yanked at her skirts. Her limbs became weak but his strong arms held her.

His arms, at least, did not lie.

"You already know," she whispered.

He pulled her closer, as he moved them through the water. Her skirts fought them both and she wound her arms more tightly around his neck, even as her heart began to ache.

"Tomorrow," he repeated roughly. "If you say it, it will be over.

Like an enchantment coming to an end. Give us one more day. One more day to swim and play. One more night to dine together. Let us pretend, for one more day. Let us have the fiction of our marriage. It is all we have holding us together. Let it hold us together one more day."

No more was he trying to kiss her. His eyes searched hers, as he tenderly brushed back her hair.

"How did you find out?" she whispered.

"I always knew."

And once more, everything she believed was swept out from under her. She had to move away or slap him or tear out his eyes, but he didn't release her, and she needed him to hold her up.

He had lied too.

Nothing was as she thought; nothing was the same. She no longer knew what was real, what was false, what was fantasy, what was true.

"I bribed a servant in your parents' house, who read your letters to Helen." As he talked, his eyes roamed over her face, as if he was trying to capture it in his mind. Their words were ending this, but still they clung to each other, their bodies not yet ready to believe the news. "I saw you arrive at that coaching inn in Warwickshire, dressed as a man. I saw Helen arrive, and go to the same room. I saw Helen in men's clothing board the stagecoach north, and then you and Miss Larke came downstairs. Ventnor's men didn't notice the switch, but I sent them back to London, just in case."

"Why? You knew the marriage would be invalid. Why?"

"I needed a marriage certificate and living bride to secure the money from my mother's trust, and I've sworn never to marry again."

She realized then that he had been moving them toward the shore, and despite her heavy skirts' protests, her feet sank into the mud. He was right: It could have waited until tomorrow. She could have waited one more day to know that he had lied to her too, that he had schemed as she had, but he had done it better, and he had won.

A dragonfly skimmed past his head, the sunlight glinting on its wings, and the waters of the lake washed peacefully around them. Everything was perfect and carefree, on this giddy summer's day. Everything but them.

"You should have told me," she said, aware of her own hypocrisy.

"Countess, we—"

"No!" She pushed away from him and lost her balance. He caught her and steadied her, before the water and hurt could carry her away. "You know my name. Use my name."

"Then it will truly end."

Again, he was right. Her name would be like the magic word that ended an enchantment. No more pretending. They would have to retreat behind the barriers of propriety and outrage and opposition. She had thought they were enemies, and then they were not, and now they would be adversaries again.

"Say it," she whispered.

"Thea."

Her name was never much more than a breath, and that was how he said it now, breathing her name like a prayer or a curse. He looked as if he had lost something, but there had never been anything to lose. They had played a game of make-believe; now the game was over, they were just cold and wet.

"I don't understand." She knew she had no right to be hurt, but the betrayal stung anyway. Everything she thought she knew was wrong, and now she knew nothing at all. "If you knew who I was, then you let them elope, Helen and Mr. Russell. Lord Ventnor will be furious."

"I hope so."

Something plopped into the water beside them, splashing them both. Thea gasped but Rafe did not so much as flinch. He turned his head, and Thea did too, and saw the tall, thin man on the bank, the breeze teasing the ends of his white hair under his hat, his arm pulled back, ready to throw another stone. Lord Ventnor.

"Speak of the Devil and he appears," Rafe said wryly. "And he does look rather furious, doesn't he?"

CHAPTER 17

Thea shivered. Even though she stared at Ventnor—and yes, a rather furious-looking Ventnor—she could hardly believe he was there.

He did not belong here, in this strange place Brinkley End had become. He was too real. She could not even fathom how he had arrived. Perhaps he had appeared in a puff of smoke the moment Rafe spoke her name and ended their enchantment.

"Get up here now, Luxborough!" Ventnor shouted.

Thea and Rafe ignored him.

"You're cold. Go inside and change," Rafe said. "I'll deal with him."

He reached for her and she yanked her arm away. "Don't touch me!"

Rafe hurtled back so fast waves washed around her. Another stone landed beside Rafe's head, the water splashing his face.

"Would you two be so courteous as to have your lovers' tiff some other time?" Ventnor called. "I demand you talk to me."

For a long while, Rafe studied her. Then, with a sigh, he

headed for the shore. Thea tried to follow, but her dress dragged against her and she slipped in the mud.

"Wait!" she cried. "My skirts."

Rafe turned. "Do you need me to carry you?"

"I despise you right now."

"Yes, but do you need me to carry you?"

"If you would."

He waded back to her. "Put your arms around my neck." She hesitated. Ventnor yelled again but neither paid him any mind. "It didn't bother you a moment ago," Rafe growled.

"A moment ago, I didn't know you were a lying, betraying, deviously deceitful liar."

"Exquisite sentiment from a woman who faked her identity, knowingly entered into a fraudulent marriage, and used my money to buy items to resell."

"It's only what you deserved."

"Probably. Now put your arms around my neck so I can bloody well get you out of here."

This time, she obeyed, and tried not to enjoy the feeling of being lifted out of the water and carried to the bank.

Ventnor sneered and shook his ebony cane at them. "You two disgust me. Canoodling in the water like a pair of stray dogs."

"Stray otters, if you please," Thea snapped.

Well, look at that. He no longer frightened her. Perhaps she was too hurt and confused and guilty to feel any fear. Or perhaps it was the effect of being in Rafe's arms, which made her feel bolder and uncaring of Ventnor's ire.

Even though Rafe was a devious, deceitful, beastly beast of a lying liar.

"Careful, Ventnor." Rafe lowered Thea to the ground beside his discarded clothes. "Or you might find yourself taking a swim too."

"Do not threaten me, you scoundrel."

"Put that on." Rafe tossed his coat to Thea. "Get inside and warm up. I'll handle him."

Water still trickling down his bare skin, Rafe shook out his breeches and yanked them on. Thea averted her eyes and fought her wet dress to shove her arms into the coat's sleeves. She gathered the lapels under her chin, and tried to work out what was going on.

"Luxborough, you have made a complete mess of everything," Ventnor said.

"Hmm?"

Ventnor pointed the silver knob of his walking stick at Thea. "That woman is not Helen Knight."

"Hmm."

"I sent you to stop Helen Knight from sneaking off to beguile Beau. You said you accomplished that by marrying her yourself, but you married the wrong woman, you blithering muttonhead!"

Rafe straightened and fastened his falls, looking as unbothered as Ventnor was riled. He shook the water from his hair and pulled on his shirt; it clung to his wet skin, but he didn't seem to care. Thea looked from one man to the other, as confused as if she had walked onstage in the middle of a play, and she did not know what the story was, or who was the hero and who was the villain, or if she was the heroine or a hapless fool.

"You sent me off to do your dirty work and expected me to obey your commands. Who's really the blithering muttonhead, Ventnor?"

"My heir is married to a shop girl because you cannot follow a simple instruction."

Rafe started gathering up his boots and the rest of his clothing. "Your heir is married to the woman of his own choosing because he could no longer tolerate you treating him like a child."

"You promised to keep Helen Knight away from Beau in exchange for the orchids."

"I lied."

"I want those orchids back."

"Oh, go away, Ventnor."

"I don't understand," Thea said to Rafe. "You seem to loathe him, but I thought you were allies. He's your father-in-law."

"A connection I would rather forget. Can you walk in those wet skirts?"

"Damn you, Luxborough. Stop talking to your harlot and listen to me!"

Rafe gestured at the viscount with a hand full of boot. "Speak of her like that again, and you will go in the lake. Thea, do you need my help?"

"I can walk. I'll have to show my legs, but the best harlots always do."

Defiantly, she lifted her sodden skirts to her knees and marched up the lawn. Rafe fell into step beside her.

"You needed a marriage certificate to get the money, and you didn't want to marry again, so an invalid marriage to me did the trick," she summarized.

"Yes. That's it."

"Then you kissed me."

"And then I stopped kissing you."

"Do not ignore me!" Ventnor stalked around in front of them. "I traveled all the way here to confront you, Luxborough."

"And now you can travel all the way back."

Thea and Rafe went around him and kept walking. Ventnor's black carriage stood outside the house, spattered with mud and pulled by a mismatched set of rented horses. Only the three matching purple footmen did not seem the worse for travel, standing smartly to attention at their approach.

"So you never meant to separate them?" Thea said to Rafe. "Helen and Beau Russell?"

"I told you, I don't care who marries whom, but I did like the idea of upsetting *him*."

"Damn you, Luxborough. I will not be ignored. You will listen to me or I shall—"

"Or what, Ventnor?" Rafe sounded irritable and bored. "What will you do this time? Hire more actors to spread your lies that I practice sorcery and poisoned Katharine?"

Thea's world tilted again. "Ventnor started the rumors? So the zealot outside your London house was William Dudley the actor?"

"Yes. Apparently, Ventnor placed scores of actors around the country. Everyone needs a hobby, and spreading rumors is his."

"But why?"

Ventnor offered her a kind, patient smile. "His lordship started it, when he published ludicrous claims that my daughter was insane."

"Yet it was you who put her in a lunatic asylum," Rafe snarled.

"No!" Thea said

Ventnor continued as if neither of them had spoken. "For the sake of my family, I could not allow such damaging allegations to pass unchallenged. Naturally, I countered by claiming that Luxborough kidnapped, brutalized, and poisoned Katharine, and thus turned her mind." With a derisive snort, he indicated Rafe with his stick. "But when he came back with those marks on his face, and his brothers' deaths making him the earl, it was only a matter of time before the gulls of the world believed he had forged some bargain with the Devil. I would never have dreamed up anything so outlandish, but I confess I played along, as I rather enjoyed the effect."

"The whole lot is nonsense," Thea said. "Rafe would never harm anyone."

"Silence!" The viscount shuddered. "How charming, Luxborough, that your harlot comes to your defense."

"Enough." Rafe dumped his clothes and marched to the carriage, sending the footmen scattering like bewigged purple chickens. He yanked open the door. "Get in before I throw you in. I'll not strike a man your age, but I have no such qualms about shooting you."

But the viscount only turned to Thea, and added, his tone affable, "Did he tell you how Katharine died? She rode off during a storm, fleeing him. Do you know why she fled?"

And Thea could not help but ask, "Why?"

Rafe looked bleak. "You know why. Katharine feared me."

"But why?"

"I don't know."

Ventnor laughed, once more shaking his ebony stick. "Because you did something to her, and that is what everyone will always believe!"

"Oh shut *up*, Ventnor."

Rafe yanked the stick out of the other man's hands, broke it over his knee, and tossed the two pieces into the carriage. Ventnor quivered with rage, spots of red appearing in his cheeks.

And then he paled.

The color drained away so abruptly that Thea feared he was about to have an apoplexy.

She followed Ventnor's gaze, wondering what had induced this effect.

Or rather, *who* had induced this effect.

Sally stood in the doorway, frozen mid-step, staring at Ventnor with a matching look of shock. She, too, was unnaturally pale, unnaturally still. Thea silently willed Sally to march at Ventnor, gun raised in her confident manner, but Sally seemed only to grow smaller and more disturbed.

"You!" Ventnor said. "But they said you were..."

Sally whirled about and ran back into the darkness of the house.

Rafe looked as puzzled as Thea felt. "How the hell do you two know each other?"

Ventnor took a deep breath, the color returning to his cheeks, and when he spoke, he only said, "You harmed my family, Luxborough, by enabling my son to marry so far beneath him. I shall ruin you."

"You will not," Thea said. "Lord Luxborough is a horrid, beastly, lying liar, but apart from that, he is kind and caring and honorable and gentle."

"Gentle? You foolish girl. He broke my walking stick."

"Yes, but he broke it very gently."

"And if you don't leave, Ventnor, I shall shoot you gently too."

Ventnor, lip curled, climbed into his carriage. As soon as Rafe had shut the door and stepped away, the footmen leaped onto the back, the coachman clucked at the horses, and the carriage made its escape.

"I still don't understand." Thea shivered in her wet clothes, while Rafe stood as impervious as a rock. "The whole time I thought he was your ally and you were doing his bidding, but the whole time you and I were actually on the same side. Nothing is as I thought it was. I worried you would be angry with me, and now I am angry with you, and I don't feel I have a right to be angry, and that makes me even angrier. And when you kissed me, it wasn't because you believed you had a right but because... And you did nice things for me, but you didn't have to do nice things, because you knew I wasn't your wife, and I felt so guilty but you..."

Rafe ran a hand through his wet hair. "It doesn't matter anymore. It's finished. Your sister is married. I got the money and the orchids. It went as planned. The game is up."

"And now?"

He looked down at the lake and then back at Thea.

"And now it's time for you to go."

RAFE WAS ALMOST grateful to Ventnor for the timely reminder of Rafe's unsuitability for marriage; when Thea was in his arms, it was easy to forget.

Everything was as it was meant to be, he lectured himself, but his eyes strayed back to the lake, as if he might catch a glimpse of a man and woman frolicking together in the water.

Blithering muttonhead, indeed.

Resolutely, he walked into the house. In the foyer, servants appeared with dry towels, and Rafe handed one to Thea without looking at her. After drying himself as best he could, he started up the stairs. A backward glance showed that Thea was struggling, burdened by the oversized coat and wet gown, her hair tumbling haphazardly around her shoulders.

"Your breeches are askew," she said. "It looks uncomfortable."

"It is."

"Good. I hope you get chafing."

He marched back down. "Do you want me to carry you up the stairs?"

"I want you to explain why Ventnor knows Sally, and why you lied to me, and what happened to Katharine."

"I already told you about Katharine."

"Except for the tiny details about the lunatic asylum and why she feared you."

Rafe muttered a dark oath. "I'm going to carry you or we'll be here all day."

"Very well. But I shan't enjoy it, and I may be compelled to scream."

"If you must."

Rafe bent and scooped her up. Everything about them was cold and damp and uncomfortable, yet her weight felt right in his arms, and her softness perfect against his body. She looped an arm around his neck, for although this was new to them, they had already mastered it. Like those kisses, like their games and conversations. They learned each other so quickly. Rafe dared himself to look at her face. Her gaze searched his, and a pang echoed through his chest. Tightening his arms around her, he closed his eyes to her beauty and emotion, but still he saw her, still he felt her. If he were a different man, he could carry his bride like this. Lay her down and show her such bliss she would never want to leave.

But he was not a different man.

He opened his eyes and headed up the stairs and toward her rooms.

THE SUNLIGHT WAS STREAMING into Thea's sitting room, where her traveling trunk crouched, gaping and empty, a pile of underclothes beside it. Rafe lowered Thea to the floor and dumped the clothes into the trunk. He went into the dressing room for another armful, and came back to see her remove everything from the trunk and hurl it across the room.

"What the hell are you doing?" He looked around at the bright, peach-colored room, the furniture dripping with sunlit stockings and shifts and the devil knew what. One stocking was curled around a vase of yellow and white roses.

"I'm not leaving until you tell me about Katharine."

"Katharine died years ago." He dropped the armful of clothes into the trunk. "She has nothing to do with anything."

"Yet you and Ventnor are still fighting over her. And that night in the portrait gallery, you said she haunts you."

"That night I was intoxicated. Nothing I said was real."

"That night you said you like me."

Avoiding her eyes, Rafe set about scooping up clothes and tossing them into the trunk, only for Thea to grab them out and fling them across the room just as fast.

"You are the very devil," he said.

"You owe me answers."

"I owe you nothing."

"You lied to me," she said.

"My only lie was pretending to believe your lies. You lied first."

She glared at him. "You put me in a position where I had no choice, when you threatened Arabella."

"Then let us call it even. Either way, it is over now." She did not agree, judging by the accusation in her face. "What is really bothering you, Thea? Are you upset because I tricked you?"

"No, it's that..." She nudged some clothes with her bare toe. "Well, we were on the same side against Ventnor. You made me think we were enemies but in fact we were allies. So it...it would have been nice. To be on the same side. That's all."

Yes, it would have been nice. So many things would have been nice. But he could not have revealed the truth back then, because back then, he could not trust her. And now he knew her, it was too late.

He scooped up a cluster of items from her dressing table, hairbrushes and whatnot, and dumped them into the nearly empty trunk. They clattered against the sides.

"What happened in America?" Thea asked.

He shook his head and roamed around, grabbing up items and

hurling them haphazardly toward the trunk. "At first, we enjoyed the adventure, though we hadn't a clue how to make a home, aristocratic offspring that we were. And then, Katharine... She changed. She turned melancholy. Didn't eat. Didn't sleep. Just started fading away before my eyes. I promised to take her home to England when I earned enough money."

"And then?"

"And then..."

Rafe paused to stare out a window and shivered, as if he were back in that cold, dreary cabin they had tried so hard to make cozy. The sunlight hurt his eyes so he turned his back on it; it forgave the slight and generously warmed his skin through his drying shirt. Thea had found a stripe of sunshine to stand in, the dust motes dancing over her white toes and damp blue skirts.

"Her melancholy passed, and I got as much work as I could. Then she changed again. One day, she spent our entire savings and more besides, buying up pots and plates and baskets of produce from the market. Hell, we had live goats and chickens running through our cabin. She said she planned to open a tavern; it would be the most popular place in the land and we'd become rich. I couldn't reason with her. I mean, she could barely cook the most basic of meals and there she was, trying to cook ten things at once, nearly burning down the house. She didn't sleep for days, just... And those blasted chickens..." She had alarmed him, with her eyes unnaturally bright and her speech impossibly fast. "Then that passed too, and she was frightened by her own behavior. There were other episodes too. When she had a shock, she lost grip on reality and feared the world meant her harm. And I..."

And he could do nothing. Nothing but hold her, and tell her everything would be all right, and secretly worry how to get her home to England. Time and again, Katharine's mind turned on her during those years, and Rafe could do nothing but watch.

He wiped his hand over his face as if he could wipe away the memory, but when he looked up, the past was still with him, and Thea's eyes were wide with concern. She looked almost comical, standing there bedraggled and barefoot, half her hair still pinned up, the rest tumbling over her shoulders. He smiled, despite everything. Oh, to forget the past and be with her now; to run his fingers through her hair and hold her against him, so that she might warm his heart the way the sun warmed his skin.

"You were so young," she said softly. She took two steps toward him, but the trunk blocked her way. "In a foreign land, with no friends, no family, no solutions. It must have been terrifying for you."

"I don't need your pity. It was Katharine who suffered. I promised to look after her but..."

He tore his eyes off her, away from that gentle sympathy that he didn't deserve.

"Lord Ventnor came," Thea prompted.

"Right. Katharine had written to her mother, and he traveled all that way to take her home. I let her go. It seemed best. Then Nicholas—the bishop, you remember—he wrote me that Ventnor had put Katharine in a lunatic asylum, so I sailed back to England to get her out. As her husband, I had rights her father did not. If you had seen her when she came out of that place..."

The memory still made him shudder: spirited Katharine turned wan and silent, shuffling along, her eyes vacant.

Rafe shoved aside the image and picked up a heavy bestiary from the table. It was open at the entry on jaguars. That, too, made his heart ache: the thought of Thea, sitting alone, reading about giant cats because she wanted to know more and he would not tell her.

"And you lived in the Dower House here," Thea said.

240

"Right. My father had died, my mother moved to the Continent, and my brother John was the earl. He let us live there."

He slammed the book shut and threw it into her trunk.

"That's not mine." She bent to remove it and hugged it to her middle. "And why never mention that Sally lived with you?"

He shrugged. "It's not worth the bother of mentioning. Sally was good for Katharine. The whole arrangement seemed to be good for her. She went weeks without an episode of any kind. I was reading about new treatments for disorders of the mind, out of France. A Quaker is trying something similar in York. I was corresponding with a French *aliéniste*, and I thought—"

"I beg your pardon? An alienist?"

"A doctor of mental illnesses. I was considering taking Katharine to the Continent. She was happy; we all were. But then —suddenly; I don't know why—her mind turned on her again. We maintained complete calm around her, and she had had no frights or shocks. Except she read that blasted Gothic novel. She believed it held messages for her. And then the crows... She kept talking about crows, saying they were coming to take her away, and accusing me of being a crow or in league with the crows, or... I don't know."

"Why did she believe you meant her harm?"

Curse you, Katharine had hissed, wild-eyed, in the grip of whatever nightmare consumed her mind, while the heavy gray storm clouds crackled and rumbled overhead. *Dark and silent as the crow, and with just as evil intent.*

"She saw a crow kill a sparrow."

"That was all?"

He sighed. "A storm was building. She was outside and I was trying to coax her back into the house. She refused, insisting I meant to murder her. I knew we had to be calm with her, but I was tired, impatient."

"Worried," Thea suggested.

He waved off her excuses. "I lost my temper and tried to grab her. She escaped and ran to the stables, didn't even saddle the horse..."

And he, the fool, he had wasted minutes fetching a vial of laudanum before going after her. Precious minutes during which she had mounted a horse and ridden away.

Thea unwrapped her arms from the bestiary and lowered the huge book to a table, frowning thoughtfully as she traced the ornate letters on its front. Just as she had traced the scars on his shoulder, a lifetime ago, back in the lake. Rafe tried to take all of her in, every angle and curve of her face and her body; he might never see her again.

She looked up and caught him studying her. Something flashed across the space between them, swift as lightning.

"Why was Ventnor so shocked to see Sally?" she asked.

"I left England the same day we buried Katharine. I don't know what happened after that."

"Did you never ask?"

"What's the blasted point? It doesn't change what happened."

He could never change the past. He could never change Katharine's death. He could never change himself.

Rafe forced himself to meet Thea's eyes, forced himself to say, "You have to go."

She lifted her chin. "Actually, I think I shall stay."

CHAPTER 18

Thea met Rafe's baffled gaze steadily. He was silhouetted against the window, his hair drying into a dark mane, the sun outlining his body under his shirt. How she wished he would accept her comfort, this strong, vital man, so caring, so hurt by life.

So determined to send her away.

Listen to him. He told her his heartbreaking story—of the young woman who endured such torment, and the young man who loved her but could not ease her pain—and then, as if none of it mattered, as if he were not a human in need of compassion or self-forgiveness—he turned around and ordered her to leave.

What else did she expect? True, she had intended to leave today, but that was before she'd discovered his deception, before she'd learned how he had suffered for his first, youthful love. It was impossible to stay angry over his lies, not now she understood his choice.

For a man such as Rafe—in his prime, titled, from an old, respected family—finding a bride would have been easy, despite his bad temper, rumors, and scars. He could have wed some wealthy lady, given her a house and allowance, and never spoken to her again. Such an arrangement would have raised no eyebrows; affection was rarely a consideration in aristocratic marriages. But instead he had chosen this ruse, preferring fraud and deception to marriage of any kind; indeed, he would have foregone the funds completely, so set was he on not taking another wife.

It was the choice of a man who was determined to have no part in the world. Thea should not take it personally, then, that he was sending her away.

It was just that she was so very tired of people sending her away.

Thea was not completely naive. She knew she had nothing to offer him, nothing but silly stories and kisses in the lake. A young woman, a passing diversion, because he was, after all, just a man. She knew this was not her home, nor ever would be.

He had said as much. And then he said it again: "You cannot stay."

"I can if I want to," she argued. "Only for a few more days. I shall leave at my own convenience. After all, you brought me here under false pretenses."

He threw up his hands. "You came here under false pretenses."

"I would never have come here at all if not for your scheme. I would have stayed quite happily at Arabella's house, pretending to be Helen, waiting for news that Helen was married and my pamphlet was printed, at which point I would have returned to London. Then you got in the way, all arrogant and earl-ish, and played with us like pieces on a board. But my pamphlet is not yet ready. When I leave, it will be on my own schedule, not yours."

He went very still. "Pamphlet? What pamphlet?"

"I wrote a pamphlet."

"You wrote a pamphlet."

"It tells the true story of what Percy Russell did to me, although I used false names and invited readers to guess whom it concerns. *The Tale of Rosamund.* Who was cruelly wronged by... You know."

Rafe said nothing. Frowning, he began to pace back and forth. He appeared vexingly unimpressed.

Thea hurried to explain. "It will be printed in time for the Prince Regent's costume party, when the whole *ton* will be in Town, and I'll have it distributed to everyone. If my plan works..."

He said nothing. Kept pacing.

"If my plan works, society will understand that Percy and his friend lied. My parents will realize they were wrong not to believe me. My reputation will be restored, and I shall return to my life."

He said nothing.

"I mean, if my plan works, I can make a new home, where nothing can be taken from me, and no one can ever send me away again. If my plan works."

He said nothing.

"Rafe, say something."

He stopped pacing. "Your plan won't work."

"Oh."

She waited. No further comment ensued.

"When I said 'say something,' I didn't mean to say that," she said. "You are meant to say it is a brilliant plan."

"It isn't a brilliant plan."

"Say it is sure to succeed."

"It is sure to fail."

And if it failed... Where would she go then? No. She could not let herself believe that.

A chill shivered over her, despite the sunlight.

"Must you be so pessimistic?" she demanded. "Is that another thing you learned at earl school? Lessons in pessimism, after your lessons in presumptuousness, perfidiousness, and pettiness."

He shook his head. "I published a pamphlet telling the truth about Katharine, but no one wanted to know. Ventnor countered with his lies, and look at the way people ate those up. Even as the lies grew more and more ridiculous, still people preferred them to the truth. Amid all the rumors you heard about me, did anyone ever mention that Katharine had a naturally occurring illness of the mind?"

"No."

"Think about that. People would rather believe in your wrongdoing than in Percy's, because that keeps their world the same as it always was."

"I'm not listening to you."

"You should. You must. Thea, this optimism of yours, it will—"

"Don't you dare mock my optimism." Anger rose in a familiar wave. "Optimism was my family's food and drink when we had little else. Optimism is how my father rose from the son of a poor warehouse clerk to a wealthy merchant. You aristocrats, never daring to get enthusiastic about anything. We cannot afford to be pessimists, did you never consider that? Of course you're miserable, when you..." She remembered herself and her cheeks heated. "Forgive me. Your loss was far greater than my own."

Dismissing her clumsy words with a shake of his head, Rafe crossed the room toward her. "I do not mock you. But have you not had enough heartache without setting yourself up for more? Your openness and *joie de vivre*—your resilience puts me to shame, and you..."

He reached out and touched her hair, his caress as light as the breeze.

"You do like me," she whispered.

"They'll crush you again, and I would hate to see you hurt."

He did not wish to see her hurt? He said those words while looking right at her, his expression so concerned? Truly, he had no idea.

She stepped back. He dropped his hand and Thea hugged her middle. "The Knight family—I believed we would always be there for each other, and I wanted so badly to do well for them. Then suddenly, everything I believed in was gone. Yet I did nothing wrong."

"I know."

"I did what I thought was right, yet I ended up punished and exiled. And I will not accept this injustice, when I have the slightest chance to put it right. You cannot understand, when you have all..." She waved an arm around her. "This. But this pamphlet, my dreams—they are all I have."

"Not quite true," he said.

He was right. She did have more: She had memories. Wonderful memories. Of him, of their kisses, their laughter, his strong arms and gentle heart, their conversations and play. How magical and marvelous that she could always take a piece of him with her, of this gentle, caring man who berated himself for failing his wife, when his only failure was that he could not see how much more he had to give. He had given Thea only a tiny piece of himself, true, but that would be enough. It had to be enough. He wasn't inviting her to stay here in his beautiful house. He wasn't inviting her into his life at all. He was telling her to leave. He was telling her...

"I beg your pardon?" she said, realizing he had spoken and she had missed the words. "What did you just say?"

"I said, you'll be rich soon."

She snorted. "The pamphlet will not make money. It will cost me dearly. I shall sell those items I bought on your account to pay for it."

"I mean your dowry. Fifteen thousand pounds. When I called on your father in London, he agreed to give it to me. My solicitor is making arrangements so it comes to you instead."

Her knees failed her, and Thea plopped down on the nearest chair.

"You villain," she said, her voice cracking. "How dare you do something like that?"

"It seemed right."

"It makes it hard for me to hate you."

"It's better for us both if you do hate me." He headed for the door. "There is no place for you here."

"I never said there was." She sat up straight and donned her most imperious look. "I shall go, of course, but when I'm good and ready, and not before."

"Fine. Stay. Go. Don't stay. Don't go. I don't care what you do."

With another shake of his head, Rafe disappeared out the door.

AFTER THEA HAD CHANGED into a dry gown and tidied up, she headed downstairs. In the foyer, a pair of maids shot her a look and whispered behind their hands before darting away. But no one came to throw her out, so she went into the library, where she found a thick letter from Arabella and tore it open.

Enclosed in Arabella's letter was a note from Helen. Thea scanned her sister's words hungrily, relieved to confirm she had married Mr. Russell at the Scottish border, as planned, and the happy couple were heading to Brighton to flaunt their marriage before fashionable society.

"Perhaps now you'll believe it's true love, for we haven't a single

regret between us," Helen wrote. "*Except one: I regret I had to leave that smelly greatcoat behind.*"

A reflection in the glass caught her eye. Thea whirled around, to face Sally and Martha.

It seemed an age before anyone spoke.

"So. You are not really the countess," Sally said. "You are neither his wife, nor his lover."

"I was pretending."

Thea's voice sounded too small and she didn't like that in herself. Whatever else happened, she had vowed that never again would she give up her voice.

"I am sorry I deceived you," she said, loud and clear. "It was to help a friend and my sister. I was pretending to be someone I am not."

To Thea's surprise, Sally responded with a broad smile. "We've all done that. What woman hasn't?"

Thea waited. Surely there would be more. Surely they would next tell her how awful she was.

But Martha only shrugged. "That explains the other matter."

"What other matter?"

"The matter of separate beds. I thought he needed some medicine to help him, but he got upset at my suggestion."

Thea thought of Rafe's hard body pressed against hers —*exceedingly desirable*, he had said—and her cheeks heated. "He was being honorable."

"If a man could impregnate a woman with a look, you would birth triplets," Martha said.

"Um." Thea thought about this. "That's rather disturbing, Martha."

The older woman only laughed.

"His lordship has agreed to let me stay a little longer," Thea added, glossing over the details of their argument. "But I should move out of the countess's chambers. If you have a smaller room?"

"Moving you will be work," Sally said. "You want to make more work for us, *my lady*?"

"Of course not. But I'm not a real lady. My name is Thea. Thea Knight."

"Have you learned to play billiards yet, Thea Knight?" Martha asked. "We'll see you after dinner."

And with that invitation, the pair turned to leave.

Thea stared at their backs, perplexed at their lack of anger. But as they seemed to have no interest in scolding her, she risked another question.

"Sally, may I ask—"

"No."

"You and Lord Ventnor seemed to know each other."

Sally hesitated, before turning back. "After Katharine died, I went to London, where I encountered Lord Ventnor. We argued, and he threatened me. I was frightened and I came back here. To my home."

"Today, you ran away from him. That must have been some argument."

"It was very unpleasant."

"About?"

Again, Sally hesitated before answering. "Katharine. It seemed to me that Ventnor did not grieve her suitably. I told him as much, and he didn't like that." She sighed. "I beg you, Thea, I prefer no questions. Even if we are friends."

Without another word, they went out.

Alone again, Thea turned to Arabella's letter, which contained an account of her trip to London to order a costume for the Prince Regent's party. The letter ended with a paragraph so astonishing that Thea had to read it twice:

I have long suspected you are withholding information and now I have proof. During our journey, we stopped in a market town, where we watched a short play performed by a traveling theatre troupe. It was astoundingly similar to your pamphlet: It told the tale of Rosamund, a winsome lass who was cruelly wronged by two dastardly knaves. (Although the ending was...surprising.) Why are they performing your story? You will write immediately and withhold nothing of your adventures.

Despite everything—or perhaps because of it—Thea began to laugh. Her impromptu performance in the coaching inn that night must have been seen by someone connected to a traveling theatre company, who thought it worthy of a repeat. Now people were hearing her story in a way she had never dreamed!

Grateful for the distraction, Thea dropped into the big leather chair and reached for quill, ink, and paper. Much of what she had withheld could not be put on paper, but Arabella deserved something for her nagging. If she wanted adventures, well, Thea could pen a whole novel of them!

Oh. *Oh.* She had never considered that. The sole purpose of her pamphlet was to clear her name; never had she imagined writing for fun. But it would be fun, wouldn't it?

And it would certainly help take her mind off...people.

It could begin as a letter, claiming to tell the true story of a young lady, who was—yes! An outcast with a secret fortune. She was kidnapped and taken to a castle by a cruel sorcerer who carried a magical ebony stick. It would be a proper castle, of course, gloomy and crumbling, with skeletons and musty books and creatures in jars. And a ghost, who came out of the portraits. No— Who came out of the lake.

Thea looked past her own reflection to the lawn and the lake beyond. Her eyes still burned with the image of Rafe, wading toward her, brandy-colored eyes intent, water trickling down those hard muscles, his body both powerful and scarred.

Suddenly, every part of her ached. Rafe did not want her, and even understanding why did not ease that hurt. One more day, he had said. What if they did have one more day? What if she went to him now and said, "Just one more evening?"

No. That would be a mistake. Rafe had turned out to be as unreliable as everything else in her world. There was no rock for her to stand on here, nothing but the same shifting sands as everywhere else. Rafe offered nothing but another adventure, to keep her entertained until she found her way home.

Thea forced her mind back to her letter.

Not a ghost, she decided, but a cursed man who came out of the lake. He was the rightful heir to the castle, but the sorcerer cursed him when he was swimming, and now he could not leave the water until the curse was broken.

Which meant he would spend most of the story nearly naked and dripping wet.

Arabella would be appalled. Excellent. Arabella was hilarious when she was appalled.

The heroine would seek to free the man in the lake from his curse and overthrow the evil sorcerer. And when the man was freed, he would take the brave, beautiful heroine in his arms and promise her—

Nothing.

Rafe wanted her, but not enough. Because no one ever wanted her enough.

Thea quashed the thought. No more self-pity. She would think about nice things and fun things, things that did not make her ache.

Resolute, she dipped her quill pen into the ink and began to write.

CHAPTER 19

Two nights. Two nights had passed and Thea still hadn't left and Rafe still hadn't talked to her. Now he was sick of his greenhouse and his plants were annoying him. Useless plants, just sitting there, doing nothing, silent and smirking and smug.

The greenhouse door opened and Martha came in.

"There are meant to be new plants arriving," he grumbled, before she could speak. "Why are they not here yet? How difficult can it be? They put the plants on the boat, they put the boat on the water, they send the boat over here. Yet here we are. No plants."

"You said the new shipment was due in September."

"So?"

Martha spread her hands. "So it is August."

"How is that relevant?"

"You are unreasonable."

"I am not."

Two nights. Two nights of lying in bed, tangled in his sheets, his argument with Thea repeating in his mind like a particularly bad play whose ending he couldn't change. Rafe had cleverly filled the previous day by demanding the land steward take him on a tour of the estate to discuss the upcoming harvests, but now he had another day to fill. And there would be another day after that, and then another. Day after day after day. With all these blasted plants. Useless, silent, sulking plants.

"Would you call me a pessimist?" he asked Martha. "Would you call me a grumpy, miserable, villainous beast?"

"No," Martha said. "I would call you things in Spanish instead."

"You're as helpful as these blasted plants."

"You know what these blasted plants are? They are hope." She indicated them with a sweep of her arm. "It is an act of great faith, to plant a seed, to nurture something fragile, yet you do that every day. And when I use these plants to make medicines, crude as they are, in the hope I can cure the sick... We are ignorant, clumsy, but still we try, and every attempt is an act of hope."

"You make hope sound like a kind of madness."

"Yes, but a madness we need to live. You have lost a lot, I know, but I think you have not lost hope."

Two nights. Two nights of staring at the dark, never daring to hope. One and a half days, staying away from Thea, because she belonged to a world where he did not. They said she passed her time in the library, writing a very long letter to her friend. They said that, and Rafe knew it was true, because he had peered through the library door. As he watched, she had paused to stare out the window, absently sweeping the end of her quill pen over her cheek, then she had laughed softly and started writing again. If he were a different man, he would have crossed that library floor, slid his hands over her shoulders. She would have tilted back her head so he could drop a kiss on her lips and ask her about her letter.

"Anyway, you have a visitor," Martha informed him

"I never have visitors."

"But this week, you have two. First that horrible viscount, now this amusing bishop. I did not like the first visitor, but this one, I like. This one, he can stay."

RAFE SPED BACK to the house, pausing only to send a maidservant for Sally, to ensure Nicholas would have everything he needed, but when he reached the doorway to the drawing room, he lingered, unnoticed.

Thea and Nicholas sat with a plate of cakes and a pot of tea, chatting like old friends. He'd forgotten how airy and appealing the drawing room could be, with its blue and white decor catching the light from the courtyard garden. Something about the scene stirred a nostalgic yearning inside him, something in the way Thea smiled at the bishop as she poured his tea. It was an odd feeling, as though Rafe had brought the greenhouse inside with him and glass walls separated him from the rest of the world; his fists clenched with an unfamiliar urge to smash them, chased by the chilling realization that he did not know how.

He stepped into the room and they saw him. Perhaps Thea was no longer angry with him, or she had forgotten she was angry, because she smiled, a smile of delight. The glass walls melted away and Rafe felt that here, he belonged.

Strange notion, considering that "here" was his own blasted house.

Then she must have remembered that she despised him, for her haughty mask came down. Before, she had donned that mask in a game that included him, but now she used it to keep him out, and he minded that. He minded very much.

"Rafe, my boy, come join us," the bishop said. "Miss Knight and I are having a delightful time."

"So I see." Rafe wandered across the blue carpet, his appetite stirred by the fragrance of the tea and fresh cakes. "What brought you here, Nicholas?"

"Thought I'd stop by to see how your marriage is coming along."

"'Stop by?' It's two days' travel." Nicholas beamed and Rafe dipped his head to study the cakes so he wouldn't look at Thea. Instead, he found himself looking at her fingers, tracing the blue flowers on the teapot's handle. "Besides, there's no marriage."

"Yet Miss Knight is still here."

"She won't leave."

"Oh, you poor boy, to be a mighty earl, yet unable to stop these helpless young women from moving into your house."

He looked up to see Nicholas wink at Thea, who grinned in response. Rafe felt a peculiar warmth at the two of them getting along so well. Then Thea glanced at Rafe. Her grin softened into a secret smile for him, and Rafe warmed for a different reason.

"Why," Nicholas continued merrily, his bright eyes seeing everything, "she might never leave."

"Oh, I'll leave." Thea tossed her head, smiles gone. "When my pamphlet is ready. Lord Pessimism here says my plan won't work, but the world will learn the truth behind my so-called scandal, when they read *The Tale of Rosamund*."

"*The Tale of Rosamund*?" Nicholas repeated. "I know that one."

"You cannot do."

"Isn't Rosamund the winsome lass—"

"Yes?" Thea prompted.

"Who was cruelly wronged—"

"Yes," Thea said.

"By two dastardly knaves?"

"Yes!" Thea clapped her hands and laughed. "Don't tell me—you saw a theatre performance of it? Arabella did too."

"Outside London. That's why the story sounded familiar: It was about that vile snot Percy Russell and your scandal, Miss Knight. Peculiar ending, though." Nicholas screwed up his face in thought. "That reminds me, Rafe. Our friend William Dudley was performing in it. I stopped for a chat, and he said he had left Ventnor's employ to join that traveling theatre troupe, and that—Oh my."

He stopped short, his eyes on the doorway. Sally stood there, her posture a mix of belligerence and uncertainty, as if she was torn between leading a charge and running away. Before Rafe could say a word, Nicholas clapped his hands.

"It's you. It is you, isn't it?" The bishop was beaming at Sally. "How did you end up here?"

Thea was frozen, teacup in midair, looking as puzzled as Rafe felt.

"You know Sally too?" Thea asked. "How does everyone know Sally?"

Nicholas still looked delighted. "'Sally,' now, is it? We know her from London. Oh my, this is too marvelous! All this time, she's been living under your noses, and no one knew because you never have visitors."

Sally was swaying, her booted feet edging along the carpet.

"The devil are you talking about, Nicholas?" Rafe said. "This is Sally Holt, my housekeeper. She was Katharine's companion."

"Perhaps she was. But this is also Miss Sarah Holloway. Once the toast of London's stage."

Rafe looked from Nicholas to Sally and back again. "You must be mistaken."

"Sarah Holloway, beloved actress in London for three seasons —or was it four?—until she mysteriously disappeared." He scratched his chin as he studied the housekeeper. "I'd never mistake that splendid red hair and that wonderful pair of—"

"Nicholas."

"—Elbows."

"But Sally Holt can't be Sarah Holloway," Thea broke in. "Certainly, the names are similar, but Sally has lived here all her life. Perhaps you saw her performing in one of the amateur productions here, and you got confused because they both have red hair. Apparently, Sally was a marvelous actress."

"Couldn't have done. I haven't visited Brinkley End in twenty years."

Rafe leaned back against the windowsill and regarded Sally, who was listening to their exchange tensely. "You never thought to mention this?"

She met his eyes coolly. "You never thought to ask. 'Tis no secret I went to London while you were gone."

"And became a famous actress?"

"Fame, by its very definition, defies secrecy."

A disingenuous reply, for Sally knew as well as he that most people on this estate and in nearby villages would never travel outside the parish and rarely saw newspapers; the theatre in London was so far removed from their rural world, it might as well be a foreign land. Sally Holt was one of their own; after returning from years in London, they would have taken her back in without a second thought.

"You never told me." Thea sounded betrayed. "I heard people talk of you, Sarah Holloway, the actress who disappeared. Is that why Lord Ventnor was so shocked to see you?"

"Ventnor," Nicholas repeated thoughtfully. "Ventnor was Sarah Holloway's patron. It was he who secured her the position at the theatre. Put lots of actresses' noses out of joint, but no one could deny she was extremely talented and beautiful."

Rafe straightened. "Ventnor was your patron?" he asked, but Sally was already turning away, saying, "If that was all, my lord, I must see to the arrangements for our guest."

"You said you and Ventnor argued over Katharine," Thea said.

Nicholas wore a rare frown. "There must be more to it than that. Rumors were circulating that one of Miss Holloway's love affairs was with Lord Ventnor's wife."

"That was a lie!" Sally cried, whirling back around.

"And she disappeared shortly after that."

Silence fell over the drawing room. Another figure appeared in the doorway: Martha, watching, her expression thoughtful. Sally's mouth was clamped shut. Pink stained her cheeks.

Then Nicholas held out his hands to Sally. "Oh, I do apologize, my dear. I thought everyone knew of your... In London—"

A spoon clattered onto a saucer. Thea was glaring at Nicholas. "So you should apologize, Bishop," she said. "Rumors and gossip are foul and horrid, and I will not have them repeated. To say that Sally had a love affair with any woman! That cannot be true."

Thea's naivety curled through the room like the steam rising from the tea. No one seemed to know where to look.

Sally cleared her throat. "It is a little bit true. As the bishop said, I did have love affairs with women. Such liaisons are more common than many realize, Thea, but no one speaks of it, because those in power prefer to hide women like me." She made a dismissive sound and her lips curled in a humorless smile. "Watch and you will see," she added, her tone harsh. "Now Lord Luxborough knows, he will turn me out."

Rafe hardly heard her. Once more, he leaned back against the windowsill, his eyes roaming unseeingly around the drawing room. Ventnor had been Sally's patron. Sally had been Katharine's companion. Ventnor had wanted Katharine locked away. Katharine had died in Rafe and Sally's care.

Around him, the others were chattering on about Sally's proclivities as though that mattered a fig. If they had met some of the people he'd met in the world, they'd be as difficult to shock as he.

"Your preferences were well known in certain circles in London," Nicholas said, reaching for his teacup. "You seemed to flaunt it, even." He glanced at Thea. "Many male hearts were broken, and a few tidy sums of money were lost by those who wagered they could change her ways."

"And here comes the sermon about sins. Do make it a good one," Sally prompted bitterly. "I expect lots of hellfire and gnashing of teeth."

Nicholas's eyes twinkled at her over his cup. "I must disappoint you, my dear. I am too familiar with human nature in all its wondrous, confusing variety to pass judgment on the ways in which we love."

"As for the rest of the rumor: I had no liaison with Lady Ventnor," Sally said. "She wanted to talk about Katharine, but Lord Ventnor had forbidden it, so we met in secret. Percy Russell saw us. It was he who started the rumors of an affair."

"About his own mother." Nicholas shook his head. "Disgusting little snot."

"The rumors upset Ventnor, and he ordered me to leave London. When I refused, he sent a man with a knife, who threatened to carve up my face if I didn't go."

"No! Sally!" Thea was on the edge of her seat. "How terrible of Lord Ventnor to believe such rumors. I grow so tired of people believing false things."

"Oh but he didn't believe them." Sally's voice dripped with scorn. "Yet people were laughing at him and Ventnor cannot bear to be laughed at. So I came back here. Here was home, and I realized I'd rather be at home than have all the fame in London."

She brushed invisible dirt off her hands. "So, my lords, if this interrogation has ended, I have errands to attend to."

"No," Rafe said. "This interrogation has not ended."

He was dimly aware of the faces turned to him, Thea, Nicholas, Martha, but all he saw was Sally, with her red hair and beautiful features and uncertain eyes. Sally, who had transformed herself after Katharine's death; Sally, who had benefited from Ventnor's help.

Sally, who spun on her heel and headed for the door. She was fast, but Rafe was faster, covering the distance in a few long strides. Martha leaped into the room as he slammed the door shut and stood before it like a sentry.

"You took favors from Ventnor," Rafe said. "Did you do favors for him too?"

Pressing her lips together, Sally looked away.

"That man put my wife in an asylum, in appalling conditions. After I freed her, he wrote me weekly, insisting I do the same. That man preferred to spread lies about me than lift a finger for her care. *That* is the man you befriended?"

"We were never friends," she snarled.

"Yet he rewarded you." He advanced on her. "What the hell did you do to Katharine that Ventnor saw fit to reward you?"

Sally's face twisted as she fought emotion, tears welling. Blood rushed in Rafe's ears and through his limbs; over it came the sound of Thea calling his name.

He ignored her. Ignored them all. Ignored everything but Sally and the guilt written on her face.

Then with a shudder, Sally covered her face with her hands and breathed, deep, ragged breaths. When she finally looked up, her eyes were red. She laughed shakily, ruefully. "I always knew this day would come, the day my past would catch up with me, and bring with it my sorrow and shame."

"You were a popular actress and well-known Sapphist, my dear," Nicholas pointed out gently. "It's sheer chance no one identified you sooner."

Sally shook her head. "I am not ashamed of either of those things, even if the world wants me to be. What haunts me is what came before."

She looked back at Rafe.

"What came before was Katharine," he said.

"Yes. Katharine."

"What did you do to her? What the hell did you do to her?"

A tiny smile touched Sally's lips, though her expression was haunted by sorrow. "I loved her. That's what I did. I loved Katharine, and that is why she is dead."

CHAPTER 20

Rafe fell back against a wall, as if he needed it to hold him up. Sally was talking nonsense. Utter claptrap. He must tell her that, tell them all that. Yell it at Thea, gawping at them with caring concern. Shout it at Nicholas, sitting forward, compassion oozing from his pores. Bellow it at Martha, drumming her fingers on the crest of a chair.

Katharine was dead because Rafe had failed to care for her. Every day for years, he had failed her. Rage surged through him, rage at Sally for trying to steal his guilt.

But as she dropped into a chair and sat like a defeated penitent with her head bowed and hands clasped, his anger dissolved as swiftly as it had risen. Whether or not Sally was right, she believed it to be true.

"Katharine never knew how I loved her," Sally said quietly. "Though love is not less real for remaining unspoken. Falling in love with someone one cannot have is a time-honored tradition; it is one thing we all have in common."

"But Ventnor—"

"Ventnor gave me no rewards." She looked up and heaved a weary sigh. "I blackmailed him."

As abruptly as if the wall had given him a shove, Rafe started pacing, propelled across the floor. "About Katharine's illness? If people didn't believe me when I told the truth, why would he fear them believing you?"

"Not that. As you said: Ventnor was terrified the world would learn the truth of Katharine's illness. Having her secluded in a country house did not ease his fears; he wanted her locked up in an asylum and forgotten." She briefly closed her eyes. "He sent men to kidnap her."

A chorus of gasps sounded through the room. Rafe stopped short, struck silent, staring at Sally.

"We were walking in the woods, and we became separated. I heard her scream, I ran and... She was fighting them off. I had a gun. I shot one, in the shoulder, and tried to shoot the other one. They ran away."

"Why the hell did you not tell me?" Rafe demanded.

"I thought I could protect her myself. I did protect her. I *did*."

"You should have told me."

Sally didn't reply. She was digging her thumb into her palm as she gazed into the distance. Into the past. The past that lived with them always. Even in this bright, airy room, the past cast its ugly shadow. This drawing room had been painted sage green in his mother's day. He could still see it, see her, his vivacious mother. And his indulgent father, his rambunctious brothers, and their guests, the constant parade of guests. All the people who had passed through this room, all the stories that had been left untold, the words unspoken, the emotions buried.

"When we lived in the Dower House," Sally finally said, "Katharine was calm and well. She was herself. Magnificent."

"Like a wild horse," Rafe said.

Sally's face brightened. "*Yes*. That was her. Those were the happiest months of my life. But you were looking for more treatments. You talked of taking her to the Continent."

"I wanted her to receive the best care."

"Do you remember, I volunteered to come with you? But you said there was no need to drag me away from my home, you'd hire someone else. I would have gone to the ends of the earth if it meant being with Katharine."

Helplessly, Rafe's eyes sought Thea. Their gazes wove together, and it was all he could do not to cross the room and lay his head in her lap. But when she half rose, as if to come to him, as if he were calling to her, he swung away to face the window. He watched her reflection, the shadowy movement as she resumed her seat.

"I'm sorry. I had no idea. If I'd known how you felt," he said to the window, to his ghostly reflection, to the lawn and lake beyond.

"Yes, if you'd known." Bitterness soured Sally's tone. "For all I knew, you would have dismissed me, had you known. My father would have put *me* in an asylum, had he known. And if you'd known what Ventnor was attempting, you would definitely have taken Katharine away. It was selfish of me, but I was so sure I could protect her."

"You did save her," came Thea's voice.

"But the shock, the fright, what it did to her mind..."

On the lawn, a large black bird landed and fluttered its glossy wings. A second bird joined it.

"The crows," Rafe said.

"The crows," Sally confirmed. "The day after the kidnapping attempt, Katharine saw them: a dozen crows, gathering in the tree outside her window."

Rafe pressed his fingers to the glass, hardly seeing the sunny scene through the memory of the storm clouds rumbling over

Katharine's head that long-past afternoon. *You are as dark and silent as the crow, and with just as evil intent.*

Sally's words washed over him. "She became convinced the crows were coming for her, to do her harm. Her conviction grew, and sentences in that Gothic novel confirmed it, and she came to believe the kidnappers were from you. I hid the book, but she found it. I put laudanum in her drink, but she must have tricked me and not taken it."

"Then she saw a crow kill a sparrow," Rafe finished, "and the coming of the storm."

He turned back around. With great effort, as though her eyeballs weighed a ton, Sally looked at him. "My error in judgment will haunt me forever. I loved her, and I killed her. If I had told you, if I had not been so selfish..."

If, if, if, if, if.

"The kidnapping attempt," Rafe said. "She must have been terrified."

Sally smiled wanly. "You would have been proud of her, the way she fought. One of those men wears my bullet hole, but the other will carry Katharine's tooth marks till the end of his days."

The image of Katharine fighting off one of Ventnor's ruffians swelled in Rafe's mind. He thumped the window frame, the sting in his knuckles driving the picture away.

"We tried so bloody hard to keep her calm," he said. "That's what they recommend. Calm. Routine. Sympathy. Sunlight. And she went months without an episode, living a normal life. Then blasted Ventnor sends his blasted ruffians..."

"It was all Ventnor's doing, then," Thea broke in. "Neither of you is responsible for her death. Ventnor's actions led to his daughter's death, and he probably doesn't even care."

"He doesn't," Sally spat with loathing. "He even said her death solved his problem." With another deep breath, she stood.

"Master Rafe—I mean, my lord. I have so many regrets. I have tried to do right by you, since you came back. I have kept this house in readiness for the day you brought home another bride, to house a new, happy family. But perhaps my reasons for that were selfish too: Because if you could free yourself of the past, maybe I could too. I shall leave, now."

Rafe shook his head. Free himself of the past? He had lost himself in the selva for that, yet still the past pursued him. Once again, his gaze strayed back toward Thea, but this time, he could not bear looking at her. This time, the walls began to close in, air became short, his legs grew heavy. Nicholas was rising to his feet, Martha was frowning at him, Thea was saying his name in an echo that shuddered through his suddenly empty skull.

"I need to think," he managed to say, eyes on the door, forcing his legs to carry him away. Something in Sally's face stopped him as he reached her side. He put a hand on her shoulder. "You loved her. I am glad of it. She deserved to be loved."

Then his legs propelled him forward again, to make his escape.

In the oppressive foyer, Rafe headed numbly for the front door, but Thea's voice, calling his name, coiled around him like a rope. If only the whole blasted world would disappear, leaving nothing but him and Thea. She would chase away his shadows, and he would chase away hers.

As he pivoted back, she skipped through the doorway toward him, easily, assuredly, their quarrels forgotten. She pressed a hand to his chest, and it felt the most natural thing in the world to trail his knuckles down her cheek.

"It wasn't you," Thea whispered, her eyes searching his.

Then Nicholas joined them, and they lowered their hands in a futile charade of propriety.

"Forgive me," Rafe said. "I need some time alone. I need to think."

Nicholas laid a hand on his sleeve. "Then take time to think. And think of how it truly was not your fault Katharine died. Not yours, nor Sally's. You have believed the wrong story all these years. This is what I tried to tell you."

A disbelieving laugh curled out of Rafe's throat. "Oh no, old man, do not pretend you ever imagined this."

"Not this exactly." Nicholas tilted his head to consider. "Fair enough. Not this at all. But I never doubted you did everything you could for Katharine."

"Yet it wasn't enough."

Nicholas and Thea exchanged a look, and Rafe's feet shuffled on the checkered floor. His four limbs fought to take him in different directions: to run to London and tear off Ventnor's head; to pull Thea into his arms and lose himself in her; to dive into the lake and swim to exhaustion; to fall to his knees and weep.

"Miss Knight, if you might give us a moment?" Nicholas said.

"Very well."

Rafe kept his eyes on Thea as she returned to the drawing room, watching until the hem of her dress disappeared.

Nicholas pulled the door shut behind her and grinned. "She's truly enchanting, isn't she, our Miss Knight?"

"Now? You want to do your matchmaking *now*?" The man was impossible. "Yes, she is enchanting, but recall she is here only so I could secure the funds to finance the medicine business. If you want happy marriages and rooms full of babies, go bother Christopher and leave me alone. I'm the man who could not protect his first wife from her own father."

He turned to leave but Nicholas caught his arm in a surprisingly firm grip. "You know, my boy, I have always wondered about this plan of yours to make medicines. I wondered how much you wish to save others because you still long to save Katharine. For years, you had to watch someone you love suffer, while you stood helplessly by. I know something of how that feels. But know that Katharine died despite your love, not because of it."

Air was growing short again, and Rafe glanced longingly at the front door. "Does this sermon have a point?"

Nicholas smiled. "Now you are in love again, and you are afraid."

"I am not."

But he was something. Something that did feel a little like fear. He was accustomed to fear as a jolting thing, direct and acute, with teeth and claws or guns and knives. This was a different kind of fear. The kind of fear that used to grip him when he witnessed Katharine's torments, when he lay awake in the dark worrying what to do. This kind of fear turned him to stone, from his shoulders to his feet, and it was difficult to breathe, with stone lungs.

"Forgive me," he said again. "I need some time alone."

Nicholas nodded and stepped away, and Rafe escaped into the air.

CRANING her neck at a window in the drawing room, Thea watched Rafe stride across the lawn toward the woods, toward his greenhouse and his plants. Only when he was gone from view did she turn back to where Sally and Martha sat silently side by side.

"This is why you feared I would dismiss you," Thea said to Sally. "The secrets you kept."

"I cannot live here," Sally said. "Not after what I have done."

"No," Thea protested. "It was not your love that killed her, but Ventnor's fear. No one blames you."

"I blame me."

Martha laid her hand over Sally's. "You loved her."

269

Sally smiled. "I used to tell Katharine that her illness was due to her having so much spirit, her human mind could not contain it."

"And when she died, you had to grieve alone," Martha said.

"I cared for nothing anymore." Sally stared down at their joined hands. "I could not bear to stay here, so I went to London. I knew I could not harm Ventnor so I used him instead. When he offered his patronage—the whole notion thrilled him, I think—I decided to live as I pleased. After all, keeping secrets had led only to heartache. But in the end, I was sent running again."

Thea growled. "Yet another reason to loathe Ventnor, for chasing you away."

Sally suddenly grinned. "The man who threatened to cut me was the same man I had shot. He told me his shoulder ached in the cold; I told him I was sorry for it, and regretted not shooting him in the heart." Her mirth faded as she shook her head. "Listen to me, talking as if I were brave, when I could not even denounce Ventnor to the world. All I can do is look after those in my care, and I never let anyone be harmed on my watch."

"You never let yourself love again either," Martha said softly. "Time has passed. You have grieved. The past cannot hold you forever."

A look fluttered between Sally and Martha, a deeply intimate exchange that made Thea hastily pivot away. She stared out the window, where Rafe had gone. How foolish of her, to have quarreled with him, to have wasted so much time.

"If only we could show the world what Ventnor truly is, if the world could stop admiring itself long enough to listen." Thea turned back to the others. "It's not right, that everyone believes lies about you, so you were forced to skulk away like a villain."

Sally snorted. "They believe the lies because they fear me, though I would do them no harm."

"They should fear you." Thea laughed at Sally's outraged expression. "After all, you are rather fearsome."

A heartbeat later, Sally laughed too. "I am rather, aren't I?"

Thea paced away from the window, powered by her growing fury. "You were threatened, and Katharine was killed, and Rafe is slandered, and I was cast out. Ventnor and Percy and their ilk merrily go about their lives, while the rest of us live like exiles because of them."

"Who are we to take on a powerful viscount?" Sally gestured at the three of them. "A Sapphic actress, a foreigner, and a scandalous outcast."

A scandalous outcast with a fortune, Thea silently amended. She had not let herself think about the money Rafe had secured for her; Pa would be displeased if she took her dowry while remaining unmarried. But fifteen thousand pounds... Oh, the mischief that could buy! Her pamphlet would be the first step. Then she'd find a way to ruin Lord Ventnor's life. And then... Well, the world offered no shortage of villains for her to bring down.

And maybe, one day, news of her activities would reach Somersetshire and Rafe would—

No. She must not start painting futures where there were none. Optimism was one thing. Delusion was another. Rafe did not want to be in the world. The world was poorer without him in it, but that was his choice. She would concentrate her effort on the things she could do, and keep such magical notions for the outlandish stories that flowed from her pen.

WITH AS MUCH consciousness as an automaton, Rafe marched in the direction of his greenhouse, but in the woods, he impulsively veered off along another path, ending up in the small clearing, standing by Katharine's grave.

Dropping into a crouch, he ran his fingers through the glossy leaves of the morning glory vine and parted them to reread the words he had ordered carved on her headstone: *Come unto Me and I will give you rest.* Perhaps he had chosen those words for himself rather than for her; in the grip of his grief and guilt, he had found some solace in the thought that finally, Katharine could know peace.

So many years had passed, taking his grief with them. He had shed it during his travels, dropping bits behind him as he roamed. Such was the nature of grief; grief for his wife, for his father, for his brother. But guilt, ah, guilt never faded. Guilt lurked always, taunting him with the intolerable injustice that he remained, when all the rest were gone.

He let the vines drop over the stone and stepped back. He had planted this morning glory the day he left England, and never tended it since. It had flourished over the years. And, he realized, it was trained to grow over the grave. He took another few steps back. The grass was trimmed. The granite headstone was clean. Someone was tending this grave carefully, and that someone was not him.

Sally.

He had never guessed her feelings; he had been insensitive and she had hid them too well. He dug into his memory, turning up images like fresh earth. Katharine teaching Sally to play cricket on the lawn. The two of them at the pianoforte at night, singing in harmony, while he and John chatted idly over their port. Their heads bent together as they read or sewed.

"You were loved," he whispered to the grave. "You were loved."

Rafe left Katharine's grave and walked. He walked and walked and walked, until the light began to fade and he returned to the house. Inside, sounds came from the dining room: Thea and Nicholas, Sally and Martha; he lingered in a hallway, listening to their muffled merriment, then he continued his walk upstairs. A tray of food had been left in his room; numbly, he ate, exhausted from turning his life over. He had been so sure he could not change the past, but later, as he slid into sleep, his past broke around him, and rebuilt itself as something new.

WHEN RAFE AWOKE, the sunlight was already a golden glow slicing through the edges of the curtains. He washed and pulled on his trousers, stockings, and shirt, wondering at the quiet, belatedly realizing it was Sunday. Only a skeleton staff worked on Sunday, and Nicholas would have gone to church. Martha traveled further, to a Catholic Mass, and Sally had taken to accompanying her. Thea would likely have joined one of the parties. Or perhaps she had left for good.

Taking a neatly pressed neckcloth from the drawer full of neatly pressed neckcloths, Rafe paused and looked around his clean room. He stepped into the silent corridor, the wooden floorboards cool through his stockings, and studied the row of windows overlooking the courtyard garden. There were too many windows—an extravagance on his father's part, given the taxes on windows and glass—but they were all spotless. The candle sconces along the wall gleamed. The door frames were polished.

He opened the next door down; this room too was fresh and tidy, albeit with signs of Nicholas's occupation. Rafe shut the door and kept walking, opening each empty room in turn. In each room, he found the same thing: The curtains were closed against the sun, but nothing was under dust covers. Everything was clean and fresh. One might think the house was fully occupied, and that the entire family and their friends would soon come crowding back. Every day, while Rafe went about his life, scores of invisible hands were keeping this house ready to welcome its inhabitants home.

I have kept this house in readiness for the day you brought home another bride, to house a new, happy family, Sally had said. *Because if you could free yourself of the past, maybe I could too.*

Then Thea had arrived.

How right she had looked in the library, in the drawing room. How easily she had slid into place, as if she was the one the house had been waiting for. Thea, an outcast wearing her sister's clothes, the merchant's daughter who had learned to walk and talk like a lady, the optimistic survivor who had a plan for fixing her life that did not include Rafe.

Rafe walked on, faster now, until he reached her rooms. He knocked. No reply. His heart thudded a violent protest. Surely she would not leave without first saying goodbye?

His chest tight, Rafe shoved open her sitting room door; her belongings were still there. He crossed to the window and looked out, over the gardens, and beyond, the woodlands and fields. And below him, a flash of yellow.

A chestnut-haired woman in a butter-yellow gown was traipsing through the flowerbeds.

Rafe pressed a palm to the glass.

If he were a different man, he would walk with her in the sunlight.

And then he remembered that everything had changed, and if everything had changed, then he could change too. If he chose.

He could choose to keep living in fear of watching someone he loved suffer. Or he could choose to be that different man.

He wheeled away from the window and ran.

CHAPTER 21

F irst, Rafe found a straw bonnet and a yellow shawl, flung across a wooden bench. He set his neckcloth down beside them and walked on.

Next, he found a pair of women's shoes and stockings. Rafe peeled off his damp stockings and laid them down. Barefoot, he walked on.

Then, he found Thea.

She was drifting through the gardens, singing to herself, fingers brushing over the flowers and leaves. Her hair was pinned up but for a few tendrils and one persistently errant lock, and her feet were white against the green grass, beneath her yellow hem. It felt like a lifetime since he had touched her; it was a wonder he had stayed away.

She spared no thoughts for him, he supposed, lost as she was in the simple pleasure of watching butterflies in a flower garden on a warm summer's day. This was her strength. It was not the kind of strength the world valued, but its power stole his breath. This was what made her a survivor: her gift for transforming the ordinary world into a wondrous, captivating place. Despite everything, no one had taken that from her. If Rafe had his way, no one ever would.

An entrancing sense of lightness swept through him, rushing through his blood as if he had swallowed a drug, but no medicine's effect was this marvelous. Every fiber in his body itched to dance. Every detail, every color, was rendered clear and crisp. The light was brighter, the bees buzzed louder, the honeysuckle smelled sweeter than ever before.

Thea gave no sign that she had seen him, but the set of her shoulders made him suspect she had. Without looking at him, she skipped behind a hedge.

Motionless, Rafe waited. Her hair appeared over the top of hedge. Then her forehead. Then her smiling blue eyes. As soon as their eyes met, she ducked.

Chuckling, he went after her. Again she skipped away, until she paused to study an orange daylily, her face half turned toward him. Her dimple told him she was fighting a smile.

He edged closer. "You have left a trail of clothing in the garden."

She laughed. "It's terrible of me, I know. No decorum at all, and the sun must be doing perfectly horrid things to my complexion. But it feels so good, doesn't it? The sun on one's skin, the air so fresh and clean, and so much sky and nature! I shall have none of this in London."

The breeze crawled over him. He gripped one wrist in the other hand so hard it hurt.

"London," he repeated.

"I must leave tomorrow, if I am to distribute my pamphlets before the Prince Regent's costume party. So never fear, I shall no longer be such a trial for you, my lord."

"You are no trial."

"No, since you never see me. I suppose, in your mind, I am already gone."

"You are never gone from my mind."

Her shoulders flinched, and the flower under her hand quivered. Slowly, she turned to face him. He read the questions in her eyes, in those expressive blue eyes that he hoped to read every day.

"Never," he repeated.

A satisfied smile spread over her face. "Never?"

"You give me no peace at all."

"Good. You deserve to be tormented mercilessly." Abruptly, her smile shifted to distress. "No, no, I don't mean that," she added in a rush. "You don't deserve it. You've already suffered in ways you did not deserve... I'm so sorry. I say these things and—"

"Hush, Thea. I know what you meant."

"Are you... Um." She nibbled at her lip and tried again. "The bishop said you needed time alone, and I understand that is your nature, to need time alone, but I did worry about you. Are you...all right?"

"Very much so," he answered and realized it was the truth. "I always thought one could not rewrite the past, but it seems the past is not set in stone. We learn new things about our history, and view it from a fresh perspective, and when we see things we hadn't known were there, everything changes. That's what you want too, isn't it? To make your parents look at what happened anew?"

Her hands were restless. "Is it possible, then?"

"If I could truly change the past, I would make it so no one had ever hurt you. If I could, I would change the whole world, so it could never hurt you again."

"I wish I could do the same for you," she said.

Ah, but she could.

He could not touch her, not yet, not when she needed to make the choice. Instead, he rested his fingers on the lily between them, and waited for her to touch him.

In the end, it was not Thea who touched him, but a butterfly. Its wings, pale blue like the English sky, rested open as it landed on the back of his hand. Thea dropped her eyes to it and sidled closer. His senses were so heightened by her closeness that he was sure he felt the butterfly's tiny feet dancing on his thick skin.

"It's good luck to have a butterfly land on you," she whispered. "If you make a wish, the butterfly will fly away and use its magic to make your wish come true."

"I've never heard that before." His voice sounded hoarse.

"Of course not. I made it up just now."

"Well, if you made it up, then it must be true."

Her lips curved playfully and her eyes dipped to linger on his mouth; he was smiling too, broadly, helplessly, undignified dimple on display.

"Will you make a wish?" she prompted.

Rafe made a wish. A wish so bold and true that the butterfly immediately took flight. He followed it with his eyes, the pale-blue butterfly fluttering off in search of his wish. Silly butterfly was going in the wrong direction. His wish stood right in front of him, saying, "Look, it left footprints."

"Hmm?"

Thea brushed her fingers over the back of his hand, and *that* left prints. Sensation rippled over his skin like the breeze on the lake, until every inch of him shimmered with the feel of her.

He caught her hand in his. "I'll tell you my wish."

"Wishes must stay secret."

"But I must tell you the wish or it cannot come true. What do the butterflies say about that?"

Another butterfly, or perhaps it was the same one, flitted past. She followed its dance with her eyes and then looked back at him.

"Butterfly says Very Well."

"My wish…"

His real wish was too important to be left to a butterfly. It fluttered inside him, tender and hushed, its delicate wings stirring up a storm in his heart. He would ask her later; it was a serious question, and not one for butterfly games.

So instead he spoke a subordinate wish. "I wish to kiss you again."

"That is your wish?"

He wasn't sure if she sounded pleased or disappointed. Perhaps he should speak his real wish, and speak it he must, because otherwise, she would leave for London the next day. But it was because she meant to leave, because she had never intended to stay, that even with the magic of a million butterflies, Rafe could not quite muster the courage to say the words. Because her answer would change everything, and if the answer was not the one he longed to hear, they would never speak again, and everything would be lost.

"May I kiss you again?" he asked.

Her lips were parted, her eyelids heavy with welcome. Her inviting gaze did not leave his, not for a heartbeat, as she whispered her answer.

"Butterfly says Yes."

But he did not kiss her. Not immediately. He did not want to rush this. He wanted every precious second to last forever.

Thea's gaze dipped to his mouth, and she moistened her lips, her innocent dart of tongue shooting a heated invitation to his groin.

With an unsteady hand, Rafe caught that errant curl and slid his fingers down its length, transferring from the silk of her hair to the satin of her throat. He fancied he could feel her pulse, racing, too fast, for him. At least as fast as his own, which skittered with the frenzy of a dragonfly. Lowering his head, he brushed a kiss over her temple. She made a sound like velvet, and his heart skittered some more.

Next, his lips grazed her cheekbone, the sweet scent of her skin snaring him like an intoxicant. He crossed to kiss her ear on the other side. Once more, she made that velvet sound.

"Are you teasing me?" she whispered.

"Why would you say that?"

He let his lips hover against her jaw and she tilted her head back in an offering. He trailed kisses down her throat, lingering to taste her skin, to sense her pulse. She buried her fingers in his hair, summoning from his throat a matching velvet moan.

"Your wish didn't say where you meant to kiss me," she murmured, breathily.

He could barely pause between kisses to reply. "I did not speak my full wish, for I did not want to upset the butterfly's delicate sensibilities."

"If butterflies hear people's deepest wishes, they cannot be too delicate or they would fall from the sky in shock."

"Would it be shocked if I said I wished to kiss you everywhere?" He planted a kiss in the hollow under her throat and dragged his mouth away, just enough to look right into her eyes. "Everywhere."

She inhaled on a gasp. Her fingers slid out of his hair and feathered over his cheeks.

"No need," she breathed. "When you kiss me in one place, I feel it everywhere."

"Do you like that?"

"I always want more. I am greedy for your kisses, the way I'm greedy for syllabub."

Rafe chuckled. "This is better than syllabub."

"I find that hard to believe. Syllabub is the very pinnacle of pleasure."

"I promise, this is better."

"Um. I'm not sure about that."

Her teasing tone danced through his veins, firing his own need for more. More teasing, more touching.

More Thea.

He slid his fingers under the edge of her bodice and over her satiny skin. The cotton yielded only enough to reveal the first enticing swell of her breasts.

Rafe pressed his hungry mouth to that glorious skin, tasted her perfection with his lips, his tongue, his teeth. With another gasp, she tangled her fingers once more in his hair, tugging at his scalp. Longing and need cascaded through him.

"And that?" He glanced up, desperate to learn everything she liked. "Do you feel that everywhere?"

She seemed fascinated by this. "As though your kisses slide under my skin and into my blood, and then they bounce around inside me, showing up in..." Her boldness failed. "Unexpected places."

"I assure you, it is not unexpected. It is extremely expected."

He had barely kissed her, and already he was almost undone, his imagination firing at the thought of her unexpected places, at the thought of planting his kisses there. Not to mention his own unexpected places, which were behaving *exactly* as expected.

Staggering a few steps, Rafe propped himself on a low stone wall to level their faces. When he parted his legs, she glided unhesitatingly between them. He held her steady at her waist, and almost immediately her hands moved over him, those irrepressible hands with their need to touch. Closing his eyes, Rafe surrendered to the warmth of the sun, and the lazy buzzing of bees, and Thea's explorations, tormenting his throat, his shoulders, his chest.

Where she stilled, her palm pressed against his muscles. "I can feel your heart beating. Hard and fast. You have a strong heart."

"You do that." He did not know if he meant that she made his heart beat fast and hard, or if she made it strong. It needed to be strong, because of the way it beat near her. "Because I want you."

"Um."

She fisted her hand in his shirt. Her breathing came jaggedly, and he opened his eyes to see her looming over him, her expression fierce.

"You like that," he growled, her ardor turning his desire savage. "You like knowing how much I want you."

"Who doesn't want to be wanted, when it's someone they want too? Someone one would pursue to the ends of the earth." Still her hands roamed, haphazardly, fighting his shirt to travel over his skin. "I liked it when you kissed my throat."

He answered with a rough sound that might have been "Yes," and threw back his head that she might brand his throat with her fury of hot kisses. Impatiently, she nudged aside his shirt to reach his collarbone. There, she bit him. He groaned against the surge of lust, his hands drifting up the curve of her waist and ribcage in an exploration of his own, pausing beneath the alluring softness of her breasts.

"Would you pursue me that far?" she asked.

"How far?"

"To the ends of the earth."

"Would you make me?"

Instead of answering, she caught his head and held him fast to kiss him, her lips plundering his, feverish, ferocious. She touched her tongue to his and retreated; he caught her and back she came, and then it was his turn to plunder, to explore her mouth with his tongue, to stroke her and madden her and let her know how intensely he wanted her. More than he wanted air, certainly, for he was light-headed by the time she broke away and brushed his hair from his forehead.

"Was it your wish to touch me too?" she whispered, her eyes searching his. "Because all these kisses, they are filling up inside me, and all these places want your touch."

His hands rode up the last few inches to cup her breasts, to seek out and tease her nipples, evoking a whimper that had him pressing his heels into the earth, grounding himself so he would not grab that yellow bodice in his fists and tear the blasted gown from her body.

They could not make love if they were not married. Of course, they would marry. But he still had to ask. She still had to say yes.

"Thea, beautiful, enchanting Thea... We can't."

"But I want more. I shan't take too much. I'll leave you what you need. I only want a bit more."

Rafe did not think he could give only a bit more. He wanted to give her everything, and take all of her.

"More of what?" he managed.

"Of you. I know you need to be alone sometimes." Her voice was tender and pleading. "But give me a glimpse of you, of the man you are when no one else is watching, when you are alone and you are purely you." She nipped his earlobe, and he made a frog-like sound that caused her to giggle. A blaze of desire seared through him, but even in the midst of this torment, Rafe had to laugh, laugh with the sheer joy of being, and being with her. When she looked into his eyes, he fancied he saw her spirit and hoped she saw his too, that he might be with her as if he were alone.

Alone with her.

The funny thing was, he had never felt less alone in his life.

"Thea, first... There's something I must do first..."

Steeling himself against the throb in his loins and the lust clawing at his limbs, Rafe slid out from between her and the wall. Her palms were pressed to her cheeks, her delicious pink lips parted, her eyes so bright she looked fevered.

But before he could ask his question, she said, "Yes," and she knew, she had answered!

And then she added, "First, you must catch me."

She took two steps backward, and then whirled about and ran. Her yellow skirts flew around her, her hair freeing itself to stream behind her.

She wanted to play, to make him work for it.

The anticipation amplified his desire, thrilling him, startling him.

And when she had gained some distance, Rafe inhaled deeply and gave chase.

CHAPTER 22

Thea did not know what she was doing.

All she knew was that every minute she passed with Rafe felt right, and today was all she had. Rafe's wish was to kiss her; he never said he wanted her to stay. He had chosen not to be in the world; she could not ask for more. No matter, she had to leave anyway, put the world right and start her life again.

But that still gave her today, and whatever memories today would bring.

She ran toward the lake, the grass springy under her bare feet. No one was around, not on a Sunday afternoon, and the quiet lent the garden an air of enchantment, as if it were magically hidden from the world. She risked a glance over her shoulder: Rafe was loping after her in pursuit. They both knew he could catch her easily if he wished. Yet he played her game.

Laughing with her scarce breath, Thea darted into a copse of trees, beyond which lay the secluded part of the lake, where she had swum alone. In the trees, she glanced around again. No Rafe. Surely he had not tired of the game so soon?

But as she reached the last of the trees, a sound had her whirling, to see Rafe, grinning and close. He pounced, catching her around the waist from behind. With a squeal, she grabbed the nearest tree. His breathing was ragged in her ear, his chest hot against her back.

I must remember this, she thought, and soaked up every sensation, seared it into her memory.

"Were you aware," he murmured, his rough breathiness curling deliciously over her ear, "that your dress is fastened with four buttons?"

"I'm aware."

"Hmm."

With gentle hands, he gathered her hair over her shoulder. Then he opened the first of her four buttons.

"One," he said.

His hair tickled her neck, his breath burned her spine, his lips caressed her skin. Everything, she reminded herself. She must remember everything. The way he touched her, his heat and his scent, the way her body clamored for more.

Another button popped open. "Two."

As his lips slid down her spine, his hands glided up her sides. He cupped her breasts again, teased her nipples. She gasped and arched, then his hands were gone.

Another button. "Three."

Her breasts wanted his touch again. Her skin wanted his kisses.

"Four."

Another breath, another kiss. Then his heat was gone, and she had only the tree under her hands and her gown gaping open and every inch of her body pulsing, burning, yearning for his touch. He surrounded her again, his hands pleasuring her breasts. Every touch sent thrilling messages express to her quim.

"Do you like that?" he murmured from behind her.

"Yes," she managed.

"Better than syllabub?"

"Um. I don't know."

With a rough laugh, he released her and she spun to face him. He looked hungry and fierce, and fully intent on her. He was smiling, a promising, mischievous smile, for her, for their game, for their secret, wicked chase, just the two of them, alone in this enchanted wood.

Laughing, she turned again to run toward the lake, but lust had weakened her limbs and she stumbled. She feared she might fall, but no— He was there. Easily, he lifted her. She released a cry of exhilaration, for she was soaring through the air, flying free yet anchored in his arms, as he carried her to the grass by the water's edge. Around them, the weeping willows tumbled in a curtain, letting in dapples of sunlight and the sound of lapping waves, keeping out the world.

Her feet were clumsy, but his hands were nimble: They skimmed over her shoulders, sliding her gown over her body until the fabric pooled at her feet. He lifted her again and then somehow, she was kneeling on the welcoming grass, her hips bracketed by his knees, like she was a queen and he was her throne, a queen wearing nothing but her shift, queen of a million unruly sensations.

His arms encircled her, as he pressed his palms onto her thighs, searing her through the thin cotton of her shift. She leaned back into him, her hands finding his powerful thighs, by her side. Closing her eyes, she dropped her head back against his shoulder.

"Oh my," she breathed.

His mouth was at her ear. "Everywhere."

The throbbing in her quim must be like a call, calling to his hands, for he slid them relentlessly up her thighs, pushing her chemise before him. He did not pause, and she lifted her hips so that he could slide the fabric up her body, and when he murmured, "Raise your arms," she complied.

Thea opened her eyes to see her chemise land on the grass in front of them, followed by his shirt. His bare arms circled her again, and she pressed her naked back to his naked chest, his heat melding with hers. She looked down at her body, exposed for the first time to a man, to the air. Rafe's weathered hands were stark against the creaminess of her skin, one hand on her thigh, the other on her belly, and both sliding upward, to where all their kisses pooled and bounced impatiently beneath her skin.

Once more, she let her eyes close, dropped her head against his shoulder, entrusted herself to him. He cupped one breast, assured and demanding and delicious, and then pressed his fingers firmly between her legs.

Pleasure spiraled through her. A high startled cry flew from her mouth. She dug her fingers into his thighs and drew ragged breaths. Not for a heartbeat did those fingers pause in their magic, as they coaxed sweet, hot sensations into wild cartwheels under her skin.

When he spoke, his breath was hot and his voice was rough.

"There is only one person in my world right now, and that is you. And only one thing, and that one thing is bringing you such pleasure, through your body and all the way to your soul, that you will never forget my touch."

"Never," she whispered in agreement.

She would remember every detail, remember how she much she craved him, his heat, his voice, his fingers doing whatever they were doing. How pleasure pooled and swelled in this relentless, transcendent torment. She felt her own wetness, caught her own scent, breathed him in, and let out the breath on a moan.

"Well?" His voice vibrated through her, and she tried to focus on what he was doing but her mind could hold onto nothing but the sensations shimmering through her like sunlight on the waves. "Better than syllabub?"

"Um." She fought for breath, caught a straggling wit. "I don't know."

Rafe's laughing groan rumbled through his chest, rumbled through her, but she regretted her answer when the next moment found her alone. But he had left her only to arrange their discarded clothing into a makeshift bed, and he gently tugged her down onto it. He leaned over her, face and hair silhouetted against the willows: another image to remember.

He lowered his head and once more she surrendered to his hot mouth and his promise to kiss her everywhere. His slow, burning kisses reached her breasts, his hair feathering over her skin; his lips trapped one nipple, that his teeth and tongue could tease it. Sensation tore through her, possessing her body so she arched and moaned and yanked at his hair. But, oh thank heaven, nothing stopped those lips of his from sliding onward, branding an inexorable trail down her writhing body.

Then she lost her grip on his hair, and lifted her head to watch, amazed, as he parted her legs with those implacable hands and settled between them. Air danced up her inner thighs to the desperately sweet pulse at her core. He met her astonished gaze, mischief and desire sparkling in those intent brandy eyes. Those unforgettable eyes did not leave hers, not for a single throb of her wayward pulse, as he pressed his hot, merciless mouth to her quim.

Intense pleasure coiled through her, making her cry out, and she caught the wicked gleam of triumph in his gaze before she collapsed back onto the ground. Her dazzled eyes blinked at the streaks of blue sky peeping through the green willows, her aroused skin sensing every playful current of air. Thea gripped the grass, as Rafe's commanding hands pinned her hips to the ground and his talented mouth teased and tasted and tormented her. Breathing eluded her; all she had were moans, and each one he answered with a growl. Blades of grass came away in her fingers, and she fumbled for something to grip, or else she would fly away, borne away by the kisses clamoring under her skin, those kisses that pulsed in her blood and supplanted her flesh, a million kisses . thronging and rioting under his mouth, threatening to break free.

Then something he did triggered their release. Bliss rippled over her, from her toes to her hair, as those million riotous kisses burst out of her, exploding into the air. She imagined them soaring through the sky, scattering in the breeze, and raining down on the world below. Still Rafe anchored her, so she did not fly away too, but remained with him, where she belonged, pulsing with bliss and hope and love.

Dazzled, she opened her eyes and met his. His expression was one of awe, and she lifted her languid fingers to touch that expression.

"You are the most beautiful thing I've ever seen," he whispered hoarsely.

"No, *you* are," she said, and he grinned.

Her body was molten, but she did not need to move, for he stretched out beside her and pulled her against him, his generous, assured hands roaming absently over her newly sensitive skin. She spread her fingers over the hairs of his chest, and wondered how it had happened, that his body had become hers too.

"Well?" he murmured. "Better than syllabub?"

"Um. Why choose?"

With a groan of laughter, Rafe collapsed onto his back, bearing her with him. She stretched to kiss to his lips: How marvelous that she could do that so easily now. That somehow, in giving her pleasure, he had given her himself.

And yet, not.

Lifting her head, Thea studied Rafe's face. His eyes were closed. The thick, dark lashes quivered against his skin, and his jaw was tense. His pulse hammered in his throat, under the last tapering lines of his scars. She understood his tension, now.

So she trailed her hand over his broad chest, the ridge of his ribcage, the muscled flat of his belly, and—

With a slap of his hand over hers, he halted her advance. His eyes were uncommonly dark, his mouth tight.

"I thought we were doing this together," she complained.

"You don't even know what 'this' is."

"I know enough. I know that I want it. That I want more of you. All of you."

Tautness hummed through him. "You want to make love with me? Now?"

"Yes. I want it all."

She wanted *him*. All of him, no holding back. This was her only chance, and such chances did not come traipsing along every day; she must seize them when she could.

Nothing lasted: She could not pick the flowers or net the butterflies or hold onto this man, or settle in his house and call it her home.

But she could have this—one perfect afternoon with the most wonderful man she had ever known.

The rules demanded that she protect her virtue, but her virtue had never protected her; she cared nothing for it now. She wanted to feel the sun on her face and the grass beneath her feet and she wanted—no, she *longed* to know how it felt to be engulfed by him.

Nearby, birds were chattering. Thea basked in the luscious wantonness of being naked, by the lake, with him.

"The way I feel when I'm with you, I want to feel it more," she said. "I want to be close to you, as close as I can get. Because I have so many pictures of you in my head, and so many memories of your touch, but I want more." She brushed her fingers over his lips. "I want to make love with you because I am greedy and I like sweet things."

"Thea." He breathed her name, as he wound his fingers in her hair and rose up beside her. "If we make love..."

"Hush. You grumble about me talking too much, but now you are talking too much."

A new light entered his eyes. "Then what would you have me do?"

She answered him with a kiss. It was slow and promising at first, but as their tongues caressed each other, a new fever seized her, breeding a desperate, insatiable hunger, a craving to press against him so completely that they became one. Rational thought took flight, freeing her hands and mouth to roam wildly over him, yearning to touch and taste every inch of him, before her only chance escaped.

In no time at all, he caught her fever, his hunger as fierce as her own. They made short work of the last of his clothes, and she was lying back, inviting his embrace, his body hovering over her. Her hand slid over his hips, brazen and reckless as she curled her ravenous fingers around his hard, satiny length.

"Thea, sweet Thea, I need you now."

Thea gripped him harder; he groaned and said, "Time for that later," and her confused mind tried to find when this "later" would be, for there was only now, and now he replaced her hand with his own and guided himself into her, pushing firmly, confidently, knowing she would welcome him. His powerful presence inside her startled her, spiked through her, then new sensations rippled outward, and she settled into rightness, because finally—at least for this brief, heavenly moment—finally, he was hers.

FINALLY, finally, she was his.

Rafe paused, to give her time, to give himself time too—time to savor this moment, this precious, sacred moment, of their bodies joined, his cock deep inside her, her face telling him her thoughts, telling him of her discomfort, her surprise, and then— So help him! Her pleasure. Her intrigue. Her wonder. Her eyes flew open, and he lost himself in their divine perfection, lost himself in her generous smile, as she shifted and tightened around him. Pleasure coursed through him, conquered him, possessed him. Thea wrapped her legs around him, took him deeper. Her fingers kneaded his back as she kissed him passionately. He gathered her close—he could not hold this position; he was not that strong—but for now, they were melded together, anchored to each other, as one.

Everything in the world was right.

Then his control failed him. He should go slowly; it was her first time, but it might as well be his first time too. Desire tore at him, overwhelming him, and he lowered her to the grass. It was their first time, but soon they would marry, and they had decades of times ahead. He would explain, she would understand, they would laugh and tease and he'd do right by her next time. The next time they made love, she would be his wife.

Rafe kept his eyes on hers and surrendered to his need, and each time he discovered her anew, he told her with his eyes that now he had found her, he would hold her fast. That now she had found him, he had come home.

Through the haze of his passion, he was aware of her crying out, of her body shuddering again and her muscles squeezing him, and he let himself go too, and filled her with his pleasure and his hope and his love.

THEA'S BODY was languid against his. A cool breeze danced over them and she shifted.

"Are you cold?" Rafe murmured. They should get dressed and go inside to plan their life together, but he liked the feel of her.

"It is a deliciously wicked sort of thrill, isn't it?" she said. "Being naked, outside. I cannot think why everyone doesn't do it all the time."

"Can you not."

She was quiet for a moment. "Actually, yes," she revised. "I can think of one or two very good reasons why not."

Rafe laughed and hugged her. Now was the time for talking, but not here under the willows, amid the disarray that followed the giddy heights of sex. He stood and helped her to her feet. Abruptly, modesty snared her: She snatched up her crumpled chemise and held it over her, her cheeks pink, her expression distressed.

He caught her face in his hands. "That was beautiful and right. Even when it is over, it is still beautiful and right."

She nodded, half smiling, but it was a wistful sort of smile, and something like confusion entered her eyes. It was the first time she'd ever made love, he reminded himself, and not to be taken lightly; the changes of the day were even more momentous for her.

He dropped a light kiss on her lips. "Come, let us dress."

They washed and helped each other dress, although their clothes were a mess.

Thea gathered her loose hair and laughed. "Oh my, we look like a pair of urchins. Will everyone know? All the staff, and Sally and... Um."

For these blessed moments, Rafe had forgotten everything and everyone but them. "Most of the staff do not work today, but the bishop and the others will be back. Wash, dress, and meet in the drawing room. We have much to discuss."

Nicholas would advise on how quickly they could marry; he would find a way to put the paperwork right. Unless Thea wanted a big church wedding; later, Rafe would ask her what she preferred.

When they were both attired properly, and behaving properly, he would propose properly. This time, she would have no cause to complain about his proposal. He would find the words to ask again, and this time, she'd say "yes."

Yet that wistful expression was in her eyes again, and before he could question it, she rose on her toes, planted a swift kiss on his lips, then dashed off toward the house.

Rafe hunted down the clothing they had left scattered through the garden, so it did not frighten any unsuspecting gardener the following day, and let his mind wander free, full of Thea and the possibilities of their life together. Hope swooped through him. Pessimist, was he? He laughed, thankful that he was, indeed, a different man after all.

CHAPTER 23

E ven after she had washed and dressed in a fresh gown, even when her nakedness was once more buttoned away and her hair restrained, Thea's body felt new and strange to her, yet newly and strangely right. Still, she felt Rafe's hands sliding over her body, their limbs tangled. Still, she felt herself engulfed in him. It was beautiful and right, he'd said. Indeed, it had been beautiful, and it had felt right.

Even when it is over, it is still beautiful and right, he had added.

Even when it was over. He, too, knew it could not last.

She indulged in sorrow for a few minutes, then pulled herself together. She had wanted memories, and now she had them. No complaining. Whatever happened next, she hoped that Rafe would not hide away from her. They could enjoy this last evening together, before she left.

Thus fortified, yet oddly nervous, Thea made her way to the drawing room. She was almost relieved that Rafe was not yet there, for she was not sure how to face him, and she jumped when someone came in. It was Gilbert, bearing a letter. He chattered out an explanation as to how he had come by it—something about the messenger and church and the bishop—but Thea hardly heard, for her name ("Miss D. Knight") was written in Ma's hand and her blood was rushing in her ears. Dimly, she was aware of thanking him and then, mercifully, he left her alone.

Ma had written! Finally! Helen must have told Ma everything. Perhaps they would say they believed her and ask her to come home now.

She would still publish the pamphlet, of course; it was only what Percy Russell deserved.

Allowing herself a small laugh, Thea stood by the French windows looking into the courtyard garden. Her heart pounding, hands shaking, Thea fumbled the letter open and began to read.

THEA WAS STANDING in the same spot when Rafe came in. He was fresh and clean-shaven, dressed well enough for dinner with a duke, in his snowy-white cravat and the wine-red waistcoat under his dark coat. She liked that waistcoat, she decided.

She would like to press her face against it, press herself against that body made for hugging, feel his arms envelop her. She lowered her hand, let the letter dangle from her fingers. How she longed for Rafe to hold her.

Until he let go of her too.

He stopped in the middle of the room and frowned. "Thea?"

"I've had a letter from Ma." Listen to her. Her voice was so bright it could serve as a chandelier. It might shatter like one too. "Lord Ventnor told her what he saw. Us together in the lake, I mean. His version of it, anyway. The version in which I am your harlot."

"You and I both know the truth," he said. "That's all that matters."

She hardly heard him. "Ma is pleased to report that Lord Ventnor has resigned himself to his son's marriage and accepted them as his in-laws. Ma and Pa dined at Ventnor House. Where it was impressed upon them that, as Ma and Pa are now part of a viscount's family, it is important for the sake of the entire family that they have nothing to do with me. They say my behavior has gone too far. I thought I was so clever, thinking no one would ever learn I was here. So much for restoring my reputation."

He shrugged impatiently and started pacing the room. "Sod them. You don't need them."

"Oh, and Pa intended to give you my 'dowry' in person, but he will not do that now." What a marvel, the way she made it sound like a colossal joke. Well, it was a colossal joke, and any moment now she would begin to laugh. She glanced at the letter, all loops and lines and utterly illegible. Funny. She'd read it only a moment ago, but now she could not make out a single word. "I cannot even demand they believe me, this time. After all, this time, Ventnor's lies have turned into truth."

She let the letter drift away from her, watched it float over the room for a few feet then land on the blue carpet.

In a rough, swift movement, Rafe scooped up the letter, screwed it into a ball, and hurled it toward the empty fireplace. It flew neatly into the gap between the ornamental fire screen and the cold grate within.

"Sod your family. Sod Ventnor and the whole blasted lot of them. You don't need any of them. We'll get married, properly, and it won't matter what anyone thinks."

Thea stared at the place where the letter had flown, then back at him. "Get married?" she repeated. She had lost her wits, it seemed; perhaps they had run away with her virtue.

Rafe certainly seemed to think so, if his incredulous expression was anything to judge by. "Of course we'll get married. We made love. An hour ago. Or had you already forgotten?"

Marrying him. Properly. Living here at Brinkley End. Could he mean it?

Well. She'd be a countess. For real, this time. Never again would she need to worry about her next meal, or where she would sleep, or what she would wear. Invitations would come flooding in. The wedding vows would work like a magic spell, transforming her from unwanted, impoverished outcast, to a desirable member of society.

And Rafe... Kind, heroic Rafe. He would be the one to save her. She would always have him nearby, to give her hugs and kisses, to dine with her and make her smile. How honorable he was. Yet if those blissful moments under the willows had turned his mind as soft and dazed as her own, he wouldn't be thinking straight. After all, if her own parents didn't want her, why would he?

"You are being honorable and self-sacrificing again," she managed to say. "Fancy that. A nobleman who is actually noble."

"I'm being... I don't..." He ran his hands through his hair, paced wildly for several steps, then threw himself into a chair that could barely contain his restless limbs. "I mean, we... You could be... Under the willows..."

"You don't owe me anything," she said softly. "Not when it won't last."

"What the hell are you talking about? Why won't it last?"

"Because nothing ever does."

"But this—" He surged to his feet again, his sentences coming in short bursts. "I want to be that man who— Hell, I am that man. To have a bride, in this home. Now I understand about the past... about Katharine... I see how my life can be different."

Despite his words, he paced like a fierce animal caged. Something squeezed her chest and she feared she would cry.

"Then how can you know?" she countered. "I am the only woman you have seen since then, and maybe you're simply relieved, or maybe after the willows you're not thinking straight."

"For crying out loud, Thea, don't tell me what I think! I know what I want." He whirled around, his arms waving. "And your pamphlet, your reputation, the lot. If you're married to me, it won't matter. Nothing in the outside world will matter."

She shook her head. All this talking and nothing made sense.

"You can't understand," she said. "You cannot know how it feels to be unable to trust the very ground on which you walk. I must put the world right, for how can I ever feel secure again, when I do not even have a safe place to stand?"

"You would be a countess. A blasted countess! Your parents would welcome you with open arms. All would be forgiven."

Quite right. They would forgive her for her scandal, though it was a malicious lie. They would forgive her for becoming Rafe's mistress, though that was not true. How magnanimous they would be, to forgive her the sins she had never committed, and overlook the mistakes she had never made.

And she would—what? She would be expected to be *grateful* for that?

But yes, if she married him, her past would be washed away and they would welcome her home.

That is, they would welcome him. When that door opened, that blue door with the brass mermaid knocker, she would enter with a ring on her hand and the Earl of Luxborough at her side.

And she would never know.

For the rest of her life, she would never know if her parents truly cared about her or truly believed her story. She would never know if Rafe truly wanted her, or if he was marrying her out of duty or kindness, or because of his relief over the revelation about Katharine and the passing novelty of Thea in his life.

For the rest of her life, she would have everything. Everything. And she would never know if it was truly hers.

As soon as she disappointed him or annoyed him or angered him, would he tire of her, send her to London, put her on the other side of the house and ignore her? If people told him stories about her, would he believe her or them?

Why, it was only yesterday that he'd discovered the truth about the past and learned to see the world differently. He was in no state to make decisions about his future, when he was still discovering his past.

If he truly wanted to marry her now, he would still want to marry her in a month. Wouldn't he? Perhaps after she left he would return to his plants and forget she had ever been here. Perhaps he would remember her sometimes, and be grateful for his escape.

Or perhaps he would think of her, and want her, and come after her.

"True," she agreed softly. "They would open the door to us, to the Earl of Luxborough and his wife."

Rafe had stopped pacing. "I don't understand what you want. Do you want to live in London?"

"I need to put the world right and know where I stand," she said. "I need my parents to believe me. I need everyone to listen and know the truth."

"Oh for crying out loud! Grow up!" Once more, his big body crashed haphazardly into a chair. "Stop being a child. You have to let go."

Again she remembered watching the release of the hot air balloon, the childhood memory Rafe had stirred. Her fear when the ropes were cut. Now she was an adult. She should not be frightened to have no anchor holding her to the ground. But here was what he did not understand: She did not even have any ground.

"You cannot understand," she said again.

"I understand you are a grown woman who cares too much what people think and are still trying to get your parents' approval."

And there it was. The annoyance—disgust even—in his voice and face was plain. Already he was sick of her. Already she had disappointed him. She had needed to wait barely ten minutes for the evidence. He did not truly want her, any more than her own family did.

"Thank you for your kindness, but I do not think marriage is necessary," she forced herself to say. "If you will lend me your carriage, I shall leave for London immediately."

His eyes flickered. He lifted his head, drew up his legs, leaned forward, elbows on his thighs. Joy skipped inside her. He would come after her.

But then he fell back into the chair. "Do you expect me to chase you? You want me to play your games again?"

"This isn't a game!"

"Because if you go, you're gone. I won't come after you."

Now she had an answer to that too. If he truly wanted to marry her, he would not say that. More lovely words that meant nothing. Yet another place whipped out from under her. She had been right not to put any trust in that.

"Of course you won't," she snapped. "You must stay here, hiding from the world, like a ghost haunting your own house."

"Another fanciful, childish notion."

"Call me childish then, if that is how you feel."

His rough laugh sounded haunted too. "You have no idea what I'm feeling right now."

Thea longed to go to him, but she would only hurt herself, so instead she ran to her room. This time, she packed, properly and neatly. This time, nothing stopped Gilbert from receiving her message and preparing the earl's carriage. Together they carried out her trunks, one filled with the items she had bought to resell, and the other filled with Helen's clothes and the cat's mask.

This time, there was nothing to stop her from leaving, no bad weather or sudden news or wild revelations.

And no Rafe, running after her, begging her not to go.

As the carriage trundled down the driveway, she twisted to catch her final view of Brinkley End. Nobody was watching her, and no one waved goodbye, and too late she remembered the bishop and Sally and Martha, but they were not there, and neither was Rafe, and nothing even seemed to care that she was gone.

CHAPTER 24

Twenty-two hours since Thea had gone. Rafe tapped at the window, and looked past his own ghostly reflection to picture the road to London. He wondered where she had spent the night, and if she had thought of him in her bed. Or maybe she was driving through without stopping, given her haste to reach her filthy, beloved London and her fickle, beloved family, and her futile, beloved pamphlet.

It was better that she was gone. If she didn't want to be here, he didn't want her here. He didn't want any of them. Why should he try to be part of the world, when the world clearly did not want him?

He was perfectly content here alone.

Except Rafe wasn't quite alone, it appeared. For he turned away from the window to see he had been joined by Queen Elizabeth. He wiped his hand over his eyes, but the apparition was still there.

Splendid. Not only had he lost the woman he loved, he'd lost his grip on reality too.

"What do you think?" the dead Tudor queen asked in Nicholas's voice.

"I always thought you'd be prettier."

"Rafe. Are you taking one of Martha's medicines?"

Rafe blinked at Nicholas over his enormous white ruff. "You're dressed as Queen Bess and you're asking if *I'm* intoxicated?"

"I'm choosing my costume for the party. I need your help."

"What party?"

"The Prince Regent is holding a costume party. Had you forgotten?"

Rafe fell into his chair. "If only I could."

If only he could forget all of it, and all the ways he had been wrong.

"Your moping becomes tiresome, Rafe. If you didn't want Thea to go, you ought to have proposed."

"I did. She turned me down."

"Ah. You failed to mention that." Nicholas sat beside him and arranged his wide skirts. "So you have a broken heart."

"I do not."

"You're in love with her."

Rafe breathed in, the air slicing his throat like razor blades. "She turned me down."

And this lovely house, ready for people to fill it. For an afternoon, Rafe had thought he would make that happen. But he was not the man for that after all. The rooms should be closed up, covers spread over the furniture and paintings, until Rafe died to make way for a new, better earl.

"This plan of hers, with the pamphlet," Nicholas said. "I confess I have my doubts about whether it will work."

"Of course it won't bloody well work. But she won't listen to me."

"Oughtn't you at least check on her, make sure she has what she needs?"

"I've already seen to it. I've written to London to give her the money from Mother's trust. I'll find another way to start that business."

"What if Thea's needs are not financial?" Nicholas persisted.

"She knows where I live."

Rafe bounced out of his chair and went back to the window. Same view as always. He couldn't even see the driveway from here.

Eventually, Nicholas stood, in a rustle of silk. "This gown is dreadfully uncomfortable. I must find something else. Will you help me?"

"No. I shall sit here and mope until this house falls down."

"An excellent plan."

"Have you a better one?"

"Come with me to London. I'm curious to see how the prodigal Marquess of Hardbury turned out. Aren't you?"

"No. And I'm not going to any blasted costume party."

"Of course you're not," the bishop said.

THEA'S TRIP to London was exactly as miserable and lonely as she had imagined it would be, however resolutely she sought to distract herself from the grim thoughts. Even when her wayward mind did not stray back to Brinkley End, her body reminded her of its change. It was not only the spots of tenderness, but something deep and intangible. A strange feeling that she could not name or identify and did not want to lose. Perhaps one's body did not easily recover from the experience of being completely engulfed in another human being.

At least in London, she had so much to keep her busy that

thinking was no longer a concern. Convincing a landlady of her respectability was troublesome, but she finally rented rooms in Soho and set about selling the items she had bought on Rafe's account. With Gilbert's help, she earned enough to settle her bills with Mr. Witherspoon and the publisher, and the rest went to pay for her lodging for the rest of the month. She had just enough coins to keep her fed until Helen returned from Brighton.

And on the second day after she arrived in London, she and Gilbert took a hackney cab to a warehouse in Spitalfields, where her pamphlets and prints had been delivered to await distribution the following day.

And oh, but her pamphlets were beautiful!

Well, the stacks of crates that held her pamphlets were beautiful.

As she stood in the dusty yard outside the warehouse, admiring the wooden crates, Thea felt a genuine smile warm her chest and shape her face, for the first time since she had left Brinkley End.

She had done this.

To be fair, Arabella had organized it, and Mr. Witherspoon had done the actual work, and Gilbert had done the heavy lifting, and she had paid for it by reselling items bought with Rafe's money. But this had happened because of her. Because she had made it happen.

Soon, men would arrive to carry the crates inside, and in the night, Mr. Witherspoon's army of delivery boys would gather. By this time tomorrow, every genteel and aristocratic household in London would have a copy of her pamphlet. Patrons of every coffeehouse would see it, and in a few days, everyone who opened a newspaper would read the advertisements. Everyone passing a print seller or bookseller would glimpse the cartoon resembling

Percy. If only Rafe were here to see it. Perhaps then he would understand.

"That's a mighty big pile of paper, miss," Gilbert said from beside her. "London won't know what hit 'em."

Thea straightened, feeling confident and proud. "I've had my time in exile. And now, now is when it ends."

"Quite right, my dear Miss Knight," someone said from the open gate.

Thea whirled, as Lord Ventnor entered, with Percy Russell at his side and half a dozen of his rough-looking men in his wake. Thea let her eyes fall onto Ventnor's ebony, silver-topped stick, and wondered how it could be, when Rafe had broken it.

Lord Ventnor smiled a chilly smile. "This is indeed where it ends."

Thea turned in a circle to keep facing Ventnor and Percy, as they entered the yard and stopped. Straightening her shoulders, she stared them down, her back to the crates as if she were protecting her treasure from a dragon. Gilbert edged closer to her side as Ventnor's men fanned out. One took his post behind Ventnor and Percy. Thea twisted to see the other men loitering near the crates.

"You, man, be gone," Ventnor said to Gilbert. "I shall not harm her."

Gilbert didn't move.

Ventnor made a dismissive sound. "Luxborough is looking after you then, Miss Knight. How touching. Adds another meaning to the word 'protector'."

"He is not my *protector* and never was."

"Cast you off, has he? Never mind. A pretty, lively thing like you, you'll find another man to take you on soon enough."

Percy snickered. "I might be interested in a new mistress. How much?"

Without thinking, Thea slapped his smirking face. Hard. It felt so satisfying that she tried to do it again, but this time Percy caught her hand. So she leaned in and kneed him in the bollocks.

Her skirts hampered her, unfortunately, but she mustered enough force to make him yelp and release her and back away. Her palm stung, and her knee was affronted at having to carry out such a repulsive task, but other than that, she felt quite good.

"You little tart!" Percy squeaked.

"You vile snot," Thea returned.

Ventnor inserted his ebony stick between them. "Now, now, children."

Percy's face turned red. "But Father! She hit me!"

"Do grow up, boy. It was exactly what you deserved after speaking to her like that." Ventnor tapped the silver end of his stick in the dust at his son's feet. "You disgust me at times, Percy. Let us not forget that it was your malicious, childish attack on Miss Knight that got us here in the first place."

Thea stared at Ventnor, stunned to have such an unexpected defender. "Then you know, my lord. You know that Percy and Francis Upton told lies about me."

"I know *now*. A cunning little pamphlet you penned, my dear." He opened one hand, palm upward, and the man behind him placed a booklet onto it. "I read it, you know. It's not too bad, for a lady author."

"How did you get a copy of that?" Thea realized she had not asked him the most obvious question. "Why are you here?"

"Not much happens in London that I don't hear about, as everyone knows I pay well for information. Someone at the publisher let me know they were printing a cartoon resembling my son, and I investigated. And here we are."

"Then you know my story is true and must be told."

Ventnor waved the pamphlet like a fan. "A conundrum. Percy

has behaved very badly, but he is my son, and I must protect my family. What happens to one member affects everyone. You would not believe the things I must do for the sake of my family."

"Oh, I'd believe it," Thea said. "Things like trying to kidnap your daughter to lock her in a lunatic asylum. Or threatening to carve up Sally Holt's face because of false rumors about your wife."

"Silence!"

"Or what, Lord Ventnor?" Thea demanded. "Will you send your ruffians after me, as you did to other defenseless women?"

"No, my dear. I shall silence you."

"No, my lord. I shall not be silenced."

"Will you not?"

Moving so quickly neither she nor Gilbert had a chance to react, Ventnor grabbed Thea by both shoulders and spun her around to face the crates. As she found her feet, it occurred to her that she had been so intent on Ventnor and Percy, she had not noticed what his men were doing.

Even then, she didn't fully understand, until the first explosion rent the air.

One explosion first, shattering wooden crates and sending booklets flying upward. Then another explosion. And another.

Thea screamed and lunged but Gilbert yelled, "Stay back, miss!" and grabbed her elbows to hold her in place, as more crates exploded.

Pamphlets and pages and splinters, flying into the air, landing, flying up, landing again.

Flames burst out of nowhere, curling around loose pages, engulfing them, hungrily seeking more, fed by dry paper and wooden splinters and further echoing blasts. Thea could not begin to imagine how it was done. All she knew was that her precious pamphlets were in a broken heap and that heap was on fire.

She shook off Gilbert, who whispered, "Oh miss, I am so sorry," and Thea tried to speak but managed only a croak. Indeed, she was silenced, as she stood surrounded by her enemies, watching it all burn.

Her words, her story, her hopes, going up in flames. A mountain of flame, climbing higher and higher, sending up a column of smoke.

How people around must be wondering at that smoke. Perhaps they would be frightened. Londoners lived in constant dread of fires. They would run to help, forming chains to carry water, to speedily douse the flames.

But Ventnor was too careful for that. Once or twice, she had outsmarted him; how pleased with herself she had been. In the end, it meant nothing. His men watched the fire carefully; they would not let it burn out of control. How cleverly Ventnor had planned this.

And so they had won. Because it wasn't about who was good or bad, who was right or wrong. It was about who held the power. All those good people listening to her story, that night in the inn with Rafe. *That's a rotten story,* they'd said. *Whoever heard of a story where the villains don't get their comeuppance?* Yet that was the story playing out right now. The good people could drink with their friends and share tales of defeated villains, while the powerful people burned down their worlds.

A breeze swirled through the yard and rose, lifting fragments of pages into the air. One landed on her, a corner of a page, and she plucked it off her dress to read the disembodied words. Other fragments flew up, rising to the top of the smoke and over the wall, fluttering off to land on houses and streets and people's heads.

A small laugh bubbled up in Thea's throat. She had succeeded after all. Her story would be spread all over London, over Hyde Park and St. Paul's, St. Martin's and the Thames. Her words would rain down on the city as ash and fragments. "What is this story that is falling from the sky?" someone would say and gather the fragments and piece them together.

No one would, of course.

No one would care about one more story from one more woman, one more lost wanderer, trying to be heard. A lone woman, saying, "but listen, please listen, this matters, this is my life." They were all trying to be heard, all wandering around their own lives, trying to tell their stories and find their way. They would brush off the ash, let the charred pages fall into the mud, and mutter some curse about the dirt of London, the city they could never leave because this was the place where dreams came true. Off they would rush in pursuit of those dreams, and never guess that someone else's dreams had, literally, gone up in smoke.

It was a grand bonfire, and Thea stared at it, even as the smoke stung her eyes, even as Ventnor strolled around in front of her. The heat burned her cheeks and she should move away, but instead she closed her eyes, and pretended the heat of the flames was the sun, and she was back at Brinkley End, ready to plunge into the cool lake. Where a pair of strong arms would hold her, keep her anchored to the ground, so she would not be lost on the breeze, like the charred fragments of her dreams.

"I don't think I'll be needing this," Ventnor said.

Thea opened her eyes to see him holding out the last remaining pamphlet. Numbly, she took it.

"A valiant attempt, my dear, but a selfish one," he added. "After all, your sister is part of my family now, and in harming my family, you would have harmed her. Family is too important. You understand that, don't you?" He turned to his men. "Make sure everything is burned, and the fire is completely extinguished with no mess left."

After a courteous bow to Thea, Ventnor stalked back through the gate, Percy trotting behind him. Around her, his men continued their work, serious and professional.

"Are you all right, miss?" Gilbert asked, his dark eyes liquid with sorrow, his battered face creased with concern.

"Of course," she said, and she was. After all, no one had tried to put her on the flames, so really, she was doing very nicely.

"I was worried he'd harm you, so I was trying to keep you safe. I never thought he'd go after the crates."

"It's all right, Gilbert." Thea turned over the pamphlet in her hand. "None of us could have imagined it. Thank you for looking after me."

"Where next, miss? You've had a terrible shock. You ought not be alone, but Miss Larke and Lady Belinda are not due into London until tomorrow and your sister is still in Brighton. Is there somewhere I can take you?"

Thea opened the pamphlet to the frontispiece. *The Tale of Rosamund.* By A Lady. This was all that remained of her story; it did not even bear her name. One last copy, and then her truth would be lost forever.

One copy was all she required.

"Warren Street." Her voice was croaky, as if she had breathed in all that smoke. "To the blue door with the brass mermaid knocker. All that remains is for me to go home."

WITH A SHAKING HAND, Thea lifted that brass mermaid and let it drop. Once. Twice. Three times. The blue door opened. The unfamiliar servant said the right things, proper and polite.

"I wish to see Mr. or Mrs. Knight," Thea said.

Smoke clung to her nostrils and coated her mouth. Her clothes must reek of it; certainly, she could smell it in her bonnet and hair. Inside her dirty glove, her palm was clammy and her fingers ached from clutching her pamphlet so tight.

"I shall see if they are home. Have you a card?"

A card. Of all the things she might have thought to bring.

Thea held out the pamphlet. "Give them that. Tell them it's their daughter Thea. Tell them I have come home."

That was enough to grant her entry to the foyer. She was not invited to remove her bonnet or gloves. She waited, and then Ma and Pa were there.

Their beloved faces were older, softer, but the same. Wary. Unwelcoming. Disappointed.

"What are you doing here?" Ma asked in a low voice, as though all of London were gathered in her foyer to overhear. "I made it clear that you are not welcome after the harm you caused this family."

"Ma, I have so much to tell you."

Pa held up the pamphlet. "What is the meaning of this?"

"That is my story." Thea's voice was too loud in the hushed foyer but she did not lower it. "Percy Russell and Francis Upton lied. I told you the truth but you wouldn't believe me. You sent me away instead. I wrote it down and had it published, so that I might restore my reputation."

Her parents exchanged a look.

"And what about the Earl of Luxborough?" Ma asked.

A thousand memories waltzed through Thea's mind, coming to pause on him smiling at her, sunlight in his brandy-colored eyes. Then his disgust and annoyance, as he sent her away. No. Not that one. She would hold onto the good memories. Those wonderful memories of him would last her. They must.

"What about him?" she said.

"Lord Ventnor described your disgraceful behavior, and we were shocked by the earl's attempt to secure your dowry when he had not the decency to marry you. Are you married to him, after all? Or at least engaged?"

"I am not."

As one, her parents stepped away from her, as if she might transmit some horrid disease.

It was Ma who spoke next. "But did Lord Luxborough... compromise you?"

"I suppose in the language of the world he did. Perhaps I erred, but it was my choice and I have no regrets."

"And he did not marry you."

"He offered. I refused."

Pa shook his head. "And you dare speak of your reputation. That is not how we raised you to behave."

Silence filled the foyer, echoing off the refined ornaments. Ma wore a cap of the finest lace, and Pa's embroidered waistcoat was silk. The very things they had fantasized about owning when they were rich. They had dreamed and planned and worked, and they had won.

But their eyes... Their eyes were cold, and not at all like Thea's memories.

How Pa's eyes would sparkle with mischief when he called his daughters "Ted" and "Harry," and winked as he sent them off do boys' work. How his face would light up with infectious optimism when he wove his bold schemes, as the family huddled around the single brazier and sipped at thin soup. And Ma, her fingers nimble as she stitched, offering ideas that earned Pa's applause, her smile indulgent at Thea's childish mischief, her bosom soft when she hugged her daughters and promised everything would be all right, for nobody could stop a Knight.

When, precisely, had everything changed? How had their buoyant hope hardened into this ruthless ambition?

"You raised me to believe our family would always be there for each other, whatever happened in the world," Thea said. "All I asked was that you believe my side of the story. Had you believed me, back then, we could have solved the problem together, as we used to do. I could have gone away, to protect Helen and the Little Ones, but not as an outcast from my own family, not to that long, lonely exile, during which you did not write me a single word. But you chose to believe my enemies. You were meant to love me, but when that love was tested, you did not stand by me. You cast me aside."

"Fine speech, Thea, but why should we believe your stories? You have confessed to your own scandalous behavior with Lord Luxborough."

"Lord Luxborough believes my stories. If he were here now, as my betrothed? If he told you I spoke the truth, would you find you believed my stories then?"

They exchanged looks. "Well," Pa said, "that would be a different matter."

Thea nodded sadly. "Because his word is worth more than mine."

"It isn't like that," Ma said. "But you always did make mischief and break rules, and, well, this is the way the world works."

"Oh, I have had quite an education in the way the world works." Thea studied her grubby pamphlet. How pathetic it was, this sorry tale, the last of its kind. She looked back up. "May I see the Little Ones?"

Pa crossed the foyer and opened the door, letting in the breeze and sounds of the street. He did not look her in the eye. "You had best go. It would not do for Lord Ventnor to learn that you were here. We cannot afford to displease him."

"Ma?"

Her mother turned away. "It is best, Thea."

Thea had nothing more to say, so she went out. The blue door closed behind her.

"Farewell," Thea whispered to the brass mermaid and returned to the waiting hack.

CHAPTER 25

V oices from the drawing room had Rafe barging through the door to see who it was. Thea, he thought. Thea had come back.

It wasn't Thea. It was a maid setting out tea and biscuits for Socrates.

The maid bobbed a curtsy and left, and Rafe sat and recalculated the hours. Thea would be in London by now. He should be with her, but she didn't want him, and he'd vowed not to chase her again, so she was in her beloved London, and he was taking tea with a dead Greek philosopher.

"Socrates?" Rafe said.

"Why not? I'm wise," Nicholas retorted. "And this toga is a sight more comfortable than that royal gown. Bit chilly though. Breeze gets right up into my—"

"Nicholas."

"—Knees."

Nicholas poured the tea. Rafe poked at a biscuit. Stale. The whole house was growing stale.

"You're really going to that costume party," Rafe said.

"Wouldn't miss it for the world. I still retain hope our Thea will triumph. I would have thought you'd want to be there."

"Thea doesn't want me there. I offered to be by her side and she refused me, though she knew my presence would make all the difference."

They would welcome home the Earl of Luxborough and his wife, she had said. He could still hear those words, as he could hear most of that blasted conversation, complete with the bitterness in her tone. A bitter edge did creep into her tone, sometimes. Unsurprising, considering what she had been through.

"I'm not sure if that poor child knows what she wants," Nicholas said.

"She's not a child."

"Very well. She's a woman. Who lost everything once, and likely fears losing it all again."

Rafe shook his head. "I offered her everything, on a silver platter. Had she agreed to be my wife, she would have never lost it."

They would welcome home the Earl of Luxborough and his wife.

The earl's wife.

Oh. Oh hell.

That was why she had turned him down.

Rafe bounded out of his chair, mind racing, replaying their conversation. Of course. What had she said? *I must put the world right, for how can I ever feel secure again, when I do not even have a safe place to stand?*

Bloody hell, yet again, how wrong he had been! Of course marrying him was no solution for her, because she was not a social climber; her dream was not to marry a man with a title, but for her parents to accept her as she was. Until she had let go of her past, she would not be ready for her future.

His heart broke all over again as realization struck its blow. She needed to do this, and she needed to do it alone. And then...

Perhaps he should have told her, that he wanted her in his life every day, that she had only to say the word and he would put everything right for her. If only he had told her that he loved her and needed her, like sunshine and water and air.

Not fair. If he had tried to hold her here, when she had unfinished business, the unresolved questions would have haunted her. She would have been haunted not by the past, but by the futures that she might have had. If he had convinced her to stay, then when times were hard—and he suspected even a happy life had hard times—then she might have doubted. "What if I had gone then?" she might have thought. "What if I had tried? Everything might be different."

If her happiness did lie in her home in London, then he had to let her find it, because her happiness had become the most important thing in his world.

But once she had done what she needed to do, she could look to her future. Rafe could only hope that he lived in her memory. That she could gaze into her memories of him and they would guide her back to him.

Oh, by all that was sacred, let her come back to him.

Wherever you are now, Thea, know that I love you, he said to her in his mind. *Come back to me, or I shall not know how to live.*

And the house—the house had to be ready. No more stale biscuits. He'd clean the whole blasted place himself. Make it ready for the day she came home.

"I understand now," Rafe said to Nicholas. "If I had married her, if she returned as the Countess of Luxborough, she would never have known what they truly thought. And Thea—she needs to know."

"And once she knows?"

"Perhaps, then, she will come back."

Nicholas absently shoved up the drooping shoulder of his toga. "You know, Rafe, my boy. If you came with me to London, she wouldn't have as far to come back."

"I'm not going to any blasted costume party."

"Of course you're not," the bishop said.

BACK AT HER LODGINGS, Thea and Gilbert found her trunk sitting on the front step and the landlady blocking her entrance, arms folded, jaw set.

"This is a respectable house," the landlady said. "I don't take women like you."

Thea looked down at her trunk, back at the woman's beady eyes. "What kind of woman do you imagine I am?"

"Exactly the kind your two gentleman callers told me you were."

"You're mistaken," Thea protested. "And I paid for the rest of the month."

"Least you should do. Now be gone."

And yet another door slammed in her face.

The crowd streamed past them. Across the street, an anomaly caught Thea's eye. Two finely dressed gentlemen stood as confidently as if that spot of London belonged to them. Some passersby took care not to jostle them, but several hopeful vendors swarmed around them, like flies on horse dung.

Yes, indeed. These two gentlemen were horse dung in human form.

Percy Russell and Francis Upton.

Her gentlemen callers, she presumed, whose lies had once more lost her a home.

They saw that she had noticed them. In unison, they doffed their hats and offered deep, mocking bows, their faces tilted up so she would not miss their malicious grins. They had everything, yet everything wasn't enough, not until they were sure others had nothing.

Gilbert was hovering. "It's getting late, miss. We must find you rooms."

"It was hard enough the first time, for a woman on her own," she said. "Maybe I can find an inn outside London."

"I know somewhere. I'll let them know you're coming."

"You don't have to."

"Miss Larke would have my head if I didn't make sure you were all right. Not to mention his lordship."

His lordship, who had let her go. If only she had stayed with him. But that had not been real either.

Gilbert lifted one handle of the large trunk. "My cousin owns a coffeehouse near here. You can wait there while I confirm this place for you. I'll bring a hack."

Numbly, because she had no better ideas, Thea lifted the other handle and together they walked to Pimm's Fine Coffee House. The place hummed with energy, from the men perched on wooden benches, each with a cup or pipe in one hand, and a page in the other. Some read quietly, others muttered in urgent conversations, and a few were in loud argument, ignored by the rest.

When Thea and Gilbert arrived, everyone paused mid-sentence and looked at them, but all decided at a glance they had no information to offer and went back to what they were doing. As Gilbert located Mrs. Pimm, Thea studied the room.

It was in coffeehouses such as this one where young Thea had loitered, dressed as a boy, running errands for a coin. She had practiced her reading on newspapers and memorized the conversations she overheard, to repeat for Pa. How she had basked when Pa's eyes lit up and he said, "Excellent. I can use that information, oh yes, indeed I can." What a team the Knight family had been.

As Thea inhaled the aroma of coffee to chase away the stink of smoke, a peculiar lightness came over her. Again, she recalled that time when her family had watched the hot air balloon, and her childish fear at knowing the balloon would no longer be anchored to the earth. All her life she had done whatever she could to stay anchored, but now her parents had definitively cut the ropes.

And Thea did not feel fear. She felt...freedom. During those three years of her exile, she could have done anything, gone anywhere. But she had not. She had stayed, stuck, her mind closed to the future, seeing only the past, trying to find her way back.

How much time she had wasted! Time she could have spent making a new home. She could do that now. Her heart skipped a little, excited by the thought.

She closed her eyes. Let the noise around her fade. Let another image swim into her mind. The lawn at Brinkley End.

"Miss? Miss Knight?"

Thea opened her eyes and blinked at the coffeehouse. Gilbert stood before her, a woman—presumably Mrs. Pimm—at his side. Before they could speak, a boy came to the door. The men fell quiet and the boy yelled out the names of the ships that had arrived in the past hour and their cargo, then accepted his coins and dashed off.

Gilbert left too. Mrs. Pimm, with the unflappable efficiency of a woman who spent her days tending to men overexcited by coffee and news, put Thea and her trunk in a corner and, unasked, served her tea with bread and jam.

"Is there anything else you need, miss?" Mrs. Pimm asked, and Thea thanked her and said "No," which was the truth, because

Gilbert and Mrs. Pimm had already given her the one thing she needed most right now: a reminder that the world still held people who knew how to be kind.

WHEN THE CARRIAGE ENTERED MAYFAIR, Thea assumed Gilbert had somehow convinced the housekeeper at Arabella's house to let her stay, but the carriage did not stop outside the Larke family's house.

This house belonged to the Earl of Luxborough.

Thea tumbled out of the carriage on weak knees, her hands jittery, a thousand butterflies in her stomach. If only those were real butterflies, and she could make wishes on them, and those wishes could come true.

But Rafe would not be here, in his London house. He would be back at Brinkley End, in his greenhouse, with his plants, and she would be forgotten.

You are never gone from my mind.

"Is his lordship in residence?" she asked, and someone said, "No."

She had known he would not be there, and indeed he wasn't, and she was crushed.

Because if you go, you're gone. I won't come after you.

She had turned him down. She could not stay here. She turned to tell Gilbert that, but the hackney cab was already moving on, and footmen were carrying her trunk inside.

So Thea let her feet carry her inside too, into that familiar hallway where Rafe had teased her about her shopping.

The usually stern butler smiled at her, with something like relief.

"We are so glad to welcome you, Miss Knight," he said, and

diplomatically avoided mentioning that he had previously addressed her as "my lady." "We've had boys looking for you."

"Looking for me?"

"Instructions from his lordship. To make sure you were safe."

"But I—I'm not the countess."

"His lordship wrote that Miss Knight always has a home here," said the butler.

He didn't explain, but only handed her off to the housekeeper, who led Thea up the stairs, talking all the while. "We'll send up supper, only a cold tray, if that will suffice, though we can send out for something hot if you wish."

"No, that's fine," Thea heard herself say.

"And you'll be glad of a bath, all that London soot and ash on you..."

Thea let the chatter wash over her, let herself be helped out of her smoke-scented clothes and into a lavender-scented robe, to wait for her bath to be ready. The smell of smoke clung to her hair.

They were still filling the bathtub when someone pressed a letter into her hand. She had only seen his precise, bold hand once before, but it was enough to know this was from Rafe. The note was short and impersonal:

As you know, our invalid marriage gave me access to a sum of ten thousand pounds. I am making arrangements to have that sum transferred to you. Present this letter to my solicitors...

Thea folded the note and put it aside. Money. He needed that money for his business, but he'd given it to her instead. Ten thousand pounds was a fortune for anyone, let alone a woman with nothing. More than enough to start her life anew.

Yet he had given her more than money: Once more, the ground had been pulled out from under her feet, but this time, Rafe was there. She had turned him down, but still he had been ready to catch her and cushion her fall. Strong and steady and sure.

"Miss?" someone said. "Miss, your bath is ready now. Would you like me to stay and help?"

"Thank you. No," Thea said. "Thank you."

The door clicked shut. Thea stood alone in a room with a steaming copper tub. She slipped off the robe and stepped into the tub. She looked down. Her smoky hair fell about her face. Through the water, her ankles were indistinct white shapes.

Oh dear heaven, she had got it all wrong.

Dropping into the water, Thea sat and hugged her knees. She breathed hard, but the hot tears came anyway. She fought them, but still they came.

Because she had got it all wrong. Too late, she realized what she had done.

She had tested him.

She had wanted to be wanted, and she wanted that so badly that she had lost all chance of having it. She had tested her parents' love, and they had failed her test. And then she had tested Rafe, and the one who failed that test was her.

All that time she'd been talking about her home in London, priding herself on forming no attachments, hiding even from herself the secret hope that he would beg her to stay. But why would he? When all she had ever said was that she wanted to leave. She liked him chasing her, but that was a game—a fun game, an erotic game, but only a game. She had played a game she didn't understand, and she had lost.

What if she had not played this foolish game? What if she had not tested him? What if she had not run in the hope he would chase her? If she had been brave and simply told him the truth: "I love you and I want to be with you always."

Because a direct statement demanded a direct response, and

Thea was not so brave as she wished. When her dream lay before her—the dream of loving and being loved; of having a safe, loving home with a strong, caring man—she had not dared to believe in it. Instead, she had run.

In the bathtub, Thea hugged her legs and pressed her eyes to her knees, and wept. The crying made her body hot, and the sobs made her sides ache, but she could not stop. When the storm had passed, the water was cooling and her hair still smelled of smoke.

Contorting herself, she sank her head beneath the surface to wet her hair, then lathered lavender-scented soap through it. By the time she was dressed again, with her hair dry and brushed and tied in a plait, and she had eaten some food and slid into bed, she felt strangely calm.

She would soon be in possession of a fortune. The first thing she would do was hire a carriage and drive to Brinkley End.

RAFE HAD nothing to do but wait. Wait and roam aimlessly, haunting his own house, until he wound up in the library, where he spied the pages Thea had left behind. He sat in that big leather chair to read them, and soon found himself engrossed in her strange, funny tale of the outcast heroine taken to a castle and the cursed, half-naked man living in the lake. Thea's voice was in every line, and, for the briefest of moments, he could fool himself that she was by his side.

"Found something to laugh at then?"

Rafe looked up to see Nicholas dressed in green and wreathed in flowers. "Puck?"

"I make a good Shakespearean sprite, don't I?" Nicholas said. "I do hope our Thea will be at the costume party."

Rafe imagined her in that cat mask. No, no masks. He longed

to see her face. He curled his fingers around the pages, then remembered himself and smoothed them out.

Nicholas flipped the green sleeves of his tunic. "I wonder if our friend William Dudley's theatre troupe is still performing that play about Rosamund. Although they really need to change the ending. If you came to London, you could see it too."

"I've already seen it," Rafe reminded him. "The original performance."

How innocent he had been back then, that first night, scowling as Thea told her story. How enthralled her audience had been. Then he and Thea had stood together in the moonlight, where she had ignored his clumsy attempts to comfort her, and cradled his face to comfort him instead.

Pain shot through him. The pages spilled from his hands and his forehead landed on the desk with a thud.

"Oh so help me," he groaned into the wood. "I miss her so bloody much."

A gentle hand squeezed his shoulder. Rafe sat back up and stared at the bishop. "I've done this all wrong, haven't I?"

"You did the best you knew how at the time."

"But what if I've lost her? What if she needs my help and I'm not there? Anything could be happening in London and I'm not bloody well there."

Rafe stared out the window. Down by the lake, Sally and Martha were strolling arm in arm, heads together as they talked. He watched them absently, two more misfits who had found a home here with him, a home he was able to offer only because he was an earl.

He had never wanted to be an earl—he'd much rather his brother was alive—but he was. The only way he could stop being an earl was to die, and he was not ready to leave this world for good. He had to decide, and decide now, whether or not he wished to be part of this world.

It was suddenly a very easy decision: This world had Thea in it, and Rafe wanted to be part of anything that had Thea in it.

Nicholas reached past him and tidied the pages. "One of the many things I admire about you, Rafe, is the way you always went after what you wanted. You never bothered yourself with what anyone else thought; you simply decided and went." He sighed dramatically. "My carriage is ready, and I must be on my way. How horrid you are, my boy, to make me travel back to London all on my lonesome."

"You are not subtle, old man."

"I am exceedingly subtle. What a shame you won't have time to pick out a costume for the party."

"I'm not going to any blasted costume party."

"Of course you're not," the bishop said, and smiled.

CHAPTER 26

The next day, Arabella and her mother arrived in London. Gilbert carried messages, Arabella came to collect her, and Thea moved again, this time to join Arabella in her family's London home.

Thea had just finished telling Arabella about the destruction of her pamphlets, earning from her friend a vehement "Curse Ventnor. I would cheerfully toss *him* on a bonfire," when they were interrupted by the delivery of Arabella's costume for the Prince Regent's party: a classical white gown designed to transform her into the Roman goddess Minerva, along with a helmet crowned with sweeping red feathers, an owl pendant, and a silver snake that would wrap around her upper arm.

Arabella busied herself with arranging the helmet's mane of plumes so they fell perfectly. "I cannot decide if it is fitting or ironic that I shall be dressed as a warrior goddess the evening I get engaged."

Thea stopped petting the silver snake. "Engaged? But you said the Marquess of Hardbury would not have you."

"Papa insists I get engaged at the party, so get engaged I shall."

"But so soon? And to whom, if not Lord Hardbury?"

"Oh, I don't know." Arabella tweaked a feather. "I shall run through my list of lords at the party and accept the first one to propose. All I ask is that he be a peer, that I may call him 'my lord' for the rest of my life and never trouble with learning his name."

Thea watched her friend's long, slender fingers aligning the feathers. Arabella was so intent on her task that a stranger might believe she found her costume more important than her engagement. Thea was not a stranger.

"Arabella, if you need help—"

"Or perhaps your earl?" Arabella interrupted smoothly. "You suggested I might have him once you finished with him. Have you finished with him?"

"No, I haven't. I'm going back to him."

"Does he want you to go back to him?"

"Yes. No. I don't know. I'm going back anyway."

Arabella's hands stilled and she pivoted away from the helmet. "Thea, what have you done?"

"I've fallen in love, that's what I've done. But I fear I have ruined it."

"Why do you say that?"

"He is giving me ten thousand pounds, which might mean he's washing his hands of me. I don't blame him because I got everything wrong. I have lost my dreams and my family, and I have enough money to start a new life, but I don't care about any of that. All I can think of is putting things right with Rafe. Even if he doesn't want me anymore, I must let him know that he is loved. I owe him that, at least, after all he has done for me. I shall see his solicitor, request an advance on the money, and use it to hire a chaise."

"Perhaps Mama could lend you funds to leave sooner."

Thea's heart skipped at the thought. She could leave tonight! And then— She looked back down at the silver snake and thought of Arabella, going off to the party in two days to get engaged against her will.

"I could share my money with you," Thea said. "You could live independently and you wouldn't need to marry Lord Wotsisname."

Arabella shook her head. "It is not the money. The Larke estate is my birthright, but the only way I can inherit it is to adhere to my father's demands."

"But remember, you said you were like a hawk, soaring free in the sky."

"Do you know how we train hawks? With a tether. The lead gets longer and longer, until eventually the tether is cut, but in the hawk's mind, it is always there." Arabella gave her a pointed look. "Wipe that concern from your face, Thea. I shall make an aristocratic marriage, as I have meant to do all my life. And I shall be able to see you more often, if you would be so kind as to make an aristocratic marriage too."

"I shall try," Thea said and tried to ignore the flutter in her stomach. But she could not abandon Arabella, even if Arabella claimed not to care. "But first I shall accompany you to the Prince Regent's costume party, if you can smuggle me in, so I can interrogate this Lord Wotsisname of yours."

ARABELLA CLEARLY DID NOT WANT Thea to interrogate Lord Wotsisname, for she disappeared the moment they were safely inside the Prince Regent's costume party, and Thea ended up wandering out onto the lawn alone, finding not a genteel party but a carnival.

Flaming torches lined the garden paths. Acrobats cartwheeled amid the guests, jugglers juggled, and up on a tight rope, rope dancers leaped and twirled. Traipsing through the crowds were jesters, who played tricks on guests or cajoled them into playing risqué games.

Everywhere, the guests' costumes created the effect of some grotesque dream. Thea's Venetian cat mask was heavy on her face, and no one gave her a second look. Although this was not a true masquerade, a few faces were covered like her own.

Thea sought a glimpse of the Prince Regent or the mysterious Marquess of Hardbury, who had been so unconscionably rude to Arabella. She overheard someone saying he had not yet arrived, and someone else claiming he was on the lawn, and someone else saying who cared about the marquess, had they heard there would be a spot of theatre inside?

Watching a play sounded as good a way as any to pass the evening until Arabella let herself be found, so Thea turned to go back inside. And then she saw him: a man wearing a giant lion's head.

Rafe!

She elbowed through the crowd, trying not to lose sight of the lion's head. All around her were people laughing, jesters dancing. An acrobat went careening past. She had to find that lion. And when she found him, she would— What would she do? Smile at him? Hug him? Oh, there he was. He was turning. She would see his face. He would see her. She would tease him, perhaps, and say—

Nothing.

The man in the lion's head had blue eyes and a red beard and was not Rafe.

Everything moved to a great distance. The mask clung to her heated face. The crowd roared and subsided, and the lion man

333

greeted a friend and wandered on. Of course it wasn't him. Too short. Too thin around the shoulders.

How silly she was, to imagine Rafe would come for her. He had said he wouldn't. Never mind. Once she got through this awful evening and secured the money, tomorrow or the next day, she would get her carriage and go home to him.

For now, she would watch the theatre.

A makeshift stage had been set up in the middle of a ballroom, surrounded by rows of chairs, with standing room behind, most spots already taken. Excited murmurs rippled through the group. "It's a surprise performance," someone said, "They decided to do it just this morning..." "It's a very modern play and quite shocking, I've heard," and "Oh dear, but doesn't Prinny hold the most dreadfully daring parties!"

Thea edged along one wall, coming to a stop by some heavy velvet curtains that sealed off an alcove, about the size of a large bed. The alcove was mercifully deserted; likely it was for the servants' use, to come and go through the door on the other side.

The beautiful mask was heavy on her face, but she dared not remove it. Especially when she saw her parents come bustling in, rosy-cheeked and excited, dressed as a medieval knight and his lady. Clearly, they were not pining for her.

Gripping the velvet curtain, Thea scanned the crowd, searching for Helen, until a drumbeat rolled through the room, and a man in thick face paint took center stage. He launched into a poetry recital, gradually winning the crowd's attention. The man looked familiar, but Thea could not place him, and her mind was puzzling it over when her roaming eyes landed on Percy Russell and Francis Upton, standing not ten yards from her. They wore elaborate outfits in the ostentatious style of the old French Court: plush coats and ornate waistcoats, with frilly cuffs and lacy cravats. Their eyes skated over her without recognition. Just as well; they would find it great sport to expose her and see her cast out.

As she watched, a footman, white wig in contrast to his brown skin, offered them a tray bearing two drinks. Percy and Francis took the glasses without acknowledging the servant, toasted each other, and tossed back the drinks in a single gulp. They dropped the glasses back on the tray, and then Percy said something to the footman that made them both laugh nastily.

Vile, dastardly knaves. Still nothing harmed or touched them. Even servants went out of their way to please them, and never mind that they were rude. Just look at that footman, heading in Thea's direction now, unfazed by their rudeness, with the empty glasses rolling around on his tray and an amused expression on his features.

Her features.

The footman was a woman. An unexpectedly familiar woman.

"Martha?" Thea blinked in surprise, and Martha jerked to a halt.

"Thea, is that you?" Martha grinned. "We hoped to see you here."

"We?" Thea looked at the empty glasses on Martha's tray. "What are you up to? I do not believe you have taken a position as footman in the Prince Regent's household."

"It is a costume party. So, I am wearing a costume." Martha shrugged and tidied the two glasses on her tray. "It is not my fault if those self-centered snots do not realize it."

"What was in those drinks?"

"I need more people for my experiments. You see, they are not completely useless."

"Oh Martha, you didn't give them your medicines! Not without them knowing!"

"Do not feel bad. It will not hurt them. Remember, it merely makes them behave as they truly are. Watch the theatre now," she added brightly, and disappeared into the crowd.

Thea was starting to feel as though someone had slipped something into her drink too, for this evening was becoming like one of those dreams populated by everyone she knew. Her parents, Percy and Francis, Martha, and there was the Bishop of Dartford, dressed as Puck, and she finally placed the man on stage as William Dudley, the actor who had pretended to be the zealot outside Rafe's house, and whom the bishop had seen performing on the road.

Then an unseen drum began to beat, slow and heavy, like a heartbeat late at night. Whispers started and faded, as a figure stalked onto the stage, face and body hidden under a black, shapeless cloak.

The drumbeat quickened. Another drum joined it, and then another, all in overlaying rhythms. The figure began to spin. The drums beat faster. Harder. Filling the room, until Thea felt her skin and bones vibrate. A flute sounded over the top, its fast, high trills weaving through the beats.

On the stage, the figure was whirling and whirling, whirling off the black cloak, whirling so that her skirts flew out, whirling so that the candlelight lit the jewels woven through her bright red hair, and her gold-colored gown glinted, and her gold satin gloves gleamed.

The drums and flute rose to a crescendo. And stopped.

The woman stood still, her arms raised in a V, her face glowing with triumph.

Stunned silence fell.

With unsteady hands, Thea yanked off her mask and stared. A moment later, England's finest were gasping and applauding and calling the woman's name.

Sarah Holloway had returned to the London stage.

That confident manner that Thea so admired was in full force tonight, as Sally—the world could call her Sarah Holloway but to Thea she would always be Sally—took command of the awestruck audience. They might rule the country, but in this moment, Sally ruled them. Ventnor had forced her to hide, but she was hiding no more. She stood before the cream of society, proud and compelling, and they loved her, whether they wanted to or not.

"My lords, ladies, and gentlemen," Sally said, her rich, melodious voice filling every corner of the cavernous room. "I present myself tonight for one special performance only."

The audience chorused their disappointment. Thea remembered that Sally had performed alongside William Dudley. That William Dudley's traveling theatre troupe had been performing on the road to London.

"A special performance for the entertainment of the Prince Regent and his esteemed guests. Tonight's play uses false names to hide its truth, for this is a true story, and the true actors walk among you in this room. Here is the puzzle and the riddle and the game: Can you unmask the truth of this story? And guess whose tale we truly tell?"

That set them all whispering. Thea's breath caught, as her eyes strayed back to Percy and Francis. The bishop had said William Dudley's troupe was performing *The Tale of Rosamund*. Excitement jolted through her.

"My lords, ladies, and gentlemen," Sally said over their murmuring. "We present a short play titled '*Win Some, Lose Some*'."

Oh. Thea forced a smile. Not her play, then. Never mind. She was happy to see Sally anyway.

But in the next breath, Sally added, "Also known as: *The Tale of Rosamund*. A winsome lass who was cruelly wronged by two dastardly knaves."

CHAPTER 27

U p on the stage, the actors took their places, and the play
    began. Thea inched back into the alcove, using the velvet
curtain to cover her face to her eyes, expecting the whole crowd to
turn, to boo and hiss and toss her out.

No one turned. No one even noticed her, for all were transfixed
by the drama unfolding on the stage. Thea let herself relax, and
take in what was happening.

Despite everything, her story was being told.

One night in a coaching inn, a man had asked to hear her
story, so Thea had stood on a chair and told her tale to a tipsy
crowd. That tale had somehow assumed a life of its own, picked
up by traveling theatre companies and performed, over and over,
so that even as her pamphlets burned and rained ash down on
London, her story lived on. To be told to the people she most
needed to hear it.

Yet not to the person she needed most.

Rafe.

Thea looked at the actors on the stage, and at the cream of

society watching, at Percy and Francis and Ma and Pa. She realized she no longer cared what any of them thought of her. The performance of this play was a victory for her, but a hollow one, for even this she would sacrifice, if it meant she could be with Rafe. Finally, she had figured out what she wanted, and she had already lost it; finally, she had grown up and now it was too late.

Not yet, she thought. It wasn't too late yet.

She'd find Arabella now, and beg, borrow, or steal money to leave London tonight. The sooner she left, the sooner she'd be at Brinkley End.

Decided, Thea drew back behind the velvet curtain and turned, almost colliding with a large man who had come too close.

He was big and broad, this man, with a great lion's head over his tousled dark hair, and an intent look in his brandy-colored eyes.

His mouth curved into a half smile.

"There you are," Rafe said.

THE ARRANGEMENTS WERE COBBLED TOGETHER SO HASTILY, there was the risk Rafe would not find her, but as all the other pieces fell into place smoothly, he had not worried too much. If he could find a tiny flower in the middle of the selva, he could find the woman he loved in the middle of the Prince Regent's party.

And like magic, he had. He had slipped through the side door into the alcove to watch the play, and there she was. His Thea. He devoured her with his eyes: her hair tumbling in delicate curls, the surprise animating her features, her expressive blue gaze.

It took all his strength not to launch himself at her and haul her into his arms. Tensing every muscle in his tortured body, Rafe prayed, yet again, that this time he had understood. That he had accurately understood Thea's reasons for leaving and what she needed. That he had finally understood *her*.

Behind her, the heavy curtains swayed and closed. On the other side of the curtains, actors performed for society. On this side of the curtain lay everything important and real.

Her eyes were suddenly swimming with tears.

"Thea?" Rafe whispered.

Somehow, his hands found hers. She clutched a fan and the Venetian cat mask, but his hands were big enough to hold hers and whatever she carried too.

"I am so sorry," she blurted out, her voice low and urgent. "I made the wrong choices. I was coming back to you. But...you're here."

"I could not wait." He drew her deeper, into a corner of the alcove. They moved together as easily as if they were both floating. "I heard Ventnor burned your pamphlets. I cannot tell you how much I regret not being there to stop him. I could have stopped him, if only I had come sooner. I'm sorry I let you down."

"But it does not matter. I'm glad he burned them, because that was how I saw the truth." Her eyes searched his, frantically. "My story, my reputation, my family: None of it matters. What mattered most was that I lost you." Her fingers weaved more tightly around his. Something fell to the floor at their feet, but neither paid it any mind. "What I mean is, I love you."

Rafe's heart stopped, jolted, tumbled through his body to his knees, and then started up again with as much fervor as if he'd sprinted a mile. Blood rushed in his ears, the audience laughed, but all the noise in the world would not stop him from hearing her words.

"I love you, Rafe, I do, and I have for a long time. I wish I had told you before. Because you should know that you are loved. That you are—you are everything. I should have simply said it, but I was too scared and I got it all wrong, and now you're here, and I don't know why you're here, but everyone's here, it's like a dream, and I'm talking too much, and I know you don't like talking, and you don't owe me anything but I love you anyway."

She breathed in deeply, raggedly. Rafe was out of breath too, though he'd not said a word.

"Say something," she whispered.

He did not dare look away from her, for fear she might disappear. "I understand now, why you had to go. You had to fight your own battles, address your past before you could look to your future. You helped me break free from my past, and you needed to do that for yourself too. I wish I had understood sooner." He freed one hand, caressed her cheek, chased away the distress haunting her eyes. "You were coming back to me?" he repeated.

"I had to. I resolved to be brave this time. To take a risk, to ask for what is mine. You said you would not come after me, so I vowed to come after you. I vowed to ask you to forgive me and give me another chance."

"Thea, know that I shall always come after you, as long as you want me. You said you cannot trust the ground on which you walk, but know this: *I* will be the earth beneath your feet." He lifted her hands, pressed his lips to her knuckles, and struggled for the words. "I've had days to craft a proper marriage proposal, to get it right this time but... I can only tell you that I love you, Thea, fiercely, truly, irrevocably. Just say you'll have me, and I will be there for you as long as you want me."

"Always," she whispered. "Which is precisely as long as I'll be there for you."

"Is that a yes?"

A broken laugh flew out of her lips, and on it rode the word he longed to hear: "Yes. Yes. Yes."

She laughed again, but she was crying too, and fighting both.

He knew how she felt for he felt it too: so much emotion that his body could hardly contain it, and his cheeks ached from smiling and his eyes stung.

"You're crying," she said.

"I am not."

This time, when she laughed, that breathy, tear-hued laugh, he captured it with his mouth. As soon as his lips touched hers, time disappeared, along with his breath, so he took hers: took her breath, took her love, and offered all of his. He wrapped his arms around her, pressing her body to his. She matched his ardor. Her hands slid around his neck, the mask dangling from her fingers thwacking him and sending his lion's head tumbling to the floor.

"We have to get out of here," Rafe muttered against her lips.

"Yes."

"Get home."

"Yes."

But that meant releasing her, and he could not bear to do that yet, could not remove his arms. Thea let her forehead fall onto his shoulder, and Rafe rested his cheek on her hair. His chest was still tight with emotion, and his body ached with desire. He reminded himself to breathe, but breathing didn't seem to matter, not when he had found her and never had to let her go.

TIME LOST MEANING, until the rising voices of the actors on the other side of the curtain reminded them to ease apart.

"Let's get out of here," Rafe muttered. He scooped up her fan, assessed the fallen lion's head and decided it could stay. "The bishop has obtained a special license and set the paperwork to rights. We can marry tonight if you wish. Unless you want a big wedding."

"All I want is you. Oh, I must tell Arabella. Oh, and Sally and Martha. And... Oh, but this was you! The theatre. Of course it was you!"

"I failed to stop Ventnor from burning your pamphlets, but I could still make your story heard. The Royal Household was eager to accommodate my request to present a play by the Luxborough Players."

"The Luxborough Players?"

Her pleasure so delighted him, the Royal Household might as well have named him king. "All the best earls and countesses own a theatre company."

She pressed a hand to his chest, her eyes concerned again. "You do so many things for me, and I do nothing for you."

"Such things are easy for me. I'm an earl, remember, whether I want it or not. And you have done everything for me. Everything." He lowered his head to kiss her again, remembered where they were, and stepped away. "Now that I know you, I know I want to be part of this world, with you. So I intend to take my seat in the House of Lords properly. There is much we must do better— improve conditions in asylums, abolish slavery, reform voting, provide education. It means we will live in London half the year, while Parliament is sitting."

Thea's eyes widened. "But all those *people*! All that *talking*!"

"It will be a trial," he agreed glumly. "But I'll be with you."

"We'll build you a darling little greenhouse here in London, where you can escape when you need time alone. And we'll spend the other half of the year at Brinkley End, I hope?"

"You will not grow bored there? You know I do not need the company of many people," he reminded her. "And if you do..."

"I would not say I need other people, although I do like them."

"And if there are no people?"

She sighed dramatically. "Then I suppose you will have to do."

She grinned and patted his cheek. "I shall write my stories. Besides, a countess can do all kinds of useful things. I could fight rumors, for example, and give a voice to those who have none. Although I doubt I'll be a very good countess, and society may not accept me."

"You will be the very best countess and society will love you. They'll deal with me if they don't."

"What about your plants and medicines?"

"Martha and I will hire others to work with her. I have agreed to let Sally and Martha live in the Dower House. It seems that they, ah, wish to set up a household together."

"*Together*, together? Well, there's a surprise. How marvelous for them."

"It is rather, isn't it?" He lowered his head then paused. "Bloody hell, if I kiss you again... Can we stop all this blasted talking and get out of here?"

They snuck up to the curtain like naughty children, and peered at the stage. It was nearing the scene at the ball, where the two dastardly knaves told society lies about Rosamund to bring about her ruin.

"I need to find the bishop," Rafe whispered, his eyes scanning the audience. "Can you see him?"

"I cannot. Oh. Percy and Francis."

Rafe ran his hand down her back. "Who are about to get their comeuppance. Do you want to watch that?"

"Um."

He glanced at her face. "What are you scheming?"

Her thoughtful look melted into a mischievous smile. "There's one more thing I need to do."

CHAPTER 28

There were many things Thea wished to say to Percy Russell and Francis Upton, but she supposed the right thing would be to warn them that they had taken an intoxicant, and might not be quite themselves.

Unless Martha's theory was right, and the medicine made them *more* themselves.

When they saw her approaching around the edges of the audience, they elbowed each other and again bowed in unison. Francis's wig fell off and he giggled.

Ah, so the medicine had taken effect.

On stage, Rosamund stood in shocked horror as she faced her disgrace. In the audience, ladies and gentlemen were murmuring to each other. Several people spied Thea stopping next to Percy, and put their heads together to start whispering anew.

"That's us up there," Percy hissed to Thea. "We did that to you. Why are those actors performing our story?"

It wasn't their story, Thea thought angrily; it was *her* story.

"Now everyone will know," she replied. "Are you sorry?"

Percy laughed, drawing more stares. It was a bit like a donkey's bray, his laugh. "It was great sport. Why be sorry?"

Francis giggled again. "The expression on your face when we lied about you at the ball!"

"It was one of my cleverest exploits!" Percy crowed.

"One of *our* cleverest," Francis corrected. "Why be sorry for that?"

"Not sorry for that!"

Thea recalled her intention to warn them they had taken an intoxicant, but clearly they did not deserve the least bit of decency from her. Their roles in society had enabled them to ruin innocents like her for sport; now, she returned the favor. Besides, this complied with her three Rules of Mischief: It served the cause of truth, they were definitely villains, and yes, she was enjoying it.

"It's true, you're very clever," Thea said. "Now everyone in society knows it. Look at them applauding, dukes and marquesses and earls. But they applaud the actors, not you."

Percy sneered. "Stupid dukes and marquesses and earls. They should be applauding me. Me! Applaud me, you fools!"

"Applaud *us*!" Francis cried. "Don't forget me, Percy."

Thea leaned close to whisper in Percy's ear. "This is your chance to ensure society knows how clever you are. Go tell them it was *your* plan. Tell them now."

"Yes, I shall!"

His feet not quite steady, Percy elbowed aside the people in his way and leaped onto the stage. He shoved away the actors; they stumbled back to watch, as Percy planted himself in the center and thumped his chest.

"It was me!" he yelled.

"Don't let Percy forget about you," Thea whispered to Francis, who nodded and ran unsteadily for the stage.

"It was a good trick, wasn't it, how I ruined Miss Knight?" Percy called out to the spectators, who were watching and whispering and watching some more. "It was my idea."

"It was my idea too," Francis whined from beside him. "Don't forget me, Percy."

Rafe was watching from the other side of the stage, Martha and Sally by his side. Martha wore that impassively curious look she got during experiments. Sally's hand was plastered over her mouth, her eyes wide with horrified amusement. Rafe's gaze shifted and found Thea's. She shrugged and he grinned.

Then her attention was caught by a man pushing to the front of the audience, recognizable by his long white hair and long black walking stick.

"Get down from there, boy," Lord Ventnor hissed at Percy. "You're drunk. You don't know what you're saying."

"Look, it's Father." Percy brayed his donkey's bray. "Father says I'm not clever, but I fooled him, I fooled you all. We told you tales about Thea Knight, and you believed us."

"Silence!" Ventnor demanded from the floor.

"You pair of disgusting oafs will stop this now," ordered another voice, as cold and crisp as a winter's night. The voice belonged to an elderly man, who was not tall but had such presence he did not need to be: the Duke of Sherbourne.

"What's that?" Percy said.

Francis squinted. "It's a duke."

"A duck, you say."

"I said duke."

"I said duck." Percy opened and shut his hand, miming a duck's beak. "Quack, quack, quack."

And, of course, Francis did too.

"Will you make this family a laughingstock?" Ventnor brandished his walking stick, cheeks red, spittle gathering around his lips. "Do not speak thus to the duke."

Percy and Francis made no sign of stopping. Instead, they bent their elbows to make flapping wings, stuck their bottoms in the air, and quacked.

Thea dragged her eyes off their ridiculous antics to study the spectators. The members of the *ton* were staring at Percy and Francis with disgust and disdain and amused scorn.

Just as they'd stared at her.

"Get down!" Ventnor appeared on the verge of tears. Thea recalled how he had misused his power to hurt others, and she cared nothing for his troubles. "Do not expose this family to further ridicule!"

"Expose!"

"Stop this farce!"

"Farts!"

Percy and Francis looked at each other and giggled. Turning their backs to the crowd, they flipped up their coat tails and fumbled for the fastenings on their breeches, while Ventnor yelled, "No, Percy, not again!" Ladies gasped and men groaned. Some turned away, some covered their eyes—or pretended to— while others stared openly, because this was not a sight they often saw.

As Percy Russell and Francis Upton dropped their breeches and exposed their round, white buttocks to the *ton*.

A QUARTET of brawny men hauled Percy and Francis away, while the ballroom erupted into a genteel uproar. The pair were unlikely to recover from their thorough disgrace. Thea pressed her lips together to hold back her cheers.

And then Lord Ventnor's voice once more cut through the hubbub. "This is an outrage!"

He had taken center stage, controlled and dignified, addressing the crowd in his practiced speaking voice. The noise faded and died. When he had the room's attention, he added, "These claims concerning my son are nothing but falsehoods and fibs."

"And yet," responded the Duke of Sherbourne, who easily commanded attention even from the floor, "your son brazenly confessed to telling malicious lies to falsely ruin Miss Knight. I do believe he admitted that right before he called me— What was it? Oh yes. A stupid, quacking duck."

"Your Grace, I must apologize. My son..."

Ventnor's narrowed eyes roamed over the audience, coming to settle on Thea. His gaze bore into her. Faces turned to see. Bodies shifted. A circle opened around her, an empty circle with her at its center, alone.

"It was Miss Knight herself who peddled this humbug about my son," Ventnor declared. "I'll wager she put something in my son's drink to alter his behavior. Why, she is nothing but Luxborough's harlot!"

Thea's skin prickled with cold, even as her blood ran hot. She straightened her spine and held her head high. It was happening all over again: the narrowing of eyes, the lifting of brows, the shoulders turning away. A plague on them. Faster than a heartbeat, they passed judgment.

The same length of time it took Rafe to bound onto the stage.

"Careful, Ventnor," Rafe said loudly. Hundreds of costumed heads swiveled toward him. "I've warned you before not to speak thus of *my wife*."

"More lies!" Ventnor pointed at her with his stick. "This woman is your—"

"Wife." Rafe loomed, his face hard and unflinching. "That lady is the Countess of Luxborough, and you will show her due respect." He eyed the audience menacingly. "You will *all* show her due respect."

Then he looked at Thea; his expression softened, and the world faded away. Her senses perceived nothing but this man, *her* man, publicly claiming her as his own.

Ventnor was still yammering. "You didn't marry her. You married the wrong woman."

Rafe's gaze didn't waver. "She is definitely the right woman."

The confusion of the audience was palpable, and through it sliced an imperious female drawl, the crisp voice rising easily above the murmurs.

"Of course they are married."

Thea dragged her eyes off Rafe, to where Arabella was gliding toward Thea as confidently as if she were indeed a warrior goddess, the crowd parting for her like water.

"I witnessed the wedding myself," Arabella added, as she reached Thea. "Would you call me a liar too, Lord Ventnor?"

"And I officiated at the wedding," declared the bishop, also planting himself at Thea's side. "Would you call me a liar too, Lord Ventnor?"

"No question of it at all," said another man. Thea was not acquainted with this speaker, but given his features and the fact that Helen held his arm, she deduced that this was Beau Russell. "Would you call me a liar too, Father?"

They were all liars, of course, but as lies went, this one was very nearly true. That gleeful half smile curved Rafe's mouth, and Thea did not even try to repress her grin. A true aristocrat would never show her feelings this way, but she didn't care. If any aristocrat wished to judge her poorly, they could do it from a nice warm seat in hell.

On the other side of the stage, Sally and Martha were waving at her. By her side stood Arabella and the bishop and Helen and

Beau, and Rafe had claimed her. What cared Thea for anyone else? She caught the Duke of Sherbourne studying her. When their eyes met, he bowed, and she responded with her most refined curtsy. With such an influential leader of society acknowledging her, everyone else would have to follow.

When the duke had turned away, Thea smiled at Arabella. "Thank you. What about your engagement?"

"Already done."

"And to whom are you engaged? What's his name?"

"Oh, some lord or other." The bluebell eyes revealed nothing, as Arabella waved a dismissive hand. "I am bored with the subject already. My wedding is not until spring, so we have time to discuss it later. Let us direct our attention to you, tonight. You have quite outdone yourself."

On her other side, Helen laughed merrily. "Indeed. Of all the mischief you have ever made, Thea, this is easily the best. But you'll have to stop making mischief once you are a countess."

Thea favored them both with her haughtiest look. "Not at all. All the best countesses make mischief, and my kind of mischief is exactly what this crowd needs."

RAFE COULD NOT HAVE FORESEEN the events of this evening; all he had done was gather up the pieces—William Dudley with his theatre company, Sally with her stage appeal, Martha with her medicines—and arrange them like dominoes, to fall as they may.

Now, the pieces lay unexpectedly like this: He and Ventnor stood on a stage, under the riveted attention of hundreds. Only a fraction of society was present, and it was hard to take them seriously given their array of ludicrous costumes, but it was enough.

It had been enough to redeem Thea. Enough to ruin the two dastardly knaves.

And it would be enough for Rafe to settle his final score.

He took three paces across the stage; faces swiveled, tracking his every move. He took three paces back; again the faces followed him, waiting for the next line. It seemed everyone enjoyed a spot of theatre, whether commoners in a tavern or members of the *haut ton*. Rafe was surprised to find this attention rather gratifying. Perhaps he should have joined his family's theatre performances as a boy.

"I grow weary of your lies, Ventnor."

Certainly Ventnor liked to put on a show, for he shuddered with self-righteous indignation. "How dare you thus impugn my honor, Luxborough! I speak only the truth."

Rafe laughed. "You, with your shiny walking stick and spotless hands, you who send ruffians to do violence in your name— You dare speak of truth and honor? Now, if we were to speak of truth..."

Ventnor's eyes narrowed. "Do not do this. You will regret it."

"This man—" Rafe addressed himself to the crowd, gesturing with a dramatic sweep of his arm. "This man tried to kidnap and imprison his daughter, my first wife, and that is why she died. All because she—"

"She died fleeing you!" Ventnor screeched. He, too, directed himself to the audience. "He poisoned her. He brutalized her. Look at him. That is the face of a brute."

"This is the face of a botanist who experienced an unfortunate encounter with a wild animal. How fanciful you are, Ventnor. Do you mean to repeat those far-fetched stories you started that I am a witch? That this cat scratch is the mark of the Devil?"

But before Ventnor could voice his predictable protests, the actor William Dudley popped onto the stage, with such exquisite timing they might have rehearsed it.

"I can testify that Lord Ventnor hired me and other actors to spread these rumors," Dudley announced.

Ventnor whirled around. "Nobody asked you, man. Away with you!"

William Dudley planted his feet and did not move, while the Duke of Sherbourne added his consequence to the stage.

"Is this true, Lord Ventnor?" the duke asked. "You paid people to spread these ludicrous, illegal rumors about the Earl of Luxborough?"

"That man is an actor," Ventnor said. "Your Grace is too wise to believe an actor."

Sally took that as her cue and glided onto the stage with such presence that everyone else might have vanished.

"Then I daresay no one will believe me either," she said, "when I confirm that Lord Ventnor sent ruffians to kidnap his daughter. I would know: I shot one in the shoulder."

Ventnor brandished his stick at her. "Do not muddy the waters. I only wanted my daughter to receive proper care. It was never my intention to cause her harm."

"Indeed, my lord." Sally made a show of thinking. "I recall you said as much to me. You said, and I quote, 'I never meant for Katharine to die.'"

"Yes. Yes!" Ventnor was nodding his head furiously. "Well done, my dear. An actress, of course, will remember the exact words. *Exactly* what I said."

"Then you said, 'Her death was not the solution I intended, but it was a solution nonetheless.'"

Gasps of horror echoed across the room. Ventnor looked about wildly, lips moving in protestations he had no chance to speak.

"Get a soul," Sally hissed, advancing on him. "You destroy

things, beautiful things, because you are incapable of seeing their beauty. You failed to see the beauty of your own daughter's life, because all you saw was your own fear and shame. You fail to see the beauty of love, because all you see is the dried, shriveled husk of your own unused heart. What a pitiful creature you are."

The air was taut with embarrassment. Something flickered in the viscount's pale eyes, the last hope of a man who did long to see beauty. A final hope that guttered and died, and once more, Ventnor sneered.

"Ignore this woman. She is a...a Sapphist!"

Sally regarded him coolly. "That did not bother you when you were my patron." She turned to the audience. "He offered his patronage so I would not reveal that he tried to kidnap his own daughter. But I can speak of it now, because he withdrew his patronage. He withdrew it by sending his ruffian to chase me away from London, under the threat of carving up my face."

The crowd was murmuring and muttering, uncertain, uncomfortable.

Straightening, Lord Ventnor wrapped his dignity around him like a cloak. "I am a peer of this realm. Am I to be tried thus, as a piece of theatre, and not in the House of Lords as is my due?"

"Enough," agreed the Duke of Sherbourne. "The Prince Regent will arrive soon, and it would be tedious to explain this farce to him. We will review these accusations later. Lords, ladies, and gentlemen, please return to your festivities. I declare tonight's theatre closed."

THEA WAS ALMOST light-headed with triumph when Rafe leaped off the stage and took her hands.

"Now that's done, let's go," he said.

She squeezed his fingers. "You were magnificent. Will anything happen to Ventnor, do you think?"

"Hard to say. The privilege of peerage protects him from punishment for most crimes."

"That's so unfair! I wish he could rot on the other side of the world."

"Many wish the same. I'll see what I can do. But we have a more important matter to attend to tonight, so let's get Nicholas and go."

Before they could speak to the bishop, a couple stepped across their path: Ma and Pa. Thea stopped short. She curled one arm around Rafe's. He wove his fingers between hers.

"By my buttons!" Pa said, a grin splitting his face. "What an extraordinary evening this has been."

"Oh Thea, what a to-do!" Ma patted Thea's shoulder. "Why did you not tell us you had married the earl? This changes everything."

They were beaming at her. Beaming! A faint growl sounded from Rafe's throat.

"You turned me out," Thea reminded them softly. "Twice."

Ma's smile faded, sorrow shadowing her face. "Thea, darling. We didn't know the truth."

"You refused to listen."

"Dearest Thea," Pa said, his eyes earnest. "I wish you would forgive us. Such foolish mistakes we made."

Thea looked from one to the other, her fingers digging into Rafe's palm. "Do you come to me because you truly regret not believing me and supporting me, or because he is an earl?"

Stark silence blanketed them. Thea was still searching for words when Helen joined them. Helen placed one hand on Thea's shoulder, one on Ma's.

"Please forgive them, Thea," Helen said. "They are our parents."

"Perhaps one day I shall forgive you, but it will not be tonight," Thea replied. "I have another family now."

Helen's hand slipped away as Thea turned her back on her parents. She concentrated on Rafe's solidity at her side, as he guided her back to Arabella and the bishop.

"I'm tired of this blasted costume party," Rafe said. "Can we go home?"

"Best if we did." The bishop's eyes twinkled as he whispered, "Now we've lied to, well, everyone, we had better get you two married."

RAFE HAD NOT BEEN to many weddings in his life, but he was fairly sure that his own, which took place that night in his townhouse, was not quite usual, given that the celebrant was a mischievous Shakespearean fairy, and the witnesses were a Roman goddess, a Royal footman, and a retired actress in a golden gown. Gilbert and the other servants crowded around too. Rafe saw only Thea, whose eyes smiled at him as they spoke their vows.

"Is that it?" Rafe demanded, shoving the signed paperwork back at Nicholas. "Are we married?"

"You are."

"Good. Then you can all get out of my house. Now."

The servants eagerly left, to celebrate in their hall. Thea crossed to say her farewells to Miss Larke, and Rafe turned to the bishop and his sparkling brown eyes.

"I told you so," Nicholas sang.

Overcome with laughter, Rafe gathered the older man into a

fierce hug. No sooner had he released him than Thea approached, grinning at them both.

"Bloody hell, don't you two start chatting, or we'll be here all night," Rafe grumbled.

"I need to thank the bishop," Thea protested.

"He'll show up soon enough, for tea and gossip, and you can thank him then."

"Besides, we need to discuss Christmas," Nicholas said. "Judith and I have decided that you will host the extended family for Christmas at Brinkley End this year."

"We will not," Rafe said, as Thea cried, "Oh yes!"

Rafe might have argued, but he spied Miss Larke wrapping a velvet cloak around her shoulders, preparing to slip out. Something in her expression compelled him to follow her.

"Miss Larke?"

She paused in the open doorway. "My lord?"

"I behaved badly toward you when we first met," he said. "The threats I made, the way I used you to manipulate Thea— I apologize for causing you distress."

She considered him coolly. "Treat Thea well, and all is forgiven."

"You were a friend to Thea when she most needed one, at risk to yourself. I am in your debt. Only say the word, and we shall not hesitate to help."

A bleak look shadowed Miss Larke's eyes, as if she might weep. But a heartbeat later, the expression passed, and she was her usual proud, aloof self.

"Good grief. Love does soften a man's brain," she drawled. "Why on earth would you imagine that I might need help?" She inclined her head. "Good night, my lord. Felicitations on your marriage."

With that, she stepped into the night.

A moment later, Sally and Martha hurtled past, calling good-byes as they ran to a waiting hack, and finally, Rafe managed to shove Nicholas out the door and slam it shut. At his look, the last of the servants melted away, and he and Thea were blessedly alone, in the blessed silence.

"Finally," Rafe said, slipping his hands around her waist. "All those blasted people are gone."

Thea smoothed her palms over his chest. "You did a lot of talking tonight."

"So I shall not talk to anyone for a week."

"You'll talk to me."

"I will." Rafe slid his hands up her arms to cradle her face. He brushed his thumbs over her lips. "I have syllabub waiting upstairs. You will not have to choose between pleasures."

A wicked gleam lit her blue eyes, sending desire shooting through his groin. She wrapped her arms around his neck and pressed her promising softness against him. "Will you feed it to me?"

Rafe ducked and scooped her into his arms, laughing at her squeals of delight.

"I shall paint it on your skin," he said. "I shall kiss you everywhere, and make love to you until all you can think of is me."

"And then?" she whispered.

Rafe tightened his arms around her. "And then I shall take you home."

EPILOGUE

To the delight of the hordes that invaded Brinkley End that December, it snowed a few days before Christmas.

Rafe arrived from his greenhouse, the cold air slicing his cheeks, and stopped short at the sight of the lawn. Or, more precisely, at the inordinately large number of children running around in the snow, squealing and yelling. Christopher and Mary had several children, and Mary's sister and husband had shown up with their children, and Thea's parents had brought the Little Ones, and while that added up to an absurd number of children, it still did not account for the masses on his lawn.

One figure parted from the others and hurled herself at him, blue eyes bright. Rafe dropped a kiss on her pink nose, and another on her pink lips, then pulled her against him and studied the screaming creatures.

Thea elbowed him. "If you keep scowling at the children like that, they'll get frightened and run away."

"There's an awful lot of them," Rafe remarked. "I think there are more than before."

"That happens with children."

"Yes, but don't they usually go through a pink, screaming stage before they get to the shouty, sticky-fingered stage?"

"Oh, I see what you mean." Thea laughed and hugged him. "The village children are here, to rehearse for the Christmas pageant."

"The Christmas pageant?"

"Had you forgotten?"

"Yes. And now I shall forget it again." With one look at her, he did indeed promptly forget the pageant and the children. "Will you skate with me today? I have news."

She answered with a broad smile, but before they could make their escape, one of the creatures came slipping and sliding across the snow toward them.

"Uncle Lucky! Uncle Lucky!" cried the creature.

Thea cast him a look. "'Uncle Lucky'?"

"Don't ask."

The creature revealed itself to be a girl, who said, "You told Charlie that crocodiles live in the lake, but I looked it up in the bestiary and they say crocodiles like hot places." She frowned anxiously at the frozen lake. "Will the poor crocodiles be all right?"

"I assure you, they are fine," Rafe replied. "In autumn, they roll in the warm mud at the bottom of the lake. Then they happily hibernate like bears until spring."

"Wonderful. I was so worried about them." She turned. "Charlie!" she screamed and Rafe winced. She ran back to the crowd, yelling, "Uncle Lucky says the crocodiles are warm and happy!"

Rafe caught Thea's look. "What? I was educating her. That's what we're meant to do with children, isn't it? Educate them?"

Laughing, Thea took his hand, and together they ran through the snow to the lake's edge, where they helped each other put on their skates. Hand in hand, they slid and circled over the ice, more or less making their way toward a cozy cabin at the far end, which Thea had prepared as Rafe's secret hideaway, should his extended family threaten to overwhelm.

"I have received news from London," Rafe said. "Lord Ventnor and Percy Russell have gone."

"Gone where?"

"An informal ducal inquiry revealed that Lord Ventnor was living beyond his means. Most of his investments failed, and what with keeping up appearances, he fell into severe debt. His solution was to help himself to the Treasury purse."

Thea's jaw dropped. "He was stealing from the government?"

"Depends whom you ask. Ventnor insists he was merely taking his due for his invaluable services. Everyone else calls it stealing."

"What will happen to him? The Crown won't seize his property or title? What about Helen and Beau?"

"His property and title remain intact. However, after some negotiations, Lord Ventnor accepted a position as governor of the colony of New Wessex. It is situated some four hundred miles west of Sydney Cove, the main center in the colony of New South Wales. Percy will accompany him, as he dare not show his face in society. Or his buttocks, for that matter. Ventnor has been instructed that he may not return to Britain until his colony generates enough money to replace the funds that he misappropriated."

Thea skidded to a halt, aghast. "How can you smile? After all he did, he gets rewarded with the governorship of a colony where he can make money?" She snorted. "What a very imperial solution: 'By George, this man is good at stealing. Send him off to steal more land for us!' I suppose he'll end up filthy rich as governor of this colony of... Where did you say?"

"New Wessex."

She nodded knowledgeably. "New Wessex. Yes. I see. Right."

"Have you ever heard of New Wessex, Countess?"

"You mentioned it just now." She glared at him. "Oh, very well. I confess I have never heard of New Wessex."

"No one has. It doesn't exist."

Thea looked at him sharply. "Then what lies four hundred miles west of Sydney Cove?"

"We don't know. No Englishman has yet ventured that far inland."

"But he..." A slow smile spread over her face. "No! Really?"

"Ventnor and Percy will spend six months sailing to the other side of the world, where they will land at Sydney Cove and inform Governor Macquarie that he, Ventnor, is the new governor of—"

"—Of a place that does not exist!" She laughed. "And Governor Ventnor may not return until he makes money from this place that does not exist. You did this?"

"As you requested: You said you wanted him to rot on the other side of the world. Although given how hot it gets in the penal colonies, he may well roast, rather than rot."

"Then they are gone, and we can forget all about them."

"I already have." Rafe skated in a slow circle around her. "I would much rather think about you, for I intend to take you into that cabin, where it is warm and cozy, and spend the rest of the day making love to you."

"Perhaps you will. But first..." She slid out of his reach, teasing him with her playful, enticing smile. "First you will have to catch me."

Thea winked, spun around on the ice, and skated away.

Rafe forced himself to wait, watching her skirts swirl around her. Love and desire filled him, leaving little room for air. He would need air, he reminded himself, for what came next.

So he breathed all the way in, and all the way out.

Then, smiling, he gave chase.

AUTHOR'S NOTE

Plants, whether for food, textiles, or medicines, were a major factor in European colonial expansion, and botany was both big business and big science. I confess that, before starting research for this story, I knew little of the history of colonial exploitation of medicinal plants, with the exception of opium. As is often the case, much of what I learned had to be omitted from the novel itself.

The plants named in Rafe's greenhouse, and their purported uses, appear in historical sources cited in books and journal articles on colonial botany and medicine. These studies examine how Europeans gathered, exploited, and tested the knowledge of enslaved and indigenous people—while often simultaneously persuading themselves that the knowledge of enslaved and indigenous people was somehow lesser, and thus erasing their expertise. Works I consulted include Londa Schiebinger's *Secret Cures of Slaves: People, Plants, and Medicine in the Eighteenth-Century Atlantic World* (2017) and *Plants and Empire: Colonial Bioprospecting in the Atlantic World* (2004). See also the list of resources on my website.

~

Cannabis came into use in medical treatments in the UK during the 19th century, although the British knew of its properties long before then, as documented in James H. Mills' *Cannabis Britannica: Empire, Trade, and Prohibition 1800-1928* (2003).

The medical and intoxicating properties of cannabis are mentioned in several texts published in the UK in the 18th and early 19th centuries (often appearing as "bhang," "bangue," or "bang"). Europeans who traveled to Asia and the Middle East had been gathering such information since the 16th century, but their accounts were often embellished or distorted to sell titillating tales of exotic vices. It was not until the 19th century that British scientists and doctors turned their serious attention to it, although work was often hampered by their prejudices against Indian medical systems and religious practices.

William Brooke O'Shaughnessy, an Irish doctor who conducted experiments using cannabis in Kolkata in the 1830s, is credited with introducing cannabis into British medicine. For subjects such as this, I work on the principle that, where one person has entered the history books for an accomplishment, many other people were conducting similar work earlier and around the same time.

The British government primarily valued cannabis plants for hemp, essential for a maritime nation that needed the fiber to manufacture sails, ropes, sacks, etc. The "hemp plant" had long been an important crop grown in Britain; for example, Queen Elizabeth I issued a decree ordering large-scale landowners to grow it. The British were therefore keen to encourage its cultivation in India, and it was a source of conflict that Indian producers resisted changing their cultivation methods.

By the 1870s, cannabis was being used in the UK to treat mental illness. At the same time, others were claiming that cannabis induced mental illness. This latter view, combined with growing international alarm about narcotics, eventually prevailed, leading to the prohibition of cannabis in the UK in 1928.

In this novel, Martha's unnamed medicine is fictional; although she based it on bhang as it was known to the British at the time, she used her own expertise to make modifications and create something new. Although I drew on accounts of William Brooke O'Shaughnessy's experiments, its effects are not intended to accurately portray the effects of cannabis or bhang.

I am indebted to a clinical psychologist for her suggestions for depictions of Katharine's condition, which would likely be diagnosed today as bipolar I disorder and psychosis. Her symptoms are not intended to be universal.

The UK implemented considerable reforms in the treatment of mental illness over the 19th century. Influencers (referred to by Rafe) were William Tuke, a Quaker and successful tea and coffee merchant, who opened the York Retreat in 1796; and Philippe Pinel, a French alienist who developed the "*traitement moral*" or moral treatment. Pinel and Tuke were working independently, but both instituted much gentler treatments than the "mad-doctors" of the day:

"Treatment at the Retreat was based on a family-like atmosphere of kindness and patience... Fixed daily routines promoted self-discipline, with importance placed on a liberal, nourishing diet, fresh air and exercise. ... Unsurprisingly, when no longer treated like wild beasts, patients responded to the same incentives, emotions and changes to their environment as people of sound mind."

writes Jill Giese in *The Maddest Place on Earth* (2018). (The "maddest place" refers to Victoria, Australia, which during the late 19th century had the highest rate of insanity in the world.)

A series of UK Parliamentary inquiries in the first half of the 19th century exposed the horrendous conditions in lunatic asylums, leading to legislative change. Unfortunately, some of the new treatments introduced proved to be as barbaric as those before reforms, and stigmas around mental illness persist to this day.

The euphemisms for sex used by the "actors" in the tavern theatre scene (Chapter 5) were taken from Jonathon Green's Timelines of Slang. See http://jonathongreen.co.uk for more.

I could go on, but I won't. I am not an historian, and my research is limited to the needs of the story and the resources available to me. For further reading, I have compiled a selection of research books, available on my website.

MV

2019

ACKNOWLEDGMENTS

My thanks to my agent, Emily Sylvan Kim, whose feedback on a very early version was invaluable in helping me find and finish this story.

The final version also benefited immeasurably from feedback from Mikaila Rushing, and feedback and editing by May Peterson.

ABOUT THE AUTHOR

Mia Vincy holds degrees in English Literature and journalism, but she has managed to overcome the negative effects of this education and now writes historical romances.

Her first novel, *A Wicked Kind of Husband*, won the 2019 RITA® award for Best Historical Romance: Long from Romance Writers of America®.

Mia's studies and former work as a journalist, communications specialist, and copyeditor took her to more than sixty countries around the world. She is now settled in Victoria, Australia.

For more, visit miavincy.com.

ALSO BY MIA VINCY

A WICKED KIND OF HUSBAND

It was the ideal marriage of convenience...until they met.

Cassandra DeWitt has seen her husband only once—on their wedding day two years earlier—and that suits her perfectly. She has no interest in the rude, badly behaved man she married only to secure her inheritance. She certainly has no interest in his ban on her going to London. Why, he'll never even know she is there.

Until he shows up in London too, and Cassandra finds herself sharing a house with the most infuriating man in England.

Joshua DeWitt has his life exactly how he wants it. He has no need of a wife disrupting everything, especially a wife intent on reforming his behavior. He certainly has no need of a wife who is intolerably amiable, insufferably reasonable ... and irresistibly kissable.

As the unlikely couple team up to battle a malicious lawsuit and launch Cassandra's wayward sister, passion flares between them. Soon the day must come for them to part ... but what if one of them wants their marriage to become real?

COMING NEXT

For news on release dates, future books, and more, sign up at
miavincy.com/news or visit miavincy.com.

A DANGEROUS KIND OF LADY

They say to keep your enemies close. They don't say *how* close.

Proud heiress Arabella Larke must marry or lose her inheritance and
everything she loves. But Arabella is determined to choose her own
husband, and for that she needs to buy time. Her solution? A fake
engagement with Guy Roth, Marquess of Hardbury, her childhood
nemesis and the one man she is sure will never want to marry her...

Made in the USA
San Bernardino, CA
11 February 2020